To Vincent,

John Conlee

ROUNDING THIRD

JOHN CONLEE

Pale Horse Books

Library of Congress Control Number: 2013911980

ISBN: 978-1-939917-04-1

Cover Art: Hugh T. McGowan
Cover Design: Sally Stiles
Author Photo: Anna Branscome

www.PaleHorseBooks.com

Also by John Conlee:

THE DRAGON STONE
A CUP OF KINDNESS
THE KING OF MUD & GRASS
IN THE SUMMER COUNTRY
THE HEATER
THE VOYAGE OF MAELDUN

"Two three the count, nobody on,
    he hit a fly ball into the stands;
roundin' third and headin' for home,
it was a brown eyed handsome man
    who won the game,
it was a brown eyed handsome man."

    Chuck Berry —
        "Brown Eyed Handsome Man"

1

Four men in Bay City Gray uniforms rested their elbows atop the protective fence at the end of the dugout. They were watching every movement of the rookie right-hander out on the mound.

Two of those four men were my closest friends — Deacon Lawler, our veteran catcher, and Jimmy Devlin, our sensational young pitcher. The third was David Rubenstein, the best pitching coach in baseball. I was the fourth.

We were watching Terry O'Grady, our top minor league pitching prospect. The kid was making his first spring-training start, pitching against the New York Yankees. Baptism by fire.

Terry got things going with three mid-90s fastballs — a called strike, a swinging strike, and a foul ball.

"All right!" Dave said. "He's finally throwing downhill. No more of that sidearm crap that only works in high school."

"Should put more dip on his curve," Deacon Lawler said, "and more hop on his heater."

"Dave, you need to shorten his stride," Jimmy said. "Not a lot, just three or four inches." Jimmy wasn't much older than the kid we were watching. In fact, they'd been teammates two years ago in Twin Falls. Now, with just one full big-league season under his belt, Jimmy had become the ace of our staff.

"What's your view, Duff?" Dave asked me. "Jimmy got a point?"

"If a humble second-sacker's opinion is worth anything in this discussion, then yes, Jimmy's got a point."

"Humble second-sacker?" Jimmy scoffed. "The words 'Ty Duffy' and 'humble' don't exactly go together. What you'd call a non sequitur. Humble my aching elbow."

"Now gosh darn it, son," the Deacon said. "Don't you go talkin' about any aching elbows. When you say stuff like that, you gotta knock on wood." He bonked his fist a couple of times against Jimmy's head. "There, that oughta take care of it."

Despite the fact the kid we were watching was "throwing

downhill," the Yankees touched him up for a run in the first and another in the second. In the third, his final inning of work, he wriggled out of a bases-loaded jam by striking out two big-name Yankees. So, while Terry O'Grady hadn't looked sensational, at least his baptismal day ended up on a positive note.

"I'd say Terry needs another season in Triple-A," I remarked.

"Yep," said Jimmy.

"Yep," said the Deacon.

"He's *close*," Dave said, "*damn* close. But you geniuses are right. Maybe he'll be back by midseason. I sure would like to see what I could do with him, given a proper chance."

The game we were watching, despite being against the hated Yankees, should have been just a run-of-the-mill spring-training baseball game. It didn't turn out that way.

In the fourth inning, Jake Weaver, a Yankees middle-man of no real importance, drilled Bobby Radley, our star right-fielder, smack in the ribs with a fast ball. It was *payback* — payback for the long bomb Bobby hit last September that ended the Yankees' season.

"Shit!" said Whitey Wiggins, our skipper. He shot a poisoned-eye glance toward Moe Torgerson, the Yankee manager, who stood stoically on the steps of their dugout with his hands jammed in his jacket pockets, his lower lip slightly protruding.

"Looks like a case of Hammurabi's Code," Jimmy Devlin said.

"Or of Leviticus 24:20," Deacon Lawler said.

"Or of 'you put one of ours in the hospital, we put one of yours in the morgue . . . ,' " I said.

" ' . . . that's the Chicago way . . . ,' " Dave said, completing the famous movie line, his Chicago-Irish accent better than mine.

As Bobby trotted down to first, some yahoo in the stands was shouting, "Don't rub it! Don't rub it!"

Right then every player and fan at George M. Steinbrenner Field in St. Pete knew what the baseball code called for. But as our pitcher, Scotty Evers, got ready to head out to the mound for the bottom half of the inning, Whitey grabbed him by the arm.

"No, son," he said, "we don't need this crap. Let it go. I'll square it with the boys. You let it go." Scotty shrugged. He knew what was expected and knew the guys would be pissed if he didn't do it. On the ball field, it's an eye for an eye and a rib for a rib.

Scotty trotted over to Bump Rhodes, the rookie catcher who was working behind the plate, and clued him in. Then he went on out to the mound to take his warm-up tosses.

When Scotty followed orders and the Yankee hitters survived the inning unmolested, the guys in our dugout were mutinous.

"What the fuck, Skipper!" said Lou Tolliver, our slugging third baseman. Lou was steamed. I figured that Whitey, being old school, must've felt their plonking of Bobby was only fair, considering the damage he'd done to them last fall.

In any case, if the Yankees were satisfied that things were now even, Whitey seemed willing to live with it. They weren't.

It was only two innings later that things heated up again. With Junior Jackson on first, Paul O'Sullivan, the Yankee cleanup hitter, rocketed a shot off the right centerfield wall. Spike Bannister, our speedy centerfielder, played the carom perfectly and rifled the ball toward the infield. Juan Flores, our shortstop, snatched it head high, spun, and flung it toward home.

The ball hopped once and snugged into the catcher's mitt a split second before Jackson reached home. Worlds collided . . . and then Junior Jackson, all 215 pounds of him, crumpled to the earth like a load of fill dirt. The umpire shot his right arm up in a dramatic gesture of "You're out!" The fans, despite most of them being Yankee fans, were ecstatic. They'd just witnessed baseball's ultimate play.

There, with the ball in his mitt and happiness all over his boyish face, stood Bump Rhodes, our rookie prospect — six-four, 240 pounds, a guy we hoped might one day be the next Carlton Fisk. Bump straddled home plate like the Colossus of Rhodes.

Jackson got up and limped off to the Yankee dugout, having just

been flattened by some totally unknown busher. Way to go, Bump!
— you big dumb stud.

But the real fireworks began in the seventh when the Yankees
called upon Big Mike Prokosch, their ace, to work a couple of
innings. As luck would have it, Lou Tolliver was due up for us. Mike
Prokosch and Lou Tolliver — two guys with a long, ugly history.

Mike's first pitch to Lou sailed high over the catcher's head,
whacking against the great plastic window set into the screen behind
home plate. That pitch was no accident — its purpose was to give
Lou a little something to think about. Then came Mike's second
pitch. It smacked Lou right in the gluteus maximus.

"God damn son of a bitch!" Lou roared out to the multitudes.
He threw his bat down in disgust.

The ump dashed out in front of the plate, but he wasn't quick
enough.

In a red rage, Lou charged around him and straight for Big Mike.
Both dugouts emptied. Within seconds a frenzied melee spilled all
over the diamond. Guys were pushing, shoving, and punching. Most
of the fighting was pretty tame stuff, actually, but not all of it. Bump
Rhodes was thrashing the life out of some poor Yankee outfielder,
and Bobby Radley was getting his own payback, pummeling a guy
with lefts and rights. That guy turned out to be Jake Weaver, the
pitcher who'd nailed Bobby back in the fouth inning.

Mike Prokosch and Lou Tolliver stood toe to toe, exchanging
blows like Tyson and Holyfield. Their long and ugly history grew
uglier by the punch.

It practically took the riot squad to put an end to this donnybrook.
As for baseball, this game was *finito*.

This being our last spring matchup with the Yankees, it would be
six more weeks before we'd see them again. That would be in late
April, when they'd come to Bay City for a regular-season series.

The fact that the Grays and the Yankees wouldn't be seeing each
other anytime soon was probably a very good thing.

2

Five months earlier the perennial cellar-dwelling Bay City Grays had stunned the baseball world by winning the AL Wild Card: the first time we'd made it into the post-season in fifteen years. Although we proceeded to lose to the Angels in the first round of the playoffs, our unanticipated success had buoyed our spirits like nothing else.

It was in the aftermath of our loss to the Angels that Deacon Lawler told us what we didn't want to be told – that it was time for him to hang it up on the game and move on with his life.

"No, son, no," Whitey had shot back. "Don't go doin' that to me, Deak. Hell, all I'm askin' ya for is one more year. That's not so much, is it? One more piddling year. You can do that for me, can't ya son?"

"I'm really sorry, Skip, but I've reached the point where I don't have much left to give. Shoot, if I did I would. No, it's time for me to be movin' inta my next line of work."

"Son, ya did wonders with Jimmy Devlin this year. I need ya to do it again."

"Skip, Jimmy doesn't need any more help from me. He's in real good hands with Dave Rubenstein. Heck, Dave did way more for the kid than I ever did."

"It's not Jimmy I need you for," Whitey said. "I need you for Bump."

"*Bump?* You talkin' about that Single-A catcher we picked up who can't hit and can't throw?" *Ouch.* Coming from the non-judgmental Deacon, those were harsh words.

Whitey said, "Ya know that story about when all the Disciples were out in that boat with Jesus and Jesus was askin' 'em to step out onto the water?"

The Deacon and I just stared at Whitey. The only times we'd ever heard him use the word "Jesus" had not been in a Biblical context.

"You know what I'm sayin', son. Okay, okay, maybe I'm askin' you to work a minor miracle. But Deacon, I have faith in you. I need you to do what I know you can do. I need you to step out on that water, son."

Boy oh boy, did Whitey Wiggins ever know how to work the Deacon. You sly old fox, Whitey, you sly old cunning old fox.

"Okay, Skip," the Deacon said with a sigh, "all I can promise is that I'll consider it. Don't know how well it'll go over with Aggie, though." Aggie was the Deacon's wife Agnes.

"Son, next year may be my last one also, and there's nothin' that would mean more to me than to see us go deeper in the playoffs than we did this year. Hell, Deacon, I know that even makin' the playoffs again is a long shot. But as Duffy here says, our chances next year are gonna be better than they've ever been. You and Duffy, Deacon, you're the two guys I always count on. Give me one more year, Deak. Hell, that's not askin' so much, is it?"

The Deacon shrugged. He was fully aware of the fact that the skipper was working him good. And the truth was – he liked it.

After losing to the Angels, I'd spent the rest of October in Ireland with Laura Morgan, who'd needed to go there in conjunction with her job at the Metropolitan Museum of Art. We'd had ourselves two event-filled weeks, to put it mildly, weeks in which Jimmy Devlin and his Irish flame Kat Brogan nearly got all of us killed. In the end we'd survived – more or less – though in Jimmy's case it was probably less. For Kat Brogan, bless her soul, had ended up crushing the lad's heart.

When Laura and I got back to New York after the long flight from Shannon Airport, she'd urged me to stay on there with her for a few more days – which was exactly what I'd hoped she'd do. So while she was at the Metropolitan Museum of Art each day, working like a mad-woman on the publicity for their upcoming exhibition on Ireland's most celebrated high crosses, I lazed about in her apartment, reading and listening to music. In the evenings we took long walks in the city or went to the movies. One night we considered seeing Bizet's *Carmen*; but then knowing that our days together were coming to an end, we decided to stay in and enjoy each other's company.

During those days neither of us felt any great need to do a lot of thinking or talking. Each of us was happy taking comfort in the other's presence. I found myself feeling closer to Laura than I'd ever felt to anyone. I sensed that she felt much the same; and to her credit, she was wise enough not to say a single word about it. She knew about Ty Duffy's tendency to light out for the territories whenever a woman started getting overly possessive.

After our five days together we said our farewells, and I took the train from Penn Station down to Bay City.

When I walked into my apartment and looked around at my own little nest, everything felt quite strange. What a lot of stuff had happened in the three weeks since I'd been there. I felt like I'd been gone a year rather than just three short weeks.

And for the first time I could remember, the sense of solitude I've always cherished when I'm alone in my apartment felt a lot more like loneliness than solitude. Ty Duffy, I said to myself, get a grip, laddie. You're the guy who takes pride in being a self-sufficient loner. Yet right at that moment I – Tyrus Raymond Cobb Duffy – had no great desire to be a self-sufficient loner.

On my answering machine were a ton of messages, the most important ones being hellos from my brother Billy, from Deacon Lawler, and from the City Opera Company, who wanted to know if I intended to renew my season tickets (*Hell yes, dummies. Hadn't I had them for the last seven years?*).

But Billy and the Deacon and the opera folks could wait until tomorrow. Tonight I needed to examine these strange feelings I'd been having. I've always firmly believed that the over-examined life isn't worth living. Tonight, though, I felt the need to sit quietly with a glass of Jameson and reflect on certain very essential matters.

I found myself feeling dauntingly alone. It was only eight hours since I'd said goodbye to Laura in New York and already I was missing her more than I wanted to admit. I missed my brother Billy; I missed the comforting presence of Deacon Lawler; and I missed my knuckle-headed pal Jimmy Devlin. And, as I frequently do, I found myself greatly missing my father.

Solitude can be one of life's greatest blessings. But right at that moment I discovered that loneliness can be a major bummer.

If introspection wasn't my long suit, neither were feelings of senti-mentality. The one big exception to that was my father, who I still missed terribly since his unexpected death seven years ago. There were times out on the ball field when I did something special that I found myself wishing my dad were there to see. During all those years Billy and I had shared with Dad after our mom had flown the coop, I'd never stopped trying to make him proud of me. And sometimes I even succeeded.

When I was seventeen and got my first driver's license, my dad would let me use our old Chevy station wagon for weekend dates. Girls had only recently become a serious interest of mine, but it didn't take long for my passion for girls to rival my passion for books, baseball, and classical music.

And as girls became a compelling interest, I couldn't help thinking about my dad and *his* relationships with women. Our mother had been out of the picture for seven or eight years, and I couldn't help wondering how Dad had been able to cope without having a woman, or women, in his life. He wasn't all that old — early forties, I guess — he was in pretty good shape and not too bad looking. Billy and I often joked about the obvious interest that women took in him. Apparently a single dad raising his young sons on his own had a lot of appeal to certain kinds of women. And over those years in which the three of us lived together, that situation hadn't much changed. As far as Billy and I could tell, though, the interest women took in Dad wasn't much reciprocated.

I remembered one night right after a PTA meeting waiting for dad out in the school corridor. The meeting had ended fifteen or twenty minutes earlier, and most of the people had already left. Where the heck was Dad? When I peeked into the cafeteria, there he was, cornered by three women, two young teachers and a very attractive single parent. "Oh," my dad said, looking in my direction, "there's my son. I'm afraid I'll have to go. It's been great chatting with you."

As I sat there in my Bay City apartment ruminating about my father, I recalled one particular Saturday night when he'd let me use the old station wagon to take a girl to the movies. Billy was spending the weekend with a friend, and Dad said he was looking forward to a quiet Saturday night. This was my first date with Amanda, a girl I'd been admiring for several weeks. I didn't know her very well, but she was great looking and had a lively personality.

On Friday and Saturday nights Dad expected me to be home by one, but since he almost always went to bed well before that, I rarely paid much attention to that one o'clock curfew. And on that particular Saturday night, after the movies my date took an unexpected turn for the better — boy, did it ever — and so it was pushing two before I got home.

Dad had left a light on for me in the living room, and when I went in, there he was, sitting in his comfortable overstuffed chair, reading.

"Getting kind of late, isn't it son?"

"Yeah, sorry. Lost track of time."

"How did it go with Amanda?"

"Actually," I said, unable not to blush, "it went really well."

"That's great," my dad said. "I hope you and Amanda were careful."

"Dad! That wasn't what I meant! We were just, you know . . . necking a little bit."

"Necking, eh? Well, I hope you at least got to second base." My father had a big grin on his face. "Just so long as you weren't rounding third." Geez, was I ever embarrassed.

My father never talked to Billy and me about sex. I think he was constitutionally unable to do such a thing. His making a joke right then about me and Mandy and our make-out session in the old station wagon was about as close as he'd ever come. And even then, it was pretty darn unexpected.

"I guess I'll be saying good night now," he said. "I'm glad you and Amanda had an enjoyable evening." This time he said that with a straight face. "I'll see you in the morning, Ty." My dad went into the kitchen and poured himself a glass of water, then climbed the stairs to his bedroom.

I was surprised he'd stayed up so late, and I was surprised by his remarks to me. And as I was turning off the porch light and the living room lights, I suddenly caught a hint of a strange fragrance. It smelled a lot like perfume. A lot like a *woman's* perfume. What in the world?

While Mandy and I had been making out in the old stationwagon parked outside her house, what had my dad been doing right here in this living room?

3

Over the winter, Jimmy Devlin and I hadn't had a whole lot of contact. Back in the fall, the day after Laura, Jimmy, and I had all flown home from Ireland, I'd phoned him in Missouri and we'd chatted for a while. Jimmy had sounded distant and subdued. Given the fact that he'd come close to being killed over there and that he'd had his heart mangled by Kathleen Brogan, that wasn't surprising. Our adventures in Ireland with Kat Brogan — and with Mick Slattery and his minions — had been harrowing for all of us, but especially for Jimmy. So Jimmy needed to be left alone to lick his wounds. Eventually, perhaps, those wounds might heal.

A little before Thanksgiving Jimmy had called me in Bay City. He'd apologized for not calling sooner and thanked me for standing by him during his tribulations in the Emerald Isle. He said he'd been a total jerk over there, and I told him he'd been no more of a jerk than any of us ever are. When I invited him to come and stay with me for a while in December, he declined with a chuckle.

"I don't think Penny's going to let me out of her sight any time soon. Maybe not even until it's time to head off for spring training." I couldn't help wondering how much Jimmy had told Penny Sutherland, his longtime hometown girlfriend, about our Ireland adventures. Whatever he said to her, I felt sure he'd left out a whole lot.

"Hey, Duff, guess what?"

"What?"

"I've been working on a changeup lately — with my dad." I could just picture Jimmy and his larger-than-life father, Henry (Hammerin' Hank) Devlin, out in the backyard like a couple of kids, firing the ball back and forth.

"Great. Straight change or circle?"

"Straight. Comin' along pretty good, too."

"Great." Last year Jimmy had been a three-pitch pitcher. His money pitch, his heater, was a four-seam fastball that he normally threw in the mid-90s. His two-seamer was clocked in the low-90s but was especially effective due to its late movement. His breaking ball was a hard slider which he usually threw off one edge of the plate or the other. If he mastered the changeup, it would make his already potent arsenal more potent than ever.

In mid-December — on Beethoven's birthday, as a matter of fact — I violated one of my sacred rules and sent Jimmy a Christmas card. The next day I got one from him; they must've crossed in the mail. Hearing from the kid brought a smile to my face, though the message on Jimmy's card, nice as it was, wasn't nearly as jaunty as the one on the card he'd sent me last year. Sadly, Jimmy Devlin appeared to have lost a lot of his jauntiness.

Also that fall Laura had asked me to come and spend Thanksgiving with her and her family in Rhode Island; I vacillated a good bit before declining her invitation. I still hadn't met her family, though I knew how much she wanted me to; but every time the prospect of doing that came up, I managed to come down with a serious case of cold feet. Laura was growing more and more exasperated with me, and I could hardly blame her.

So instead of spending Thanksgiving with Laura in Rhode Island, I came and spent the first week of December with her in New York. During my visit we did all the things we usually did — took long walks, visited museums and bookstores, saw a couple of operas at Lincoln Center, even ice skated at Rockefeller Center.

But as delightful as that week was, something was missing. We both knew that those days together, pleasant as they were, weren't as magical as the days we'd spent together in Dublin earlier in the fall. The reason, I felt sure, was my refusal to come at Thanksgiving. That had hurt her. I did what I could to make it up to her. I didn't succeed.

"Sometimes, Ty Duffy," she said one night, "I'd like to grab you by the scruff of the neck and give you a good shake."

◆ ◆ ◆

Just before Christmas I made my annual visit to Manassas to spend the holidays with my brother Billy and his wife Sarah. It was cold and snowy the whole time, which didn't prevent Billy and me from enjoying a massive snowball free-for-all with the neighborhood kids. When we came back in the house that Christmas Eve afternoon, all wet and rosy-cheeked, Sarah just shook her head. She didn't need to say what she was thinking about a couple of thirty-year-old knuckleheads who'd never grown up, knuckleheads who probably never would grow up.

Just before supper the phone rang. The caller was our mother, calling from Ireland. Neither Billy nor I had heard a peep from her all fall. The last time I'd seen her was when Mick Slattery's boyos had whisked her, the unconscious Mick, and my mother's well-heeled friend off in their yacht en route to the hospital in Dingle — the culminating events of what had been a very tumultuous day out on the Great Blasket.

After that, so far as I knew, she'd gone back to Kinsale with her yacht-owning companion. I hadn't known how to contact her there; and given the tenor of the note she'd left for me at the hospital in Dingle, I figured she had no great desire to hear from her first-born son anyway.

But during our conversation that Christmas Eve she didn't even bring up those dramatic events, events which must've been harrowing for her. My mother, though, has always been resilient, so by then she'd probably put all of that behind her. Throughout her adult life she'd had her share of scrapes, difficulties from which she'd always managed to extricate herself.

"Mom, a couple of months ago I saw on the news that a missing piece of the Anne Frank diary turned up out of the blue at the National Library of Ireland. I wonder where in the world *that* came from? They said all the experts have to work with is a photocopy. It should give those folks a challenge, trying to figure out if it's authentic."

Over the line came my mother's familiar, deep-throated laugh. I think she was pleased that she'd gone at least partway in satisfying her son's ethical principles. Not to the point where she might risk her full payday, though.

"How are things in Kinsale, Mom?"

"They're good, Ty, good as could be. I've enjoyed these last few months — no thanks to you!" There came her familiar laugh again. "But an attractive opportunity has come up in Amsterdam, so I'll be off to the Continent right after New Year's."

I'd wondered how long things would hold steady for her in Ireland. Her joyrides never seemed to last for long. For my good old mom, it was time to be moving on.

"You think you might get back here any time soon?"

She hesitated, then said, "No, probably not any time soon. Things have been going quite well for me over here. You wouldn't want me to tempt fate by changing my routine, would you? Don't you ball players believe in sticking to your routines so as not to tempt fate?"

"Mom, I would never want you to tempt fate. Still, Billy and I would love to see you sometime." At that remark, Billy made a gruesome face, a face I remembered seeing on the cute little mug of an eight-year-old boy.

"I'll see what I can do, Ty. Maybe I can come before the end of the summer. Maybe I'll get another chance to see you play in a ball game. Or if Billy and Sarah come to Wimbledon again, maybe I can see them in England."

Clearly, my mother had no intention of returning to the U.S. any time soon.

After the holidays I returned to Waverly College, my alma mater, to teach a writing class during the January term. I'd done that the year before for the first time, so this time I went into it with a clearer idea of what I'd let myself in for. And this time I think I may have contributed some things of value to the students. Anyway, that's how it felt to me and how I hoped it felt to them. I also began to form real friendships with a couple of my students, which pleased me. But this time around my eyes were opened in another way.

On the basis of last year's experiences, I'd created for myself an idyllic notion of what university life was like — a notion that everyone there was free to be themselves and to pursue their interests to their hearts' content. But this time that ideal came face to face with reality as I discovered that the people comprising this world weren't immune to all the small-mindedness and petty vices the rest of us fall prey to. I came to realize that some of these gentle, humane, and enlightened folks could backbite with the best of them.

Buried in the groves of academe, I'd discovered, were some real land mines, and if one weren't careful he could get his effin' leg blown off. I managed to tread lightly and leave Waverly with limbs intact. But this fresh realization caused me to do some reevaluating. Now I had second thoughts about whether I'd want to pursue an academic career when my ball-playing days drew to an end.

When pitchers and catchers reported to camp in February, I did too. Call me an eager beaver. I was eager to see Jimmy, eager to see Deacon Lawler, and eager to have a glimpse at this big lump of a kid named Bump Rhodes. His real first name wasn't Bump, of course. It turned out to be Edgar. Hearing that, I wondered if this strapping young Tarzan had been named for Edgar Rice Burroughs. Not likely, though the idea amused me.

That first night in Florida, Jimmy and I went out to eat at the Taj Mahal restaurant, just like old times.

"Jimmy," I said, after we'd ordered and the waiter had set two large bottles of Indian beer in front of us, "what was Tarzan's English name?"

Jimmy pursed his lips and stroked his chin while he pondered the matter. Then he shot me a knowing grin. "Lord Greystoke," he said.

"Guess I'm buying," I said.

"Guess you are."

Jimmy and I had a lot of catching up to do, but it took us awhile to get around to it. After the long hiatus that followed our Ireland experiences, neither of us was quite sure how we should start in on things. But by the time we'd finished our second bottles of Kingfisher Lager, we'd begun to get our friendship back on track. Nonetheless, it still seemed clear to me that Jimmy Devlin had lost a lot of his youthful exuberance. Jimmy was now a sadder man. Maybe, just maybe, he was a wiser one.

"How's the changeup coming?" I said.

"Did I tell you about that? Man, it's coming along great. Just about there, Duff. My dad is smarter than he looks, you know. He showed me the right grip, real loose and far back in my hand. Yeah, it's just about there. Rubenstein'll be shocked and awed."

Jimmy's enthusiasm, at least in regard to this topic, was what I'd hoped to see. Hearing the kid enthusing about pitching brought a smile to my heart.

"How's Laura?" he asked me. "You two tight as ever?"

"She's doing great," I said, "at least I think she is. I haven't seen her since December. I'd hoped to go up to New York last weekend, but she begged off. She's been rushing about like a crazed thing, with the Celtic cross exhibition opening in three weeks — just in time for St. Patrick's Day. What about Penny? How's she doing?"

"Oh, Penny's just fine, Duff. Though I'm damned glad the season's finally getting here," Jimmy said, his old grin peeping through just a little bit. "Penny's a really great person . . . but I do get tired of her constant hovering. Know what I mean?" I nodded in agreement, though the truth was I'd never let a woman get to the hovering stage. Before things reached that point, I'd always managed to light out for the territories.

"Okay, Jimmy, here's the big question. So how's your old man?"

"My old man? My old man is my old man, same as always. About as unchanging as the tides, or the man in the moon."

"It was great getting to know him last year. He's a colorful fellow, Mr. Henry Devlin. No dull moments around your father."

"Nope," Jimmy said, his grin breaking through once more. "Speaking of which, my dear old dad gave me something to pass along to you. It's out in the car. Dad said, 'You give this to ol' Banjo, son, whenever you get a chance to. Ol' Banjo, he's gonna like it.' "

"Cool. What is it?"

"A CD, my friend, what else would it be?"

"A CD? It wouldn't be the new recording of *Turandot* I've been looking for, would it?"

"Not bloody likely. No, it's Merle Haggard's Greatest Hits."

"Merle friggin' Haggard. A perfect memento of our barbecue night last year in Kansas City. That is really cool." I meant it, too. From Jimmy's father, that CD was the perfect gift. Way better than the *Turandot*.

"Jimmy," I said, feeling it was time to take the plunge and move into deeper waters, "have you heard from Kathleen Brogan? Any idea what's going on with her?"

Jimmy hesitated a bit before replying. "Kat? Well . . . yeah . . . I got a letter from her back in November." I remembered the letters she'd sent him last year care of me; and I found myself imagining their subtle lavender fragrance.

"Oh yeah? What did she say?"

"Duff, it was all a crock. All bullshit. Apologies and half-assed explanations and feeble rationalizations. A big load of crapola. She was oh so sincerely sorry. Well, fuck that."

"C'mon, man, that doesn't sound fair."

"Hell no it isn't fair. The hell with being fair."

"Did you write her back?"

"Hell no I didn't write her back. What the hell for? She wasn't going to leave her boyos. All a matter of personal honor. Shoot, Ty, Kat has what she's always wanted. She's become the real big deal in that neck of the woods, the lads all kowtowing to her like she was Queen Maeve the Magnificent. Or the fucking Queen of the May.

Or some damn thing." Since Jimmy was on a roll, I knew better than to say a word.

"No, Ty, the hell with her. Better to let bygones be bygones." Yeah, it really sounded like Jimmy was doing that! "Duff, that damn woman ripped my guts out. I'll tell you one thing. I sure as hell am never going to let that happen to me again."

Good thing I'm not a betting man, I said inwardly, 'cuz if I were a betting man . . . .

"Did she say anything about Mick Slattery? Did King Mick make a full recovery?"

"At the time Kat wrote her letter, Mick was still on the mend. But I got the impression that Kat and Mick's relationship, whatever it was, had shifted in Kat's favor." Jimmy closed down for a little while; but then he said, "Damn it, Ty, Kat said she still loved me. She said she hoped the day would come when we could still be together." We both sat there in silence, mulling that one over.

Finally I said, "What about the lads? She say anything about them? She say anything about how they're feeling toward you now?"

"Nah, not really. Nothing specific anyway. But she told me to be careful, and that she'd do all she could to keep a firm hand on things over there. I took that to mean things hadn't exactly quieted down."

And I took it to mean there were folks in Ireland who still had payback very much on their minds. When it comes to harboring long-term animosities, there are no better haters than the Irish.

I couldn't help remembering that one of the last things Kat had said to Jimmy in Ireland was, "They'll be comin' for ya, Jimmy." She'd said that over *there* she couldn't protect him. I wondered who in the world was supposed to protect him over *here?*

Jimmy Devlin, after all, was the man who'd taken down Mick Slattery. And that, I felt sure, was something for which he could never be forgiven.

4

The night before position players were due in camp, Jimmy, Deacon, and I went out to an early movie. Bump Rhodes, the rookie catcher and the Deacon's new protégé, tagged along.

It was a Coen Brothers' comedy, and while I prefer their darker dramas, the movie had Bump in stitches from start to finish. Every time he guffawed, the rest of us couldn't help bursting into laughter with him. It felt good to laugh, and it felt good to hear Jimmy Devlin laughing. Sharing laughs is one of the best ways for people to bond, and Jimmy, the Deacon, and I were on our way to bonding with Bump.

Afterwards, in high spirits, we went to eat at a local café — four large men crammed into one small booth. At six-one, 180, I was the shrimp of the group. Bump ordered two BLTs, a large order of fries, an order of onion rings, and a large RC Cola; Jimmy ordered a rib-eye steak sandwich, fries, and a tossed salad; the Deacon ordered barbecued ribs and coleslaw; and I went with a large Greek salad with extra Feta, dressing on the side. Jimmy and I shared a pitcher of draft beer. Bump and the Deacon both stuck to soft drinks.

Bump eyed my salad suspiciously, not quite sure what to make of it. "Rabbit food?" he hazarded. I wrinkled my nose and twitched my ears.

"So, where you from, Bumpster?" Jimmy asked him.

"Well . . . I s'pose you could say I'm from L.A."

"L.A.?" Jimmy said.

The Deacon and I looked at each other and silently mouthed, "L.A.?" Deacon Lawler was from L.A., but none of us believed for a second that this kid was from L.A.

"Yeah, L.A.," Bump said. "You know, . . . lower Alabama." Then all four of us broke into laughter.

Unlike the rest of us, who were college grads, Bump had gone straight from high school to playing professional baseball. Now, having just turned twenty-one, he already had three years of pro ball under his belt. Our organization had picked him up at the end of last season, hoping he was ready to make a great leap forward. He appeared to have the raw talent to do that, though to date his offensive stats were a mixed-bag. In A-ball last year he'd batted a mere .235, though he'd belted out twenty-three round-trippers. Over the last month of the season, when he'd been moved up to Double-A, he'd batted a whopping .210, and yet he'd hit seven more HRs. His biggest problem seemed to be making contact. The big lout struck out nearly half the time.

So the Deacon's job this season was to form and mold the kid into a big league catcher. And my job, I discovered to my dismay, was to diagnose his batting problems and turn him into a semi-respectable hitter. Since I'd achieved a .311 career average over my eight seasons in the bigs, it was blithely assumed that I knew everything there was to know about hitting. Yeah sure, I said to myself, I *do* know a few things about hitting. And one thing I know quite well is that you can't put in what God has left out. When it came to Bump Rhodes' talent for hitting, it appeared that the Deity had been downright parsimonious.

I wasn't sure who was going to have the tougher chore, the Deacon or me. As it turned out, it was both of us.

Throughout our post-movie meal, Bump Rhodes hadn't been able to keep his eyes off the tight blouse of the young waitress who'd served our food and who'd just brought the check.

"Whoa, baby," Bump said, admiring her round little bottom as she sashayed away. "I'll bet you wouldn't say no to that, would ya Jimmy? Nice little rump, man. Gives you a quiver in the liver."

"What?" said Jimmy, who'd been studying the check the waitress had left on the table.

"*That,*" Bump said again, gesturing with his head in the direction of the waitress, "you wouldn't say no to *that.*"

Finally getting Bump's drift, Jimmy said, "Bump, you know, don't you, that during the season we all swear a solemn vow of celibacy? Deacon told you about that, didn't he?"

"A vow of what?"

"Celibacy. You know — no sex. Deak, you told Bump about that, didn't you?" Bump's eyes got big.

"Come on," he said, "you're pullin' my leg. You are, right?" The look on his face said he wasn't quite sure.

"Blame the Deacon," I said, "it was his idea. See, we had this big team meeting after the All-Star break last year when we were really playing badly, and that was when the Deacon got this weird notion about all of us agreeing to have no sex. Some of the guys weren't so happy about it — Lou Tolliver really hated it — but in the end, we all agreed to try it out for a few weeks. And damned it if that wasn't when we got hot, winning fifteen out of eighteen."

"Turned our season around," Jimmy said. "Did you know that from the first of August on last year, the Bay City Grays had the best record in all of baseball?"

Bump looked totally nonplussed. He glanced at Deacon Lawler for any hint of confirmation, but the Deacon just gave him a noncommittal shrug.

"What about the married guys?" Bump said.

"Didn't change things much for them," Jimmy said. "It was us young guys who had the toughest time."

"Shoot," Bump said. "You guys are pullin' my leg, right?"

Late on the night of March 15th, the night before St. Patrick's Eve, I called Laura in New York. The exhibition on Celtic crosses would open to the public the next day, and the night before it did, the museum had thrown a special gala for patrons and honored guests, including a lot of Irish dignitaries.

It was pushing midnight when I called, and Laura sounded exhilarated, exhausted, and hugely relieved. She said everything had gone like clockwork, and that to her great relief, none of her worst fears had materialized. Now she could relax and enjoy the fruits of her labors.

"It's over," she said. "Whew! — that's the sound of a gigantic sigh of relief. Right at this moment I'm sitting here in the dark sipping a glass of merlot and listening to Mozart's Clarinet Concerto. There's only one thing I can think of that could make things even more to my liking."

I smiled to myself, picturing her there in the dim light of her living room, her legs tucked beneath her on her sofa, the sounds of one of Mozart's most melodic works filling the room.

"It's just about three weeks till I see you," I said. "You're still coming, aren't you?"

"Yes, I'm *pretty* sure that will still work. And if for some reason it doesn't, I'll be there for the Yankee series."

We'd talked about Laura coming and staying with me during the second week in April, in time for her to see our home opener. This year we'd start the season on the road with a series in Toronto and another in Boston. Then we'd have a two-week home stay, ending with our much-anticipated showdown with the Yankees.

"I've got an idea," I said hopefully. "Maybe you could come both times."

I heard Laura's low laugh. "Not too likely," she said. "But one of them, for sure."

"So everything went like clockwork? I'll bet you were the star of the show, with compliments galore." Again I heard her soft laughter.

"It went as well as we could have hoped. Compliments? Oh, well, who cares about compliments?" I could tell from her tone that she'd received tons of compliments and that she'd liked it. Why shouldn't she? After all her months of hard work — work which prevented me from seeing her as much as I'd've liked — those people damn well better appreciate her.

"Ty, there's one thing about tonight I need to tell you. Among our honored guests was someone you're acquainted with."

"Oh yeah?"

"Um hum. It was your old friend Seamus Byrne."

I let that sink in a moment. "Good old Seamus, huh? So, how's my favorite Irish solicitor? He speak to you?"

"Oh, yes. Oozing Celtic charm from every pore. What was it Kat said about him, that he could charm the birds right off the trees? He told me how terribly sorry he was he hadn't had a chance to show me around his beloved Dublin town."

"What'd you say?"

"Oh, just how much I'd enjoyed our too-brief visit to Dublin and how much it had meant to me to see some of those wonderful ancient sites you and I went to."

"He say anything about any of our mutual acquaintances?"

"Not a word. Solicitor Byrne was all sweetness and light. No hidden warnings or innuendos or anything like that. He said he'd recently come back to the Boston office of their law firm for another lengthy stint. He asked about you, Ty, said he hoped he'd see both of us in the near future."

"Good old Seamus," I said. "Gosh, maybe I'll have the good fortune to run into him when we're playing Boston in April." I sure as hell hoped not.

5

The plan for the Grays was to go north carrying a trio of catchers. We could afford that luxury for the first month, since in the early going, as a result of open dates and rainouts, we planned to go mostly with a four-man pitching rotation. The plan was for Deacon Lawler to catch Jimmy's games; Miguel Torres, our backup catcher, to catch Stan Foubert and Jack Fletcher's games; and Bump Rhodes to catch our fourth starter, Alfred King. Alfred was a two-pitch pitcher — four-seam fastball and hard slider — which would make it easier for Bump to handle the catching chores.

That was the original plan. But because of Bump's poor hitting during the spring, that plan went the way the best-laid plans often do. Aside from his moment of glory when he'd flattened Junior Jackson in their collision at the plate, Bump's only other moment of glory was a 450-foot home run he launched off some no-name minor-league lefty who'd had a short-lived tryout with the Mets.

During the spring Bump had gone 0-for-16 against right-handed pitchers and just 3-for-13 vs. lefties, including that one towering home run. In batting practice, Bump did great against righties. The kid's long belts produced as many oohs and ahs as those of our biggest boppers, Todd Cottington and Lou Tolliver. But when he was up against real pitching, Bump was a lamb to the slaughter. So by the time we broke camp the thinking had changed — Bump would only play when we faced a left-handed pitcher. That way he'd have a fighting chance of keeping his batting average above the Mendoza Line.

Still, for those who had eyes to see, it was plain enough why Pete Paulson, our GM, and Whitey Wiggins, our manager, had wanted to pick up this kid and why they still held high hopes for him. Bump Rhodes had athletic gifts galore. Besides his size and strength, he was remarkably agile behind the plate with quick feet and soft hands.

The big lug's greatest liability was his throwing. His arm was plenty powerful, that wasn't the problem. The problem was that when he fired the ball in the direction of second base, there was a chance it would end up in the centerfield bleachers. There were times during the spring when he didn't just overthrow second base, he overthrew the guy backing up second base. And there were a couple of times when his throws to second nearly decapitated our terrified pitchers.

But the kid really cared. The kid worked his ass off. The kid drank in everything the Deacon taught him. And by the time those six weeks in Florida came to an end . . . he hadn't made a shred of progress. Bump Rhodes was simply *not* a big-league catcher. Not even close.

There was no doubt by the end of spring training, though, that Jimmy Devlin was a big-league pitcher. Last year's AL Rookie of the Year was performing at a phenomenal level. Jimmy was focused, determined, and all business. He'd come to camp in tip-top shape, he'd looked invincible in his spring outings, and he was primed to have a career year. James Patrick Devlin was ready to pick up the Bay City Grays, put us on his shoulders, and carry us all the way to the World Series.

And it scared the heck out of me. Maybe it was great for Jimmy, and maybe it was great for the team, but it sure as blazes wasn't great for me. Where was that goofy kid who'd bought me a Harp Lager in a New York hotel bar a year and a half ago and called me "Mr. Duffy"? Where was my grinning young amigo who'd endeared himself to me so quickly? I sure did miss him.

When I'd been a kid, my first great love after baseball had been books. All the usual suspects — Jules Verne, Alexandre Dumas, Arthur Conan Doyle, J.R.R. Tolkien, Robert Louis Stevenson. A little later I developed my second great love, classical music. Maybe it was heaven sent, because it certainly fell out of the sky.

It started one day when my dad, my brother, and I headed off on a spur-of-the-moment camping trip. During the drive I fiddled with the car radio, trying to find a ball game. What I stumbled on instead was the Saturday afternoon opera broadcast from New York. As my ears drank in the "Anvil Chorus" from Verdi's *Il Trovatore*, I was hooked just like that. Verdi's operas enthralled me, and he was my first great musical hero, though it wasn't long before Beethoven and Mozart entered the picture. To this day, those three guys are my holy trinity.

The truth was that up until that time I'd been a total ignoramus about classical music. Shedding my ignorance was a slow process, but over the following months I began to wade deeper into the fascinating waters of real music. I had a long way to go to achieve any degree of sophistication in my musical tastes. At the beginning I just knew what I liked when I heard it. I had zero knowledge of the composers or of the stylistic characteristics of the periods in which they composed.

I got some initial guidance from the comments of FM radio announcers, and I began to check out library books and read about music and composers. I wasn't much into the technicalities of the music, but I found the accounts of the composers' lives intriguing. But most of all, it was the music that I loved.

My father and my brother, those knuckleheads, found my fascination with classical music a matter for endless ribbing. In our house there'd never been any shortage of music: sixties rock and roll; Motown; Folk Revival stuff; even some Broadway shows. But we had almost nothing in the way of classical music, aside from maybe Gershwin's *Porgy and Bess*. I assumed (wrongly, as it turned out) that my dad was as ignorant about classical music as I'd been.

Which is why I was hugely surprised when I opened my dad's presents to me on my eleventh birthday. There, in my young short-stop's hands, were two glorious albums of classical music, albums I treasure to this day. I treasure them because my father gave them to me but also because of what they were.

One of the albums had three Beethoven piano concertos,

the First, the Third, and the Fifth. I'd been slow to warm up to piano music, but this stuff was so fantastic it knocked me on my backside.

And darned if the other album wasn't even better. It was a recording of Schubert's "Unfinished Symphony." By then I'd heard of Schubert, though I wasn't familiar with his works. At that point in my musical education, I didn't think it was possible there could be any symphonies out there that could rival Beethoven's Third or Mozart's Forty-First. In the next hour I learned differently. This Schubert fellow, whoever he was, had entered the competition big time.

But the real question was — how in the world had my Beatles-loving dad known that these two albums would be just what the doctor ordered? A lucky guess? Had he asked someone for suggestions? Or did my dear old dad know more about classical music than he'd let on?

"Dad," I said, "how come it's called the unfinished symphony?"

"Take a look at the liner notes, Tyrus. See, it only has two movements, one in B minor and one in E major."

"Uh . . . okay. So what if it only has two movements?"

"Where are the other movements?"

"Uh . . . I guess there aren't any others."

"That's why it's call unfinished. Symphonies have four movements."

"How come it only has two?"

"That's a great mystery. No one knows for sure what happened. Schubert did write a scherzo movement but he only orchestrated a couple pages of it. That movement is usually ignored. When the symphony's performed, it's almost always performed as a work in two movements." How did my dad know this stuff?

Anyway, I listened to Schubert's wondrous symphony three times that day. It seemed pretty darn perfect just as it was; still, I wouldn't have minded if there had been more.

◆◆◆

We soon discovered that Bump Rhodes could offer some very startling insights. When he saw how well Lou Tolliver and Bobby Radley had been hitting early in the spring, he remarked, "You can always count on those dark-haired guys to do great in the cool spring months. Wait until it's sweltering in July and August. Those guys'll wilt like lettuce. That's when us light-haired guys'll take over and show 'em what hittin' is all about. Us light-haired guys are the real hot-weather hitters."

"Light-haired guys hit better in hot weather than dark-haired guys?" Jimmy said disbelievingly.

"Oh yeah, " Bump said, "it's an established fact. You could look it up."

"You could look it up? And where would you go to look up something like that?"

"What about the bald-headed guys?" I asked. "When do they hit best?"

"Depends what color their hair was when they had some."

"Bump," Jimmy said, not being able to restrain himself, "sorry, man, but what you're spouting is pure tosh."

"Huh?"

"Tosh," Jimmy said again.

"That mean you're doubtin' me?"

"Yep."

"Thought you might be," said Bump.

One day Bump said, "They're always callin' it a diamond, but it ain't really a diamond. It's just a plain old ordinary square a-perched up on one end."

"I didn't know your middle name was Euclid," I said.

"It ain't Euclid," Bump said, "it's Eustace. I'm Edgar Eustace Rhodes, though o'course folks just call me Bump."

"Eustace as in Saint Eustace?" Deacon Lawler said.

"Eustace as in Eustace Station, London?" Jimmy said.

"That's Euston Station," I said, "not Eustace Station."

"Whatever," Jimmy said.

"Nah, it's Eustace as in Uncle Eustace," Bump said.

"So, Mr. Geometrician," Jimmy said, "how 'bout telling us the difference between a diamond and a square that's a-perched up on one end."

"Diamonds are skinnier," Bump said.

"I thought they were fatter," I said.

"Those are the expensive ones," Bump said. "I'm talkin' 'bout the cheaper ones. They're skinnier."

"What about the middle-priced ones?" Jimmy said, "the ones that aren't fat and aren't skinny?"

"Those are the ones that are square," Bump said.

"Thanks for clearing that up, Euclid," I said.

6

Most parents of teen-aged sons experience the late-night phone call, the one where the voice on the other end of the phone says, "Sir, you'd better come down to the station and pick up your son." My dad got that call the night after Billy and his tennis pals at Pocahontas High School won the state championship. A guy on the team had scored a keg of beer, with the result that those knuckleheads spent a chunk of the evening off in the woods celebrating their victory — celebrating until the local constabulary got wind of what was going on and hauled those happy high-schoolers off to the hoosegow.

The night before we broke camp and headed north, it was the Bay City Grays' turn to get that phone call. I'd been reading late and was just dozing off when I heard a tap at the door.

"Duff, you still awake?" It was Deacon Lawler

"I am *now*," I said, mumble-grumble.

"Could you help me go and collect a few of our teammates? Three of 'em have gone and got their sorry selves arrested."

"Let me guess," I said. "That wouldn't be Nick, Zook, and Bump, would it?" Around eleven-thirty, when most of us were leaving the club where we'd been frolicking, that happy trio had insisted on staying behind. I wasn't sure that was a good idea, given the condition they were in, but they promised that when their end-of-spring-training celebration had run its course, they'd take a cab back to camp. Apparently they found themselves a different form of transportation.

I pulled on a pair of sweatpants and a sweatshirt and stepped out in the corridor, just as another door opened and Jimmy Devlin's head appeared. "What's up, fellas?"

"The Deacon and I are off to retrieve Ping, Pang, and Pong from the local drunk tank," I said.

"Ping, Pang, and Pong?"

"Nick, Zook, and Bump," the Deacon said.

"Ah, *that* Ping, Pang, and Pong. You dudes want a little assistance?"

"A little assistance would be a very good thing," the Deacon said. "That'll make one of 'em for each of us."

When we got to the station, as the Deacon dealt with all the paperwork, Jimmy and I studied the wanted posters. "Shoot," I said, "not a single photo of Jim Breyreitz anywhere." I was referring to the Yankee catcher, my arch nemesis.

"Maybe the fuzz have already nabbed the loser," Jimmy said. "Hey, even a blind pig snuffles up a truffle once in a while."

From down in the direction of the cells came a loud, drunken voice. "Whatta 'bout my phone call? Whatta 'bout my court-appointed attorney? Don't us law-'bidin' citerzens got no rights 'round here? Ain't nobody ever heard of habeas carcass?" The loud, drunken voice belonged to Zook Zulaski, and one got the impression the jerk might've had previous experience in surroundings not unlike his current surroundings.

When we reached their cell, Zook Zulaski was clinging to the bars like an inebriated orangutan. Nick Gurganis was slumped off in one corner of the cell looking very zonked out. And Bump was sitting on the floor, his legs splayed, staring off into space with a dazed look on his face and softly singing to himself: ". . . *ain't no bugs on me . . . ain't no bugs on me; / I don't know 'bout the rest of you mugs, / But there ain't no bugs on me.*" I knew that Bump, good Southern Baptist boy that he was, was not normally a drinker. Nick and Zook must've been corrupting our young innocent from the backside of nowhere. Live and learn, Bump, live and learn.

After we'd extracted our trio of teammates from the long arm of the law and manhandled them into the team van, Nick flopped down on the rear seat and immediately fell asleep. Zook climbed in beside me on the second seat, still muttering away about his citizen's rights. "Geez, Duffy, didn't even Morandize me. Geez, Duffy, didn't know I was livin' in the Soviet Union. Did you, Duffy?"

Bump was sitting on the front seat beside the Deacon, completely zombified, still softly crooning: " . . . *ain't no lobsters on me . . . ain't no lobsters on me; / I don't know 'bout the rest of you mobsters, / But there ain't no lobsters on me.*" I didn't know if what Bump was singing was a real song or if this was just drunken improvisation.

Back at our training facility, we steered them as best we could toward their assigned rooms. Zook, as I tossed him roughly into his room, was still mumbling something about writs of habeas carcass, bills of restrainder, and ex-post factory laws. Jimmy opened Nick's door, carefully aimed his body, then shoved him in the direction of his bed. Nick took three stumbling steps and sprawled face down on his bed.

It took all three of us to get Bump through the door and onto his bed. For a moment he lay there softly singing: " . . . *ain't no ticks on me . . . ain't no ticks on me; / I don't know 'bout the rest of you . . .* " — and then Bump Rhodes became an inert blob. "Good night, sweet prince," I whispered, "and flights of angels sing thee to thy rest."

Home sweet home — if only for the briefest of respites. One night, and then it would be off to Toronto for Opening Day.

At least I could unpack a bit before repacking. And I could listen to some Mozart. And sleep in my own bed. And have a long and leisurely chat with Laura from the privacy of my own apartment. I might even do a little laundry. Okay . . . maybe the laundry could wait.

I went over and said hi to my neighbor Chuck, who'd been dutifully collecting my mail. Our deal was that I fed his cat when he was away and he collected my mail when I was away. It was a lot more convenient to have Chuck do it than have the post office hold it for me.

I got along good with Chuck's cat, whose name was Boog. I liked Boog a lot, and he always seemed to like me; every time I fed him I wondered if maybe if I shouldn't go to the SPCA and get a cat of my own. A cat, I thought, would give me a little bit of company but not too much company. But, because I was away so often during the summer, it didn't seem like it would be fair to the creature to be left alone so much. Other than our mail-and-cat arrangement, Chuck and I had little interaction. We both believed that good fences make good neighbors. Chuck, I couldn't help noticing, seemed to have a rather curious personal life; but I did my best not to notice too much.

I took the box of mail into my dining nook and plopped it down on the table. Then I took a long, steamy shower in my very own bathroom. Then I put on my very own fresh 'jamas and bathrobe. Damnation, I almost felt like a new man.

I tried calling Laura in New York but only got her answering machine. Hmm. Maybe she had something on tonight I'd forgotten about. I felt a twinge of concern. Well, maybe she'd call me later.

I poured myself a splash of Jameson and thumbed through my CDs. I pulled out an album of Beethoven piano sonatas and was about to put it on when I changed my mind. Instead, I reached for something I hadn't played in a long time: Jackson Browne's *For Everyman*. I had a sudden desire to hear the song "These Days." It was a song that forced me to think about all the things I'd failed to do for Laura, all the things I could've easily done but hadn't.

I sipped my whiskey and listened to the bittersweet lyrics, staring out at the darkening night sky. The next thing I knew, it was morning.

In the morning when I checked my answering machine for messages, there were none. Usually that makes me happy. Today, not so much.

I slugged down a large mug of strong black coffee and went through my stack of mail. Two-thirds of it found a home in the trash. The bills I set aside to attend to later. There were only a few personal letters; I'd take a look at them before driving to the ball park to catch the team bus to the airport.

That's when I spotted the letter. With the Eire stamp. With the faint whiff of lavender. It wasn't addressed to Jimmy Devlin, care of Ty Duffy, like the ones I had before. This one was addressed to Ty Duffy.

I poured a second mug of coffee. Figured I'd need it. Then I tore open the envelope and extracted the letter. There was no doubt who it was from. Kathleen Brogan. Kat.

Kat had impressed me in Ireland last fall – with her intelligence, her fierce independence, her beauty, and her daring. She'd also confused the hell out of me. The minds of women remain terra incognita for many men, and Kat's mind was a classic case in point. Why she'd done what she'd done over there in Ireland had mystified Jimmy and me. Laura had been more understanding and forgiving of Kat. But Jimmy Devlin had been deeply hurt. To him her actions had seemed a betrayal. And the lad was still trying like anything to get her out of his system. He was failing miserably, though he continued to fight the good fight.

Now – since Jimmy had refused to respond to any of her overtures – Kat wanted my help. I was her last hope. Kat, I said to myself, if you're turning to me for help, that's the action of a desperate woman.

What Kat wanted was simple enough. Encourage Jimmy to call her or write to her. She felt, and she was probably right, that once the ice was broken again with Jimmy, she could take things from there. She knew what I knew – that Jimmy Devlin was still crazy about her. But he was also a thick-skulled, obstinate knucklehead who had his pride.

But the question in my mind was, was re-connecting with Kat really the best thing for Jimmy? Mightn't it just screw the lad up once again? And mightn't it put the lad, yet again, in harm's way with Mick Slattery's cadre of loyal louts? And mightn't it cause havoc with Jimmy's pitching, which would cause havoc for the Bay City Grays? Thanks a lot, Kat, for mucking up my neat and tidy little life.

7

On the flight to Toronto, Jimmy and I got in a pair of cribbage games. I won the first but got skunked in the second. Lousy bugger — loading his crib with sevens and eights and coming away with double runs!

Most of the guys dozed or listened to their headsets during the flight, but Bump Rhodes kept getting up and wandering around in the aisle, chatting with the flight attendants, using the toilet, getting more soft drinks, you name it. The lad was excited. This was his first trip with a major-league ball club; he simply didn't know what to do with himself.

Once more I couldn't help wondering why the kid was even here. Why were Pete Paulson, our GM, and Whitey Wiggins, our skipper, so enamored of him? Okay, he had the physical attributes you'd want in a catcher and maybe some of the inner qualities, too. But for goodness sakes, his hitting was abysmal. They say you can make stats say anything. But not Bump's. There was *no way* you could make his minor-league hitting stats say anything other than that he was a mediocre minor leaguer. Even saying that was giving him every benefit of the doubt.

So why were the head honchos so eager to get this kid to the big leagues? I must've been missing something. Because to me, Bump Rhodes had all the markings of another promising young ball player who, in the end, would turn out not to be good enough.

Jimmy must've been reading my mind. "Duff, what in hell were they thinking inviting Bump to come north with the big club? They think we need comic relief or something? Shit, I hope Pete Paulson isn't sleeping with Bump's momma."

Jimmy had an impish gleam in his big brown eyes. It pleased me to see him cracking jokes. That augured well.

"It's a mystery wrapped in an enigma inside of a riddle," I said.

"What it is," Jimmy said "is a load of tosh."

◆ ◆ ◆

Jimmy Devlin took the hill for us in our opener against the Blue Jays, and last year's Rookie of the Year gave us seven shutout innings as we snagged a six-to-one win. Lou Tolliver bashed a two-run homer, Deacon Lawler added a solo shot, and Bobby Radley and I each chipped in with a pair of singles. In the top of the ninth, Whitey sent Bump up to pinch hit for the Deacon.

As Bump strode toward the plate, Dave Rubenstein, the Deacon, Jimmy, and I watched with hope in our hearts. Maybe the kid would surprise us.

Bump took three mighty hacks — came up Canada dry — and headed back to the dugout, fulfilling our expectations.

"Don't think we're lookin' at the next Gabby Hartnett," Dave said.

"Nope," Jimmy said. "Nor the next Bill Dickey."

"Not even the next Sherm Lollar," Deacon Lawler said.

"Do you think just maybe . . . ," I said, "Bump could be . . . the next Bob Uecker?"

"A real possibility," Dave said, and Deak and Jimmy nodded.

After the game Deacon, Jimmy, and me, with the Bumpster in tow, went off to celebrate our first victory in our own wholesome fashion. Wholesome, anyway, in contrast to how Lou, Spike, Todd, Nick, Zook, and some of the others chose to celebrate.

Jimmy, rather than being pumped after his classy performance, seemed sullen and morose, though three beers into things he brightened up a bit. But Edgar Eustace Rhodes had enough high spirits for the four of us. Despite K-ing in his first official at-bat in the big leagues, Bump could barely contain himself — for the lad had just fulfilled his boyhood dream: Bump Rhodes was officially a big-league ball player. He might have gone oh-for-one, but no matter. Bump Rhodes was now a part of MLB history.

With his boundless energy, Bump was practically bouncing off the walls of the restaurant. And when his food arrived, he turned that energy to devouring one of the biggest, bloodiest steaks I'd ever laid eyes on. As if he needed any more testosterone.

"Good golly, Bump," Jimmy said, eyeing his food, "in truth, dude, you are a troglodyte."

"He is," I said, "but he's *our* troglodyte." Bump was grinning like we'd just complimented him.

We were about five minutes into our meal when I noticed that Bump was holding his knife in his left hand as he sawed away at the mountain of bovine flesh filling his plate.

"Bump, you aren't a natural lefty, are you?"

"A lefty? Nah. Just in regard to my politics. Ha, ha." Ha, ha was right; Bump was as apolitical as the fork in his right hand.

"Seriously. You realize you're cutting with your left hand, don't you?"

"Makes it easier," Bump said. "That way I don't have to switch my knife with my fork." Using his knife, Bump tapped his forehead, signifying he'd thought the whole thing through.

"I'm a lefty," Jimmy said, "but even I don't cut with my left. I keep my fork in my left and cut with my right."

"Most righties cut with their right also," I insisted. "I don't think anybody cuts with their left."

"Guess I'm just weird," Bump said.

"Can't argue with that," Jimmy said.

"Bump," I said, "just out of curiosity, which eye is your dominant eye?"

The kid, using his left hand, had just cut a big chunk of steak and deposited it in his gaping maw, so we waited patiently for awhile, admiring his powerfully masticating jaws.

Then Bump said, "Huh?"

"I was asking you about your dominant eye. For most people, their right eye is their dominant eye. You're right-eyed too, right?"

"I got two darn good eyes," Bump averred, "both of 'em twenty-twenty. I don't have no blasted dominant eye. Both of them eyes of mine are dominant. Neither of 'em takes a back seat to the other."

"Bump, just about everyone has a dominant eye. There's no need for your non-dominant eye to take it personally."

Jimmy and the Deacon were taking all this in without comment, not sure where I was going with it. I wasn't sure myself, though a kernel of an idea had begun to form.

"Okay, do this for me," I said. "Take your right hand and point it up at the corner of the room where the wall and the ceiling meet."

Giving me a funny look, Bump raised his arm and pointed his finger at where I'd said.

"Okay, now close your right eye." Bump scrunched up his eye. "Is your finger still pointing at the corner? Or did it move?"

"Still at the corner."

"Aha. Okay, now open your right eye and close your left."

"Holy Molasses!" Bump said. "Whatta ya know about that!"

"I'm guessing your finger moved."

"Duffy, you're one smart feller, you know that?"

"I guess that means your left eye's the dominant one."

" . . . well . . . it don't make much of a matter, does it? I mean, so what if it is?"

"For most people it doesn't matter at all. For you, it could." Bump just stared at me opaquely.

"Bump," Deacon said, finally getting in on this, "did you ever try hitting left-handed? Or did you ever try switch-hitting?"

Bump, his chewing momentarily in abeyance, covered his upper lip with his lower lip, then shook his head no.

"Not even as a kid playing whiffle ball in the back yard?"

"Oh well, o' course I did a little of that."

"How'd you do from the left side?"

"I don't know . . . okay, I guess. You know, I didn't really think a lot about it. It was just goofin' around."

"Bump, Duffy may be on to something. It might be interesting to see what you could do hitting from the left side."

"Cripes, Deacon, you ain't goin' ta turn me into a lefty, are ya?"

"Shoot, Bump," Jimmy said, entering the fray, "since you can't hit righties worth a lick, you could hardly do any worse going up to the plate as a lefty." Bump's eyes darted angrily at Jimmy, then darted angrily back at me and the Deacon.

"I *can* hit righties, darn it," Bump muttered, more to himself than to us. "I *can*, darn it."

"Bump," Jimmy said, realizing he needed to make amends for his last comment, "it's lefties that you can hit. Lefties. And you hit 'em good, too. Nobody wants to change that. But what Duffy and the Deacon are suggesting just might be worth thinking about. To be an everyday player, Bump, you've got to be able to hit righties."

"I can learn to hit 'em," said an aggrieved Bump. "I can, darn it. I'm young. I can learn."

"Yes," said the Deacon, "that's right. You're young and you can learn. But look. Let me and Duffy do a little experimenting. Nothing may come of it, we realize that. And for now we'll keep this to ourselves, if you want. But listen, son, you're okay with us trying a few things out, aren't you?" When Bump didn't say anything, Deacon repeated himself. "You are, aren't you?"

Bump stared glumly at the table top. Then he lifted his head and looked for a long moment straight into the Deacon's face. Finally Bump Rhodes slowly nodded his head.

And thus began The Great Experiment.

On Tuesday afternoon a couple of hours before pre-game BP, Deacon and I led Bump to the batting cage beneath the stadium.

"I'll set it at seventy-five," Deak said. Bump had brought three bats of different weights, not sure which one would feel most comfortable. Switch-hitters rarely use the same bat from different sides of the plate.

Bump picked one and took a few left-handed practice cuts. "This feels weird. This plan of yours ain't a-gonna work. I can tell you right now, it ain't a-gonna work."

"Get your rear in there, Edgar. Let's see what you can do," I said. "Choke up a few inches till you get the knack of it."

"Choke up? Shoot. Never choked up in my life." Bump looked skeptical, but he stepped up to the dish and readied himself for the pitch. He let a couple go by before taking a hesitant swing. He foul-tipped it straight back into the net.

"You got wood on your first swing!" I shouted.

"Some wood," Bump grumped.

He watched a couple more, then missed altogether on his second full cut. "Shoot," he said. Bump gritted his teeth. He let three more go by, then nailed the next one dead-center, lining the ball straight back off the top of the pitching machine.

"I got you, you son of a gun!" Bump sang out.

"Don't go breaking the machine!" the Deacon shouted. Bump grinned and gritted his teeth even harder.

We kept at it for another twenty minutes. Bump had several swings and misses and a lot of fouls, but he also squared up quite a few and ripped 'em good.

"Put it up to eighty," Bump yelled. "Think I'm ready."

"Tomorrow," Deacon said. "That's enough for now. Bump, I like what I see. How you feeling, kid?" Bump looked disappointed. He was warming up nicely to our little experiment and wasn't ready to call it a day.

"Look at that!" Bump said, studying his hands. "Gettin' a gol-darn blister. Guess you gotta form different callouses hitting from the left side. Never woulda thunk it." Bump was the only guy on the Grays' roster who refused to wear batting gloves. In the entire big leagues, there were only three or four such guys. Old School guys, that's for sure.

"Like the feel of the wood against the palms of my big paws," Bump said. "Puts me and the bat at one. Heck, I even like it when I hit a real stinger. Gives me a quiver in the liver."

"You don't actually sleep with your bat, do you?" I said.

" 'Course I do," Bump said, giving me a broad grin. "Me 'n' Betsy, man, me 'n' Betsy."

"You call your bat *Betsy?*"

" 'Course I do. What else would I call her? Hey, you guys reckon I can hit some lefty during regular BP?"

"No," the Deacon and I both said.

"Aw . . . And why not, for cripe sakes?"

"We're just gettin' our toes in the water, son," Deak said. "Liked what we saw today. But let's not go rushin' things."

On Wednesday afternoon we spent forty-five minutes with Bump in the batting cage. He was squaring up the ball well at 75 mph, so we notched the speed up to 80. Before long he was making pretty solid contact with most of those pitches, too. The lad was thrilled.

"Triple!" he shouted, after he clouted one really good. ". . . oh, man, crappy little blooper! . . . hey-hey, double off the Green Monster! . . . now that there's what ya call a dinger, my friends, a dinger! You can touch 'em all, baby, you can touch 'em all!"

When we set the machine at 85, Bump struggled to make solid contact, so we decided to knock off for the day.

"C'mon, I was just gettin' the hang of it. Let's keep going."

"Tomorrow," Deak said. "That's enough for now."

"How about pre-game BP?"

"No!" Deacon and I said.

We split our final pair of games in Toronto, losing Wednesday night by six to four, then winning Thursday afternoon eight to four. Neither Stan Foubert nor Jumpin' Jack were especially sharp, but they didn't get knocked around, either. The highlights for us were Todd Cottington's pair of homers and Bobby Radley's pair of sensational catches. The second one, on Thursday afternoon, a full-extension, sliding grab, was a game-saver. The Deacon worked behind the plate in the first two games and Miguel Torres caught the afternoon game on get-away day. For three days, Bump Rhodes had bullpen-catcher duty. But Bump Rhodes wasn't complaining. Bump Rhodes was a big-league catcher, and he seemed perfectly content to bide his time.

8

The Red Sox were three and oh after sweeping their home-opening series versus Tampa Bay. We came into Boston at two and one, following our decent start in Toronto. Jorge Comellas would take the hill for us on Friday evening, Alfred King would pitch on Saturday, and then Jimmy Devlin would go against Pedro Ordoñez on Sunday, a much-anticipated matchup of aces.

Fenway Park was packed and noisy on Friday night. The energy level, as usual, was like nowhere else. Boston fans can get ugly, but they have a real passion for the game and for their beloved Sox — they are baseball's truest fans, a smidgen ahead of Cubs, Cardinals, and Yankee fans.

Juan Flores got things going for us in the top of the first, slapping a double to right-center. I tried to punch a slider on the outside corner to right but grounded to second, moving Juan over to third. When Lou Tolliver swatted a towering fly to deep center, Juan tagged up and scored easily. It was a good start.

In the bottom of the first, Jorge Comellas, the Tijuana Teaser, did his finest Luis Tiant imitation, confusing the Sox hitters with an amazing variety of junk. He set them down in order.

As I trotted toward our dugout, I glanced up at the seats. A year ago when I'd done that, I'd spotted a gorgeous auburn-haired lass sitting six or seven rows above our dugout — a lass who turned out to be Kat Brogan, a lass who did a wondrous job of dumping a boatload of trouble on Jimmy Devlin and on me. Tonight, Kat Brogan wasn't sitting there. Softly to myself I said, "*Whew*."

It had been an eventful year — eventful both good and bad — since that night. It was a year in which Jimmy Devlin landed himself in deep "shite" with the loyal louts of Mr. Michael Slattery. A year in which Laura Morgan, inexplicably, chose to come back into the life of Ty Duffy. A year in which my inimitable mother stumbled upon a lost literary work and parlayed it into a lapful of greenback dollars.

A year, against all odds, in which the Bay City Grays stopped being bottom-feeders and emerged as bona fide contenders.

But a lot remained unresolved. Jimmy and Kat, for sure. And I'd begun to feel pretty uncertain about where things actually stood between Laura and me. I *really* did not want to blow it with Laura. Not this time. Not like I'd done once before.

Jorge worked out of jams a couple of times in the fourth and the seventh, and we came through for him with several additional runs. Jesus Hernandez came in in the bottom of the ninth and closed things out. Final Score: Grays 5, Red Sox 2.

After the game I took a break from my teammates and followed my usual post-game routine in Boston, making the rounds of all my favorite record stores.

I didn't find anything I couldn't live without, but I picked up a few CDs, including recordings of *Hansel and Gretel* and *The Marriage of Figaro* I didn't already have. I also picked up a couple Mark Knopfler CDs. My brother Billy is a Dire Straits fan, but I prefer Knopfler's solo stuff — gentle tunes with great guitar riffs.

It was nearly twelve-thirty when I got back to the hotel, and as I crossed the lobby heading for the elevators I heard a deep voice say "Mr. Duffy?" I spun around and found myself staring into the face of a man who looked vaguely familiar. He was stocky, about five-ten, with thinning sandy-colored hair.

"Might I have a brief word, sor?" He smiled faintly as he watched a shock of recognition cross my face. The man I was looking at I had last seen lying unconscious on the cold stone jetty of an island off the west coast of Ireland. His name was Michael Slattery.

"Mr. Slattery?" I said, dumbfounded.

"Mick to me friends," he said, extending his hand. I took it and gave it a minor shake. "Think we could sit over there?" he said, gesturing with his head toward a quiet corner of the lobby.

"Uh, sure," I said, "that'll be okay — though I hadn't realized you counted me among your friends."

"Then we need to get that changed," he said. "In this sad, short, brutish life of ours we need all the friends we can get."

"Well," I said, sitting down and beginning to get over my initial shock, "in this sad, short, brutish life of ours there are friends and then there are friends."

"And Jimmy Devlin, I imagine, is one of the latter. That's grand, sor, grand. Just how it oughtta be. No finer quality than loyalty to one's pals, is there?"

When I didn't say anything in response, Mick Slattery just sat there staring at me, a watery smile on his thin-lipped face. I couldn't help noticing a faint scar high on his forehead, a scar that curved up through the thin hair in his receding hairline; and I couldn't help remembering the circumstances that had caused the scar to exist.

"Kathleen Brogan's doing really well," he finally said.

"That's great," I said. "I'm glad to hear it. Can't say I know her very well, but to the extent that I do, I like her quite a lot."

"She's a remarkable lass," Slattery said, "like a daughter to me. There was a time when I considered her father my closest friend in the world." For just a second he looked grim, and I couldn't help intuiting that something must've caused a serious rift between the two of them. Could it have been Kat herself? I wondered. I knew that Kat's father had been dead for at least a decade, though I knew nothing of the circumstances of his death. For a fleeting moment I wondered if he hadn't died of natural causes.

Who, really, was this man? Long before I'd ever met Kat, I knew Mick Slattery by reputation, or by reputations, since they varied widely depending on who was talking; but I certainly didn't know him. My one previous encounter with him — that day out there on the Great Blasket — was hardly auspicious, as I watched him terrorize my mother and browbeat Kat Brogan, while at the same time inspire fear and fierce loyalty in his foot soldiers. No, I really didn't know Mick Slattery. But I suspected that the real Mick was closer to being Genghis Khan than Gandhi.

"Listen, lad, it's Kat I wish to speak to you about. She's been through quite a rough patch these last few years. But as I just told you, lately she's been doin' grand. Tell you the truth, that lass has been makin' my life a bed of roses, runnin' things like she's been doin'. Hell, sor, I feel a bit like me own boyos have kicked me to the curb," and he gave a soft chuckle. "Them boyos of mine seem to prefer Kat to me. Hell, can't say I blame 'em." Somebody, I felt sure, was leading up to something.

"So, here's the deal. You say you like Kathleen Brogan, and I want more than anything to believe you. Assuming it's true, then you, like me, want what's best for Kat." He paused and stared at me, waiting for me to give him some sign of agreement. I just sat there and stared back at him. I knew the bastard was trying to manipulate me. And there's nothing I hate more than knowing that someone's trying to manipulate me.

"What's best for Kat right now is that she keep on doing exactly what she's been doing," he said. "What isn't best for Kat is for her to get involved with your pal Devlin again. I don't know if she's had any contact with him recently. But I sincerely believe that if she did, that would be an unfortunate development for all concerned. It would undermine all the fine progress the lass has made."

Like the Tar Baby in that old Uncle Remus story, I just sat there keeping my own counsel. Like the Tar Baby, I wasn't sayin' nothin'.

"So . . . what might you be knowin' about the matter, sor?" said Slattery, deciding it was time to give the Tar Baby a little poke with a stick.

Finally I said, "Jimmy's business is his own, Mr. Slattery, and my business is my own. I don't mind his, and he doesn't mind mine. As far as Kat Brogan is concerned, all I can tell you is I don't think he's had any contact with her — none that I know of, anyway. And it's my impression he doesn't intend to have any. As far as I know, Jimmy believes he's finished with Kat Brogan."

I wasn't *exactly* lying. I felt certain Jimmy hadn't made any attempt to contact Kat. I believed that part of what I was saying was absolutely true. On the other hand, I was far from certain that Jimmy was finished with Kat. There's a passage in Malory where Merlin tells Arthur that when a man's heart is set, he's loath to change his mind. I felt pretty sure that Jimmy's heart was set, whether he realized it or not.

"I very much hope what you say is so," he said. "If the lad is truly finished with Kathleen, that's a grand and excellent thing. Would you happen to know, by the way, if she's tried to contact him? He hasn't made mention of that to you, has he?"

I remembered Jimmy telling me about the letter she'd sent him last fall, a letter he'd refused to answer. And I felt sure she must've sent him others since then, ones he'd similarly refused to answer. That was why she'd finally sent one to me, a letter I'd been sitting on for the last five days while I figured out what the hell do about it. Although Mick Slattery didn't know it or intend it, he was inadvertently helping me make up my mind in a fashion that might not be to his liking.

"Like I said, Jimmy's business is his and my business is mine. He hasn't mentioned Kat to me for several months, and far as I know, Jimmy and Kat are kaput." On the literal level my claim was absolutely true. And yet it was a claim I didn't believe for one tiny second.

Mick Slattery got to his feet and held out his hand, signaling the end of our conversation. "I hope you are right, sor. I sincerely do. Thank you for taking the time to speak with me."

I remained sitting there by myself for a few more minutes. Damnation, I thought, the great man himself had come to see me. Taking matters into his own hands. This was obviously something that was hugely important to him. Kat Brogan, obviously, was hugely important to him.

It was a damned good thing, I reflected, that Jimmy hadn't responded to Kat's overtures. And yet I couldn't see Jimmy sticking to that noble resolve much longer. I knew him too well to believe that. He could be stubborn and obstinate, but Kat had insinuated herself deeply into his heart.

Well damn it, Jimmy, it looks like we're back to playing with fire. But damn it, who did Mick Slattery think he was, trying to control people's lives? And damn it, who the hell did he think he was — trying to manipulate me!

On a cool, drizzly Saturday night we lost a tough one. Alfred King gave us seven strong innings and we were up three-two going into the bottom of the eighth. If our setup guy, Joe Oliver, could only hold the lead, we'd have Jesus Hernandez to close things out in the bottom of the ninth. Only four games into the season and already Jesus had racked up a pair of saves. But it didn't happen that way. J.O. retired the first two guys, then gave up a walk followed by a homer that disappeared in the direction of the Citgo sign way behind the Green Monster. When we went down in order in the top of the ninth, that was all she wrote. Sox 4, Grays 3.

The loss dampened our spirits. Except for Bump. The kid, making his first big-league start, had caught the entire game. That wasn't too much of a challenge, since eighty percent of Alfred's pitches were fast balls. And facing the Sox's left-handed pitcher, Bump Rhodes had collected his first major-league hit, a line-drive single up the middle. Now Bump had the ball to prove it — the first baseball for his trophy case. He was grinning like a kid on a Yuletide morning.

From out of the showers resounded Bump's joyful noise — "Jo-lene . . . Jo-lene . . . Jo-lene . . . Jo-leeeene!"

"Hey, Dolly Parton," yelled Zook Zulaski, "how 'bout shutting the fuck up!" Like Bump, Zook had started his first game of the season, giving Nick Gurganis a night off. Unlike Bump, Zook had taken the collar.

Bump stepped out of the showers with a towel wrapped around his waist. He didn't bear the slightest resemblance to Dolly Parton.

"You got a problem with my singing?" he said.

"Just shut the fuck up, okay?" Zook gave Bump a meaningful

look. "Else I'll have to shut you up."

Bump thought about that for a moment. Then he said, "You'll have to shut me up? Sakes alive, Zook, you and what army?"

"Hey, you two," the Deacon said, "leave it alone. Save all that crap for when we face the Yankees." But Zook Zulaski wasn't in the mood to leave it alone.

"We just lost us a ball game, Rook. So how come you're so fuckin' cheerful?"

"I'm so cheerful," Bump said, "because I just got me a freakin' base hit. That's how come. So how many freakin' base hits did you get?" Coming from a brash, upstart rookie, those were fighting words.

Bobby Radley and Deacon Lawler quickly stepped in between the two of them.

"Cool it, dammit," Bobby said. "You're teammates. Teammates don't fight teammates."

"With the Bay City Grays," I said, "it's all for one and one for all." Good old Alexander Dumas. I knew the bastard would come in handy one day.

"Duff's right," the Deacon said. "We can yell at each other. We can give each other all the crapola in the world. But that's as far as it goes. Save the rough stuff for when we need it. Like when we play the Yankees."

"Sorry," Bump said, looking shamefaced. "All my fault, Zook. I promise ya, man, I won't be singing no more Dolly Parton. You got my word on that." Zook still looked pretty pissed off.

"Shake on it, you knuckleheads," the Deacon said.

"All for one and one for all," Bump said, taking Zook's hand and shaking it. "Right?"

"Yeah, right . . . d'Artagnan," Zook said — which took every one of us by surprise.

Bump, Jimmy, and I went out to get a quick bite at a little place I knew on the fringes of Beacon Hill. We didn't plan to make a late night of it. Jimmy would be going for us tomorrow, and on nights before he pitched he liked to get his beauty rest.

"Who would have thought," I said, "that Zook Zulaski, who's never read a book in his life, would have heard of d'Artagnan. How'd he come up with that?"

"Movies?" Bump said.

"Nope," Jimmy said. "Video games."

"Seriously?"

"Oh yeah. Zook's been hooked on video games since forever. No tellin' all the cool stuff he's picked up from that."

"Video games!" Bump scoffed. "I say pah to video games."

"You're not into video games?"

"Video games are shite," Bump said, "pure and simple."

"Bump, I'm shocked. Where'd you learn a word like that?"

"From you, Duff, from you. I figured if you used it, it must be okay for me to use it."

"Well, crap. The last thing I want to be is a corrupter of America's youth."

"Duff," Jimmy said, "I think it's a bit late to be worrying about that."

Bump must've felt bad about his run-in with Zook, since he apologized to us about a dozen times. "Hey, no sweat, bubba," Jimmy said. "Forget it. Though I would've been curious to see how a little dust-up between you two Neanderthals would've come out."

"Jimmy," Bump said, "you don't really have no doubts 'bout how it would've come out, do you?"

"Bump, Zook is no pushover."

"Cripe sakes, Jimmy, I'd've flattened the poor feller."

"You really think so?"

"Hey, I ain't a-whistlin' Dixie here, ya know."

"You're a big-time pugilist?" I said.

"Don't know what that means," Bump said. "But when it comes to a little rough and tumble, you boys're lookin' at the King of Conuceh County."

King Edgar? I thought. Wasn't Edgar the last guy standing at the end of *King Lear?* After everybody and his brother were dead?

An hour or so later we were trekking across The Boston Common, heading in what I hoped was the direction of our hotel.

"You know where in heck we are, Duff?" Bump asked, sounding a bit dubious.

"Hey, I have a pretty good general idea," I said, irritated at having my navigational skills questioned.

"If Duffy can't do it, nobody can," Jimmy said.

"Twenty dollars says I can get us there in under ten minutes," I said.

"I ain't no bettin' man," Bump said. "'Sides, it's against the rules of baseball."

"It's against the rules of Nature not to be a betting man, Bump," Jimmy said.

"Guess I'm just a freak of Nature," Bump said.

"More than likely," Jimmy said.

We passed close to the big pond where they have those swan boats that tourists and young families enjoy. Seeing them always makes me think of Wagner's *Lohengrin.* Maybe, I mused to myself, Bump Rhodes is really just some long-lost Grail Knight who's reappeared from the mists of antiquity. Maybe a white dove will come floating down from heaven and pull Bump and his swan boat off to the Grail Castle where he will heal the Maimed King and put an end to the Waste Land.

Amidst my flights of fancy, suddenly looming up in the mirky darkness ahead of us were three and a half hulking Grendel-monsters. The big ones bore a strong likeness to the three Irish toughs who'd roughed us up last year in the hotel hallway. The smaller one bore a resemblance to that little piece of crap named Molloy, a little piece of crap whose manhood I'd once threatened to remove. Maybe tonight I'd get a chance to make good on that threat.

This could hardly be accidental. My guess was that Mick Slattery decided to put a little exclamation point on the discussion we'd had the night before. He was sending me and Jimmy a reminder that Kat Brogan was strictly off limits.

"Shit," Jimmy said, seeing what I'd already seen.

"You thinkin' these fellers might mean trouble?" Bump said.

"You can be pretty sure of that," Jimmy said. "Whatta ya say, Duff? Shall we make a run for it? We can surely outrun the oafs."

"Discretion is often the better part of valor," I said.

"Now don't you be a-worryin'," Bump said. "I can deal with these fellers if need be. Heck, maybe they don't mean us no harm a-tall."

"Uh . . . ," said Jimmy, ". . . I'm fairly sure they do."

"Hello, there," Bump called out to the approaching trio and a half. "Nice night for a stroll, eh fellas?"

"Forget the other arseholes," one of them said. "It's feckin' Devlin we want."

"Now hold on there, fellers," Bump said. "No need to be precipitatin' nothin'."

"Get lost, ya feckin' gobshite," came the reply. Now the Grendel-monsters were at very close quarters.

"You just keep behind me," Bump said to me and Jimmy. "I can deal with 'em." And then Edgar Eustace Rhodes went into action. My word, did he ever. No wonder he claimed to be the King of Conuceh County.

With his left foot, Bump suddenly kicked the right-most monster on the inside of his knee, felling him like a screaming tree. In the next instant he'd smashed his right elbow into the jaw of the middle monster while at practically the same time he threw his left fist, with 240 pounds of solid muscle behind it, into the upper-chest area of the guy on the left. *Wham, slam, bam.*

The third guy slumped down onto his knees, his body paralyzed by the stunning blow to his chest. The other two were writhing on the ground, one with a useless leg, one with what was more than likely a broken jaw. It'd taken a whole second and a half for Bump Rhodes to make chopped liver out of Mick Slattery's trio of barroom brawlers.

By then little Molloy was fleeing the scene like a frightened jackrabbit. Good thing for him and his testicles he was.

"Did you say you knew how to get us back to the hotel?" a wide-eyed Jimmy said to me.

"I believe I did, yes. Perhaps we should endeavor to do that."

"Thanks, Bump," Jimmy said, as we hurried along across Boston Common toward Tremont Street. "You know, Bump, I'm guessing it was a damn good thing Zook decided to shake your hand instead of trying to shut your mouth."

"I don't enjoy hurtin' folks," Bump said. "I don't do it less'n they deserve it. Those fellers back there, I'm guessin' they deserved it."

"More than most," I said.

9

For the last three years when the Grays had been on the road, I'd chosen to room alone. This year I was back to having a roomie. A roomie named Jimmy Devlin. That had been my decision. With the Deacon now having Bump under his wing, Jimmy had been cut adrift. I figured it might be better if someone was keeping an eye out for the lad.

When I suggested to Jimmy that we might room together, he shot me a squinty-eyed look and uttered those immortal words: "Why don't you get stuffed, amigo." *Ouch.* It was verbatim what I'd said to him a year and a half earlier when he'd asked if we might room together. Seeing the look on my face, Jimmy couldn't help laughing gleefully. "Take that, ya son of a bitch."

"Guess I deserved it."

"Guess you did. But okay, sure, I suppose I could put up with you — just as long as you're not some kind of a snoring bastard."

"Uh . . . well . . . I'll do me best, me bucko."

"Your best had better be pretty damn good."

So when Jimmy and I got back to our hotel room following those startling events on The Boston Common, we exchanged wide-eyed looks as if to say, "Did we just witness what we think we just witnessed?"

"That Bumpster of ours," Jimmy said "is one lean, mean fighting machine."

"Jason Bourne, Jackie Chan, and Cuchulainn rolled into one."

"I still have no clue why the guy's even with the ball club, but right this moment I'm glad he is."

"Maybe that's why he's here. Sent to be your guardian angel."

"If he was, he's one tough son-of-a-bitch of an angel."

"You think Lou Tolliver could take him?"

"Lou? Not a chance in hell."

"How 'bout Honest Jack Strachan?" I said, referring to Mick Slattery's right-hand guy.

"Shoot, Honest Jack? Hell, Duffy, even you were man enough to take Honest Jack." Jimmy was referring to what had occurred last fall on the Great Blasket when I knocked Jack Strachan into the sea and the two of us had come mighty close to drowning.

"Well, how 'bout me?" I said "You think *I* could take him?"

Jimmy looked at me and mouthed the word, "*You?*" Then both burst into laughter. I'm not sure which of us was laughing the hardest.

"Whatta ya think, Jimmy," I said after we'd calmed down, "you think Bump could take John Wayne?" I said that because I knew how much Jimmy loved *The Quiet Man*, a film with one of the all-time great movie fights.

Jimmy pondered that one for awhile. "Nah," he said at last, "don't think so — not the Duke. Good as Bump is, he couldn't take the Duke. Not even the King of Conuceh County could take the Duke."

Later that night as I was dropping off to sleep, I remembered my earlier musings about *Lohengrin* and the crazy notion that Bump Rhodes might be destined to be some sort of a Grail Knight. Considering the events that had transpired during the evening, maybe that notion wasn't quite as ludicrous as it had seemed.

On a bright, crisp Sunday afternoon Jimmy Devlin took the mound against the Boston Red Sox and the celebrated Pedro Ordoñez. The matchup pitted last year's Rookie of the Year versus last year's AL Cy Young winner.

In the bottom of the first Jimmy struggled, giving up a walk, a single, and a two-run double. The Sox held on to that two-to-nothing score until the top of the sixth. That was when Todd Cottington singled, Bobby Radley tripled him home, and Spike Bannister scored Bobby with a sac fly. Suddenly it was a two-two ball game. It stayed that way until the top of the eighth.

Juan Flores led off for us and Pedro's first pitch clipped him on the elbow. With our speedy lead-off man on first, we had several options: sacrifice bunt, straight steal, hit-and-run, or none of the above. On the first pitch to me I squared around to bunt, then took a half-swing and punched the ball over the head of the charging third baseman. *Got you, you bastard!* Juan scampered all the way round to third.

Now we had runners on first and third and nobody out – a sweet situation for Lou Tolliver. The only problem was that Lou hadn't had a hit off Pedro in a month of Sundays – and this was Sunday. Predictably, Lou went down on strikes.

With left-handed hitting Todd Cottington coming up, the Sox made the call to their bullpen, bringing in a crafty lefty named Link Longley; Link's job, nine times out of ten, was to retire a single left-handed batter. As usual, Link did his job well, fanning Todd on four pitches. *Crap.* Now, our baserunners still on first and third, we had two down.

With switch-hitting Bobby Radley stepping to the plate, the Sox decided to keep Longley in to make Bobby hit from the right side. That was what did them in. Link missed his spot, leaving a slider hanging in the middle of the plate. Bobby's mammoth home run cleared both the fence and the seats in left-center.

"You can touch 'em all, baby, you can touch 'em all!" Bump shouted gleefully from the dugout. With one swift swing of Bobby's shillelagh, we'd leapt in front five to two.

In the bottom of the ninth, Jesus Hernandez slammed the door on the Sox. And so the Bay City Grays exited Beantown after taking two of three from the Red Sox. Our record on the young season stood at four and two, after winning a pair of road series against two first-class ball clubs.

But most important of all, Jimmy Devlin was alive and well and physically intact. Thanks to Bump Rhodes, Jimmy's new-found, two-fisted guardian angel.

Now it was back to Bay City for our home opener.

10

We were a happy bunch on the short flight back to Bay City. We'd played solid ball out on the road, our hopes were high as an elephant's eye, and we were heading for the comforts of home. And, with Monday an off-day, we could catch our breaths before battling the Blue Jays in our home opener on Tuesday night.

When I reached my apartment there was a note stuck to my door. It was from my neighbor Chuck: "Having a few folks over. Why don't you pop in?" I wasn't much in the mood for socializing, but I supposed I should make an effort to be neighborly. Besides, Chuck always lays out a nice spread and that would save me having to rustle up my own grub.

I showered and changed, then called Laura in New York. My call went straight to her machine, which was no surprise. On Sunday evenings she often had museum-related functions she needed to attend. Anyway, I *supposed* that was it. I snatched up a bottle of wine and headed next door to Chuck's.

"Tyrus, come on in, man, come on in. Glad you could make it. Give me a quick moment and I'll be back to introduce you around. You know where things are; go and help yourself. I'll be right back, okay?" And Chuck flitted off.

I carried the bottle of wine into Chuck's kitchen and then rummaged through his refrigerator in search of a proper bottle of beer. No Harp Lager, but Anchor Steam would do just fine. As I was popping it open, I felt something rubbing against my leg. It was Boog, Chuck's cat.

"Someone seems to like you," said an amused-sounding female voice from behind me.

"Boog and I are pals," I said, turning around. There before me stood a short, shapely, blondish young woman wearing jeans and a western-style plaid shirt with button-down pockets. A short, shapely, blondish woman with a warm smile and dark brown eyes.

"Hello," she said, "I'm Sandy." She held out her hand.

"I'm Duff," I said.

"Pleased to meet you, Duff."

"Pleased to meet you too. Is that Sandy with a big S, small a, small n, big D, double e?"

She laughed. "No, but I know what you're talking about. Sorry to disappoint you, but I'm just regular old Sandy. Doesn't even have an i on the end of it. And I'm not Sandra, either. I'm plain old Sandy all the way." She had a mild Southern accent. Not deep South like Bump, more like Kentucky or Tennessee.

Boog was twisting his lithe self in and out around my legs, purring happily. I reached down and gave his sides a gentle rub.

"I'm the next door neighbor," I said by way of explanation. "I look after Boog when Chuck is out of town."

"Lucky Boog," Sandy said with a wide smile. "So, you're the ball player?"

"I guess I am," I said. "But who are these folks, anyway? This one of Chuck's theatrical groups?"

"Musical groups," she said.

"They don't look a lot like opera singers."

"No, not so much," she said with a laugh. "We're the Blue Ridge Mountain Reivers."

"You steal from people?"

"No, we sing to them. Actually, I'm the one who does most of the singing. I'm the lead singer in the group."

"You guys from Nashville?"

"Yes sir, we are," she said proudly. "You may not've heard of us, but you will, I can promise you that."

"I'm more of a classical music guy, but my father liked some of the great country singers — Johnny Cash, Merle Haggard, guys like that. Let's see, I'm trying to think of female singers he liked. Umm . . . Barbara Mandrell? Does that sound possible?"

" 'Sleeping Single in a Double Bed'," Sandy said.

"Let's see . . . 'I Was Country When Country Wasn't Cool'? " I said, trying to hold up my end.

"My, but you're an impressive fella." As she spoke, I couldn't help noticing the small flecks of gold that glinted in her dark brown eyes.

"We're having three performances here this week," she said. "It would be great if you could come to one of them. We're playing on Monday, Tuesday, and Thursday."

"That *might* be possible. I'll get the details from Chuck. Maybe I could come with a few teammates after one of our games."

"Maybe some of us could come and see your Wednesday game when we're not performing," Sandy said. "It'd be fun. I played softball myself all the way through high school. Second base."

Yikes, I said to myself. Maybe it's time to be extricating myself from this pleasant little encounter. It was getting just a bit too close for comfort.

Fortunately, that was when Chuck came and dragged me into the living room to meet the rest of the Blue Ridge Mountain Reivers — Luke, Randy, Big Un, and Slim: mandolin, banjo, guitar, and washboard. Easy-going guys who enjoyed doing all the talking, thank goodness.

Before I left, I made sure to fill myself good with several tasty French bread sandwiches loaded with slices of ham and cheese, slathered with Dijon mustard and topped with lettuce and tomatoes. Damn nice nosh, Chuck, definitely my kind of stuff.

As I headed for the door, Boog tracked me down and rubbed his goodbyes against my ankles. And from across the room, Sandy gave me a big farewell wave and an even bigger smile.

"Come and see us," she mouthed at me. "I'll try," I mouthed back at her.

Just as I stepped through the door to my apartment, I heard the phone ring.

"Ty, it's me," Laura said. "Sorry to disappear on you again. Chrissie called this afternoon and offered me her extra ticket to see

Cosi fan tutte. I couldn't turn it down."

"You'd better not have turned it down. One never turns down Mozart. I just wish I could have been there also."

"You were in Fenway beating the socks off the Sox," she said. "That's even better than listening to Mozart."

"Probably about a tossup," I said. It felt good to be joking and joshing with Laura Morgan, the person who meant more to me than anyone else.

Late on Monday morning, the Deacon and I spent an hour with Bump in the batting cage. We started him off at 80, but by the time we'd finished he was up to 90; and by the sound of the bat meeting the ball, you could tell he was making great contact on a lot of pitches.

"Fellers, I think it's time for me to take some real BP," Bump declared. "Enough of this batting-cage stuff. Ya know what I mean?"

"We're *getting* there," the Deacon admitted, "we're certainly *getting* there."

"Shoot, Deak, we *are* there, gosh darn it."

"We're close," the Deacon replied calmly. I knew he was pleased with Bump's progress. But I also knew he was determined not to rush things too much. Whacking the crap out of the grooved tosses of a pitching machine in private was one thing. Hitting live pitching in full view of teammates and fans was quite another.

"Hey Deak," I said, "after our team practice this afternoon, how about I throw to the kid for ten or fifteen minutes out on the field?"

"Now you're talkin'," Bump chirped.

Deacon Lawler frowned at me, then shrugged. "Who's going to shag all the balls?"

"Well, heck, I'll pick 'em up all over the gol-darn stadium," Bump sang out. "All 'cept the ones I knock way up inta the seats." Bump Rhodes was in full-joy mode.

So following our regular team workout, four of us hung around and waited for all the other guys to clear out. Our Big Experiment was still under wraps, and we wanted to keep it that way — to save Bump from any possible embarrassment, but also because we weren't sure how it would all go down with the powers that be.

Bump stood close to the screen in front of the seats behind home plate and I stood just behind the plate, armed with a huge white bucket of baseballs. Deacon trotted out to right center, Jimmy to left center.

I threw Bump the entire bucket, starting off by grooving the ball at a moderate speed, then stepping up the velocity a bit, then firing him my very best fast balls. Not exactly high heat, but they were fast enough to be challenging. As soon as Bump got comfortable, he began knocking my vaunted fast ball all over the lot.

"Now I see why you never became a pitcher," he yelled out at me. "You ain't got much of a heater, Duff."

"Now you see why I don't have to throw farther than from second base to first," I yelled back.

"C'mon, Duff, you got more gas than that, don'cha? Let's see what ya really got." Hey, you little punk! Watch it! — or I might just show you my very best knock-down pitch!

Bump put on quite a display, spraying balls all around the outfield. Facing me was a far cry from facing real pitching, but his swing was fluid and natural. Yes, Bump Rhodes showed real signs of becoming a decent left-handed hitter. For the first time I began to think that our Great Experiment might actually work. In just a little over a week the kid had made astonishing progress. In athletic parlance, Bump was truly "a natural."

"C'mon, Duffy, you can throw harder than that, can't ya?"

"Gird your loins, rookie, here it comes!"

I threw Bump a sharp-breaking curve ball that dipped in under his hands. The muscle-bound knucklehead nearly broke his back swinging at it. Jimmy and Deacon were laughing their asses off as Bump Rhodes picked himself up.

"You foxy old devil!" he yelled at me. "Lemme see that one again."

"You want it, you got it!" I yelled back at him. I went into my windup, such as it was, and this time threw him my very best knuckleball. Unfortunately, it didn't knuckle.

Bump Rhodes drove the pitch high over the right-field scoreboard. We heard the ball ricochet off the side of a brick building and come bouncing back toward the stands. Bump must've hit it a good 440 feet. "You can touch 'em all!" came Bump's joyous cackle.

"Nice knuckler!" Jimmy yelled at me from the outfield. "You gotta teach me that one."

As we were dressing after our secret workout, Bump asked us what we were doing tonight. When we didn't have games scheduled, the kid was always at loose ends. Finding things to do on his own was kind of beyond him. He wasn't much of a reader, he scoffed at Zook and his video games, and one can only watch so much TV. So sometimes we'd take him with us to the movies or the bowling alley.

"How'd you like to hear a bluegrass group play tonight?" I said.

"Bluegrass? That would be great, Duff. I'd love to do that."

"Jimmy? Deacon? How 'bout you guys? Bluegrass? Irish beer? Celtic topless dancers?"

"Who's playing?"

"Not anybody you'd know, but they're supposed to be good. They're called The Reivers."

"They steal from people?" Jimmy said.

"No, they sing to them."

"The Weavers?" the Deacon said. "Pete Seeger and those guys?"

"Uh, no, Deak. I don't think those guys have performed in the last half century."

"When I was a kid," he said, "we had one of their albums."

So did we, an old record my father'd inherited from his father. One of those songs I remembered well. When my father was putting me and Billy to bed — we were maybe five or six — he'd tell us a story and sing to us. One of his favorites was "Goodnight, Irene." I still sing it in the shower.

At that moment Dave Rubenstein strolled in, stopped, and stared at us. "What the heck are the four stooges still doing here? Practice ended two hours ago."

"First ones on the field, last ones off," I said.

"Hey coach," Bump said, "guess what we're doing tonight? We're going to hear The Reivers."

"The Reivers?" Dave said. "Do they steal from people?"

"Why does everyone say that?" Bump asked, looking perplexed.

11

We were sitting in Milligan's, a small club that looks out on the Inner Harbor. Me, Jimmy, Deacon, Bump, and maybe eighty or ninety other folks, a lot of whom were wearing Reivers tee-shirts. "Need ta get me one of them tee-shirts," Bump said. "Think they have one big enough for me?"

I'd met most of the folks in the group the other night at Chuck's, though now out on the stage there were a few more of them — two additional guitar players and a fiddle player. The fiddle player was a lanky young woman. My new friend Sandy, the lead singer, was the only one of the group without an instrument.

Our table was off to one side near the front, and when Sandy spotted us, she gave us a wave.

"Friend of yours?" Jimmy asked.

"More an acquaintance."

"Cute as a button," Bump said, grinning at me.

When the emcee announced them, the crowd broke into a raucous cheer and Bump was right there with them. The Alabama Kid was here to have fun, no doubt about that, for he'd already downed his second RC Cola. Bump Rhodes was on a roll.

The Reivers' first number was a lively instrumental, probably what you'd call rockabilly. Right away the audience was clapping in rhythm along with Sandy, who was dancing an Irish jig, Appalachian style, weaving in and out among the members of the group.

"Wow!" said Bump, "look at her, man. Boy, I'll bet you wouldn't say no to that!"

"Her name's Sandy," I said. "When they take their break, maybe I can introduce you."

"No, Duff, not her. The other one."

"The fiddle player?"

"Oh yeah, man, the fiddle player!" To be honest, I hadn't paid her much notice. Now I did. She was taller than Sandy and not quite so pleasingly rounded. Her long, raven-black hair was tied back in a ponytail that hung halfway down her back. Whereas Sandy was wearing jeans and a plaid shirt like the night before at Chuck's, the fiddle player was wearing black leather pants and a dark purple tee-shirt. Sandy was all pinky-cheeked; the fiddle player's face was as pale as a lily flower.

"Ya like that, huh?" said Jimmy.

"Oh golly yes," said Bump. "Don't you?"

"Actually," Jimmy said, "I'll confess that I do. But since you saw her first, amigo, I promise to steer clear. Duff, we ought to do all we can to help our young amigo out, don't you think?"

"Don't you fellas be teasing the lad," the Deacon said.

"Who's teasing?" Jimmy said. "It's time our young friend got himself some serious action."

"He came, he saw, he got some serious action," I said. Bump was blushing like anything.

"You ever had a girl?" Jimmy asked Bump. "I mean, did you ever have a girlfriend?"

"Well, shoot, 'course I've had a girlfriend. Shoot, I've had me a couple o' girlfriends." But the lad did not choose to elaborate.

When the group was taking their break, Sandy and the fiddle player came over to our table; serendipitously, the fiddle player pulled up a chair right next to Bump. Sandy and I made introductions all around, and when she introduced the fiddle player she said, "This is Vi, hottest Celtic fiddle in the Virginias and Carolinas."

"Vi?" said Bump.

"Vi's short for Violet," the young woman said in a soft, low voice.

"Violet," Bump said. "What a lovely name. Suits you to a tee." Then he suddenly blushed, fearing she might think he was referring to her tight tee-shirt.

Into my mind popped a picture of Violetta, the pale-faced heroine of *La Traviata*. My word, was this going to be another instance of life imitating art?

"I have five sisters," she said. "Each of us named for a flower."

"And you got the best one," Bump said. "Absolutely fits you."

"Maybe you-all could stick around for a while after we finish our last set?" Sandy said. "That'd give us a chance to have a proper visit."

"Sure we could," Bump said. "That'd be okay, wouldn't it Deak?"

The Deacon had been taking all of this in quietly, a slightly bemused look on his face.

"Sure it would," he said. "Sandy, I'm going to buy the lad a Reivers tee-shirt."

"Think they'll have any triple-X's?"

"I doubt if they've had a run on them," she said, looking around the room. There wasn't a man there who came close to being as big as Bump. "Maybe you could buy our CD also," she said.

"Yeah, Deak, buy the CD," the kid said. "I'll pay ya back."

"No, this one's on me."

"While you're at it, Deak, buy a couple for me," I said. "I'll give one to Jimmy's father. He'll love these guys."

"You love us too, don't you?" Sandy said.

"I sure do," I said. "That's why I want Deacon to buy two. One of 'ems for me."

"I'm glad you love us," she said. "That pleases me a lot."

I saw Jimmy looking at me warily out of the corner of his eye. You are absolutely right, I said to him inside my head. Ty Duffy needs to be treading very, very cautiously. Indeed, Ty Duffy might be well advised to be heading for the hills — the *hills*, not the Blue Ridge Mountains.

And then came the Bay City *Home Opener* — a large and hopeful crowd; a rousing rendition of the National Anthem; the throwing out of the ceremonial first pitch; a series of introductions. It would be hard to say who got the biggest ovation as we lined up along the first-base line. Whitey Wiggins? Deacon Lawler? Jimmy Devlin?

Bobby Radley? Mine was pretty good too, and it felt *great*.

In the game, Stan Foubert, unlike last week, was every bit the wily veteran hurler he was. He was spotting the ball with pinpoint precision and mixing his pitches with the subtlety of a French chef. Stan took the win, Jesus picked up the save (his fourth), and Lou Tolliver served up the game-winning hits. By day's end the Bay City Grays stood atop the AL East with a record of five and two.

On my way home, I stopped and picked up Chinese takeout. I planned to eat, relax, and listen to music. After all the folderol of our home opener, I wanted an evening of solitude.

As I re-heated my food, I listened to the voice messages on my machine – congratulations from Laura, from my brother Billy, and from an old college pal. Then I listened to the last one.

"Hey, Duff," came a woman's voice I didn't recognize. "Hope you don't mind my calling you. I just wanted to tell you how great it made us feel that you came to hear us play last night. That was really sweet of you guys. But also, I wanted to apologize. We were planning to come to your game tomorrow night, but things have gone so well that Chuck's booked us for an extra night. So, no ball game. I hope you'll give us a rain check. Anyway, you haven't seen the last of The Blue Ridge Mountain Reivers. And I hope we haven't seen the last of you. Duff, I hope I haven't seen the last of you. Okay, talk to you soon."

Oh, boy, what had I gotten myself into?

During pre-game batting practice on Wednesday evening, Jimmy, Dave Rubenstein, and I were admiring the jaw-dropping power of Lou Tolliver and Bump Rhodes, whose soaring shots had the fans scurrying for souvenirs in the left field seats. Bump, of course, was hitting right-handed. His lefty efforts were still a secret, deep and dark.

"Bump's a batting practice star," Dave said. "Too bad he can't hit real pitching. I've seen a lot of guys like that, guys who look like world-beaters in BP but are strikeout artists in games."

"Dave," Jimmy said, "do you have any clue why the kid's even here? He's a great kid and all, but man, a big leaguer? Give me a break."

"You don't know why he's here? It's simple. Rule 5 is why he's here."

"*What?*" I said. "Bump's a Rule 5 player? I thought he came up through our own minor league system."

"He did and he didn't. We nabbed him last June from the Pirates. Since they hadn't protected him, we snatched him up. He spent most of last season with our single-A club, but now, if we intend to hold on to him, we have to keep him on our twenty-five man roster. Look, fellas, it wasn't my idea. I disclaim any and all responsibility."

"Somebody actually think the guy can play?" Jimmy said.

"It's because our minor-league catching corps is woefully thin. With the Deacon reaching the end, our cupboard is pretty bare. Miguel's a solid backup but he's not an everyday guy. There's no one down in the system close to being ready. Bump, at least, has raw potential. Anyway, that's what Pete and Whitey think."

"Raw is right," Jimmy said.

"Well," Dave said, "maybe it's wishful thinking, but I think I've seen some improvement lately. His throwing's definitely better, and his hitting . . . umm . . . it's not *totally* horrible."

"Deacon's been working hard with him," I said, "that's for sure."

"Why doesn't Zemeckis shell out a few bucks and buy us a free-agent catcher?" Jimmy said. "No, never mind. I know the answer to that one — the fucking skinflint." Jimmy's attitude toward the Gray's parsimonious owner wasn't his alone. We all shared it.

But Dave was right. Bump's throwing had improved a little bit. And then, I thought, there's also the matter of Bump's left-handed hitting. Just wait till they see that! It was still too soon to say, but maybe The Big Experiment would actually result in something.

◆ ◆ ◆

On Wednesday night Jumpin' Jack Fletcher had his A-game working. With the bottom dropping out of his sinker, he induced ground ball after ground ball. I had seven assists, and Juan and I turned three double plays. The Grays didn't do a lot of hitting, but we came away winners, 3 to 1. This time Spike Bannister, our center fielder, was the batting star; he doubled and tripled and figured in all three of our runs. During the first two weeks of the season the Bay City Grays had been spreading the glory around.

On Thursday afternoon, with Jorge Comellas out on the hill for us, it was an entirely different story. Jorge's success depends on finesse, guile, and deception, but on that afternoon they were in short supply. The Jays knocked Jorge all over the lot and thumped us, 10 to 4.

Still, in that series, just like in the previous two, we'd won two out of three. Two out of three is .667 and in baseball, .667 wins pennants. Six wins and three losses ain't nothin' to sneeze at. Any team in baseball will take such a record.

Our second home series was against Tampa Bay, who, like us, was a team on the rise. They had an unruly bunch of youngsters who were feeling their oats. The AL East is a killer of a division, but the kids on the Rays didn't seem daunted. They battled us tooth and nail in all three games, and we were fortunate to win two of them.

On Friday night the Rays roughed up Alfred King by ignoring all his other pitches and sitting on his fast ball. Bump caught the entire game and went one-for-four, collecting his second big-league hit. He also threw out a guy attempting to steal, another first for the kid. But the Rays won the game.

Jimmy was in full command on Saturday. He tossed a complete game, allowing just one run on five hits and two walks. The big surprise for the Rays' hitters, and for us too, was Jimmy's new changeup, which kept their batters off stride.

"Duff," he chirped after the third inning, "did I tell you my dad and I worked all winter on my new changeup?"

"Not more than twenty or thirty times," I said.

On Sunday afternoon Stan Foubert reprised his performance of the previous Tuesday. The French chef was out there slicing and dicing with the best of 'em. Miguel Torres, our backup catcher, hit a three-run shot in the fifth inning, and the Rays never recovered. We came away with a 5-2 victory.

And so with two weeks of the season now in the books, the Bay City Grays were still playing at a .667 clip. And that was mighty sweet.

12

The Yankees and the Grays hadn't encountered each other since their donnybrook back in mid-March. Going into the last weekend of April, the Yankees' season thus far had been downright mediocre. They were ten and nine, in third place in the division. We, on the other hand, were sitting atop the AL East at twelve and six. It was way too early for our records to mean a whole lot; and yet a win in April counts just as much as a win in September.

During the weekend series, each team would trot out their top three hurlers. It would be Jimmy Devlin versus Randy Smalley, Stan Foubert versus Big Mike Prokosch, and Jumpin' Jack Fletcher versus R.J. Dickerson, a recent free-agent acquisition.

One thing was for sure — on this final weekend in April, Bay City would be rockin'. The series had been sold out for weeks and anticipation was rampant throughout the city. The Grays did not intend to let their fans down.

Just about everyone was in town for the big showdown. Jimmy Devlin's father and mother had flown in from Missouri, along with Penny Sutherland, Jimmy's hometown sweetheart. Deacon Lawler's wife Agnes had come all the way from Southern California, a real rarity. Bump Rhodes' parents had driven up from lower Alabama in their pickup truck with built-in camper; Bump wasn't likely to play in the series, but they wanted to be there anyway. My brother Billy and my sister-in-law Sarah, who were on spring break from the high school where they taught, arrived on my doorstep on Wednesday evening. I welcomed them with brotherly love.

But for all those who *were* there, one most crucial person wasn't. Laura had called on Tuesday night to give me the bad news. At short notice, the museum was sending her and a couple of others to Florence to lay groundwork for an important exhibition. She would be in Europe from Thursday until the following Wednesday. She said she hadn't had any choice and hoped I'd understand. She said she felt terrible about it. Believe me, she wasn't the only one who felt terrible about it.

Thursday was an off-day for us, and for weeks I'd been planning to host — along with Laura — a social gathering at my apartment that evening, for all our family members and guests who'd gathered from the corners of the orb. Well shoot, with or without Laura, I was still going to have that party. Fortunately, I had Sarah to lend a hand; and fortunately, I'd lined up an excellent catering outfit to take care of the big stuff.

When I got back from practice, I showered and gave my place the once over. To me, things looked mighty good, thanks to Sarah, whose presence was a great comfort in light of Laura's absence.

There were more people jammed into my apartment than ever before. I hoped it wouldn't explode. Lou Tolliver and a willowy blonde turned up at six-thirty on the dot. Lou must've been hungry. My brother Billy also looked hungry as he eyed Lou's leggy blonde; she was definitely an eyeful. Nick, Bobby, and the Deacon arrived with their wives, and a little after that Bump showed up with his parents.

Bump's father was a shy little man probably more at home with his mule than with thirty complete strangers. Shyness wasn't a problem for Bump's mother, who reminded me of Ma Kettle from those '40s movies. A conversation with her was easy because she did all the talking. Bump took after his mother more than his father.

I was an inexperienced host, but it didn't matter. Most of these folks knew each other, and we were all members of the Bay City Grays "family." Maybe not Lou's blonde, though about a dozen ballplayers were eager to welcome her in.

Jimmy and his parents finally arrived, along with Penny Sutherland. I'd been looking forward to seeing Jimmy's father. He always says I'm a stitch — "you're a stitch, Banjo" — but he's the one who's a real stitch.

Penny Sutherland looked terrific. She'd clearly made an effort to spiff up her image. She wore a fetching and rather revealing dress, something she hadn't bought off the rack. Her hair was styled, and she exuded some very subtle fragrance. It struck me that Penny must've sensed she was in a battle for the heart of her guy. Since Jimmy would never have told her about Kat, Penny must've intuitued there was another powerful tug on Jimmy Devlin's affections. What Penny surely didn't know, though, was that her rival was the most beautiful woman in all of Ireland. Penny was a decided underdog in this contest. After all, how you gonna keep 'em down on the farm after they've seen Kat Brogan? Still, Penny Sutherland, bless her, was fighting the good fight.

"Nice spread ya got goin' here, Banjo," Jimmy's father said, surveying the wonders before him — ham biscuits, egg rolls, chicken wings, various dips, coleslaw, potato salad, you name it.

"Not quite Nebuchadnezzar's Feast, but in the same ballpark."

"Not quite Belshazzar's, either," Deacon Lawler said. "I'm Jimmy's catcher, sir," he said, extending his hand. "Maybe you remember me?"

"Course I 'member you, Deacon. We met last year in Kansas City, son. So you went and caught me a-scramblin' my Nebuchadnezzar with my Belshazzar, did ya?"

"They were father and son, sir, like you and Jimmy. Though they weren't quite as nice as you two are."

"I hope no huge hand's going to suddenly appear and start scribbling all over my wall," I said. "I had the place re-painted just last year."

"You know what I'd like to see that hand write?" Lou Tolliver said. "Yankees Suck!"

Lou's vulgar remark produced smirks and chuckles. The only one who seemed shocked was the Deacon's wife, Agnes, who got a little red in the face and diverted her eyes. The Deacon reached out and patted her arm, his eyes shining with affection. Deacon Lawler was our rock, and his wife Agnes was his.

At one point in my big social event my neighbor Chuck popped in. He was a fish out of water amongst all those ballplayers and their lovely ladies, but Chuck, to my great admiration, was pretty adept at every social situation. Nothing ever fazed Chuck. He didn't stay long, but his brief visit lifted a few eyebrows, especially when he embraced me warmly just before he left.

"Nice neighbor ya got there, Banjo," Jimmy's father said to me.

"Chuck's a really good guy," I said. "I value his friendship."

"I'd have ta say the two of you are quite a bit different," Henry Devlin said. "But I don't have no problem with guys being a bit different."

Dave Rubenstein finally arrived, accompanied by his long-time girlfriend Rachel. I'd met her a couple of times in New York, where she worked as an attorney. Rachel was a New Yorker through and through, having gone from the Bensonhurst section of Brooklyn to Hunter College to Yale Law School, and then back to Manhattan. Her dark beauty made quite a contrast to that of Lou's blond bombshell.

"Wow," Bump whispered to me. "That there gal's quite a looker. Makes me think of Violet, ya know? Shoot, Duff, how come you and me are the only fellas here who don't have no lookers? Man oh man, I sure do wish Violet was here. And I'm bettin' you're wishin' that Sandy gal was here, too."

"Yeah," I said, "there are a lot of attractive women floating around in this apartment. But you're right, on this particular night you and me appear to be the odd men out." Bump, though, was wrong in thinking I might be wishing Sandy was here. It was someone else I was wishing was here.

"Well say, Banjo, I really do like that picture ya got hanging in your study," Jimmy's father said, a little while later.

"Which one's that?"

"It's that gas station one, Titus. Really takes me back." We walked down the hall and into my study, where we stood together and looked at an Edward Hopper print I've always liked. It shows a man standing in front of three old-fashioned gas pumps with the flying red horse emblem of Mobil Gas on top of them. The backdrop for the gas station is a generic rural setting, with a darkening sky out beyond some woods.

"I remember old gas stations just like that one, back when I was a kid. Off in the Missouri countryside. Makes me feel kinda sad to look at it. But it sure does take me back."

"It could be just about anywhere," I said. "Hopper lived in New England, but that could just as easily be Missouri as a lot of other places. And I agree with you about making you feel kind of sad. Sad and nostalgic. For me it conveys an intense feeling of loneliness. I think that's why I bought it."

"You ain't lonely, are ya, Banjo?"

"Oh well, only now and then."

"Banjo, I can't tell ya how much your lookin' after Jimmy means to the wife and me. You been a really good friend to the boy. Means a whole lot to us."

"Henry," I said, putting my hand gently on his shoulder, "what you just said means a whole lot to me."

Despite the fact that they were just one game over .500, the Yankees came into town loaded with super-stars. All their key guys were healthy: outfielders Paul O'Sullivan and Mickey Waters; first-baseman Gino Giannelli; shortstop Darren Jennings; and their DH, Junior Jackson. And over the winter, as usual, they'd reloaded with fresh studs — Japanese outfielder Yuki Tanaka, who'd led Japan's Central League in batting; power-pitching right-hander R.J. Dickerson, who'd notched eighteen wins for Houston last year; and most importantly, home-run-hitting third baseman Arturo "El Bombo" Carrasco, who'd bashed thirty-nine long bombs for the Texas Rangers last season. With the addition of Dickerson, the Yankees had a starting threesome — Smalley, Prokosch, and Dickerson — that was unmatched in baseball.

What the Bay City Grays had was exactly what we'd had at

the end of last season. No important new faces, no big-name free agents. But to our credit what we had was a bunch of eager young guys who'd come up together through our own system. We had Jimmy Devlin, Jesus Hernandez, Todd Cottington, Bobby Radley, Jorge Comellas, and Alfred King — to go along with Lou, Spike, Juan, the Deacon, and me.

We didn't have the best lineup money can buy. But we had scrappy guys who'd play their hearts out for a slice of pizza and a cold beer. And now we had a new secret weapon. Because now, though still under wraps, we had Edgar Eustace "Bump" Rhodes. Oh yes, we had the Bumpster — our own personal Grail Knight.

The first two games in our series against the Yankees were hugely disappointing — no brawls, no managers tossed, not even a close game. And the Yankees whupped us both times.

Going into Friday's game, Jimmy had been three and oh, with an ERA under 2.00. Afterward, he was three and one, though the game hadn't much damaged his ERA. Jimmy pitched well, but Randy Smalley pitched better, and the Yankees won four to nothing. The hitting star for the Yankees was El Bombo Carrasco. With two guys on, he turned on Jimmy's ninety-seven mile fastball and lasered it in the upper-deck in left center.

It was a similar story on Saturday, as the Yankees' Mike Prokosch outpitched Stan Foubert. We scored first when Juan led off with a single, I followed with another single, and Lou doubled to left center, scoring Juan and me. But that was it. Big Mike settled in and pitched the next seven innings on cruise control. This time the final score was six to two.

Those losses seriously dampened the ardor of our fans. The simple fact was, the Yankees had way more talent than we had. But, there was still one game left in the series.

On Sunday afternoon for some reason Whitey decided to let Bump do the catching. That was mighty strange, since he'd be facing a *right*-handed pitcher and since he'd never caught Jumpin'

Jack before. But *maybe* there was method in Whitey's madness. Never one to manage by the book, Whitey always did what his gut told him to do. Maybe, though, he was doing what his heart told him to do.

Our loyal fans still stuck by us. They were out in full force, and every few minutes they broke into their "Let's go, Grays!" chant. And in the top of the first we gave 'em something to cheer about.

Mickey Waters, the Yankees' leadoff guy, opened the game by looping a soft single to left center. On the first pitch to Darren Jennings, Mickey broke for second. Bump snatched Jack's pitch and fired a bullet to second. I slapped my glove down in front of the outfield corner of the bag, knowing that Mickey would slide headfirst and try to snag the corner of the bag with his left hand. My tag beat him by a fraction of a second, and the umpire nailed the call. Mickey was "Out!"

Darren Jennings, the Yankee shortstop, then lined a solid single to right, bringing up left-handed hitting Paul O'Sullivan. I slid over toward first and Juan moved over close to the bag at second. On the second pitch to O'Sullivan, Jennings took off for second. Once more Bump fired the ball down to second, and this time it was Juan who put the tag on the runner. Two Yankee hits and two Yankee base-runners gunned down by Bump Rhodes.

I could hear Jimmy's leather-lunged father and my brother Billy lustily heaping abuse on the Yankees — like a tenor and a baritone belting out a duet from *Carmen*.

With two down and none on, O'Sullivan rocketed a shot in my direction. I dove to my left and speared it in the web of my glove. In their half of the first, the Yankees had hit three shots and had nothing to show for it.

In the bottom of the first, Juan again started us off by singling up the middle. And when I stepped into the batter's box, who should I find there behind the dish but my dear old pal, Jimmy Breyreitz. This was the first game he'd worked in the series, since he was in the process of being phased out as the Yankees' starting catcher. His knees were pretty well shot, though he was still a dangerous hitter with men on base.

Breyreitz was fussing and fuming over the pitch that Juan had hit. Apparently Dickerson hadn't located it where Breyreitz wanted it. "What a dickhead," the jerk muttered.

"You just call R.J. a *dickhead?*" I said.

"Hell yes, I did, and you're a dickhead too, Duffy."

"Just shut up and play ball, Jimmy," the umpire said.

"Dickhead," Breyreitz muttered to himself.

On R.J.'s second pitch to me, Juan swiped second. Breyreitz's throw was late and off the mark.

"Nice effort," I said.

"That dickhead's way too slow to the plate with men on base," Breyreitz said. "Wasn't my fault."

"Never is," I said.

"Shut up, dickhead."

Eventually, after working the count full and then fouling off three pitches, I garnered a walk. That gave us two on and none out, and on the very next pitch, Juan and I pulled off a double steal. This time Breyreitz's throw was on time but high, and Juan slipped in beneath El Bombo's glove. Second and third, nobody out.

With Lou at the plate, the Yankees chose not to issue an intentional walk and not to draw their infield in. Lou proceeded to hit a chopper to Phil Dorset at second, allowing Juan to score and me to advance to third. Now we were up, one to nothing. And when Todd Cottington flew out to the warning track in right, I tagged and trotted in with the run. End of the first inning: Grays 2, Yankees 0.

But it didn't stay that way. The Yankees scored one in the fourth on Junior Jackson's solo homer, and tied the game up in the top of the seventh on El Bombo's third blast of the series. So going into the bottom of the seventh the score was knotted at two apiece.

With two men down, Bump Rhodes would be coming to bat for the third time. Facing the potent right-handed offerings of R.J.

Dickerson, Bump had fanned feebly in his first two at-bats. Now coming up with the game all even, Bump walked slowly toward the right-hander's batter's box. Then all of a sudden he *stopped*.

Bump stood there for a moment looking deep in thought. And then, instead of stepping into the right-hander's box, he walked around behind the umpire and entered the left-hander's box.

"What the hell!" Whitey spat out. "Bump, what're ya doin', son?"

Bump's impulsive action took us all by surprise. The Deacon and I exchanged startled looks. Up till then Bump hadn't even taken regular batting practice from the left side, just those few impromptu sessions I'd thrown to him on the sly. Up till then no one else had even known of our Big Experiment. What the heck was the knucklehead thinking? Bump Rhodes was nowhere close to being ready to face big-league pitching from the left side. And especially not from the likes of R.J. Dickerson.

Bump, I silently implored, please don't do this; it's really going to screw things up. Bump's left-handed hitting had come a long way, and his confidence had grown by leaps and bounds during the past week or so — but there was no way in hell he was ready for this.

A buzz began slowly building in the stands as the fans who were attentive to such things began realizing that something weird was going on. Now all the players in both dugouts were on their feet lining the protective railings, curious to see how this unexpected development would play out.

Bump stood stock-still in the batter's box having assumed his left-hander's stance. Then R.J. looked in for the sign, nodded, and went into his windup. He fired a fastball straight down the chute. Ninety-four miles per hour, a good ten miles an hour faster than anything Bump had seen from me. Bump just stood there like an inert rock as the ball thumped into Breyreitz's glove. The umpire's right arm shot out. *Strike one*. Bump hadn't even twitched.

Once again Dickerson looked in for the sign and once again he went into his windup. Again it was a mid-90s fastball, right down the pike.

Suddenly, Bump's bat flicked. Totally without warning, the mongoose had attacked the cobra! And the sound of the bat hitting the ball was like nothing you have ever heard. Not unless you've heard the Trump of Doom.

Bump was as stunned as everyone else. Before you could even bat an eye, the ball disappeared into the ether. Those few fans who saw it — and only a few with extremely sharp eyes actually saw it — would remember it for the rest of their lives.

"*Holy shit!*" Whitey's startled outcry expressed what every one of us was thinking.

His swing completed, Bump stood frozen in the batter's box — like a Greek statue or an Arthurian knight who'd just vanquished his foe.

For the briefest moment there was silence on the face of the earth. Then the stadium erupted.

Bump still stood there. He looked over toward the Deacon and me for guidance.

"Touch 'em all, you lunkhead!" I shouted at him, "touch 'em all!"

Bump grinned sheepishly, then tossed his bat aside and proceeded to touch 'em all.

Bump Rhodes had belted his first big-league home run. And as it turned out, he'd won the game for us.

But the ball he'd hit was never found.

"A real shame no one ever found that dang ball," Jimmy's father said after the game. "A kid oughta have his first home-run ball."

"I don't think there was any ball to be found," Jimmy said. "I think Bump flat out vaporized it."

"No one could find it," I said, "because it came down in the never-never land of the Grail Castle."

As if choreographed, Jimmy and his father both shot me pitying looks. I'd never realized before how much Jimmy looked like his father.

"Titus," Jimmy's father said, "you been listenin' to too many o' them danged opry things. Better stick to Merle Haggard, son. He'll keep you grounded in the real world."

That was probably good advice.

We'd be ending the first month of the season with a three-game series in Cleveland before flying on to New York for our return series with the Yankees. Most of the folks who'd turned up for the first Yankee series had now departed for destinations known or unknown; just a few of the faithful planned to stick with us for the coming week. That included Jimmy's father, but not Penny Sutherland.

"Never been to Cleveland before, Banjo," Mr. Devlin said to me. "What should I know about the place?"

"I'm told they have a lot of Indians there," I said, repeating a feeble joke I'd used on a pixie of a fellow I'd encountered last fall in Dublin, a fellow who claimed he liked Cleveland though he'd never actually been there. My joke had sailed right past my Dublin acquaintance, but Mr. Devlin gave it a polite chuckle. "And then there's the Rock 'n Roll Hall of Fame," I said. "I'm sure you won't want to miss that."

"I'm sure I won't," he replied, sardonically.

Despite Bump's heroic homer against the Yankees, Whitey sat him for the whole three-game series in Cleveland. And as the dust settled in the days following Bump's magical moment in the sun, pretty much everyone had come to the conclusion that his monumental blast had been an aberration — nothing more than a fluke. But at least now Bump was openly taking pre-game batting practice from both sides of the plate. That was progress of a sort, I guess, though his left-handed hitting still had a long ways to go. He was woefully inconsistent from that side, even against the extremely hittable pitches served up in batting practice.

In the Cleveland series we returned to our previous pattern of winning two out of three. On Tuesday night Alfred King notched a solid win, then on Wednesday night Jimmy, bouncing back from his loss to the Yankees, tossed a complete game in our five-to-one win, making his record on the young season four and one. He was firmly on his way to making the AL All-Star squad. We dropped the final game on Thursday afternoon when our bats let us down: Cleveland four, Bay City one.

We were a month into the season and still hadn't swept a series; but none of us were unhappy about carrying a fifteen and eight record as we headed into the merry month of May.

13

On the first Thursday in May, our evening flight to New York got in ahead of schedule, and we arrived at our hotel an hour earlier than expected. Laura and I had planned to meet for lunch at the museum on Friday, but now, since it was only 9 o'clock, the notion flitted through my head that maybe we could get together for a while tonight. Hope springs eternal in a young man's heart.

I phoned Laura's apartment, then tried her cell phone, getting no answer on either one. I left messages telling her I was already here and asking her to call me if she got a chance.

That's when I thought, what the heck, it's only ten blocks from our hotel to her apartment building on the Upper East Side. I'll give my legs a stretch and stroll on over there. Maybe I'll get lucky and she'll be back by the time I get there. If not, I'll still have a pleasant early-spring jaunt through the streets of one of the world's great cities.

But while I was en route I began having second thoughts. Maybe this wasn't such a hot idea. I liked the idea of surprising Laura. But what if I was the one who got surprised? Laura and I hadn't seen each other since before the start of spring training. And since the season had started, she hadn't once come to Bay City. Was I being obtuse about how things truly stood between the two of us? I really hoped not.

And then there I was, standing outside her building. I paused for a moment and looked up at her fourth-floor apartment, whose windows faced the street. I felt like a high-schooler driving past his girlfriend's house on the off-chance she might be home — something I'd done back in the eleventh grade when I was first dating Mandy. When it comes to matters of the heart, some of us don't get much beyond the eleventh grade.

It looked like there were dim lights on inside her apartment — which didn't mean she was back, since she'd probably left a few on when she went out. Anyway, since I was there, I bit the bullet and pressed the intercom button. Maybe I'd get lucky and hear her voice. In fact, I did.

"Yes?"

"Laura, it's me. I tried to call. I guess you didn't you get my messages."

There was a long pause. "Ty? Is that you? No . . . um . . . no, I haven't checked my messages. So no, I didn't get them." Then there was another pause.

I had a terrible feeling that I'd picked a very bad time to be showing up on my girlfriend's doorstep. You dunderhead, I thought — your girlfriend isn't alone.

"Hey, I'm sorry, Laura. I didn't mean to barge in unannounced. We got in early and I was eager to see you. Sorry, bad idea. Listen, I'll see you tomorrow as we planned. If that's still on."

There was another long pause. Over the intercom I could clearly hear Laura's huge sigh. "Ty . . . ," she finally said, "maybe it would be best for all of us if you just came on up."

Best for *all* of us? What did she mean by that? Just who are *all* of us, I couldn't help wondering. Maybe I didn't want to know.

"Ty," she said, "I'm going to buzz you in." And then she did. I reached out and pulled the door open, wondering if that was a particularly good idea. If I went up to her apartment, I would soon discover who all of us really were. Courage has never been one of my strong points. Nonetheless, I steeled myself for whatever was in store and went on in. It's always better to know the truth . . . I guess.

I rapped softly on Laura's door, and she opened it so quickly I knew she'd been waiting there. We both stood looking at each other for a moment, neither of us speaking. Finally she reached out and took my hand. "Ty, please come in." She leaned forward and brushed my cheek with a soft kiss. Then she began pulling me toward her living room.

The lights in the room were dim, but as I looked across at her sofa — a sofa on which Laura and I had shared quite a few tender moments — I could tell that someone was sitting there looking at me.

In the dim light I realized it was a woman. A woman named Kat Brogan.

The shock of seeing Kat left me speechless. I'm not sure who I thought I might find in Laura's apartment. Whoever it was, it *wasn't* Kathleen Brogan.

"Hello, Ty Duffy," Kat said. "I trust you're doin' well."

"Hello, Kat," I said, trying to gather my wits. For several seconds the three of us remained enveloped in silence.

"Sit down Ty, won't you please?" Laura said. "Would you like a glass of merlot?"

"That would be great," I said.

As Laura was getting a glass for me, I gazed once more at Kat Brogan. In the dim light of the apartment she looked more stunning than ever. The reddish glow of the glass of wine she held in front of her complemented her classic Irish complexion and her wavy, slightly tousled, auburn hair, one tendril of which brushed her left cheek.

"I guess it would be stupid to ask what brings you here. You must've known we were playing in New York."

"I've been in Boston for the last few days," Kat said, "trying to sort out some things that Seamus Byrne — our mutual friend, Seamus — has royally mucked up."

"Good old solicitor Byrne," I said, "a fellow who's dear to our hearts."

"Oh, I'm sure he is," Kat said with a chuckle. "Mick should've sent good old Seamus packing years ago. But of course Mick's loyalties to family and friends run deep. Looks like he'll leave the job of sacking Seamus to me. Thanks, Mick. So typical. If you need someone to do your dirty work, get a woman to do it. Then the lads can't blame it on you.

"But to answer your question, yes, I knew you were playing here.

My flight back to Ireland isn't until Monday night. So I had a few extra days to play with."

As I sipped my wine, I eyed both Kat and Laura over the rim of the glass — two of the loveliest women I'd ever seen. One of them I was crazy about. And one of them scared the bejesus out of me.

"Did ya get my letter?" Kat said.

"Yes, I got it."

"D'ya think Jimmy will see me?"

"No, Kat, not willingly. He's convinced that you betrayed him. He hasn't forgiven you and he doesn't want to."

"I have to talk to him," Kat said. "I have to have a chance to explain things to him, make him understand. Things happened too quickly over there. There are explanations, Ty Duffy. If I can talk to Jimmy, I know I can make him understand. He'll forgive me. I know he will."

Um hum, I knew that too. But was that what I wanted to happen? If Jimmy were to forgive Kat, where would that leave us? And where would that take us? Nowhere good, it seemed to me.

"Ty," Laura said, "can't you get Jimmy to come and see Kat? Wouldn't that be best?" What the heck, I thought, now you guys are double-teaming me?

"Jimmy won't come," I said, "not if he knows Kat's here. The only way I could get him here would be to trick him into it. Is that what you want?"

"If you have to," Kat said, "yes."

"Dammit, Kat, don't you understand that you broke his heart?"

"Give me a chance to mend it. What I did over there — if you'll just think about it for a moment, Ty Duffy — was for the good of everyone. Jimmy couldn't have stayed in Ireland, not after he'd taken down Mick Slattery. He'd've been a dead man walking. And I couldn't have gone off with Jimmy. That would have made things even worse. Jimmy would have paid a terrible price. You know that's true.

"But now things are gettin' more settled and sorted. Mick's

back on his feet, the enterprises are thrivin', the lads're feelin' good about things — "

"Oh, yeah," I said, "God's in his heaven, all's right with the world." Not hardly, I thought. A couple of weeks ago in Boston, Mick Slattery made it quite clear to me that things weren't settled and sorted. And that they wouldn't be, not if Jimmy and Kat had anything more to do with each other.

"Of course things aren't perfect," Kat went on. "But they're vastly better. Mick knows that I'm my own person, and he's okay with it. He understands he can't go around decidin' things for me. Our relationship has shifted. I truly believe that. And I believe that eventually — not just yet, mind you, but eventually — it's going to be possible for Jimmy and me to be together. If that's something Jimmy still wants. All I want is the chance to make him know that that's what I still want."

Kat was painting a rosy picture of her new relationship with Mick Slattery. And I think she believed it, too. Mick must've done a hell of a good selling job. Or maybe he thought portraying himself as a kinder, gentler Mick was the best way to bring Kat back into the fold. It smacked of the old velvet glove trick, the old velvet glove concealing a fist of iron.

"What about Sunday after your last game?" Laura said. "Couldn't you and Jimmy come over for an early supper?" Laura, drat her, was definitely in league with Kat.

Inside my head I said, "Laura, do we want Jimmy falling under Kat's spell once again?" And inside my head came her response. "You don't believe that Jimmy has ever escaped being under Kat's spell, do you?"

"Listen, you two, let me ponder the matter a little bit, okay?" Of course they both knew, as I did, what the result of my pondering would be. Women, god love 'em, have a remarkable talent for getting what they want.

"Kat," I said, wanting to change the subject, "can I ask you something? Something kind of personal?"

"Ask whatever you like."

"Kat . . . what was it that happened to your father?" Now it was Kat's turn to look uncomfortable. Well, good. I was tired of being the one on the defensive.

"Why d'ya want to know?" she replied rather guardedly. This was a sensitive area, and I knew I'd better tread lightly.

"I was very close to my own father," I said. "His untimely death knocked me for a loop. I still haven't come to terms with it, and maybe I never will. There are times when I miss him so much I can hardly stand it. It seemed to me that missing our fathers was something you and I might have in common. You were probably even younger than I was when you lost your dad."

"Twelve. I'd just turned twelve. The accident occurred two weeks after my birthday. After Da's death, me mam only lived another six months. Died of a broken heart, she did. So there I was with no parents and no siblings. Just kindly Ned Taafe and my very old granny." I remembered Ned Taafe from our adventures last October in Dingle, when he'd taken us in his boat out to the Great Blasket.

"And, o' course, there was Mick. Ned and Mick, me da's two closest childhood chums. Neddy'd stayed home in Caherciveen and worked his boat. But not Mick. Oh, no, not Mick. He quickly moved on to other things. And he dragged me da along with him." I had at least some slight notion what those "other things" might be. I wondered how deeply into them Kat's dad had been dragged.

"How did he die?" Laura said softly, asking the question I'd been hesitant to ask.

"It was the cruel sea that took 'im," she said, "as it takes so many. It takes 'em and then gives 'em back. Oh yes, the sea always gives up its dead." Kat seemed lost in painful memories, and Laura and I both knew better than to press her any further; though both of us wanted to know more.

Laura refilled our glasses and then we sat there for a while in silence, each of us lost in our own thoughts.

"I probably ought to go," I said at last. "But please. Don't come to any of our games this weekend. That would be a bad idea. Watch 'em on TV. Jimmy and I will be here for dinner on Sunday evening. Okay?"

"That's brilliant," Kat said, looking happier than she had since I'd arrived at Laura's apartment. "You're a grand man, Ty Duffy, a grand, grand man."

Not so grand as all that, I said to myself.

14

I had a lot to think about as I walked slowly back to the hotel. I had just agreed to bring Jimmy for dinner on Sunday, and I didn't feel so happy about that. I felt like I'd just sold my best pal down the river. Kat had called me a grand, grand man; *that* was a laugh. I felt strangely akin to the verminous creatures scurrying beneath the city streets.

By the time I'd reached the hotel, my thoughts had done a one-eighty. If Jimmy didn't want to see Kat, then dammit, I would respect that. I hate it when people try to manipulate me — people like my mother, like Mick Slattery, like Kathleen Brogan. Yet here I was, about to do the same thing to my closest friend. *No.* I wasn't going to do it. I wasn't going to trick Jimmy into having dinner at Laura's. Not unless seeing Kat was something that Jimmy Devlin really wanted to do. If Jimmy wanted to do it, then okay, let the chips fall where they may.

"Where the heck you been, Fidelio?" Jimmy said, with unintentional irony. "Let's see. You wandered over to Lincoln Center to check out all the opera crapola they got going on over there. Correctimento?"

"Not quite. I did take a long walk, though. Needed to clear my head, stretch my legs, get a few of the kinks out. And if I were to speak truthfully, as I occasionally do, I might confess that I worked in a brief visit with Laura."

As Jimmy looked at me, I saw a hint of sadness creep into his big brown puppy-dog's eyes. "Ya know, Duff, I envy you, man. You're one lucky fella. With that Laura gal of yours, you got yourself a pretty terrific woman. I'm happy for you, you bastard. But I envy you, too. Still and all, you're a guy who deserves to have a terrific woman."

"So are you," I said. "And maybe you have one, too."

"Who? *Penny?* Shoot, Tyrus, yeah, I do have Penny. Good old

Penny. She's a great kid, our bright and shiny Penny. She's been a wonderful friend to me for a damn long time. But here's the truth, Duff. To me, Penny will always just be Penny. You know what I mean?"

"She looked great last week," I said.

"She did, didn't she? Don't know what's come over her lately."

"Wanted to look her best for you. Wanted to impress your teammates. Wanted you to realize she's an attractive, sexy woman, not just some little kid you grew up with."

Jimmy still looked sad. "I wish I felt differently about Penny. I wish I cared about her the way you care about Laura. Hell's bells, Duff, Penny deserves more from a guy than I can ever give her."

"How come you can't give her more?" Jimmy just sat there without saying anything. "Jimmy," I said, "is it because of Kat? Is Kat the reason you can't give Penny more?"

Jimmy sat there looking at the floor, bouncing his fists softly against his thighs, his lips compressed in a sad grimace. Finally he lifted his head and looked at me, then nodded slowly. "Yes, I think that's probably it," he said. "Yes, it's probably because of Kat. God damn Kat."

"Have you heard from her lately?"

He slowly shook his head no. "Nope, not lately. Kat finally got the message. I told her over and over to go away and leave me the hell alone. And now, damn it, she's gone and done it."

He sat there in silence a little longer, then said, "A woman I don't love but really like and greatly admire is never going to give up on me. And a woman I can't stop thinking about — a woman who buried a god damn dagger in my heart — has finally gotten the message and given me up for a lost cause. Now that she's gone and done just what I told her to do, I'm more miserable than I've ever been in my life. So, how do you like them apples, amigo?"

"Are you saying you didn't want Kat to go away?"

"Hell no, I didn't want Kat to go away. That woman is the bane of my existence, but Jesus, Ty, what will I do without her?"

"Jimmy, sorry to be a densehead. But just for the sake of clarification, are you telling me you want to have Kat back?"

"What the hell you think I've been saying, densehead?"

"What if you could get her back?"

"Forget it, dude. No way I'm ever going to grovel. I'm no fucking groveler. I told Kat over and over to leave me the hell alone; it took a lot of persuading, but now she's been persuaded. Kat is gone — and that's the fact, Jack."

"No," I said, "I'm not so sure about that."

For a second I wondered if I should tell Jimmy that Kat was in town; that she wanted to see him more than anything; that at this very moment she was in Laura's apartment. But if I did, what reaction would it provoke? There was a good chance, I feared, that it would provoke a strongly negative reaction, that it would just push Jimmy right back to square one. So, as I usually do, I kept my own counsel.

Our series with the Yankees in New York proved to be the mirror image of our series a week earlier in Bay City. In our place, they'd taken two of three; in their place, we took two of three.

The really memorable game occurred on Friday night. In the top of the first, Juan Flores got things going for us by slicing a leadoff single to left. Then it was my turn to bat.

"Hello, stupid," Breyreitz said as I stepped into the batter's box.

"Hello, handsome," I said cheerfully.

"Get stuffed, faggot," Breyreitz muttered.

After I'd worked the count to two and one, Juan took off for second. Breyreitz had trouble getting rid of the ball before firing a bullet to Jennings at second. Juan's foot slid in beneath the tag.

"Shit, Mr. All-Star," Breyreitz said in disgust, "put the fuckin' tag on the asshole."

"That was on you, pal," I said. "You gotta get rid of it quicker."

"Screw you, jerkoff," came the predictable reply. "And don't *ever* call me pal."

With the count at three and one, I was looking for a fastball on the inner half of the plate. If I got it, I intended to put a hurt on it. And damned if I didn't get it. It was right in my wheelhouse — to the extent that I have a wheelhouse. I smacked a high line drive toward the left-field corner, and I hit it so well that it carried all the way into the stands just to the fair side of the foul pole. It was my first home run of the season. And man, was it ever sweet.

When I came up again in the third, Juan was already at second, having led off the inning with a double to left center.

"Hello, stupid," Breyreitz said.

"Hello, stupid," I replied.

"There's an echo in here," the umpire said.

This time once again I did something I almost never do; I swung at the first pitch. In an entire season, I swing at the first pitch maybe five or six times. Pitchers, knowing I'm not a first-ball hitter, often start things off by laying one right down the middle in order to get ahead in the count. And that's what this guy did. And what I did was rip a single right back up the middle. Juan scored easily, giving us a three to nothing lead.

When I stepped in in the fifth inning, for once in his life Breyreitz kept his mouth shut. He'd mouthed off twice and twice I'd had hits. I guess he thought he'd try something different. Never a bad idea.

This time it was Nick Gurganis who was perched on second. Nick had worked a leadoff walk, and Juan had laid down a perfect sacrifice bunt.

"There's an open base, pal," I said. "What about an intentional pass?" Breyreitz just spat in the dirt in front of home plate, grunted, and scratched his inner thigh. I'd never known the guy to be so quiet.

I took a called strike and then a ball, and then came the third pitch, a slider on the outside corner. It kind of hung there for a split second giving me time to put the barrel of the bat on the ball and make some really good contact. The ball shot off the bat and soared toward the right-field corner. It didn't stop soaring until it'd landed eight rows back in the lower deck. Holy Moses, I'd hit another home run, this time an opposite-field home run. From out in the bullpen I could hear Bump shouting, "Touch 'em all, Duffy, touch 'em all!"

Did I say the Friday night game was a memorable game? For me, it was absolutely memorable. It was the first time in my entire life I'd hit two home runs in a game. I'd never done that as a kid, as a high-schooler, as a college player, as a pro. *Never*. And now I'd gone and done it in Yankee Stadium versus the hated Yankees. Believe me, it doesn't get any better than that.

As I trotted toward the dugout after touching them all, Lou Tolliver grinned at me and said, "God damn, slugger, why don't you kill the rally while you're at it. I hate hitting behind bastards like you." Then Lou gave me an affectionate necklock.

In the dugout my teammates mobbed me. And from out of the stands I heard the voice of Jimmy's father, who'd loyally stuck with us since the previous weekend. "Ya got good wood on that one, Banjo, *darn* good wood!" My own father wasn't there to watch me; but Jimmy's father damn well was. And his praise meant a ton to me.

After dropping a close game on Saturday night — we went down four to three — on Sunday afternoon we *stuck it* to the hated Yankees. For us it was Home Run Derby. Lou hit a pair, and Todd, Spike, Bobby and I each hit one. For me, three round-trippers in a three-game series was my personal ML record. And as I was circling the bases with a huge grin on my face, I could hear a few wise-ass fans chanting "ster-oids! ster-oids!" That was a laugh. Scrawny little me on the 'roids. But hey, maybe that was something I should think about!

With Monday an open day, some of the guys were heading back to Bay City on that Sunday night and some weren't. Using my powers of persuasion, I talked Jimmy into hanging around for the evening in NYC. Laura had invited us both for dinner, I said, and then maybe the three of us could take in a movie — or something.

Or something was right. Jimmy Devlin, the innocent lamb, had no idea that Laura Morgan and I were leading him down the garden path — right to where a ravenous wolf awaited him. An extraordinarily attractive ravenous wolf. But I wouldn't be doing it, I told myself, if it wasn't what Jimmy wanted. That was what he'd told me, wasn't it? I'd even asked him for clarification, hadn't I? Yet my inner voice of conscience still nagged at me. Shut up, I said. I'm doing the right thing.

At six-thirty, Jimmy and I stood outside Laura's apartment building. I still had qualms about whether or not I was selling out my best friend. And about whether I was compromising my last bit of integrity.

"Why are you hesitating?" Jimmy said. "Ring the damn bell."

"Sorry. Don't mind me. I was just thinking about something."

"Well, don't think. I'm hungry, man."

So I rang and Laura buzzed us in. As we went up to her apartment, my second thoughts hadn't disappeared. But it was kind of late for turning back.

Laura opened the door, gave us welcoming pecks, and ushered us into her dimly lit living room.

It took Jimmy a moment to realize that someone else was there. And when he did, his first words were, "What the bloody hell! Duffy, you lying son of a goddamn bitch!"

"Jimmy, Jimmy, Jimmy . . . ," Kat said softly, getting up and coming across to him. Before he could do anything she had her arms around him. Jimmy stood there stiff as a board.

"Damn it, Kat, I told you I didn't want to see you!" Jimmy blurted out. "Can't you take a god-damned hint?"

Kat didn't say anything more at that point. She just clung to Jimmy, tears streaming down her beautiful Irish face.

"Damn it, Kat, don't go crying, for goodness sake!"

"Oh, Jimmy," she said in a tear-filled voice, "you hafta be fair to me, laddie. You have ta give me a chance to explain it all to you."

"Explain *what*? Why you turned your back on me? Why you preferred Mick and his mucky minions to me?"

Kat placed her hands on the sides of Jimmy's face and turned it so they were staring into each other's eyes a few inches apart.

"Oh, laddie," she said, "I did it because you mean so very much to me. I did it because I had to protect you. I did it in hopes that you and I might still have a chance ta be together." Then her tears began to flow once more. Kat was a real pro at employing a woman's most powerful weapon.

"Shit, Kat, don't cry. I hate that. Please don't do that."

"C'mere, Jimmy," she said, taking him by the hand and leading him over to the sofa. "C'mere and lay your head in my lap. I need ya ta listen to me. Be fair ta me, lad. Listen ta me for five minutes. That's all I'm askin' of ya."

Jimmy Devlin was a goner. He'd mounted a modicum of resistance but now his resolve was used up.

"Kat," Laura said, "Ty and I are going to leave the two of you alone for a while. We'll see you later, okay?"

"Thanks, Laura. That'd be grand."

Jimmy and I exchanged brief glances; I gave him a little shoulder shrug as if to say, hey, don't blame me, I just do what I'm told. Jimmy returned my shoulder shrug with a small one of his own. He appeared to be reconciled to the situation.

Out on the street, I asked Laura what we should do now.

"I suspect you're hungry," she said. "Why don't we go somewhere and get ourselves a bite to eat. Then, maybe we can take a long walk through the city."

"What about them? Jimmy was totally famished. I thought we were going to have dinner with them?"

"No, they'll be fine by themselves."

"Well, okay."

"I have an idea," Laura said. "After we've had something to eat and stretched our legs a bit, why don't you and I go back and spend some time together in your hotel room? It's been a while since we've had a chance to do that."

Even Ty Duffy isn't so naïve as not to glom on to the meaning of Laura Morgan's words. And what she was suggesting appealed so much I came close to suggesting we skip the meal, skip the walk, and head straight back to the hotel.

But then another little thought flitted through my mind. "What if Jimmy comes back to the room while we're still there?"

"Jimmy won't be coming back to the room tonight," Laura said. "Jimmy will be otherwise occupied."

"Oh . . . I get it. You know, being otherwise occupied sounds like quite a nice way to spend an evening."

"It does, doesn't it?"

It was around eleven-thirty or twelve when the telephone rang in my hotel room. I was half-asleep and planned to ignore it.

"You'd better get that," Laura said from somewhere down beneath the covers. So I reached out and snatched the bloody thing.

"Yes?" I said. It was Jimmy. He said he just wanted to let me know he wouldn't be coming back to the room tonight; that he didn't want me to be worried about him; that he'd meet me at Penn Station in the morning; that he hoped I wouldn't mind gathering up his things and bringing them to the train.

"Nope," I said, "don't mind a bit. No worries, muchacho." Then we both hung up.

"That was Jimmy?" Laura said.

"Yep. Not coming back tonight."

"There's a surprise," she said. Laura was still semi-buried in the covers, with just her face peeping out, framed partly by her light brown hair. Her blue eyes twinkled at me. The way she was looking up at me with warm affection made me think of Boog the cat.

"C'mere," she said softly, extending a hand toward me.

When a very attractive woman who's lying in your bed tells you to "C'mere," it's usually a good idea to oblige. Especially if it's *this* very attractive woman. So, without a second thought I did.

On the train ride down to Bay City, while Jimmy slept, I leaned back in my seat and reflected on the events of the weekend.

The least complicated part was reflecting on the baseball games we'd played, though my sudden power surge had certainly left me flummoxed. Maybe all my anxieties about Laura and about Jimmy and Kat had juiced me up somehow. But the crucial thing for me now was to put those home runs I'd socked completely out of my mind. I'd seen far too many players knock a few dingers and then start thinking they were the next Babe Ruth. Nothing screws a guy up more than getting home-run fever. I knew that if Bump's momentous homer the week before had been an aberration — and I wasn't so sure about that — my trio of home runs against the Yankees was truly an aberration.

As for Laura and me — wow — all my doubts and fears had been assuaged in one fell swoop. How could I ever have doubted her? We seemed to be back on the firmest footing we'd been on in a long, long time. And boy, was I happy about that.

But as for Jimmy and Kathleen Brogan . . . yes, there was the rub. Jimmy, it appeared, had had his heart mended just like that. Kat had won him back — as Laura and I had known she would — and now the lad was absolutely beside himself with joy. That was a very good thing, wasn't it? How could it not be a very good thing?

But what would happen when Mick Slattery got wind of it? When it came to Mick, I felt certain that Kat had it completely wrong. She believed that Mick had undergone a real change; and that she was the one who was now in control of that relationship.

I didn't believe that for a second. The Mick who'd interviewed me in Boston was not a kinder, gentler Mick. Mick Slattery, I fervently believed, was still the Bastard of the World.

15

When I got back to my apartment after our team practice on Monday afternoon, I found a note taped to my front door. "Can't use my opera ticket for tonight. Maybe you'd like to have it? Chuck."

The cheeky bastard. The opera ticket he was offering me was *my* opera ticket. Once our baseball season is underway, I give my tickets for the remainder of the opera season to Chuck; and if he can't use them, he passes them along to clients.

I was bushed, but what the heck; maybe I'd go anyway. *Der Fliegende Holländer* — "The Flying Dutchman" — is a personal favorite. Since Chuck had left me just the one ticket, I guessed he'd found someone to take the other one.

I'd just reached my seat when the orchestra launched into the overture. Sitting next to me in my other seat was a woman I didn't know. She offered me a smile, then turned her attention to the music. I could smell her fragrance, something lovely but old-fashioned. Arpège? It was like something my mother might wear.

I turned my attention to the music also. Wagner's overtures and preludes are my favorite parts, always making me wish the guy had written some symphonies. As for this opera, I'd always liked the myth behind it, about the sea captain who said the wrong thing at the wrong time and doomed himself to sail the seas forever — or until he could find redemption through the love of a woman.

During the first act I leaned back and closed my eyes. Enveloped by the music, I allowed my mind to wander. Maybe it was the woman's perfume that sparked a particular memory. I found myself taken back to a time when I was eight years old, standing way out in center field and wearing a faded blue baseball jersey. I was a member of the mighty Blue Dodgers, a team for eight, nine, and ten-year-olds. It was the only year that I ever played in the outfield.

My mother and father were in the stands watching along with all the other kids' parents. So was my six-year-old brother Billy. It was the final inning of the game and we led our arch rivals, the Red Rangers, by two runs. There was one out, but now the sacks were filled with Rangers, and coming up to bat was a tall skinny nine-year-old who'd already socked one way over my head.

My teenaged coach kept motioning me back. "Deeper!" he finally yelled at me, "You gotta play deeper!" Dutifully, I retreated to the deepest recesses of center field.

My pal Tommy launched the pitch and the skinny kid belted it. But not over my head. He belted it straight up.

Crap, I was playing too *deep*. I charged toward the infield for all I was worth.

The ball went up and up. It reached its apogee and for a split second seemed to hang there. Then down it came.

Maybe twenty feet in back of the second-base bag the ball rocketed toward the earth. It rocketed toward the earth and landed right smack in the webbing of the small glove at the end of my outstretched arm. I *had* it. I'd *caught* it.

Still on my feet, my momentum carried me straight toward second base — where the runner had failed to tag up! The father who was coaching third base was desperately shouting at the kid to "go back to second, go back to second!" But it was too late.

I easily beat him to the bag. An unassisted double play. The game was over. The Blue Dodgers had defeated their arch rivals. And it was all due to me.

Our ecstatic players and fans were bouncing around on our side of the field like Mexican jumping beans. "Hey Duffy," our young coach yelled at me, "thought I told you not to play so deep!" He gave me a vigorous high-five. "Great catch, Ty, that was a really great catch!"

My mom and dad were as tickled as anyone. Billy was the liveliest jumping bean of the bunch.

"That was wonderful, Tyrus," my mother said, hugging me against her. "Rudolph Nureyev couldn't have done it more gracefully."

"Nureyev?" my father said. "Hah. That was pure Willie Mays."

"Nuh uh," Billy said, punching me on the arm, "that was pure Ty Duffy."

The four of us were all laughter and smiles. It felt great. It felt just the way everything ought to feel between members of a loving family. On that particular day, for just a little while, that was really how things felt.

It was about three weeks later that my mother suddenly up and scarpered. Never to return. And never again to see me play baseball until I was in the major leagues, fifteen years later.

Mom's sudden departure inflicted some very deep wounds on all of us. The truth is that my brother has never forgiven her. I halfway have . . . I suppose.

In the end we all managed to survive. My dad, my brother, and I went on to have a dozen great years together in our all-male household. It didn't take long for Billy and me to adjust to the absence of our mom. We were resilient, resourceful kids, and we cherished the close bond we shared. Dad was harder to read. I don't believe that he rebounded as easily as we had. Deep down, I think, he remained a deeply wounded man. Wagner's Flying Dutchman, in the end, found redemption in the unswerving love of a woman. My father never did.

My thoughts wandered on to Wagner's other operas, particularly to Parsifal and Lohengrin, and to my absurd notion that Bump Rhodes had some connection to them. Parsifal was the German version of the knight named Perceval, the rustic Welsh lad who'd had all the right stuff to be a Grail Knight — spiritual and sexual purity. Bump Rhodes was cut out of the same cloth as Perceval the Welshman. Bump — who hailed from the hinterlands of lower Alabama; who called himself the King of Conuceh County; who never drank (except on one memorable occasion) anything stronger than RC Cola; who suffered from unrequited love for a young woman named Violet. It was all just a little too weird. Or maybe me, with my fixed ideas, was the one who was just a little too weird.

As the applause marking the end of the first half of the program subsided, the woman sitting beside me said, "Would you care to join me for a glass of wine?"

"Yes, I'd be pleased to join you," I said, and that was more or less the truth.

"I'm Alyssa," she said, as we perched ourselves on high stools beside a tiny, round-topped table. "And you, I believe, are Ty Duffy — Ty Duffy the baseball player."

I held a finger up in front of my lips. "Not so loud," I whispered. "I'm traveling incognito. Some folks tend to ridicule my operatic enthusiasms."

"Mum's the word," she said, holding her finger up in front of her lips. "Anyway, no one looking at you right at this moment would imagine for a second that you are a ball player."

"How am I supposed to take *that* observation? Don't know whether to feel flattered or insulted."

"Take it in any way you like," she said, her eyes smiling brightly.

As I looked at her, it suddenly struck me how much this Alyssa woman reminded me of my own mother, both in mannerisms and appearance. She was stylishly attired and quite attractive for a woman who was probably in her mid-fifties; and she knew it, too. And like my mother she had striking eyes, though hers were more of a smoky blue color than my mother's grayish-green.

"How long have you known Chuck?" I asked her.

"All his life," she said. "I'm his mother."

"Seriously? That hardly seems possible."

"You're quite the gentleman, Mr. Duffy, and I appreciate the gesture. Charles has told me a good deal about you. But not how kind you can be."

"That darn Chuck's been telling tales on me?"

"You've made quite an impression on my dear son, you know. Probably because the two of you are so different."

"Not so different," I said. "Maybe in a few outward things; but inside, we probably share most of the same needs and insecurities."

"Are you saying that you're a manly man who's capable of having tender feelings?"

"Absolutely not. Never had a tender feeling in my life."

"Of course you haven't," she said. "But I have to say I find your manliness quite appealing. In fact, quite alluring."

"Alyssa, are you flirting with me?"

"You can let a fifty-six year-old woman have her fun, can't you?"

"I can," I said. "Up to a point, anyway."

"I wonder what point that would be?" she said, a twinkle in her eye. Then she took a sip of her wine.

Chuck, you slimy bugger, I said to myself, what the hell you doin' to me, mate?

"Don't look so nervous, Ty," she said. "Charles asked me to jolly you up a bit. He said you'd been looking quite forlorn recently. He thinks you've been having girlfriend troubles. I'm sorry if I've gotten carried away with my jollying."

"That's okay," I said, feeling relieved that this had all been a put-on. "It's not every day an attractive and fascinating woman takes an interest in me. As for my being forlorn, Chuck was right about that; though that's all been sorted out quite agreeably."

"That's wonderful," she said, placing her hand on top of mine. "I wasn't sure how far I might have to go in my efforts to cheer you up. Though I have to confess, it would've been fun to find out."

Just then the house lights dimmed, alerting us to the fact that the opera was about to start again. Which was none too soon for me.

During my junior year at Waverly College my father and I lived alone together for the first time. Billy had gone off to Vanderbilt on a full-ride tennis scholarship and was having such a good time that he rarely came home. For the previous dozen years, ever since my mother had skedaddled, it had been the three of us living together. And then, suddenly, it was just Dad and me.

It was a trying year in some ways but also a special year. I enjoyed my classes, enjoyed dating girls, and enjoyed playing my final season of college baseball before going pro. And then there was Dad. He tried to leave me alone, but of course he couldn't. You need to get a life, Dad, I was always thinking; but even if you don't, please, please keep your mitts off of mine. But maybe, unbeknownst to me, my father had more of a life than I'd been aware of; and I'd been so busy leading my own I hadn't realized it.

One day as my Shakespeare class was ending, my professor, an attractive young woman some of us had fantasies about, nabbed me as I was leaving the room. "Ty," she said, "if you aren't rushing off to another class, could I speak to you a moment?"

"Sure," I said, wondering what she might want. I didn't think she could have any complaints since I hadn't missed any classes and I'd made an A— on the mid-term exam. It was true that I didn't speak up much in class, but neither did a lot of students.

"I just wanted to ask you if you know J. J. Duffy."

Wow, where did that come from? "Yes," I said, "I kind of do. He's a close relative."

"He's your father?"

"Yes, that's right, he is."

"I just wanted to say that my grandfather thinks the world of him."

"Uh . . . okay."

"I guess you know he's been volunteering at the Cedar Grove retirement home, going along with some of the residents on their trips to museums, ball games, the zoo?"

" Uh, well, that sounds like the kind of thing he might do."

"And it's greatly appreciated. Everyone at the home thinks your father is a wonderful man."

"Uh . . . thanks, professor. I'm kind of partial to him myself."

At supper that evening I gave my dad a hard time about the good deeds I'd gotten wind of. He just shrugged. Oh sure, he said, he'd been helping out one afternoon a week at the retirement home. No big deal. Someone had mentioned they needed volunteers and he thought it was something he could do.

"Dad, do you know my Shakespeare professor? Professor Stevenson? Cynthia Stevenson?"

My dad did something completely uncharacteristic. He blushed. "Let me see," he said, pretending like he was wracking his brain, "is she the young woman whose grandfather is in the home? Comes there sometimes with two older women?"

"Dad, I've no clue who she comes with. I've never been there."

"If she's the one I'm thinking of, she's a very caring young woman. Her grandfather really appreciates her visits. How is she as a professor? Is she pretty good?"

"Yeah, Dad, she is. She's really excellent in the classroom." Typically for a guy my age, I wondered where else she might be excellent — and if my dad might have reason to know. Nah. Of course not. Don't be silly. And yet I couldn't help thinking that would be really cool. Go for it, Dad.

In any case, I realized then that my father, who seemed so familiar to me, still must have had a few secrets. There were some private recesses tucked away that Billy and I knew nothing about. I found myself liking the idea that my father was not a completely open book. There weren't many mysteries about my father, but maybe there were a few. Well, damn it, Dad, good for you.

I had no desire to probe into my father's mysteries. They were none of my business. But there was a different dad-mystery that I really did want to probe into, the mystery of what had happened to Kat Brogan's father. What had been his relationship to Mick Slattery? What were the details of his fatal accident? And how did all that bear on the question of Mick's relationship to Kat?

Other than the little bit Kat had told Laura and me in New York, I knew nothing at all about the circumstances of Kat's father's death. My instincts told me it wasn't an accident, told me that Mick Slattery had been behind it in one fashion or another. His death, they told me, was payback. For what, I didn't know. But I suspected that whatever it was, Kat Brogan was at the center of it.

16

In baseball there's a common phenomenon known as the June swoon. Usually it involves a player who's had a great first two months and then tails off dramatically. It can also involve an entire team, when just about everyone goes into a slump at the same time.

With the exception of Jimmy Devlin, during the month of June the Bay City Grays descended into the midst of a collective swoon — we were mired in what John Bunyan called the Slough of Despond. We stopped hitting; we stopped pitching; and we'd lost all our swagger. By the third week of June, we'd plummeted from first to fourth, now just two games over .500. And our won-lost record wasn't the worst of it.

In Chicago, Bobby Radley broke a bone in his wrist diving for a ball. He'd be out at least a month. In Detroit, Lou and Juan collided going for a foul pop-up. Lou was okay, but Juan broke his collarbone. He'd be out six weeks. In Kansas City, Nick Gurganis pulled a hamstring running to first base. He'd be out a week, or more likely, two. Sometimes when it rains it's goddamn cats and dogs. The All-Star break couldn't come soon enough. But the disasters weren't over.

In our first game back in Bay City after a long road trip to the Midwest, Deacon Lawler took a wicked foul tip off his throwing hand. His thumb was broken, his season was over, and very probably, his career. In the same game, Jumpin' Jack Fletcher suddenly felt something tear in his throwing shoulder. Like the Deacon's, Jack's season was finished.

And so, in all probability, was the Bay City Grays' season. In those disastrous two weeks, our promising season had gone to the Hot Place in a hand-held basket.

But we still had one bright ray of hope — James Patrick Devlin. Jimmy was mowin' 'em down better than ever. His record was nine and two, and he was a shoo-in for the AL All-Star team. And then, to everyone's amazement, a second ray of hope suddenly emerged — a shiny beam named Edgar Eustace "Bump" Rhodes. Bump Rhodes was our Man on the White Mule.

That third week in June, back home in Bay City, we began our first round of interleague play with a series versus the D-Backs, which was followed by one against the Rockies. Despite losing the Deacon and Jumpin' Jack in the second game that week, we still managed to win four of those six games, thanks to strong pitching from Jimmy, Alfred King, and Jorge Comellas; and thanks to a game in which our listless bats inexplicably came alive and we knocked out fifteen runs, our season high. The game featured a right-handed homer from Bump and an inside-the-park homer from the fleet-footed Zook Zulaski.

But the best thing for me about the week was Laura Morgan's visit to Bay City. We hadn't been able to see each other since the weekend in New York in early May, but I think we both knew, following that weekend, that things between us were back to where each of us wanted them to be.

We enjoyed a truly idyllic weekend together. Laura, what a good sport, attended all three of our games. I guess her presence must have inspired me, because I went five for ten and hit my first home run since New York.

On Saturday morning we ate a late breakfast at Maggie's Grill. On Saturday afternoon I introduced Laura to my neighbor Chuck and to Boog the cat. Laura hit it off with both of them. And during the entire weekend, we didn't run into Seamus Byrne a single time. Thank goodness for minor miracles.

Before the weekend was over, Laura had extracted from me a promise to go with her to her parents' house in Rhode Island during the All-Star break in July — assuming I wasn't selected for the team, which seemed a pretty good bet, since I was currently third in the voting at my position. I made that promise in good faith, too. What the hell was I thinking?

♦♦♦

The last week in June we headed out west for our second week of interleague play. First to San Diego for a three-game series with the Padres; then on to L.A. for three games versus the first-place Dodgers.

What a raggle-taggle team we'd become. Whitey'd had to put Zook in right in place of Bobby Radley; he'd put a young guy called up from Triple-A in left to replace Nick Gurganis; and now Manny del Rio, our utility guy, was in at short replacing Juan Flores. Bump Rhodes, to everyone's consternation, had assumed the job of being our starting catcher. Terry O'Grady — a young triple-A pitcher that Dave Rubenstein had liked the looks of in spring training — was called up to take Jumpin' Jack Fletcher's spot in our starting rotation. Lou, Spike, Todd, and I were the only regulars still in our starting lineup.

Since Dave believed Terry O'Grady was ready to go, Terry would make his first big-league start for us in San Diego. It was a logical move, since Petco Park is a pitcher's park and since the Padres are a weak-hitting team. Who better to build one's confidence against? Plus, Terry was a local kid, having grown up in Encinitas, just up the road from San Diego. So he'd have a huge contingent of fans to root him on.

San Diego is a beautiful city boasting a perfect natural harbor and near-perfect weather. It's not so overwhelming as L.A., and much more of a piece. As far as I know, it has only one major flaw — most of the locals could care less about baseball. The Padres have a spectacular new ballpark in an excellent location; and although they are a small-budget franchise, they have an impressive crop of young pitchers. All in all, the team has real positives. But only their hard-core fans realize all the things they have to be excited about.

Bump Rhodes was a guy who had things to be excited about, too — he was making his first trip to California, he was the starting catcher on a big-league team, and he had actually begun playing like one. Yes, Bump had a lot to be excited about. And over the next four months, he was going to have more to be excited about than any of us could have imagined.

As for Jimmy Devlin, since his successful reunion with Kat in New York he'd shucked off all his moroseness. If Jimmy had been pitching well before that reunion, afterward he was pitching even better. Exactly what was going on now between him and Kat I didn't know. He didn't say, and I didn't ask. Whatever it was, I could tell he felt good about it. Seeing Kat had removed a huge burden from the lad's shoulders.

But always in the back of my mind was the fear that someone else was going to get wind of the renewed Jimmy and Kat relationship. When that happened, the shit would hit the fan. If only that could wait until the season was over. But of course it couldn't.

Our hotel was located in San Diego's Gaslamp Quarter, only a short walk from Petco Park. Once a notoriously seedy section of the city – in fact, the red light district – it was now a trendy area of pretentious restaurants and watering holes, stylishly done, but about as authentic as the set for a Hollywood western. But what would you expect? This was Southern California.

"This place is great!" Bump chirped as we meandered along 5th Ave., not far from our hotel. "Look! There's an Irish pub. See it, the Blarney Castle? There's no way you fellers can pass up an Irish pub."

Jimmy looked at me and shrugged a "why not?" "They're sure to have Guinness on tap," he said. "Maybe Harp and Smithwick's, too."

"They probably do," I said. "But I'm not so sure about RC Cola."

"You can't always have everything," Bump said philosophically.

When we stepped inside Jimmy said, "Jesus, Mary, and Joseph, it's just like being in County Cork."

"Oh yes," I said, "just."

To their credit, the pub owners had done a creditable job of recreating the ambiance of an Irish pub. Not quite as scruffy, perhaps, but dark, rough wooden tables and booths, lots of Irish-looking crap all over the walls, and a little nook where they could have live music, though on this Monday evening they didn't. Even a few of its employees, judging from their accents, hailed from the Auld Sod.

"Would ya look at what the cat drug in," said a voice from out of my past. Standing next to our booth was a hatchet-faced man whom I'd last laid eyes on as he was leaving the small hospital in Dingle, Ireland. It was Honest Jack Strachan, Mick Slattery's right-hand man. "If it ain't Ty Duffy and the elusive Jimmy Devlin, two o' me all-time favorites. What'll ya be havin', lads? The drinks're on me."

"Irish hospitality, eh Jack?" I said. "Well, you can make mine a pint of Guinness."

"Mine, too," said Jimmy.

"Nothing for me, thanks," said the Deacon, his broken right thumb still sporting a splint. The Deacon eyed Jack Strachan rather dubiously.

"Think I could have a Coke?" Bump said shyly.

"What brings you here, Jack? Last place I would've expected to see you."

"Seamus and me've been here a couple o' days on business. We own this place, ya know, 'long with a few others."

"Catchy name you've given the place," I said.

"Weren't my doin'," Jack said with a shoulder shrug.

"You want to join us? We could reminisce about old times."

"Nah, nah. But if you'd give me half a sec I'd like ta give Jimmy-boy here a little message. Then I'll be on me way."

Jimmy and Jack stared at each other for a lengthy moment before Jack continued. "Laddie, Mick says he's up to date on recent developments. Says it might behoove you — his word, not mine — ta think things through a bit. Says he wants no harm ta come ta nobody. He knows your ball team has had a run o' bad luck lately.

He'd rather not see you have any more." Then Jack clammed up, letting his words sink in.

Jimmy sat there staring right back at Jack, not saying anything. It was Bump who finally spoke up.

"That don't sound so nice to me, mister," he said. "Sounds like some kinda gosh-darn threat. That what that was?"

Jack, for the first time, turned his attention to Bump. "Don't know who you are, lad. You some knight in shining armor or somet'ing? This don't involve you, lad; so you'd best keep your young mug out of it."

"Mister," Bump said, "if it involves my teammate, it involves me."

Bump's remark caused Jack Strachan to smile. Bump's sentiments must've appealed to Jack's Celtic warrior code. "Good for you, laddie, good for you," he said.

Then turning to me he said, "Mick's mighty disappointed in you, Duffy. He thought the two of you had an understanding."

"No, we did not. If he thought that, he was seriously mistaken."

"Well . . . anyway . . . I guess you've all got the message. Oh, here," he said to me, handing me a slip of paper and shooting me a meaningful look. "In case you think it might be good for me 'n you to have a little chat." I shoved it in my jacket pocket without a glance.

"I'm off then, lads," he said. "Hope ta talk ta ya soon, Duffy."

"Nothing like Irish hospitality, Jack," I said to his departing back.

When he was gone, Jimmy turned to Bump and said, "Nice going, d'Artagnan, I appreciated that."

Bump still sat there, working hard to put two and two together. Finally he said, "Does that there feller have anything to do with those other fellers who gave us a hard time in Boston?"

"Oh yes," I said, "not much doubt about that."

"I kinda thought so," said Bump. "Guess they must think there's some reason to be keepin' an eye on all of us."

"That's how it looks to me," I said.

Jimmy, staring glumly into the dark depths of his Guinness, made wet circles on the table with his glass.

As the four of us walked back through the Gaslamp Quarter to the Marriott, Jimmy said, "Running into Jack Strachan like that — I'm guessing it was no coincidence."

"Nope," I said, "I don't think it was any coincidence."

"You Irish cousins of mine," Bump said, "you fellers just can't help rubbin' each other the wrong way, can ya?"

"Irish cousins of yours?" said Jimmy. "How do you figure we're your Irish cousins?"

"Well," Bump said, "I'm a Welshman. And o' course the Welsh and the Irish are pretty close kin. So I reckon that makes me your cousin."

"You're *Welsh*? How do you figure you're Welsh, Alabama-boy?"

"Couple of things. First off, 'cause I'm descended from the Welsh Indians. You heard of them, right? And second off, I'm Welsh 'cause I'm descended from my great granddaddy, Jesse Jones, the Welsh baseball player."

"Jesse James?"

"Shoot no, not Jesse *James*, Jesse *Jones*. Also known as Broadway Jones. My great granddaddy was a pitcher. And if he hadn'ta got hurt, he woulda been a real good one, too."

"Broadway Jones, huh?" said Jimmy. "I hate to tell you, but that sounds like a load of tosh."

"Nope, ain't no tosh about it. It's the gospel truth."

"I never knew," I said, "that before there was Broadway Joe there was Broadway Jones."

"Yep, there was. It's the gospel truth."

That night I went on-line and looked up Broadway Jones. Bump was right; there really was a guy with that name who pitched in a few games in 1923. His full name was Jesse Frank Jones. His old man must've been as good at naming his sons as mine had been.

"Hey, Duffy," Jimmy said, "while you're at it, look up the Welsh Indians. I mean, who the hell are the Welsh Indians?"

I didn't need to look them up. I already knew the old yarn about the Welsh Indians, who'd supposedly descended from a twelfth-century Welsh prince. After the guy had accidentally stumbled upon the New World, he'd gone back to North Wales and gathered up a group. They'd sailed off west across the Atlantic, but nothing was ever heard of them again. Then in America's early days, rumors of a tribe of light-skinned Indians, Indians who spoke a language that sounded like Welsh, started surfacing. Thomas Jefferson even told Lewis and Clark to keep an eye out for them on their famous trek into the west.

Right at that moment, though, a different thought insinuated itself into my brain. For here was Bump Rhodes, claiming to be a Welshman. And I knew damn well that Perceval, the Arthurian Grail Knight, had been a Welshman. Geez, Bump, you aren't reliving one of your past lives, are you? Oh, man, me and my stupid ideas. Give it a rest, Duff, give it a rest.

As I was getting ready for bed, I reached into my jacket pocket and fished out the little slip of paper Jack Strachan had given me. I unfolded it and took a look: "Call me," it said, followed by what I supposed was a cell phone number. I re-folded it and put it back in my pocket.

17

Jimmy was dead to the world as I slipped quietly out of our hotel room a little before eight in the morning. Not a morning person, our Jimmy.

I headed down the street that led toward Petco Park, then turned right onto a broad sidewalk beside which ran a set of tracks for a bright and shiny old-timey trolley. It looked charming, but a trolley ride wasn't what I needed. I needed a vigorous walk.

As I headed in the direction of San Diego's harbor, the sky was gray and heavy with moisture, what locals call the marine layer, which rolls in at night off the Pacific. It would burn off by late morning, and then the city would luxuriate in its famous sunshine the rest of the day.

I walked a couple of miles along the waterfront past an assortment of piers and naval ships, docked ferries, restaurants, and fishing boats, before turning around and starting back. By then it was after nine, and I was feeling a serious need for coffee.

A place called The Brickyard snagged my attention, so I popped in for a look. It had a few tables inside and quite a few more outside in a courtyard facing the trolley tracks. I ordered a large black coffee and some sort of fancy bagel melt, then carried my provender to one of the outside tables.

As I sipped coffee I glanced at the sports section of the local newspaper, then spent a few minutes knocking out the daily crossword. Not too challenging, though one clue had eluded me.

A tall guy in a black windbreaker that said SDSU took a seat at a nearby table and nodded his hello to me. Then he took a second look at me, and I knew what that meant — the guy had recognized me. That rarely happened, even in Bay City, and I hadn't expected it to happen in San Diego. The guy must've been a serious baseball fan. Fortunately, he was considerate enough to leave me alone.

The Brickyard was a popular place, and it wasn't long before all the outside tables were occupied. I figured I should give mine up, having been there for maybe forty-five minutes. I'd better trek back to the hotel and see if young Jimmy might actually be up and at 'em.

"So, are you all set to face Jude tonight?" the SDSU guy said to me, finally getting up his nerve to give voice to his thoughts. He was referring to Jude Pevensey, the ace of the Padres' staff and the moundsman we'd face in tonight's game. I looked over at the SDSU guy and grimaced.

"I don't even want to think about facing Jude," I said. "You got any words of wisdom?"

"Swing at the first hittable pitch," he said. "Don't let him get two strikes on you unless you know how to hit a very good slider."

"I don't know anybody who does," I said. I got up slowly from my chair and snatched up my newspaper, which was still folded to the crossword puzzle.

"You wouldn't know a seven-letter word meaning glacial debris, would you?" I asked. "In Ireland they call the ridges left by the glaciers eskers. Not enough letters, and too obscure anyway."

He gave it a moment's thought, then said, "How about moraine?"

I gave him a thumbs up, filled in the answer, and left.

For a Tuesday night game in San Diego, it was a terrific crowd. That was partly due to Jude Pevensey pitching for the Padres and partly due to Jorge Comellas pitching for the Grays. It was the Tijuana Teaser versus Jude the Dude. It was junk-ball city versus classic power-pitching.

The atmosphere was one I'd never experienced before — it was like we were playing in some Latin American country. Thousands of fans had come up from Mexico and were making their presence known visually and orally. They were dancing and chanting and waving green and red Mexican flags. They'd come to support their hombre.

The Bay City Grays don't have a boatload of Latin players, but Whitey put in every one we had. Miguel Torres would be behind the plate, Manny del Rio at short in place of the injured Juan Flores, and Hector Gomez, the Triple-A kid, was in left. When the P.A. announcer read out our lineup, those guys all got huge ovations. But the biggest ovation was for our pitcher, Jorge Comellas.

Whitey had Manny leading off, and Jude the Dude quickly blew him away with four straight blazing fastballs. Jude's first four pitches to me were fastballs also, two in the zone and two just missing. Having watched every one of them, I now faced a two-two count. Pevensey had fired eight straight heaters, four to Manny and four to me. It was time, I felt sure, for his vaunted slider.

What was it the guy in the SDSU windbreaker had said? Do anything you can to avoid Jake's slider? No way, Hoss, I said to myself. I'm looking slider, and if I get it I'm putting the wood to it. And there it was. *Wicked.* Right on the outside corner — right where he wanted it and right where I'd expected it. I lashed at the ball and caught it good. As it shot off the bat and headed toward right center, I was thinking double, maybe even three-bagger. Then I had to think again. The Padres' center fielder, who'd been shading me slightly to right, was off at the crack of the bat. The little so-and-so was sprinting his ass off. At the last possible moment he laid out horizontally and plucked the ball from the ether — a spectacular grab. The Padres fans were on their feet, roaring their approbation. *Mierda.*

I circled the first-base bag and jogged back across the infield toward the visitors' dugout. As I passed behind the mound, Jude and I exchanged glances. He gave me a tight little smile knowing I'd outguessed him and thankful he had a damned jackrabbit in center field. But his smile also meant it wouldn't happen again. And it didn't. My next three trips to the plate resulted in a grounder to second, a strikeout, and a weak fly to left. I went oh-for-four on the night.

Jorge's assortment of slow, tantalizing pitches — curves, splitters, knuckle-curves, and the occasional fastball — had the Padres' hitters off-stride all night. They got a scratch hit here and a walk there but didn't mount a real threat until the bottom of the eighth inning. Then, with the score still zero-zero, the top of their order was coming up.

Offensively, the Padres consist of one magnificent warrior surrounded by a middling assortment of lesser spear-carriers. Their one great warrior is a left-handed power hitter named Martín Montanez, a guy with one of the sweetest swings in the Bigs. Jorge'd worked cautiously to him all night, walking him twice and getting him to line out once. Now he couldn't afford to walk him. With one on and one out, if he walked Montanez it would move the potential winning run into scoring position. This was clearly the moment for Whitey to take Jorge out and bring in our lefty reliever Joe Oliver. But Whitey didn't. It was a bad managerial move, yet a move that bespoke Whitey's humanity. Win or lose, Whitey wanted this to be Jorge's game.

And it almost worked. Jorge flirted with the corners and got Martin to foul a couple off. But when the count went full, Jorge had no choice but to come in with one, so he tried sneaking a fastball by Montanez on the outside corner.

Martín flicked his wrists and the ball shot on a line toward left. Hector Gomez broke in two steps, saw the error of his ways, and retreated. He was too late. The line drive rose rather than dipped and passed above his outstretched glove by a foot and a half. Then it caromed off the wall and went past him in the opposite direction. The runner scored easily and Montanez went all the way to third as Hector ran down the ball. When the next hitter lofted a lazy fly to right, Montanez tagged and scored, and the Padres had taken a two-zero lead over the Grays.

As we came to bat in the top of the ninth, it was "T-Time." That is to say, Jude Pevensey made way for a guy with an even more astoundingly British name, Clive Tiverton, the Padres' ace closer, who was simply known as Big T. "What *time* is it?" the P.A. system blared out. "It's T-Time!" the Padres fans shouted at the top of their lungs, as Clive jogged in from the center field bullpen.

Big T struck out the first two guys who came up and then faced Bump, who was pinch hitting for Jorge Comellas. Bump swung and missed twice, then hammered a shot to deep center. But that damn jackrabbit out there ran it down, making an over-the-shoulder grab. This night's game was in the books.

After the game I slipped off by myself for the meeting I'd arranged with Jack Strachan back at the Irish pub. I felt an odd kinship with Jack, a guy I'd nearly killed before turning around and saving his life. That was last October, in the frigid waters off the Great Blasket Island on the west coast of Ireland. It was as close to a heroic moment as I'd had in my life, a life largely unburdened with heroic moments.

Jack was already there, sitting alone in the same booth we'd sat in the night before. He was sipping a pint of Guinness; another full pint was across from him, lying in wait for me.

"Gracias, Jack-quito," I said, lifting my glass.

"De nada, amigo," he said.

"Amigo?"

"Sure, why the hell not?" he said.

"Hey, amigo," I said, "you don't still have that lumber-jack plaid shirt of mine, do you? The one I lent you last year out on the Great Blasket? I sure do miss that damn thing."

"Nah, not no more," Jack said, smiling. "Too big for me, it was. Almost big enough for me to swim in." Jack flashed me a big grin. "Nah, dropped it off at the Oxfam shop, I did."

"Just as long as it found a good home."

Then we sat there in silence for a lengthy moment, each of us eyeing the other cautiously. Finally I said, "How ya comin' with your swimming lessons?"

Jack laughed. It was a laughing matter and it wasn't a laughing matter — since I'd nearly drowned the guy, and then in trying to save him, he'd nearly drowned me.

"It's strange, isn't it," he said, "in a small country surrounded by water and filled with loughs and rivers, how few Irishmen can swim. Many a good man's gone to a watery grave because of it."

Jack's remark brought to mind Kat's father. Okay then, I thought, might as well to go ahead and take the plunge. If there was someone besides Mick Slattery who was likely to know, it was Jack Strachan.

"Hey, Jack," I said, "did you know Kat Brogan's father?"

"Kev? Oh yeah, knew 'im like a brother. I wasn't as close to 'im as Mick was, but we was good pals, Kevin Brogan and me. They don't come any better'n Kev."

"Did something happen between Kev and Mick?" I said. "Did they have some kind of a falling out?"

Jack gave me a tight-lipped stare. Yes, I thought, remembering the first time I'd met him in Dublin, this is a fellow with a lean and hungry look, the kind of guy me and Julius Caesar need to watch out for.

"Whenever Kat's mentioned her father," I said, "I've always sensed a real bitterness toward Mick. I could be wrong, but that's how it's seemed." I shut up, hoping that Jack would take the bait. Damned if he didn't.

"Only one thing happened between Mick and Kev," he finally said. "Niamh."

"Niamh?"

"Oh yes, Niamh O'Connell, as she used ta be. Duffy, if you think Kat is a beautiful woman, ya shoulda seen Niamh. The four of 'em grew up together — Kev, Mick, Niamh, and Ned Taafe. I didn't know them then; but thick as thieves they was. We all knew that one day Mick and Niamh would get married. Then Niamh ups and marries Kev. Jesus, Mary, and Joseph. Poor Mick was overjoyed at the good fortune of his two closest friends — and he never forgave either of them."

"Was that when Mick went off and got himself involved with the Irish Republican Army?"

"Nah, he and Kev were already deep into that shite. Believe me, you don't wanna know. Mick was a rising star, Kev his loyal sidekick. A fine team they made. But after Niamh and Kev got married, Mick just bided his time, though we all knew Kev's days were numbered. But, hell, I've said too much a'ready. So I'd best say na more about them good old days."

Jack was confirming what I'd long suspected. I didn't need to know the specifics of what had happened to Kev. I now felt sure that Mick Slattery, in his inimitable fashion, had made certain arrangements for Kevin Brogan. And if I knew that, Kat Brogan surely knew it also.

Now that she was a woman, a woman who'd come into a position of power and responsibility, what was Kat going to do about it? *Not nothing.* Jack had said that Mick had bided his time before taking revenge on Kev. I couldn't help wondering if Kat Brogan was biding her time as well.

"Your pal Devlin," Jack said, turning to the real subject of our rendezvous, "Mick's got 'im in his gun sights. Devlin's had his chances to back off; now it's just a matter of time. If you're in the line of fire, he'll take you out, too. That goes for the lad you had with you the other night, the one who mussed up the boyos in Boston."

"In his gun sights?"

"You know what I mean."

"This isn't the wild west of Ireland," I said.

"It's Mick Slattery we're talkin' about here. He's a law unto himself. You don't cross Mick Slattery. Not ever."

"Who's going to do his dirty work — you?"

"Not in a million years. I tried that once, and some spritely young fella knocked me into the sea and nearly drowned my skinny arse." Jack was grinning at me.

"Look, Duffy, I like ya, lad. You saved Devlin once. I admire ya for it. But don't stretch your luck. Anyway, maybe it ain't the absolute end for Devlin. But his comeuppance is a-comin' in a very big way. Ya can't stop it. Ya don't wanna stand in front of a runaway train."

"Shite," I said.

"Oh yeh," Jack said, "that pretty much sums it up."

When I got back to our hotel room I found a note from Jimmy which said, "Watching video with Terry." What it meant was that Jimmy, Dave Rubenstein, Deacon, and probably Bump, were all with Terry O'Grady, studying the Padres' hitters in preparation for tomorrow night's game, Terry's big-league debut. We had thorough scouting reports on every batter, and tonight Terry had charted Jorge's pitches. But as useful as each of those things was, these days there was no substitute for watching video footage.

I slipped quietly into the video room at Petco Park, not wanting to disturb the brain trust. It was Jimmy who was doing most of the talking. My young pal, who was no older than Terry in actual years, was way ahead of him in experience and knowledge. Jimmy Devlin, despite his other immature ways, knew a hell of a lot about pitching.

"See the hole?" he said. "Inside corner, thigh-high? Get him looking for an outside pitch, then bust him right in there. He won't have a chance." Terry nodded. "You got that, Bump?" Jimmy said. Bump nodded. Bump would be calling the pitches tomorrow night for Terry.

They moved on to studying Montanez. I doubted very much if there were any holes in that guy's sweet swing. But Jimmy, acting like he thought his name was Christy Mathewson, had some ideas. "He'll expect you to pitch around him but he'll be looking for a mistake. You leave the ball out over the plate and he'll make you pay. Like most great left-handed hitters — with the exception of Bump here — the pitch he prefers is the low inside fastball. That's the one he can really drive to right. Inside, keep the ball up. Outside, keep the ball down. If you get two strikes on him, you can come down the middle with a fastball but no lower than shoulder high. If he can catch up to your high heat, he's a better man than any of us, Gunga Din."

I leaned against the wall in the back of the room, looking at these friends of mine with a smile in my heart. Damn it, I said to myself, this is what it's all about. A close-knit group of guys all pulling together, trying to make something work. Guys who love the game and who care deeply about each other. Terry was a California surfer dude, Jimmy a Missouri small-town kid, Bump a lower Alabama farm boy, Deacon the only true Christian I'd ever met in my life, and Dave Rubenstein an Ivy-League genius who'd rather coach baseball than make a mint on Wall Street. What a goddamn motley crew. But Christ almighty, how I loved these guys.

When they'd finished up, we all headed back together, making the short walk from Petco Park to the Marriot. Somewhere off in the distance a clock chimed the hour. Two A.M.

"We have heard the chimes of midnight, Master Shallow," I said.

"That we have," Jimmy replied, "that we have."

"I think it's two," Bump said, "not midnight."

"They're quoting Shakespeare," the Deacon said softly to Bump.

"Well, shoot," Bump said, "I knew that."

The next night proved to be the turning point in our season. We'd been in a god-awful funk for the last three weeks, what with injuries, a spate of losses, and a pathetic dearth of offensive firepower. But it was the night before, when Jorge lost that tough one to Jude Pevensey, that would be our low watermark. From then on, the Bay City Grays were on the rise. God Almighty, from that point on the Bay City Grays had begun the long trek back.

On Wednesday night Terry O'Grady gave us a huge lift in his major-league debut, allowing just six Padres hits and a lone run in his seven innings of work. The Grays, God bless 'em, had finally rediscovered their truant hitting shoes. Lou Tolliver belted a pair of homers. Bump hit a mighty blast to straight-a-way center that nearly made it all the way into the park-at-the-park, his ball causing a mad scramble among the kids and picnickers out there. And our veteran second-sacker, a guy named Ty Duffy, actually lifted a high fly ball to left that ended up on the first balcony of the Western Metal Supply Company, adding a bit of spice to the meals of those who were dining there.

We followed that game the next night with a two-to-one win as wily Stan Foubert baffled the Padres' hitters with the pinpoint accuracy of his deft mixture of curves, sliders, and cutters. In recent months Stan had been showing signs of his age; but on that night, Stan was still the man.

After that tough first loss in San Diego, things on our West Coast trip were looking up. Now it was on to L.A. and a big weekend series with the NL West-leading Dodgers.

18

On Friday afternoon, as I was setting off for Dodger Stadium, I saw that the door to Deacon and Bump's room was slightly ajar. I paused outside of it for a moment and listened to the music coming from the room. A woman with a slightly husky voice was singing: "*Just a song at twilight, / When the lights are low / And the flick'ring shadows, / Softly come and go.*"

The voice sounded familiar. Then I remembered the Blue Ridge Mountain Reivers album we'd all bought copies of back in the spring. The song was from that album, and the singer was Violet. She was normally one of the group's backup singers, but on the BRMR's rendition of the old ballad she'd sung the lead. I'd only listened to the CD a couple of times, but this was one of the cuts I'd liked: "Love's Old Sweet Song."

I waited till the song was finished and then shouted, "Bump, you in there?" The music immediately went off and a sheepish-looking Bump Rhodes stuck his head out.

"Listening to some tunes?" I said.

"Yeah . . . just a little bit." His head nodded up and down.

"It sounded great."

"Yeah . . . I like it," his head still nodding.

"Beautiful old tune."

"Yeah." Bump was obviously in a talkative mood.

"Was that Violet?"

"Yeah . . . Vi," he said, still nodding.

"You still in contact with her?"

"Yeah, just a bit." Then, hesitantly, "Actually, I'm gonna see her tonight."

"Seriously?"

"Yeah. They're all a-gonna be at our game."

"They're in L.A.?" I said stupidly.

"On tour. Got gigs Saturday and Sunday but not tonight."

"Then maybe the Grays'll have a few fans tonight."

"And you're gonna have one special one." Now Bump was grinning.

"Yep, me and Big Un. We've become very close pals," I said, referring to the group's mandolin player.

"Nope, ain't Big Un I'm talking about."

I knew it wasn't Big Un he was talking about. It was Sandy he was talking about. Well hell, what's a guy supposed to do? Some women just can't take a gosh-darn hint.

I love ball parks. New or old, large or small, full or empty. I love to go back to ball parks where I once played, and I love to go to ball parks I've never been to before. I love minor league ball parks and Little League ball parks. I love high school ball fields, college ball fields, inner-city recreational fields. I love driving through remote areas in the countryside and happening upon some rural country ball field — maybe it's still in use; or maybe it's completely dilapidated, the wooden stands rotted away and weeds growing all over the field. It doesn't matter. People played here once. They laughed and jawed and ran the bases. Here games were lost and won. Here people had sad moments. And here they had moments in the sun.

Of all the great major league ball parks, Dodger Stadium is one of the most magical. On this nearly smogless day, I stood on the top row of the upper deck directly behind home plate drinking in the scene before me, a scene of symmetrical perfection. The San Gabriel Mountains formed a spectacular backdrop for the ball park. It was a couple of hours before we'd take pre-game batting practice, and I had the stadium nearly to myself. I'd been in professional baseball for over ten years and yet, because I'd always been in the AL, this would be my first time playing in this hallowed place.

I gazed at the far-off mountains, then drew my eye in like the lens of a camera, focusing on the stadium itself. The low single tier of bleachers beyond the outfield walls and the pair of matching scoreboards centered behind the seats in left-center and right-center. The blue outfield walls with their symmetrical dimensions, and the light-brown dirt of the warning track. The great expanse of green grass and the two perfectly chalked foul lines converging upon home plate. The three gleaming white bases set down like small square gems in the well-groomed infield dirt. At the center of the cross-mown infield grass, the pitcher's mound with its bright-white rubber slab amidst the encircling dirt — the pitcher's mound, the jewel in the crown. It was an awe-inspiring sight. Small wonder they call it a diamond.

Dodger Stadium, with its multiple grandstand decks and its banks of seats neatly arranged in a variety of pastel colors. The quintessential Southern California ball park, tucked snuggly into Chavez Ravine, with the city of Los Angeles just beyond the ridge behind it and the San Fernando Valley stretching out to the left in front of it. It wasn't Kubla Khan's pleasure dome in Xanadu, it was Walter O'Malley's in Shangri-la. Where Sandy Koufax once pitched a perfect game, where Kirk Gibson hit one of the most celebrated home runs in World Series history, where Fernando Valenzuela and Mike Piazza had their fabulous rookie seasons. Where, in a few hours, the Bay City Grays would be taking on the legendary Trolley-Dodgers, once the pride of the borough of Brooklyn, and for the last half century, the pride of greater L.A.

Sadly, the game that Friday night proved terribly anticlimactic. In fact, for the Bay City Grays it was a shambles. Poor Alfred King had his worst outing of the season. His control was shaky, and he couldn't find the strike zone with his breaking ball to save his soul. That meant the Dodger batters could sit on his fast ball, which they did, knocking him all over the lot. So with two outs in the bottom of the third, Whitey strolled out and took the ball out of Alfred's hand, replacing him with Zach Collins, one of our not-so-good middle relievers.

After the first three innings we were down by six runs, and we never got back into the game, despite the fact that Bump and I both homered. Between the two of us, we garnered seven base hits. So at least Bump and I had managed to give our contingent of loyal rooters, including the Blue Ridge Mountain Reivers, a few things to cheer about.

After the seventh inning the stadium had begun to clear out. Dodger fans are notorious for arriving late and leaving early, and on this Friday night they'd certainly done that. Not many were left by the top of the ninth to see Bump mash a monstrous home run that caromed off the right-centerfield scoreboard, a good 475 feet from home plate. The final score was ten to five, and my only consolation was that I'd gone four for four, which meant that my career batting average in Dodger Stadium was an immaculate 1.000. Maybe I should quit while I'm ahead, I thought.

"Shoot," Bump said when we were back in the clubhouse, "sure wish we coulda done a lot better tonight. Still 'n all, I guess them two gorgeous women kinda inspired you 'n me, eh Duff?" Bump looked pretty happy, all things considered. "You know, kinda got our juices flowin'." Bump's were definitely flowing. Mine, maybe not so much.

Sandy and I were sitting in the front seat of the Reivers' van looking out at the moon-lit sands of the beach at Will Rogers State Park. Bump and Violet were off somewhere sinking their toes in the sand or dipping their ankles in the surf. Bump seemed to have the notion that Sandy and I wanted to be alone. There was no doubt that he and Violet wanted to be alone.

"Ty," Sandy said, looking at me earnestly, "I want you to understand that I am *not* a girl who can't take a hint. I know you're not interested in getting involved with me. And to be honest with you, the last thing I want right now is to get seriously involved with a guy. I don't need that. I've got other plans, and relationships with men are only lurking out there on the periphery."

Sandy was an attractive woman, and I was definitely attracted.

Given my weaknesses and my proclivities, it was a huge relief to hear what she'd just said.

"Under other circumstances," I replied, "getting involved with you is something I would've wanted a great deal. But as you've guessed, yes, I'm in a serious relationship right now, one that means more to me than any relationship I've ever been in. The last thing I want to do is mess it up."

Sandy didn't say anything for a moment. Then finally she said softly, "She's a lucky woman, Ty, a lucky damn woman."

Then after a lengthy moment she said, "Would you come and walk on the beach with me for a while? Could we just share a few moments together and be the kind of friends we can be? Then you go on with your life and I go on with mine. Would that be okay?"

"That would be okay," I said.

"Good," she said. Then she reached out and took my face between her two hands and drew my lips toward hers. Umm, a delightfully chaste kiss. Delightful, anyway, though maybe not so chaste.

I woke up on Saturday morning with the overture to *Tannhäuser* sounding in my head. As I showered, I went back and forth between whistling and singing the melodic strains of Wagner. When I came out of the bathroom, Jimmy had the pillow pulled over his head. Guess my amigo wasn't in the mood for music this morning. Some folks just don't appreciate a good tune when they hear one.

I headed down to breakfast by myself, still humming away. It was a beautiful L.A. morning. Through the large plate glass windows of the Ritz-Carlton Hotel dining room I could see a few stray puffy clouds scudding gently above the San Gabriel Mountains. Not a bit of smog. L.A. had made a lot of progress in that regard.

"Are you a Wagner man?" a voice said from behind me.

"To some extent," I said, turning around to take a look at the speaker. "Certain bits, anyway." The speaker was a tweedy-looking gentleman who was probably in his sixties. His long graying hair curled over his ears and he wore a navy-blue knitted necktie over a titanium-gray shirt. He reminded me of some of those dusty old English professors back at Waverly College.

"Are *you* a Wagner man?" I said.

"I put him to good use quite regularly," he replied.

"You're a musician?" I proffered tentatively.

"Probably more accurate to say a composer. Film scores, actually."

"Wow. Anything I might have heard of?"

"Perhaps." Then he named several famous films that I had certainly heard of.

"Geez. I remember how much I liked the music in *The Pathfinder*. That was you, huh?

"That was mostly me; along with all the bits and pieces from the classical composers I, um, made use of."

"Which didn't stop you from winning an Academy Award."

"No, it didn't. Come join me," he said. So I did.

"You must not live in L.A., if you're staying here," I said.

"No. I live in London. I'm just here for a few days trying to convince the folks at Universal not to make too many changes to my latest score."

"Good luck with that," I said.

"Oh, they'll probably come around," he said. "And in all fairness, sometimes their suggestions are quite good."

"Do you remember the baseball film *The Natural*? The one with Robert Redford? What did you think of that score?"

"I certainly do remember that striking score. After all, one of mine was in the running that year, too. Without a doubt, Newman did a masterful job. He wove together those themes from Aaron Copland and Virgil Thompson with consummate skill." I had to laugh at that.

"Do all you film score guys make it a habit to pillage the classics?"

"My dear sir, us 'film score guys' are equal-opportunity pillagers.

We don't just pillage from the classics, we find our sources of inspiration wherever we can find them. For *Pathfinder*, actually, it was mostly Irish folk tunes."

"Perhaps along with a dollop of Vaughn Williams," I said.

"Ha, ha. Oh yes, along with a goodly dollop of Vaughn Williams."

When I got back to the room, Jimmy was noshing on his room service breakfast and poring over his notes on the Dodger batters in preparation for tonight's game. While Bump and I had frolicked at the beach last night, Jimmy and the Deacon had been studying video tape of the Dodger batters. They were all new to Jimmy, but when it came to reading hitters, my young confrere was wise beyond his years.

Jimmy's biggest concern about tonight's game wasn't facing the Dodgers' heavy-hitting lineup, it was having to bat himself — his first such experience this season. Last year he'd batted five times in the interleague games we'd played in NL parks; he struck out four times and tapped weakly back to the pitcher once, his only contact. Determined to make a better showing this year, he'd taken a lot of extra batting practice. And *bunting* practice, in case he was called upon to scarifice.

Jimmy threw lefty and batted lefty; and Bump, after watching Jimmy flailing away futilely in BP, hazarded a suggestion: "Why not give it a try from the other side of the plate, Irish boy? Don't look like ya got much chance from that side." Jimmy's reply was just a bit vulgar.

That Saturday night our Irish boy named James Patrick Devlin tossed a game to remember — a complete game shutout in which he yielded just two hits and gave up just a pair of walks. A total of four base runners, none of whom even reached second base.

The guy doing the hurling for the Dodgers wasn't half bad either. He held us down good, retiring nine of our first ten batters. But in the fourth I led off with a single and then Lou Tolliver deposited a mighty blast in the left field bleachers. In the seventh we picked up an insurance run when Jimmy Devlin blooped a ball down the right field line that landed just fair and scored Zook Zulaski all the way from first. It was Jimmy's first big-league hit and his first career RBI. Now we would never hear the end of it.

So we'd knotted the series at a game apiece. Sunday would be the rubber game.

In the clubhouse after the game I discovered a note taped to my locker. I'd had a phone message from Laura: "Ty. Call me as soon as you can," it said. Holy crap. I hate messages like that. They scare the bejesus out of me. I can't remember receiving a single message like that that ever portended good news.

I rummaged about and eventually located my errant cell phone, then searched out a quiet corner where I could talk to Laura with a degree of privacy.

Laura answered the phone after the first ring. "Ty?"

"Hey, you," I said. "What in the dickens are you doing still up with the night owls? Must be two in the morning in your neck of the woods."

"Ty," she said, "something terrible has happened."

"Laura, are you *okay?*"

"I'm fine," she said.

"Laura, what's happened?"

"It's Mick. Mick Slattery."

"Mick? What about Mick?"

"Ty . . . Mick Slattery is . . . dead."

On the night flight back to Bay City the Grays were whooping it up — we'd taken two of three from the Padres and two of three from the L.A. Bums. Even Whitey Wiggins was getting into it, entertaining the troops by belting out a drunken version of Dean Martin's "That's Amore." Whitey's Italian sounded terrific — though I couldn't make out a single word.

And yet, two rather important members of the team weren't

doing much whooping. A couple of guys named Devlin and Duffy.

The night before Laura had told me the shocking news about Mick Slattery. And it wasn't until Jimmy and I were noshing on our room-service breakfast Sunday morning that I found the right moment to tell him about Mick's demise.

When I had, Jimmy'd just sat there in stunned silence. Finally he stammered — "Jesus, Duff. Are you really tellin' me that Mick Slattery is *dead*?" About six different emotions struggled for possession of my young friend's face.

"How the hell did it happen? You know any of the details?"

"Nope. Laura didn't know them either." All she'd known was what her mother had told her, that there'd been a boating accident somewhere off Cape Cod in which Mick Slattery had disappeared. He'd apparenlty drowned.

Jimmy continued staring at me. "Jesus, Duff. If it's really true, I don't know whether to be glad or sad. I hardly knew the bastard. I didn't like him, that's for sure, but I never would've wished him dead."

I glanced at Jimmy out of the corner of one eye, remembering that fateful incident on Great Blasket when Jimmy Devlin blew Mick Slattery away with a fast ball right down the chute, firing a golf-ball-sized rock straight at Mick's head. That was one occasion, I think, when Jimmy Devlin might well have wished Mick Slattery dead.

"Um . . . Duff? There's no chance it was anything other than an accident, is there?"

There it was, the sixty-four shilling question; the very same question that had been rattling around in my head ever since I'd talked to Laura.

"I haven't a clue," I said. "All I know is what Laura's mother heard on the news. Big story in Boston, apparently, though not much of one in New York. But even if it wasn't an accident, I'd say you've got a fairly decent alibi, being 3,000 miles away playing in a ball game before 40,000 eyewitnesses. Kat does too, I guess, being 3,000 miles away in Ireland. If there's a culprit lurking in the bushes, maybe it's our old pal Seamus Byrne. 'It was solicitor Byrne in the scullery with the carving knife,' " I intoned, making a feeble effort to lighten the mood. But the look on Jimmy's face told me he had other thoughts.

"Oh God, Duff," he finally said. "You said Kat's in Ireland. But she isn't. She's in Boston. Flew back a week ago. I talked to her on Thursday morning."

"In *Boston*? Oh, man. How'd she sound?"

"Pissed off was how she sounded. She'd come back because Mick had totally screwed something up. Apparently Kat'd worked her ass off on some big property deal in Ireland involving a hotel and a golf course, and then Mick, without even consulting her, torpedoed the whole thing. Kat believed it wasn't that Mick didn't like the deal, he just wanted to show her up in front of the boyos. You know, let 'em know he was still the big man. Anyway, the two of 'em had a major row about it. Sounded like the whole thing was a huge clash of egos." Jimmy paused to catch his breath.

"Hell, Duff, I wish Kat would wash her hands of all those creeps. She never will, though," he said with a sigh. "It's in her blood — her god-damn Irish blood."

"Yes," I replied, shrugging my shoulders, "I'm sure you're right." Here's to the Irish and their god-damn blood, I said to myself, raising a toast with my glass of grapefruit juice.

19

After our late-night flight, I reached my apartment in the wee hours and crawled longingly into my own soft bed. I lay my weary head down to sleep the sleep of the just.

I slept till noon. No team practice was scheduled, and I planned to skip my usual off-day workout at the gym. All I wanted was a quiet day of reading, lazing, and listening to music. I wanted to luxuriate in soul-soothing solitude.

About 12:45, as I was savoring my first cup of strong black coffee — three scoops Colombian, two scoops Nicaraguan — the jangle of the phone burst the silence. I considered ignoring it, then reluctantly picked the blamed thing up, thinking it might be Laura with up-to-date news on Mick.

"Banjo?" came a familiar voice. "Ya heard the news? You're a-goin' with the boy to the All-Star Game!" Jimmy Devlin's father sounded pretty darn excited.

"*What?*"

"You're the startin' second sacker, Banjo. Shoulda been all along. Now ya are."

"What about Dorset and Castilla?"

"Both of 'em injured."

"Oh, man."

"So you're it, kiddo. Shoulda been all along. If Jimmy's out there as the startin' AL pitcher, that'll mean two Bay City Grays in the startin' lineup. I tell ya, Banjo, been a darn long time since that's a-happened."

"That's great news, Henry. I guess. The only thing is — I've made other plans."

"Then you'll hafta be changin' 'em. Can't not be playin' in the All-Star Game."

In fact, that was the agreement I'd made with Laura — I'd go to Rhode Island and meet her parents *if* I wasn't playing in the

All-Star Game. When we decided that, I was a distant third in the voting, so it seemed a safe bet. I'd been steeling myself for days. Now that would be all for naught.

"Hey Banjo," came Mr. Devlin's voice. "You still there?"

"Yeah, sorry. I'm still here. It's just that your news kind of complicates things for me."

"Well now Banjo, makin' the all-star team can't be anything but good news, can it?"

"Oh yeah? How about telling that to my girlfriend."

"If she's any kind of a girlfriend, Titus, shoot, she'll be all for you playin' in that game. Heck, Titus, give me her phone number and I'll set her straight."

"I'll bet you would, too," I said with a laugh.

Within half an hour of Mr. Devlin's call I got the official confirmation. The flunky who called from the MLB office congratulated me on being a three-time all-star. It didn't thrill me like it had my first time, but it still felt good.

But . . . what about Laura and meeting her parents in Rhode Island? It was time to face the music, so, breathing a sigh, I picked up the phone and called Laura at the museum in New York.

"Mr. Duffy, sir," she said, when they'd tracked her down, "this is only the second time you've ever called me at work. Something important must be up."

"Uh, yeah. Laura, they've just added me to the AL all-star team. They want me to start at second base."

There was a pause at the other end of the line. "They have? They do?"

"I'm afraid so."

"And what did you tell them?"

"I told them I'd let them know by tonight."

"Ty . . . thank goodness you didn't tell them no. I would have been upset if you'd turned them down. I'd hate to see you miss out on such a great honor because of me. Promise me you'll play."

"Seriously?"

"Of course seriously. Every little boy dreams of playing in an All-Star Game. You can't pass that up. You weren't actually thinking about telling them no, were you?"

"Actually, I was."

There was another pause on the line. "Thank you for not saying yes until you'd talked to me. But it's important that you play."

"What about Rhode Island?"

"Rhode Island isn't going anywhere. There'll be other opportunities for Rhode Island."

What a lucky stiff I am. What did I do to deserve a woman like Laura Morgan? I've often wondered why she sticks it out with a bum like me. Still, nothing in the world pleases me more.

Whew. After all of that, I finally had a chance to crawl back under the covers and escape for a couple of hours to Oxfordshire, England, and enjoy the company of Inspector Morse and the loyal Sergeant Lewis — one thoroughly complex bloke (Morse) and one thoroughly admirable bloke (Lewis). Eventually, I laid the book down and slipped blissfully into the land of slumber.

Later, in the twilight hours, Guiseppe Verdi and John Jameson replaced Morse and Lewis as my amiable companions — *Don Carlo* and a glass of Irish whiskey. As I listened and sipped, I stared out at the darkening skyline of Bay City. When the opera got to "*Dio, che nell'alma infondere,*" I closed my eyes and drank deeply. The music, the whiskey, and the view put me in a very mellow mood. I thought about how incredibly fortunate I was to have a woman like Laura Morgan.

Then, as the final sips of the Jameson passed through my lips, I found myself thinking about Kat Brogan and about the late, lamented Mick Slattery. I hadn't learned anything more about what'd happened to Mick. But whatever had happened, I felt certain that in one sense or another Kat Brogan had been in the middle of it. A beautiful, fascinating, enigmatic woman, Kathleen Brogan — *la belle dame sans merci.*

My own Laura Faye Morgan is no tender little flower — once, during our first romantic go-around, Laura had told me she hoped I'd take a flying leap off the George Washington Bridge; and that if I needed help, she'd come along and give me a push. But Laura Morgan, thank my lucky stars, is *not* Kat Brogan.

On Tuesday morning I emptied out my travel bag, thinking I might actually do some laundry. Remembering my father's advice to always check the pockets first, I carefully extracted coins, wadded up receipts, movie stubs, and cough drop wrappers. And also a little piece of paper on which was scrawled Honest Jack Strachan's cell phone number. "Call me," it said. San Diego seemed a long time ago though it was just a week.

Then the thought struck me. Maybe, if I treaded cautiously, I might be able to get Honest Jack to tell me more about what had happened to Mick. Jack Strachan was hardly my pal, but he was closest thing I had to a friend amongst that sprawling clan of unruly Irishmen. If anyone knew the truth about what had happened out there on that boat, it would probably be Jack.

After five rings I was about to give up when a voice answered.

"Yes?" it said.

"Jack? That you?"

"What if it is?" came his gruff reply.

"Jack, it's Ty Duffy."

"I told ya, Duffy, I don't still got yor bloody, feckin' shirt. I took it to the Oxfam shop. Now would ya stop houndin' me about the ugly feckin' thing!" Then Jack laughed. So did I.

"Good one, Jack. But listen, I was just calling to tell you how sorry I was to hear about Mick. How're things going with you and the boys?"

"Ah shite, Duffy, t'ings ain't so good. Wish that night woulda never happened. One o' the worst of me life."

"Were you there? I thought you'd still be out on the west coast."

"I were there all right. Pretty much all of us were there. Me, Kat, Seamus, Mick, Rory, Declan — hell, it were Uncle Tom Cobbley and all."

"Rory, Declan?" I said. "Don't think I know Rory or Declan. They a couple of the boyos?"

"Nah, nah, Rory and Declan are Mick's worthless feckin' nephews."

"Where'd they come from?"

"Ah, well, Mick's been groomin' Rory for a while now. You know, since the accident last fall. Gettin' him all lined up to be takin' things over, should there be a need. His brother Declan's a worthless piece o' shite, and frankly, Rory's not much better. But you know Mick, always lookin' out for kith and kin." If Mick was in the process of grooming Rory for future glory, I wondered what that said about Mick's plans for Kat.

"Jack, if you don't mind my asking, what happened on the boat that night? You guys having a wild party?"

"Ah, yah, celebratin' the Feast of St. Peter. Patron saint of us fishing lads. So we all went out onta the water to celebrate him proper like. All half crocked we was, hell, even Mick. Not so usual for him. Mick had been in a foul mood recently, so I guess he was feelin' the need to be lettin' loose a bit. That's what did 'im in. Never woulda fallen overboard otherwise. Mick never was much of a drinkin' man. Not like some, anyway."

"Did you see it happen?"

"Nah, nobody did. Probably coulda saved him in that case. Nah, wasn't right off anybody realized Mick weren't there. When we did, it was too feckin' late."

"What a terrible thing," I said. "I'm really sorry, Jack." Jack remained silent for several seconds.

"Yah," he finally said. "Well, we won't be seein' his like again, will we?"

"Jack, I mean it, you have my deepest sympathies." Mick Slattery had inspired the fiercest loyalties in Jack, and I knew that his death had been a terrible blow.

Not once in our brief conversation did Jack express any doubts about Mick's death being an accident. But Jack was nobody's fool. Surely he had the same suspicions as the rest of us. After all, Kat's father had died in a boating accident off the west coast of Ireland, and now Mick had met a similar fate off the east coast of the U.S. There was real symmetry in that pair of accidental deaths — a fearful symmetry. Still, assuming that Jack did have some serious suspicions, he wasn't about to voice them to an outsider like me.

Anyway, now that Mick was out of the picture, I wondered which direction Jack's loyalties would swing. Which one of that pack of rapscallions would win Jack's support? Maybe Rory, though I wasn't so sure about that. Maybe Kat? I wasn't so sure about that, either; especially not if he suspected she'd had a hand in Mick's death. In that case, Jack would be one very dangerous bloke.

Jack Strachan was an emotionally stout fellow, but his grief over Mick's death would be real and potent. Grief, I knew from my own experience, is the one human emotion few of us know how to cope with. My father once told me there was "no reasoning with grief. All you can do," he said, "is let it wear away slowly, like an inscription on a graveyard stone." Ironically, it was with my father's own death that I discovered the truth of his words.

20

On Tuesday night, Jimmy won his twelfth game of the season and Bump bashed out a pair of doubles and tossed out two guys trying to steal. I managed a base knock on a slider that didn't slide and garnered a pair of walks in my five trips to the plate. Our recent winning spate had put us back in the pennant chase, so the four amigos were in a jovial mood as we sat in one of our favorite watering holes, a grungy little pizza place called Salvatore's.

"Okay, my sagacious compatriots," Deacon Lawler declared, "it's Tuesday quiz night at Salvatore's. And the game tonight is going to be great Italians."

"Great Italians, eh?" I said. "Okay, I'll go with Dante Alighieri."

"I'll go with Federico Fellini," Jimmy said.

"I'll go with Chef Boy-ar-dee," Bump said, without missing a beat.

"No, no, witless wonders! Great Italian *ball* players. And you can't use Lazzeri or the DiMaggio brothers. *Ball* players, witless wonders, *ball* players."

"I thought that seemed a little easy," Bump said — the guy who'd given us Chef Boy-ar-dee as an example of a great Italian.

"Since we're eating at Salvatore's," I said, "I'll go with Sal the Barber Maglie."

"I'll go with Joe Pepitone," Jimmy said. "You know, in honor of Sal's famous pepperoni pizza."

"*Pepitone . . . ?*" I said. "A *great* Italian?"

"He counts," Jimmy shot back, "Pepitone counts!"

Bump was rubbing his chin, deep in thought. "Okay," he said at last, "I'll go with Cookie Lavagetto — just to keep the food thing going."

"Wow!" the rest of us said in unison, staring at Bump with open admiration. Bump looked mightily pleased at himself, knowing he'd come up with a cooler answer than Jimmy or I had.

"What orifice did you pull that one out of?" Jimmy said.

"This orifice," Bump said, pointing to his mouth. "Not the one you were thinking of."

"Bump," Jimmy said, "sometimes you are one funny guy."

Now, as we neared the mid-point in the season, Bump and Jimmy still weren't entirely comfortable with each other; and yet I could see they'd begun to form a curious kind of attachment. That was a good thing, since it was possible they'd be battery mates for a long time to come. But Jimmy still couldn't restrain his impish impulse to needle the innocent lad who was the pride of lower Alabama.

"Hey Bump," he said, "how come your nickname is Bump? I thought all ball players named Rhodes were called Dusty? How'd you come to be Bump?" Bump chose not to respond; instead, he just sat there doing a passable imitation of the Mona Lisa.

Finally Bump spoke up, though not exactly giving Jimmy a direct answer. "Ya see, one day I was just a-sittin' there on a log," he said, "and my poor ol' mama, she really wanted me to get a move on it. So she went 'n hollered at me: 'Hey you lazy boy, don't you be sittin' there like a bump on a log! You get a move on it, lazy boy!' "

"You're making that up," Jimmy scoffed. "That's too good to be true." Bump was grinning, mightily pleased with himself.

"In high school," Bump said, "they took to callin' me The Thumper. Sometimes it was Bump the Thump."

"You are so full of it . . . Mr. Bump the Lump! I don't believe for a second you were ever called The Thumper! And certainly not Bump the Thump."

"The heck I wasn't. Shoot, I can show you a clipping with the headline, 'Thumper Carries Whachahoochie to State Crown.' "

"Whacha-*whatchie?*"

"Whachahoochie."

It was 1:30 before the four of us went our separate ways, Bump and the Deacon back to the Deacon's small townhouse where Bump had his own bedroom; Jimmy to his long-term hotel room close to the ball park; and me back to my downtown apartment.

I'd parked my car on a side street a block and a half from Sal's, and as I strolled toward it, I discovered I didn't have the street to myself. Two guys were lounging on some brownstone steps right next to where I'd parked. I had a feeling the dudes were waiting for me.

"Evening," I said to them. They got to their feet and approached me. One was small and dapper, one was huge and slovenly.

"You the ball player with the high I.Q.?" the dapper one said.

"No, that's someone else," I said.

The slovenly one grunted and started making boxing moves right in front of me, throwing a series of left and right jabs in mid-air. Then all of a sudden he threw a haymaker straight at me, his fist the size of a small asteroid. I ducked and he just barely grazed my ear. *Ouch.*

The dapper guy chuckled. "Geez, Lennie, you missed 'im. He's too quick for you, son. This one's quick as an alley cat." Lennie grunted.

With my back against my car I assumed a boxer's stance too, my two fists held up in front of me.

"Uh oh, Lennie, looks like we got us a fighter," the dapper guy said. "A fighter with a high I.Q."

"I think you've got the wrong guy," I said — though I maintained my boxer's stance.

"Think you can take him, Lennie? He's not exactly small, is he?" Lennie grunted. "Must be at least a light-heavyweight. What are you, Lennie, 225? You only got thirty or forty pounds on him. And remember, he's quick as an alley cat. He's a real athlete, too, probably works out three, four times a week. Been doing his reps in a gym while you've been doin' yours in Rosie's Bar and Grill. This don't look like a fair fight to me, Lennie. Maybe we should just let him go before he damages you." Then he chuckled. Lennie just grunted.

"Okay, listen, Duffy," the dapper guy said, "it's time we stopped foolin' with you and got down to business. I'm George and this here's Lennie." George and Lennie? Sounded vaguely like something out of Steinbeck.

"This is strictly business, Duffy, nothing personal. We're here because of your mother. Turns out she owes the guys who hired us big time. Seems she waltzed off with some stuff wasn't hers to waltz off with. Our employers didn't appreciate that. Trouble is, we can't find her. Like you, she's quick as a goddamn alley cat. Must run in the family. Now we have to resort to Plan B. Plan B, I'm sorry to say, is you. It's a case of the sins of the mother being visited upon the son. Not fair, but there it is. So this is our way of saying hello. We'll be back in touch with you real soon with all the details."

"This has got to be a mistake," I said, finally lowering my guard. "My mother's been in Europe for over a year. She couldn't have done what you say. She hasn't set foot in this country for a long, long time. I know that for a fact."

"Not this country, Duffy, Canada," the George guy replied. "Clare Laughlin's your mother, right?"

"So I'm told," I said with a grimace.

"Look, Duffy, it's just a couple hundred g's. That's chump change for a rich ballplayer like you. And you got six weeks to scrape it up, too. You can do that for dear old mom, right?" Lennie grinned at George's words. I wasn't grinning.

"Who you working for?"

"Don't worry about that. This is just a preliminary chat. We'll be back in touch with all the details. C'mon, son," the dapper guy who called himself George said, placing his hand on Large Lennie's shoulder. "I know you could've taken him, Lennie. Not tonight, but you still might get your chance." Lennie grunted, then grinned.

After they were gone, I stood for a while leaning against my car. What the bloody hell? I thought. For crissake, Mom, what the heck have you gone and done now?

I felt my ear, which was throbbing. Geez, good thing I'm quick as an alley cat or it wouldn't just be my ear that was throbbing.

21

That last week before the all-star break we continued playing good ball. We took three straight from the Indians and two of three from the White Sox; and now our walking wounded had begun straggling back. Nick Gurganis, our regular left fielder, was the first to return, and he returned with panache, going eleven for twenty-four, with a homer, a triple, two doubles, and seven RBI. Nice to have you back, Nicholas. After the break, when Bobby Radley and Juan Flores came off the DL, we'd be close to full strength.

Our wins that week moved us to seven games over .500. So the Bay City Grays went into the break just five back of the Red Sox and three of the Yankees — the teams we'd face when the season resumed.

I thought a lot that week about my mother and about my late-night encounter with George and Lennie — if that was really their names. But in the following days I heard nothing more from them. Maybe they'd tracked down my mother and worked things out. Or maybe George had had an attack of conscience and realized it was totally unfair to put the screws on me for something I had nothing to do with. Yeah, and maybe Bump Rhodes would be the guy to finally break Joe D's fifty-six game hit streak.

After our last game on Sunday, Jimmy and I took the train to New York, since the All-Star Game would be played in the Mets' new stadium. Laura insisted we stay at her apartment during the break, and we'd accepted her offer. I planned to stay on in New York after the Tuesday night game; Jimmy planned to head on up to Boston and spend a couple of days with Kat before our weekend series with the Sox.

On Monday morning I didn't wake up until long after Laura had left for work. I'd finished my second cup of coffee before Jimmy, who was sleeping in the living room on Laura's sofa, raised his tousled head, blinked his eyes at me a few times, and then shambled toward the bathroom.

After Jimmy showered, dressed, and gulped down some break-fast, I grabbed up the grocery list and the reusable shopping bags Laura had left on her kitchen table. Then the two of us set off for Gristedes on Second Avenue, a couple of blocks away.

As we walked, Jimmy ran his eyes over Laura's list and sighed. "Guess we'll be eating healthy for a couple days. Hope it won't be too much of a shock to your system, Duff. At least she's got 'beer' on the list. Though I wonder why there's a question mark after it?"

"Probably means it's optional."

Jimmy pulled a ballpoint pen from his pocket and crossed out the question mark.

It was a typical mid-summer's day in the Metropolis. Delivery trucks crowded the sidewalks, cabs honked, joggers sped or slogged past us, dog-walkers paused to clean up their messes, young mothers and grannies shepherded youngsters — it was the sidewalks of New York.

At mid-morning Gristedes wasn't jam-packed, so we meandered along the aisles, keeping an eye out for the various items on Laura's list. I didn't mind that Jimmy was liberally supplementing Laura's healthy stuff with ball player food. He was making sure a couple of strapping young men weren't going to starve to death in the next couple of days.

"Ray's Pizza?" Jimmy said when we'd finished the shopping. "Might be our last chance for some real food."

"Good idea." Jimmy and I gorged on Ray's famous pizza, then headed back to Laura's apartment, saving the last couple of slices for our late-afternoon snack.

Starting for the NL in the Tuesday night affair was a wiry little guy with flowing dark locks. His name was Tim Elphinstone, and in this age of huge pitchers he was an anomaly. He was officially listed at five-nine and 160 pounds, which was giving him every benefit of the doubt. His nickname, not surprisingly, was "the Elf." He was last year's NL Cy Young winner, and he was in the running again. I'd never batted against him, but since I was hitting sixth in the AL lineup, I had a chance to study him before I got to the dish. Good thing, since he'd retired the first five guys by the time I stepped in.

It was the top of the second in a nothing-to-nothing game. Neither Jimmy Devlin nor Tim Elphinstone had allowed a hit. On this sultry summer night in Queens, both of them had great stuff. I watched closely from the on-deck circle as the Elf blended fastballs, sliders, and a wicked changeup to Matt Woodward of the Angels, who was hitting ahead of me. Matt whiffed on the Elf's wicked changeup. If I got one of those, I'd be ready for it. I hoped.

The Elf started me off with a mid-90s heater on the outside corner. Strike one. He followed that up with another one that backed me off the plate, a ball inside, then another just off the plate. Ball two. Then came what looked like an inside fastball but was a hard slider that broke across the inside corner. Strike two. At that point I'd seen four pitches and still hadn't got the bat off my shoulder. With the count two and two, the Elf threw his hard slider on the outside corner, and I almost bit. My instinct was to swing, but somehow I held back, knowing I might have taken a third strike. The ball broke just off the plate and the ump got the call right. Full count. Now for the payoff pitch.

I hoped for a fastball on the inner half. If he went with the slider, my goose was incinerated. I got what I wanted, a fastball on the inner half. It was up — the proverbial "high hard one." But I'd anticipated it and damn if I didn't clock it. Right on the sweet spot. The result was the longest home run of my career, a good twenty rows up in the leftfield seats.

In my two previous all-star appearances, I'd stroked a pair of singles. Now I'd smacked the most impressive dinger of my baseball career. Maybe I was a little bit glad to be playing in this All-Star Game after all.

Jimmy Devlin worked two perfect innings before being taken out.

In my second and final turn at bat, now against a fire-balling lefty, I hit a routine grounder to the shortstop, Clayton Washington, who plays for the Reds. But who cared? I'd whacked a mighty home run that gave the AL the lead, a lead it never relinquished.

We ended up winning four to one, another win for the American League. Jimmy, who'd had six up and six down, was the game's MVP.

22

Regular play would resume for us with three games vs. the Red Sox, so on Wednesday morning Jimmy headed to Boston while I stayed for another two days in New York.

After Laura'd left for work, I called my apartment in Bay City to check my answering machine. I knew there'd be some warm messages and some amusing ones after my performance last night, and there were. But it was the message from my brother Billy that caused me some real concern: "Ty, call just as soon as you can."

I rummaged through my belongings, located my cellphone, and rang my brother in Manassas.

"Man, Tyrus," Billy said, "you been juicing or what? Where'd all that power come from? You've already got twelve home runs on the season and now you go and hit an absolute bomb in the All-Star game? Good gravy, dude, you knocked the stuffing out of it. Did you see the look on Elphinstone's face? The poor sap thought he had it by you, only to have it land thirty rows up in the seats. I almost felt sorry for the little punk."

"Billy, the message you left on my answering machine. What's up with that? Has something happened?"

"Yeah, maybe. Listen, a couple of weeks ago a guy called asking about Mom. Wanted to know how to contact her. I asked him who wanted to know, and he gave me some song and dance about business matters. I told him I didn't know how to contact her and that I believed she was out of the country. I figured it wouldn't hurt to give him that much. He said thanks and hung up.

"So far so good. Then a couple of days ago someone called and said he was doing a survey about preschools. Asked about Marian's preschool. Wanted me to confirm the name of the school she goes to. I told him it was none of his effing business, and he apologized for upsetting me. But here's the thing — I'm almost certain it was the same guy who'd called asking about Mom."

Crap. Looks like George and Lennie are preparing Plan C, I thought. I'm Plan B, and now Marian, my precious little niece, is going to be Plan C – though I wasn't about to say that to Billy. Damn it, Mom, sometimes I wouldn't mind wringing that lovely, selfish neck of yours!

"Billy," I said, "maybe the two guys just had similar voices."

"I didn't say anything to Sarah. Thought I should mention it to you first. Ty, do you know much about Mom's recent activities? Has she done something even stupider than usual?" I hated to dissemble with my own brother, but as usual I felt the need to shield my mother from Billy's hostility.

"Not that I know of," I said. "She's been completely in-communicado. I don't where she is, but like you told the guy on the phone, somewhere other than the U. S. of A. Central Europe, probably. Prague's become a big favorite with her."

"If this guy contacts you, you'll tell me, right? I sure as hell don't feel like taking any chances with my daughter."

"Gosh, no," I said. "Billy, I'll let you know if I hear from him. I promise."

And I will, too, I told myself, I will. But let's not get ahead of ourselves. I felt pretty sure George and Lennie wouldn't go to Plan C until they'd exhausted Plan B. In fact, Plan C was probably just a ploy to make certain that Plan B worked. Anyway, no good would come from scaring the dickens out of Billy and Sarah. Plan C, I felt sure, would be off the table once Plan B had worked. And Plan B was going to work because one stupidly dutiful son had already decided to cough up the dough to bail his mother out. That stupidly dutiful son was also a devoted uncle who planned to make absolutely certain nothing bad would happen to his niece.

But I did have to hand it to George. The sneaky little bastard knew all along that his backup plan would be just the ticket to force me to play ball. Well hell, playing ball was something I was quite used to doing.

Okay, Mom, I said to myself, looks like I'll be hauling your chestnuts out of the fire yet again; this time to the tune of some pretty big bucks. And Mom, don't go telling me you'll pay me back. I'm very feckin' tired of that sad old song. Sing something else for a change. And then I remembered that when it comes to singing my mother has a tin ear. Figures.

About four-thirty on Wednesday afternoon the buzzer to Laura's apartment rang. Laura wasn't due back from work for another hour, and I wasn't sure what to do. For starters, I did nothing. Then it rang again. Go away! When it rang yet again I thought, okay, maybe it's important.

"Yes?" I said, pressing the intercom button.

"Oh . . . hello. It's Janet Morgan. Laura's mother. Umm . . . is this Ty?"

"Uh . . . yeah . . . right the first guess," I said. "Okay, uh here, let me buzz you in."

"Thank you, Ty."

If Mohammad wasn't going to go to the mountain, the mountain was going to come to him. But maybe I was being presumptuous.

Entering Laura's apartment a few moments later was the woman who was Laura's mother. I knew a good bit about her — probably a lot more than Laura knew about my mother — though I hadn't yet met Laura's mother face to face.

"Thank you, Ty," she said again as she entered Laura's living room. She smiled and extended her hand, which I took. "It's very nice to finally meet you. I hope you won't mind if I just set myself down for a moment. Those city sidewalks take a toll on a person's feet."

She set her small armload of packages down, then subsided onto Laura's sofa. "Whew. That feels better already."

"Would you like something cold to drink?"

"A glass of ice water would be wonderful."

"You got it." I was back in a jiffy with two large glasses of ice water.

She looked at me and smiled with a pair of light blue eyes that were virtually identical to Laura's. They say that if you want to know what a woman will look like in twenty-five years, take a good look at her mother. If this was Laura in twenty-five years, you'd get no complaints from me. She looked terrific. No aspirations at being a fashion plate like my own mother; but not exactly some fusty-looking blue-stocking, either. She wore a short-sleeved, cranberry-colored shirt over beige slacks and no jewelry of any kind, not even earrings, watch, or rings.

I guessed she was maybe an inch or two shorter than Laura and maybe a few pounds heavier; but she looked fit and glowing with good health. And I couldn't help noticing the rather devious twinkle behind her glasses as she looked me over. Yes, this was the woman who'd wanted to name her daughter after one of the most complex and enigmatic characters in Arthurian literature, Arthur's half-sister, Morgan le Fay.

"Laura should be back from work in a little while," I said. "She didn't tell me you were coming. But it's great to finally meet you."

"I didn't know myself," she replied. "I'm afraid I sometimes do things rather impulsively. A colleague of mine was receiving an award at a luncheon downtown, and afterward I decided to stay in the city and do some shopping. Then, since it was getting on toward late afternoon, I thought maybe I'd stop by and say hello to Laura; and to you, if you were still here after the game last night. We saw your home run, by the way. It was certainly a mighty clout."

"Thanks, I got lucky. But I'm sorry to say, rumor has it you are a Red Sox fan. Say it ain't so."

"Oh yes . . . yes, it is certainly so. You grow up in Rhode Island, it's pretty much an unavoidable fate."

"But not for Laura."

"No, not for that child. We raised her to have a mind of her own, and darned if it didn't turn out that way. But you seem to have succeeded in turning her into a baseball fan after all. Better late than never."

"I don't think she's completely sold on baseball just yet, but her interest in the game is growing. Maybe one day she'll make it to true fandom."

"So perhaps your influence on her hasn't been such a bad thing."

"It's her influence on me that hasn't been such a bad thing," I said, hoping that didn't sound too glib, though it probably did.

This woman was definitely sizing me up. And I wanted like anything to make a favorable impression. No matter what they say about first impressions being deceiving, I really wanted to make a favorable impression on this woman.

"Laura said you were an English major in college."

"That was a quite a while back," I said. I sat down in Laura's favorite reading chair, the corner of a coffee table between us.

"She says you're a fan of Sir Thomas Malory. Of *Le Morte D'Arthur*."

"Since I was about ten, I guess. Read a few modernized excerpts in a book that had a lot of great illustrations. Then I read some big chunks of it in high school. I read it in its entirety in college, reading it for the first time in Malory's original language — the only way to do it properly. Now, I'll admit, I re-read it every three or four years."

"And what about the work don't you like?" she said. Her unexpected question gave me some pause.

"What *don't* I like? I like pretty much everything about it. It comes pretty close to being a perfect work, I think."

"No, it certainly isn't a perfect work," she said firmly. She took off her glasses, set them on the coffee table, and looked straight at me, her clasped hands beneath her chin. "Tell me what you don't like about it." And she looked at me with that devious glint in her eyes. *Crap*. I hadn't reckoned on taking my Ph.D. oral exam this afternoon. Did I need to pass it in order to win this woman's favor?

"Okay . . . what don't I like about *Le Morte D'Arthur*. Well . . .

okay . . . I have to admit that I'm not too wild about his depiction of Sir Perceval; Perceval comes across as kind of a second-rate Galahad, like a slightly tarnished Grail Knight. Even the third of the Grail Knights, Sir Bors, is more interesting than Perceval.

"I much prefer Chretien de Troyes' Perceval to Malory's. In Chretien he's an innocent, naïve kid who has no clue who he really is. After he totally messes up at the Grail Castle, we can only hope he'll eventually get a chance to make things right again."

Janet Morgan was sitting there grinning like a gargoyle, albeit an attractive gargole. "I knew there would be something you didn't like. And I have to say, Ty Duffy, that I pretty much agree with you."

Does that mean, I thought, that it's okay to date your daughter?

About a quarter to six we heard Laura's key in the door.

"Hello, honey!" Janet Morgan called out to her.

"Mom? Ty? Well, look at you two. Taken over my apartment like you think you own the place. Which, I guess, you sort of do," she said, looking at her mother, "since you helped out so generously with the deposit." Though small, Laura's apartment had to cost a bundle; and there was no way she could afford it on her museum salary alone. We'd never discussed her finances, but I suspected some parental assistance was involved.

Laura and her mother hugged and kissed each other on the cheek, then Laura latched on to my arm and clutched it possessively, which felt plenty good to me. "Guess I don't need to introduce you to my guy," she said. "When did you get here, Mom? Have you two been having yourselves a good natter? Mom, can you stay for supper?" Laura's hugging my arm and calling me "her guy" gave me a warm feeling.

"Yes, we've been having quite a good natter," she said, and I nodded my agreement. "But I'll have to say no to supper. I need to catch the seven o'clock train. But I can stay for a few more minutes."

The dynamics between mothers and daughters intrigue me. I

know a lot about the dynamics between fathers and sons, but in my growing up years relationships between mothers and daughters were far beyond my range of experience. So I just sat there looking and listening. And as I did, I realized that I felt unexpectedly comfortable in the presence of these two women. Breaking the ice with Laura's mother hadn't been nearly as traumatic as I'd feared it might be. I felt that I'd managed to get off to a fairly good start with her. Janet Morgan was definitely a force to be reckoned with, as I'd known she would be. But then, what woman isn't?

23

It was late morning on Friday, and Kat, Jimmy, and I were picnicking in The Boston Common, not far from the duck boats that always made me think of *Lohengrin*. For a day in mid-July, it was surprisingly pleasant. It promised to be a beautiful evening in Fenway Park for our series opener against the Sox.

Kat was as lovely as ever but her mood was subdued. Mick's unexpected death and its aftermath seemed to've cast a pall over her. I would pump Jimmy later to find out what he'd learned about Mick's so-called accident. And maybe I could do a slight bit of probing on my own right now.

"A week or two ago," I said to Kat, "Jimmy told me you'd been excited about a business deal you'd been working on in Ireland. What was that about?"

"Ah, Ty Duffy, it woulda been such a grand and lovely deal," Kat said, perking up a bit. "Yes, it would've been so brilliant." I smiled at her but kept mum, not wanting to interrupt her.

"We had us a grand opportunity, the chance to buy a five-star hotel just on the outskirts of Galway City. A truly charming old place with a first-class restaurant and a lovely golf course. It would've all been so brilliant, Ty Duffy. A big step up from Mick's middling chain of tourist motels. Ya know, Ireland's economy is certainly hurtin' right now, but it's tourism that's keeping us afloat. The hotel's in the perfect location, too. Close to one of Ireland's most vibrant cities, close to some of our most famous tourist destinations — the Cliffs of Moher, the Aran Islands, Connemara — and within an hour's drive of maybe fifteen or twenty other golf courses. Oh, it would've been so very brilliant." Now Jimmy was grinning at Kat, pleased to see her come to life.

"Where's the deal stand now? Is it dead? Or could it still be made?" I asked.

"Ah, well, Mick in his wisdom told 'em no. The price were too high, he insisted, though that were a load of hooey. Nah, the price weren't too high, the price were fantastic."

"Do you think the opportunity might still be there?"

"Gettin' everyone to agree on anything big right now is out of the question, things bein' so unsettled. And since Mick said no, no one would want to insult his memory by doin' the very thing he didn't want us to do. Nah, 'fraid it's not a real possibility anymore."

"What I mean is, do you think the hotel is still for sale? I mean, what if a different group of investors wanted to take a shot at buying it? Not Mick Slattery Enterprises, or whatever you guys are; but, say, an anonymous group of American investors?" Jimmy and Kat were both startled by what I seemed to be suggesting. Frankly, so was I.

"What if someone," I blathered on, "I'm not naming any names, mind you, could come up with a sizable down payment to secure whatever loan might be necessary?"

"And what if I wanted to be a minor shareholder?" Jimmy chipped in, getting into the spirit of the thing. "I could probably pay for a broom closet or one of the loos." Jimmy and Kat's faces bore bright, excited looks. Guess I'd lit a spark in these two youngsters; as if they needed any more sparks being lit in them. Still, it was great to see the glow returning to Kat's cheeks.

I didn't know why that notion had suddenly popped into my mind, or even if I was serious about this. Nor did I know what kind of money we might be talking about. But I knew one thing — Larry Berkman, my close friend and trusted financial advisor — was going to think I'd gone bonkers, first asking him to set aside two hundred thousand (to bail my accursed mother out of her dangerous situation); and then to come up with who-knew-how-much to secure a loan that would probably be in the millions. Man, good thing I'd just received a tidy little bonus for participating in the All-Star Game; and a *really* good thing I'd been a penny-pinching bastard for the last ten years. Anyway, I thought, what the hell. It's only money.

◆ ◆ ◆

When I got back to our hotel room after the game that Friday night
— a game in which the Sox had bested us 5-3 and I'd gone hitless —
I noticed the message light blinking on the telephone. I figured out
which button to push and then listened to a voice I'd last heard on
a dark street in Bay City. It belonged to smarmy little George.

"This the ballplayer with the elevated IQ? If it ain't, put the
phone down, doofus, and fetch the brainiac. So Duffy, you there
now? Okay, listen up. There's a new little problem that's come up.
Result is we're gonna need that money sooner than I told ya. All ya
got is ten days. Sorry about that. Also, it's gonna be a bit more than
I told ya before. Don't go blaming me, blame it on your sweetie-pie
mom. That mom of yours, Duffy, she's one shifty piece of work.
Anyway, soon's you fellas are back in Bay City, me and Lennie're
gonna come-a-callin'. It'd be a good idea if you could have the bread
ready for us. Cash. As it turns out, it'll have to be two twenty-five.
Thanks to your mom's latest fandango. Quick as an alley cat, that
mother of yours.

"Oh, and Duffy. Sorry 'bout the game tonight, pal. But ya can't
win 'em all, can ya?"

I'd been wondering when I would hear from George again. Now
I had. I wondered, too, what the hell Mom had done to piss 'em
off even more. Thanks, Mom, that's an extra twenty-five thousand
you just cost me. So Mom, why don't you go and take a very long
catnap.

Before I went and forked over this kind of dough, I'd been
hoping I could get some kind of written agreement from these guys
to show we'd paid for the items my mother had allegedly purloined.
Something that would make them our legal possessions. That was
probably wishful thinking. Still, one could always hope.

In the meantime, I figured I would also try to track Mom down
and see what she had to say about all of this. I felt sure whatever she
told me would mostly be a load of tosh. Still, it was worth a try. *If* I
could manage to track her down, a pretty big if.

Figuring I should probably get right on it, I spent the best part of an hour making phone calls to half a dozen hotels in various central European cities, places I knew Mom had stayed in the past. No luck, but I left messages asking her to call me. Maybe she would get one of them and actually call me back, though I wasn't especially hopeful.

Jimmy and Kat had met up after the game and gone off together, so I really didn't expect to see him back tonight. But about one-thirty he came draggling in. He looked plenty upset, too. Considering George's phone message and my futile efforts to contact my mother, that made a pair of us.

"You look like a guy who could use a drink," I said.

"Hell yes, I am."

"That goes for me, too."

We trekked down to the hotel bar, found ourselves a quiet corner, and started on some serious drinking. Jimmy ordered himself a draft of Killian's Red. For me it was a whiskey night.

"Well, Duff, got my first taste of Rory McManus tonight," Jimmy said, after drinking off about a third of his draft. "What a feckin' loser. Mick's little shite of a nephew was acting like he's the new sheriff in town, or some feckin' thing. Thinks he's the one everybody has to kowtow to; seems to think he owns Kat Brogan. Duff, I came this close to pasting the little prick. Kat stopped me just in time, probably a good thing for the both of us.

"Those guys, Duff — Rory and Declan and some of the others — they're going out of their way to treat Kat like dirt. After all she's done for them this year, being so loyal to them and keeping everything together. There's gratitude for you. But Kat's been playing a waiting game. Knowing what losers Rory and Declan really are, she figures the boyos will reach the same conclusion. That *might* happen, but those laddies are a pretty dense bunch. Good old Seamus, he's already in there kissing their pink little Irish arses."

"How come they're being so mean to Kat?"

"Because that's how they think Rory wants 'em to treat her. Whatever Rory wants, Rory gets. And because a lot of them suspect that Kat was involved in Mick's death. They blame her, Duff. They don't think it was an accident." And dense as they may well be, I thought, they could be right.

"Was Jack there?" I asked.

"Honest Jack," Jimmy said, nodding. "Yep, he was there. Looks like he's about the only ally Kat's got amongst the Mick Slattery clan. He was real quiet but definitely keeping a sharp eye out. I could tell he's no fan of Rory. Jack loved Mick, and Rory is no Mick. Mick was smart and tough and domineering, but he was no preening pretty boy. Feckin' Rory thinks the world's in love with him; and he thinks Kat's in love with him, too, because awhile back they'd had a little fling. Rory thinks he's got her wrapped around his finger. Boy, is he wrong about that."

"How'd they treat you?"

"Like a total non-entity. Like I wasn't even there. But the hostility in the air, you could have cut it with a knife."

"That's better than beating the shit out of you."

"Well, yeah."

"Do you think there's any chance Kat might finally extricate herself from that bunch?"

"Man, how I wish that would happen. But I don't plan to push her. I hope she'll decide to try it. And if she does, I just hope those boyos will let her slip quietly away. That doesn't seem to be their style, though."

No, it doesn't. But one can always hope.

Larry Berkman was aghast. "*How* much?"

"I'm guessing two million, at least."

"Two million *dollars?*"

"No," I said. "Two million *euros.*" Larry was silent for a moment, letting that sink in. It was ten-fifteen on Saturday morning, and I'd caught Larry on the sixth tee at the Westchester Country Club. For a guy in his profession, that wasn't unusual.

"Um . . . Duffy, my boy, that would require taking some serious whacks at your portfolio."

"But it wouldn't leave me destitute?"

"No, not destitute."

In all of baseball, I'm the most frugal guy I know. No fancy homes, cars, girlfriends, watches, diamond ear studs; no drug habit, no alimony, no child support payments; no fripperies or frivolities of any kind, unless you count great sound equipment and a pint-sized Library of Congress of CDs, which I don't count. So most of my annual salary — which is pretty decent though nowhere close to being up there with the big boys — goes straight into my investments, which Larry oversees for me. For the past four or five years, I've probably lived on no more than a tenth of what I make.

"Larry," I said, "I'm not about to blow my wad on something foolish. I'm as careful with a dollar as any client you have."

"Careful?" Larry scoffed. "Duffy, you're the biggest cheapskate I know!" We both laughed, knowing it was probably so.

"C'mon, Larry, that's not kind. Call me frugal, thrifty, or even parsimonious. But don't call me a cheapskate."

"Let's just say you're not a spendthrift," Larry replied.

I went ahead and filled him in on what I knew about the possible hotel deal, singing the praises of a place I knew practically nothing about, especially playing up the golf course angle and the prospect that the hotel could come up with some great package deals for groups of Americans who wanted to tackle some of Ireland's choicest courses.

"What's this place called?" Larry asked. "It isn't Fawlty Towers, is it?"

"That would pack 'em in. No, it's the Glen Tiernan Priory Hotel. Pretty classy, eh?"

I heard Larry breathe out a big sigh. "Okay, let me make a few inquiries. I have a couple of contacts who can probably check things out. If things look as promising as you say, then we can talk about it. Hell, Duffy, if it even comes close to looking as promising as you say, maybe I'll want in on the action myself. Maybe get some free golf out of the deal."

Larry was a semi-serious golfer. He'd lured me into playing with him a few times, and being no golfer myself, I'd blithely assumed that my superior athleticism would carry the day. That hadn't been the case. And Larry, the sneaky bastard, liked to play for quite a few bucks a hole, too. Larry Berkman enjoyed holding on tightly to my money, one way or another.

24

In the shower after our Saturday night game, Bump was singing lustily — *I have fallen for another, she can make her own way home!"* — a lyric from a song by the Saw Doctors. Bump was ebullient. Batting lefthanded, he'd smashed a pair of homers into the right-field seats at Fenway, one of them nearly reaching the red seat marking Ted Williams' longest home run. That gave Bump eight taters on the season, four from each side of the plate. Although his batting average was only .243, it was slowly climbing. Against all odds, this big lump of a kid was turning out to be a big-league ball player. So go ahead and sing your heart out, Bump. There are moments in life when you just have to dance as if no one is watching.

"Hey d'Artagnan," Zook Zulaski shouted at Bump. "Whatta ya mean, 'She can make her own way home?' What kind a guy would do that? I thought you were a man of honor."

"It's just a song," Bump said.

"So you've fallen for another, huh? Geez, Bump, don't think I want anything to do with an asshole like you."

"Those're just words from a song," Bump said.

"Just words from a song? d'Artagnan, you're an embarrassment to the team. And you were the one spouting all that 'all for one and one for all' bullshit."

"I'm not d'Artagnan," Bump said.

"Not d'Artagnan? Then who the hell are you?"

"Monsieur, I am Edmond Dantès."

"Oh, well, thanks for clearing that up, frog-breath."

"He used to be d'Artagnan," I said. "But now he's the Count of Monte Cristo."

"Bump," the Deacon said, "I thought you were Welsh. Now you're telling us you're French?"

"I thought you were the Thumper," Jimmy said.

"I thought you were the King of Conuceh County," I said.

"I am French, I am Welsh, I am a king and a count and a thumper; I am a bubble in beer; I am a string in a harp. I am a man with a thousand faces. I am here; I am there; I am *gone*." And as he said "gone," he snapped his fingers.

Bump's little peroration left us with our mouths agape.

Finally Zook said, "Dude, you are totally full of shit."

At eight-thirty on Sunday morning, the phone rang in our hotel room. Jimmy groaned, pulled a pillow over his head, and went back to sleep.

"Yes?" I said into the receiver.

"Ty?"

"Mom?"

"It's me, honey. They told me at the hotel you'd called. I hope I didn't wake you. I get confused by the time differences."

"That's okay. Time to be up anyway. We have pre-game batting practice in a couple of hours."

"Why did you need to get in touch with me, Ty? I hope everything is okay."

"Is everything okay with you?"

"Of course, honey, things with me are good."

"You're a hard one to track down, Mom."

"I've been moving around a bit." My mother laughed. "You know, here today, gone tomorrow."

"Sounds like a fun life."

"It has its moments."

"In your recent moving around — any chance that included Canada?"

For several seconds my mother didn't reply. Then she said cautiously, "Why do you ask?"

"You wouldn't know anything about some missing art works, would you? A Turner watercolor and a Picasso drawing? Some guys have been nosing about, wanting to get paid for them. Seems these items suddenly up and disappeared. Right about the time a woman named Clare Laughlin did a bunk."

The silence at the other end of the line was palpable. My mother was taking longer than usual to concoct her "explanation." I couldn't wait to hear what she would come up with. Of course she could simply plead ignorance. Somehow, though, I doubted it. That would be too simple.

"Ty, I think I know the items you are talking about. They were part of a big estate sale I attended in Canada a month or so ago. I did buy a few things, but most of the really good things were out of my price range. I certainly couldn't afford the Turner or the Picasso."

"You couldn't afford them so you walked off with them instead?"

"Ty Duffy, how could you say such a thing to your mother!" In my mother's voice I heard shock, dismay, indignation.

"So what are you saying, Mom? That you know nothing at all about what happened to the items?"

"No," she said at last, "I'm not saying that. It was a friend of mine who bought them. For tax purposes, he asked me to hang on to them until he'd found buyers." Yeah, I thought, *that* sounds really plausible.

"Mom, we are both in a lot of trouble. Those items were valued at two hundred thousand, and some folks want their money."

"Two hundred thousand? They certainly weren't worth that!"

"So how much did you sell them for?"

"I didn't sell them, Tyrus, my business associate sold them. And I'm not telling you for how much."

"Hey!" Jimmy mumbled from beneath his bed covers, "some of us are trying to get some sleep around here." I ignored him. It was time for him to haul his lazy carcass out of bed anyway.

"Mother, I need two hundred thousand dollars from you, and I need it immediately. I'm not kidding. This is serious stuff."

"Honey, I don't have it. That's the truth, I honestly don't. Ty," she said, and of course I knew exactly what was coming next, "do you think you could lend it to me? I mean, could you take care of it on your end? Then, just as soon as I can, I will square things with you. Honey, that's my solemn pledge. I know I've made you promises before that I haven't kept. This one I will keep. I swear it."

And then I surprised myself. "No, mother, I won't. That's it. No more free rides. Nada, zilch, finito, kaput. Mom, you are on your own. And I'm telling you, these guys will be coming for you. If I don't get that money really soon and get these guys off our backs, they will be coming for you. I can't protect you anymore. It's time for you to reap what you've sown." What a heartless bastard I'd become.

"Honey! I promise you! I'll pay you just as soon as I can. Ty, please — do this for me!"

"Sorry, can't do it. Not this time. This time you're on your own." And I hung up the phone.

Of course I would pay them. I wasn't about to take any chances with my little niece Marian. But I wasn't going to tell my mother anything about that. The hell with her. Let her squirm. Might be good for her. Might build her character. Lord knows, she needed a little character building. Okay, a lot of character building.

I got back to my apartment about nine on Wednesday night, following our three-game series in New York. We hadn't done great in New York, dropping two of three to the Bombers, but before that we'd won two out of three in Boston. Playing .500 ball on the road against two really tough clubs is easy to live with.

I set my bag down just inside my door and noticed the neat stack of mail on my hall table, the handiwork of my neighbor. So I nipped out again and tapped on Chuck's door, just to let him know I was back and to thank him for looking after things.

"Ty," he said, beaming a smile at me, "you missed my mother by about ten minutes, you unlucky dog. Looks like you've made another conquest, Tyrus. So I went ahead and arranged a little opera date just for the two of you. Hope that's okay." I *think* he was joshing me.

As we stood there by the open door, Boog the cat was rubbing up against my ankles and purring to beat the band. I reached down and rubbed him on the sides of his face beneath his ears.

"Boog likes you better than me, Duffy," Chuck said, making a face. "Just one of the many reasons I hate you so much."

"Sorry I missed your mother," I said.

"Yes, I'm sure you are. Come on in for a minute, won't you? Listen, Tyrus, I have a few things to tell you. Nothing to do with Mother." No, but I had a premonition it might have something to do with *my* mother. And I was right.

"Duffy, a couple of . . . what should I call 'em . . . *cretins?* . . . stopped by here earlier today. Wondered if I knew when you would be back. I don't know how they got into the building, but our security is so pathetic I guess it's no big surprise. Anyway, I tried to give them the cold shoulder, but the slimy little one wouldn't take no for an answer. He was extremely rude to me, Ty, the little scum rag. They didn't say when they plan to come back. But I know they are eager to track you down. Not friends of yours, I hope?"

"Hardly friends."

"Anything I can do? I know a few people who might be able to, uh, you know . . . discourage them?"

"What? Chuck, you never cease to astonish me."

"Well goodness gracious, I certainly *hope* not."

"Discourage them, huh. That's an intriguing offer. Don't think it will come to that. But I'll keep it in mind."

"You aren't in any trouble, are you? Is there anything you want to talk about?"

"No, I'm not in any trouble; at least I don't think I am. But someone I care about is, I'm afraid. But no, Chuck, I don't want to talk about it. Thanks, though. You're a great neighbor."

"I hope I'm more than a neighbor," Chuck said.

"Anyway, tell your mother I'm sorry I missed her."

"Oh yes, I'm sure you are. Well, sir, you take care, okay? Seriously, Tyrus, you stay safe."

"I'll do everything I can to oblige," I said.

Thursday was an off day, and aside from the team's workout, I had nothing scheduled. I planned to talk again with Larry Berkman and then with the guy I work with at my local bank. George had said they wanted their money in cash, but I wasn't sure I would comply with their wishes. Not unless they would give me something on paper to document the transaction: a handwritten receipt, a canceled check, something. My position would be "no paperwork, no cash transaction. Otherwise, you blokes can try to get the money directly from my cursed mother."

The phone rang about 1:30 and I figured it would be George. It was a woman's voice, and it took me a second to recognize it.

"Hello, Ty," Sandy said. "Sorry to keep turning up like a bad penny. I need a big favor, and I couldn't think of anyone else to ask. Would you be willing to come with Bump to our show tonight?" I hadn't known The Reivers were playing in Bay City. Neither Bump nor Chuck had said anything about it.

"Um . . . I guess so," I said, trying to muster some enthusiasm.

"That's the easy part," she said. "Here's the hard part. There's a guy, one of our backers, who refuses to leave me alone. You remember when I told you I was a gal who could take a hint? I am, Ty, I mean that. But this guy isn't. Because I'm not involved with anyone right now and because he has a vested interest in our group, he thinks I'm fair game. I've told him over and over I'm not interested. But he refuses to get the message."

"What do you want me to do? Take him out in the back alley and. . . ."

"No, nothing like that. Just come to the show, and I'll sit with you at the breaks. Then if he sees us leave together after the show, he'll get the message. That's all I want. I think that's all it should take for him to finally wise up."

Yikes, I thought, I have problems of my own right now. Do I really want to get myself involved in someone else's problems as well? That didn't seem like such a great idea.

"Ty? Do you think you could you help me out?"

"Uh . . . sure. I'll track down Bump and see if we can go together."

"I knew you'd come through," she said. "You're a terrific guy, Ty Duffy."

Oh yes, I thought, I'm a real sweetheart of a guy. Mother Theresa ain't got nothin' on me.

For once in my life I got what seemed like good news — from Larry Berkman, my financial advisor. He'd heard back from his sources in Ireland and the reports he'd received on the hotel had been glowing. He thought that buying the hotel wasn't just a sound investment, it was an outstanding opportunity. Apparently Kathleen Brogan had been right all along, despite Mick Slattery's contrary opinion.

I listened patiently as Larry waxed enthusiastic about a lot of stuff I didn't understand — limited corporations and partnerships, the complexities of overseas investments, Irish tax laws, and the like. Larry said he could put together a group of investors for us if we wanted him to, and that I could decide what percentage owner I wanted to be. He said he wouldn't mind having a small piece of the action himself. Well hell, if Larry wanted in, it had to be a pretty good deal.

So it began to look as though Kat Brogan might end up being the proud possessor of a five-star hotel after all. That is, if she didn't wind up in the slammer for having offed Mick Slattery. Or if the laddies didn't decide to take matters into their own hands and exact harsh retribution upon Kat. It seemed to me that either of those things remained distinct possibilities.

25

George and Lennie turned up around five, a-tap, tap, tapping at my chamber door. Chuck was right about our building's worthless security system.

I didn't want them in my apartment, but we could hardly have the conversation we were about to have out in the hallway.

"Cool pad," George said, feasting his eyes. Lennie grunted.

I motioned them toward my living room sofa, hoping big Lennie's huge corpus wouldn't scrunch the poor thing. George, instead of sitting on the sofa, balanced himself on the arm rest at one end, his short legs not quite reaching the carpet. Make yourself at home, George — slimy bugger.

George stared at me for a moment, a big smile on his verminous mug. Finally he said cheerily, "Money?" And he held out his cupped hands in front of him.

"Contract?" I said. "No contracto, no dinero."

"Ha, ha, ha. Duffy, you are an amusing hombre. But I am going to surprise you, my friend." And he took out an envelope and extracted a piece of paper which he unfolded and then read out loud: "Paid in full for two exquisite works of art." Above it was a space for the date, beneath it a line on which was written "$225,000."

"We can date it and both sign it," he said. "Just as soon as you fork over the scratch."

"Two exquisite works of art?" I said. "That's pretty damn vague."

"You are exactly right. And that's all the further we plan to go." Frankly, I was surprised they'd been willing to go that far. "So there is contracto. So where is dinero?"

"Sign it and date it," I said. "Then I'll get the money."

"Lennie," George said, "I don't think the fella trusts us." Lennie grunted.

No, I did not trust them! If I just gave them the money, what was to keep them from tearing up the so-called contract and walking away? I didn't just fall off the turnip wagon, you know.

"Back in a sec," I said. I took the piece of paper to my study where I have a small lock box in which I keep important papers. I tucked it away, then pulled out the double plastic bag containing the money they wanted in cash. I had actually carried it home from the bank on my person, no Brink's truck in sight. That was a bit nerve-wracking, but also kind of exciting. Now and then you have to live on the edge.

Back in the living room, I handed over the bag.

"Want to count it, Lennie?" George said. "No, that's right, you can't count that high." Lennie gave George a narrow-eyed look, suspecting he might've just been insulted.

Then turning to me George said, "You know what, Duffy? Just to show you what trusting guys we are, we won't even count it. Come on, Lennie, let's make like bananas and split." A grin appeared on Lennie's face and George shot me a big wink. Both of us knew that old chestnut was right at Lennie's level.

As they were going out my apartment door, George turned back to take a parting shot.

"You know, Duffy, you must really love your mother. Such filial devotion is quite touching. Ha, ha, ha. Really quite touching."

The Blue Ridge Mountain Reivers were in fine fettle. Luke, Randy, Big Un, and the other musicians up on the small stage were really going at it. Violet's Celtic fiddle was zinging, and Sandy's vocals were spritely. The first night I'd met her she'd said, "You may not have heard of us yet, but you will." It looked like she was right, for in just four or five months their fame had grown by leaps and bounds. As I watched them now and watched her now, I realized that if another wonderful woman didn't have such a powerful claim on my heart, this one might be worth taking a chance on. Those were thoughts I needed to steer clear of.

Bump sat there in his BRMR tee-shirt nursing his RC Cola and loving every minute of the evening. Tonight it was just the two of us. Bump was there to see Violet, and I was there to be seen with Sandy. I wasn't sure if her little stratagem would succeed, but I felt obliged to give it a try. As a friend, I owed her that much.

There was a second group scheduled to play, and when they came on for their first set, the Reivers had an hour's break. Violet and Sandy, along with Big Un and Luke, came and crowded around the table Bump and I had commandeered. Sandy cozied up at my side and placed her arm across my back, her hand resting atop my left shoulder. I didn't mind, knowing it was all part of our little charade.

The other group was playing more traditional Bluegrass, and their banjo player was laying on some viciously hot licks. They played a couple of rollicking instrumental pieces, as folks clapped along, then suddenly modulated into a slow and gentle number, this one accompanied by subtle vocal harmonies. That's when several couples got up to dance. Just as I was working up my nerve to ask Sandy if she wanted to dance, I realized someone had come over and was standing by our table.

He was a big man, taller and wider than me, with a slight bit of paunch and thinning dark hair. I put him in his early forties. He was dressed in a western shirt and blue jeans and wore a fancy pair of cowboy boots. I had a pretty good idea who he must be.

"Would you mind if I danced with the little lady?" he said to me, in a deep baritone voice. Sandy had a slightly apprehensive look on her face, and I didn't know if her apprehension was because I might say no and provoke a confrontation; or because I might say yes and put her at the mercy of this man she wanted to avoid.

"Uh, sure," I said. "I guess that's okay." Sandy, not looking terribly happy, gave me a tiny nod, indicating her agreement.

After they melted into the slowly dancing throng, Violet dragged a reluctant Bump out into the throng as well. Luke had wandered off, which left just me and Big Un sitting at the table.

"Hey, Big Un," I said, "want to dance?"

"Well . . . maybe we shouldn't," he replied with a grin.

"In that case," I said, "perhaps I'll just go and cut in."

"Think that's a good idea?"

"I have no idea," I said. "Guess we'll find out."

I threaded my way through the throng, shouldered past Bump and Violet who were clutching each other awkwardly but intimately, and finally located the couple I was searching for. I tapped the big fella on the shoulder and gave Sandy a hopeful look.

The guy just ignored me and pulled Sandy closer to him. I took that for a bad sign. But what the hell, in for a penny, in for a pound. I tapped him again, this time so hard he couldn't pretend he was unaware of my intentions.

"Watch it," he growled.

"Mind if I cut in?" I offered politely.

"Hell yes, I mind! This is my dance! Wait your goddamn turn."

"I think it's my turn now," I said. "You've had yours."

Letting loose of Sandy, the big guy twirled around and gave me an opened-handed slap across my face, a slap that could be heard — and probably felt — all the way to Peoria. Geez, it was an impressive wallop. It staggered me but I didn't leave my feet. Before I could mount any kind of response, my arms were grabbed from behind. The big guy obviously had a couple of confederates ready to hand. I struggled to free myself but to no avail.

The big guy stepped up to me and slapped me again, a right, a left, and another right.

I could taste blood trickling from my nose and a corner of my mouth. "You son of a bitch," I blurted juicily.

But in the next moment my own pair of confederates had arrived — Bump and Big Un — each of them grabbing one of the guys who'd been pinning my arms. My arms now free, it was time to see if they worked.

The big guy was in the process of swinging at me again, and this time I blocked his blow with my left arm and brought my right fist up in a mighty uppercut into his midsection. The guy was big, but he had obviously been neglecting his crunches; his belly was so flabby it felt like my fist might make it all the way to his backbone.

His face went apoplectic. Geez, I hoped his eyes wouldn't pop out. And when he doubled over in front of me, I couldn't help bringing my knee straight up into his face. For the big fellow, that was the coup de grâce. Now I wasn't the only one bleeding from the nose and mouth.

Bump and Big Un were in a furious tussle with the club's security guys, and in the next moment I felt myself being slammed to the ground with about three or four guys piling on top of me. They wrenched my hands behind my back and slapped on a pair of handcuffs. I guess Bay City's finest were now on the scene as well. Good thing. Some unruly folks might well turn up in a club like this one.

I'd never been arrested before. A first time for everything, I guess.

Big Un and Bump and I soon found ourselves ensconced in the back of the paddy wagon, heading for the city lockup.

"Think the Deacon will be disappointed in me?" Bump asked.

"For coming to the rescue of a teammate? Bump, he'll be proud of you. All for one and one for all, man." He would, I think. But as for the officials of Major League Baseball, and our team owner, and our general manager — our head honchos were going to be most unhappy with the pair of us. Bump Rhodes and I, no doubt, would be receiving some hefty fines. But whatever Bump's fine would be, I intended to pay it.

At the station house, when the cops realized who we were, they decided to release us on our own recognizance. They gave us a stern warning, then sent us forth to sin no more. That was the good news. The bad news was that there'd been a couple of photographers at the nightclub who'd snapped photos during our little fracas; and they were waiting outside to photograph us again as we tried to slip quietly off into the night.

26

By early August we were hot on the heels of the Yanks and Sox, tied for first three games ahead of us. Jimmy had been on cruise control, his won-loss record fifteen and four, his ERA just a pinch over 2.00. Terry O'Grady, our California surfer dude, had come into his own, going four and one since being called up; and Alfred King and Jorge Comellas continued giving us solid starts nearly every time out. The only one faltering was Stan Foubert; the years were catching up to our crafty veteran.

At the end of July, Kat Brogan had flown back to Ireland where she was quietly laying the groundwork for the ownership transfer of the Glen Tiernan Priory Hotel to its new group of owners. At the same time, she was trying to reduce her involvement in overseeing the Mick Slattery empire. That was the tricky bit, since until Rory returned to Ireland from Boston, she was still responsible for running things.

Our playing schedule during August had us finishing up our yearly play versus the West Coast teams in Anaheim, Oakland, and Seattle. In September we'd do battle with the teams in our own division, including home-and-home series against the Yankees and the Red Sox. Like last year, those games would surely determine who made it to the postseason and who went home. It promised to be another pressure-packed finale to the season. For a ballplayer like me who's spent most of his career on forgettable teams, it doesn't get any better than that. Those are the opportunities we live for.

We got back from Seattle in the wee hours of a Monday morning. As usual, Chuck had performed his mail duties to perfection, and I would have ignored the neat little stack on my front hall table if a small slip on top hadn't caught my eye. I glanced at it and learned there was a package at the post office I'd need to sign for. From my mother? I *hoped* not. But first I needed sleep; I'd trot on over there in the afternoon and find out what was up with that.

Seven hours and two strong cups of coffee later, dressed in shorts, a Blue Ridge Mountain Reivers tee-shirt, and sneakers, I traversed the sweltering streets of Bay City en route to the P.O. Along the way several people said hello to me and congratulated me on our great road trip to the West, where we'd won seven of nine games. After years of anonymity, I almost felt like a celebrity. Given a choice, I preferred the anonymity.

The post office guy handed me a medium-sized package, flattish and heavy. I noticed it'd been sent from Austria and was insured for $100,000. It was from my mother. Just great, Mom, another purloined objet d'art for me to squirrel away for you. Mom, get yourself a bank cache in the Caymans and leave me out of it.

I trekked on back to my apartment and poured myself a third cup of coffee. It was going to be a four or five cup kind of day. Then I set to opening the package.

Inside the outer wrapping was a sturdy packing crate, and taped to the front of it was a business-sized envelope. I removed it, opened it, and extracted a bank draft — for $50,000 and made out to me. The note said, "Ty, paying you back. Thanks for your wonderful help." Wow, Mom, never expected that! But Mom, it's $225,000 you owe me, not $50,000. Still, since I hadn't expected to see a single penny of my money, that made me fifty big ones to the good.

I set about disassembling the packing crate. The last time my mother had sent me a package from Europe she'd given me strict instructions not to open it, instructions I'd ignored. This time there were no such instructions.

Inside, in stiff brown paper, was a framed print. It was a misty image of a small ruined castle perched on a hilltop overlooking a body of water, maybe a lake or a seacoast. And then, as I was holding it up and admiring it, the penny suddenly dropped. This was no print. This was an original watercolor. Holy Moses and the Moss-Gatherers, it was the J. M. W. Turner watercolor, one of the "exquisite works of art" for which I'd paid two hundred and twenty-five thousand dollars.

Taped to the back of it was another note: "Thought you would like this. Consider it my gift to you. Love, Mother."

You have to hand it to my feckin' mother. I guess she believed that the money and the Turner watercolor balanced the scales. Not really, since the Turner wasn't likely to be worth $175,000 — which was probably why she could stand to part with it. The Picasso drawing, on the other hand, the other "exquisite work of art," I felt sure had had plenty of value, and I suspected she must have made a boatload when she unloaded the thing. She had to have — if in a fit of generosity she was sending me fifty thousand dollars and the Turner watercolor to boot.

But look. No reason to be a cynic. I hadn't expected to have any return on my transaction with George and Lennie, other than making damn sure nothing bad happened to my niece, and maybe hoping at the same time nothing bad happened to my mother. Getting a chunk of my money back was purely a bonus. And to tell you the truth, I really liked the Turner watercolor. I'd never owned a real work of art before. This one was very much to my taste.

So, let it be said that my mother was not totally without scruples. Not totally.

Bump Rhodes, after the night on which he and I had been run in for disorderly conduct, had come to view himself in a whole new light. Now he was no longer some hick kid from Podunk Valley. Now he was a worldly fellow who had a sexy girlfriend; who'd come close to actually having a rap sheet; who'd had his picture on the front page of *The Sun*; and who'd received his first big-league fine. Bump was eternally grateful to me for my elevating influence.

But the Deacon and I were grateful for something else entirely — Bump's remarkable performance on the ball field.

Right before our eyes, the hapless, hopeless kid we'd seen in spring training had blossomed into a major-leaguer. Our skipper,

Whitey Wiggins, and our GM, Pete Paulson, had been true believers all along. The rest of us doubters and skeptics, including Jimmy Devlin, had now come around. Even Bump himself was coming around, finally realizing he could play some ball. Bump Rhodes had begun to believe in himself.

All season long Jimmy had used Miguel Torres as his personal catcher, never Bump, who'd been limited to catching Stan Foubert, Alfred King, and Terry O'Grady. But now Jimmy was willing to have Bump behind the dish when he pitched. That said a lot for Bump.

If our disorderly conduct escapade had done Bump Rhodes a wagon-load of good, the same couldn't be said for me. I'd had a lot of explaining to do to Laura, who'd seen the tabloid accounts that described "a love triangle" gone wrong. When she called me asking what this business was all about, I fell back on telling her the truth. I believed she was a person who would know the truth when she heard it and would be able to handle it.

"Ty," she said after my rambling explanation, "all of that seems a little bit implausible. More like a daytime soap than real life."

"Maybe so," I said. "But Laura, it's what really happened. I was only trying to help a friend who'd asked for my help."

"A *friend?*" she said.

"Yes, a friend."

"A *close* friend?"

"A friend. Just a friend."

Laura remained quiet. Then I heard her sigh. "Okay," she said at last, "I'll take your word for it." She was silent again for a few seconds. "Ty," she said at last, "please don't ever let me see your exploits splashed all over the tabloid press. If I do. . . ."

That was surely an ultimatum. "Thanks a whole lot for the vote of confidence," I said.

"Ty Duffy," Laura said softly, "I hope you realize that you can be a very exasperating man."

"Yes," I replied, "I realize that. But listen. I'll admit that in my roughly three decades of life I've done some things I wish I hadn't done. Laura, this wasn't one of them. Maybe my actions were stupid, but my intentions were entirely honorable."

"There's some road that's paved with honorable intentions," Laura said.

"Yes," I said, "I've heard that. Is it the one that runs from L.A. to Vegas?"

"I don't think that's the one."

"No, perhaps it isn't."

27

It was mid-August and Jimmy's father and Penny Sutherland were coming to Bay City for our weekend series with the Royals. Since I have more room than Jimmy, they'd agreed to stay with me. That would allow me get in some lively verbal badinage with Jimmy's father and would give Jimmy some breathing room in regard to Penny, whom he always accuses of "hovering." I didn't mind Penny hovering here for a few days. Penny's a good cook, and I'd grown tired of frozen pizzas and Chinese takeout. I could go for some wholesome meatloaf, corn, and mashed potatoes with gravy.

So on a Thursday afternoon, an open day for us, Jimmy and I met Penny and Jimmy's dad at the Bay City International Airport.

"I brung ya a surprise, Banjo," Jimmy's dad said, after hugging the tar out of each of us.

"I have one for you too, sir, back at my apartment."

"It damn well better be bourbon and not none of that Irish stuff you're always forcing down my gullet."

"I hope it's better than that," I said.

"Better than bourbon? Well shoot, now ya got me excited."

Penny clutched Jimmy, who half-heartedly reciprocated. Then she hugged me as well. As she embraced me, I couldn't help noticing her fragrance. I didn't recognize it, but it was quite appealing.

Remembering how embarrassingly bare my cupboard had been last year when Penny and Mr. Devlin had stayed with me after Jimmy's injury, this time I'd stocked my larder with everything Penny could possibly want. I knew she'd be charging in there with the intention of cooking up a storm. Wanting to impress her, I'd bought every fruit and vegetable that grows on God's green earth; several kinds of meat — fish and fowl, swine and kine — and a bunch of different dessert makings. I elevated Kroger's stock all by myself.

"Would you mind if I cooked dinner for us this evening?" Penny ventured shyly, after they'd stashed their bags in the rooms where they'd be sleeping.

"No need for you to do that. I thought we'd all go out somewhere, just the four of us."

"I'd really like to cook, if you don't mind. Then we can have ourselves a lazy evening here."

"I guess that works for me," I said. "Is that okay with everyone else?" Jimmy's dad was glancing at me out of the corner of his eye, doing his best not to guffaw.

"That gal Penny, she's a mighty good cook," he offered with a mostly straight face.

"Hey Penny," said Jimmy, "I've got an idea. Why don't you make us some supper."

By then Penny realized there was a male conspiracy going on in my apartment.

"Okay, wise guys," she said. "Maybe we should take Ty up on his invitation to eat out."

"No!" we all shouted in unison. "We want home cooked!"

"All right, if you insist on it." Penny peeked into my fridge and quickly took stock of things.

"How does pork chops, green beans, scalloped potatoes, and spinach salad sound to everyone?" she said.

"And what for dessert?" Jimmy's father asked.

Over dinner Jimmy father's asked me if I'd been staying out of trouble lately. "Hope you been mindin' your p's and q's, Banjo. Not gettin' into no fights nor anything."

"Doing my best, but it isn't always easy with knuckleheads like your son leading me astray. But listen, Henry, have I got a deal for you. How would you like to invest in a hotel in Ireland? Trust me, sir, it's the opportunity of a lifetime."

"In Ireland? Why, my great-great-granddaddy come over here from Ireland. That was during that god-awful famine they had over there. Know the one I mean?"

"I do. So that's when the Devlins came, '47 or '48. You all got here before the Duffys. We were a couple of decades after that."

"Johnnies-come-lately," Jimmy said.

"But Henry, what about the hotel? You want in on it?"

"Don't think I got that kinda money lyin' around, Titus. Sure wish I did."

"Well, there's one person at this table who'll soon be rolling in the green stuff," I said, glancing at Jimmy. Last year Jimmy had made the minimum major league salary. This year they'd bumped it up just a little bit. Next year his salary would be approaching mine, and in the near future, if he kept going at the rate he was going, it would be astronomical. Jimmy was still a good ways from free agency, but when he got there, I only hoped he'd sign me on as his agent. Ten percent of what he was going to get would be sweet.

As we noshed on our home-cooked meal, Jimmy and I told Mr. Devlin and Penny Sutherland all about the financial venture we'd embarked upon in Ireland. Well, actually, we didn't tell them *all* about it. We managed to leave out one aspect of it — the one pertaining to a woman named Kathleen Brogan.

I doubted if Henry Devlin even knew of Kat's existence. Nor did Penny, at least not specifically; though I felt sure she'd intuited that she had a formidable rival out there somewhere. And Penny, after her fashion, was preparing to do battle with that rival. I liked Penny Sutherland a lot. And to be honest, I wasn't sure how I really felt about Kat Brogan. But in a battle between the two of them for the body and soul of Jimmy Devlin, Penny Sutherland wasn't likely to come out on top. Kat Brogan was in a league of her own.

After putting away double servings of vanilla ice cream covered with chocolate syrup and sprinkled with walnuts, Jimmy's father galumphed down the hall to my bedroom where he'd be sleeping (I'd moved to my study) to retrieve the gift he'd brought me.

"So here's what I brung ya, Banjo," he said, handing me a large, flattish, rectangular-shaped package wrapped in butcher paper. I kind of suspected it might be something to hang on a wall.

"Is it a microwave?" I said, feeling it tentatively. "How did you know I needed a new microwave?"

When I'd torn the paper off, what I'd uncovered was a framed photo of me in full stride just connecting with a baseball. It was a shot of me knocking that home run I'd hit in the All-Star Game. And even to my own humble eyes it was a thing of beauty. One of my sacred rules has always been to display no showy baseball memorabilia anywhere in my apartment. Guess that was just another of my sacred rules that was doomed to fall by the wayside. Those Devlins, father and son, were good at corrupting me.

"Wow," I said. "Who's that handsome guy?"

"Not so handsome," Mr. Devlin said, winking at me. "But he ain't half bad with the whoopin' stick. Looks like he kinda clobbered this here one. I thought about gettin' ya another of those prints ya got in there, you know, like that one of the gas station I like. But then I thought, well shoot, that there boy needs some baseball stuff on his walls. He ain't got enough baseball stuff."

"I don't? I never noticed that before."

"Like fun you ain't. Banjo, you know you ain't supposed to hide your lamp under a bushel. You do too much hiding your lamp, son."

"Hah!" Jimmy scoffed. "You don't know the guy like I do, Dad. Duffy's excessive modesty is just a perverted form of vanity."

"Oh, now son, old Titus here, he surely ain't no pervert."

"Listen," I said, "now it's my turn to bestow some gifts." And in the next moment I'd fetched a pair of items from my study, handing one to Jimmy's father and one to Penny.

"Ty, you didn't need to get me anything," Penny said. But I could tell she was pleased that I did and curious to know what it was.

Jimmy's father was already unwrapping his. "Don't think it's a microwave oven," he said, feeling the small package. When he'd removed the last bits of paper, there in his hand was a boxed set of Johnny Cash's final recordings, called "Unearthed," which he'd made just a few months before his death.

"Well doggone it, Banjo, this sure is swell. Yep, it sure is. Even better than your bourbon, son. Though come to think of it, I could use just another little splash." It was Penny who jumped up and attended to his needs.

"C'mon, Penny, let's see what ya got there," Henry Devlin said, gesturing with his glass toward the small package I'd handed her.

Back in her seat, Penny opened the tiny packet. Inside was a small, plush-covered jewelry box. She lifted the lid and gazed upon a bejeweled and intricately worked Celtic cross on a silver chain.

"Oh my," she gasped. "How beautiful. Oh Ty, I don't know what to say."

"Just a little bit of Ireland to share with you," I said.

I saw Jimmy looking at me askance. Being no dummy, he'd figured out that I was trying to level the playing field a bit for Penny in her unfair competition with Kat Brogan. And if he felt a twinge of jealousy at my having lavished an expensive gift on his own personal hometown honey, well, all the better.

For the next hour and a half we listened to Johnny Cash and sipped our bourbon. Then, after we'd made a final check of the evening ball scores, Jimmy said it was time for him to be heading off. Penny stooped over him and gave him a little peck on the lips. Then she said goodnight to Mr. Devlin. And then, just before going down the hall to my guest room, she came over to where I was sitting and gave me a long and lingering hug.

"Thank you, Ty," she said softly, "for such a beautiful, special gift." Once more I inhaled her lovely fragrance. Once more I noticed Jimmy giving me a peevish look. Penny Sutherland had a plan. And maybe, just maybe, it was starting to work.

I was up early, but Penny was in the kitchen ahead of me.

"Coffee?" she said. "Strong and black?" She poured me a mug, and it was nearly as good as what I make myself.

"Thanks," I said. "Tastes just right."

"Breakfast?"

"Half a grapefruit and an English muffin with honey," I said.

"No sausages and scrambled eggs?"

"Not today. Save 'em for you-know-who."

Penny and I sat in my little breakfast nook and visited like we'd done before. She did most of the talking, something she had little chance to do when Jimmy's father was around. She told me about her school in Missouri and how this year she'd be teaching third grade. Then she asked about the hotel in Ireland, and I filled her in as best I could, being careful not to touch upon certain topics.

"Jimmy won't have to go over there after the season is over, will he?"

"I'm not sure. We haven't discussed it, but since I'm the primary backer, I'll need to go. Frankly, I'm pretty excited about it. It's something entirely new to me."

Penny smiled at me in a show of interest. I sensed, though, that the subject made her uneasy. As well it should.

An hour and a half later I left Penny to her own devices — Jimmy's dad was still nowhere to be seen — and trekked off to a local bookstore-café called Shakespeare & Coffee, a riff on the name of a famous Paris bookstore. It had a small selection of new books and CDs, a rack of gift cards, a lot of posters and the like; but its real attraction to me was its huge stock of second-hand books and great coffee. During the off-season I spent many a morning here, though I didn't get here so often in the summer.

I snagged half a dozen used books that looked promising and sat at a small table sipping Sumatran coffee. I perused the books slowly, hoping one or two would grab me. From over the sound system came Billie Holiday singing "Detour Ahead." A leggy brunet was sitting at the table next to me, though I tried not to notice.

Then I sensed a hulking presence at one of the card racks. When I glanced over, there stood my amiable compatriot who hailed from lower Alabama. Bump Rhodes in Shakespeare & Coffee? I hadn't expected *that*.

"Bump," I said, sotto voce. "What's up?"

"Hey there, Duff," he said, coming over and sitting down across from me. "Am I glad to see you. Need some help." Out of the corner of my eye I noticed the leggy brunet checking us out.

"You looking for a card?"

"Yeah. But they're all so dumb. Can't find one I like."

"Birthday card for Violet?"

"How'd you know?"

"Lucky guess. Why don't you get a blank one and write your own message?"

"They have blank ones?" I went to the rack and picked out three or four I thought might be suitable and placed them in front of Bump.

"I like this one," he said, "all them purplie flowers. But what should I write? Don't want to write something dumb like " 'roses are red, violets are blue.' "

"No. Just write what you feel."

Bump thought for a bit, then scrawled a few lines on a napkin. "How's about this?"

I turned the napkin around and had a look: "Roses love sunshine, violets love dew, angels in heaven know I love you."

"Good job, Bump. That'll work." Maybe a bit sappy, but it wasn't so awfully bad, and it fitted Bump. Besides, for me the words struck a sentimental chord. They were from an old folk song called "Down in the Valley," a song my father sometimes sang to Billy and me when he was putting two tired little knuckleheads to bed.

A cheerful Bump Rhodes purchased his card, waved me a farewell, then headed off to mail it to Violet. I took a few more moments to finish my coffee and decide on the books. As I did that, I enjoyed the sight of the leggy brunet as she meandered toward the door. Before she exited, she cast a brief glance back in my direction.

Erring on the side of caution, I stayed right where I was for the next five minutes. When I went up to the counter to pay for my books, the music coming over the sound system was Van Morrison singing "Days Like This."

28

Jimmy Devlin was out on the hill, going for his eighteenth win, most in the majors. The Royals were a good hitting club, but Jimmy cruised through his seven innings yielding just two runs on six hits. His heater was sizzling and his new changeup baffled the KC batters. Scotty Evers entered in the eighth and gave up a run, then Joe Oliver set the Royals down in order in the ninth. No need to use Jesus Hernandez, our closer, in so lopsided a game. Bobby Radley was the hitting star, going three for five and knocking in four runs. We won 8 to 3 without breaking a sweat. In Boston, the Sox fell to the Rangers, putting us only one game out of first.

Our clubhouse was rocking. Bump was singing in the shower as usual, and now Zook Zulaski was singing along with him — "Jolene, Jo-lene, Jo-lene, Jo-le-ee-ene" — with Bump's tenor voice and Zook's light baritone blending neatly together.

"It's the music of the spheres," I said to Deacon Lawler.

"More like two cats caterwauling," he replied with a grin.

Jimmy had dressed in a hurry and left, not inviting me to join him, his dad, and Penny. I wondered if Jimmy felt I'd been spending too much time with Penny Sutherland lately.

The Deacon, Bump, and I went and grabbed a quick sandwich, then I headed back to my apartment to call Laura. I only got her answering machine, so I left a cheery message and said I'd try again tomorrow. I knew that since that little nightclub fandango I wasn't entirely in Laura's good books. To achieve that Ty Duffy needed to be on his best behavior and then some. But the bloke was trying hard, so give him a little credit, okay?

I went into my study where I'd been sleeping while my guests were here and sprawled on my daybed to read one of the books I'd bought that morning, one of the later novels in Patrick O'Brian's series about Jack Aubrey and Stephen Maturin. I'd read it before, but some things get even better on subsequent readings. Lucky Jack was definitely my guy; but it was from the complexities of Stephen Maturin that I'd gained insights into the Irish.

An hour later I heard Penny and Mr. Devlin come in and say their good nights. I wondered about their evening. How had Jimmy treated Penny — with warmth and affection, or like a jealous schoolboy? I wondered if Penny and Mr. Devlin thought it odd that I hadn't joined them after the game. I wondered if Penny Sutherland might have any reasons to be gloating just a little bit tonight.

On Tuesday night, Whitey Wiggins, Deacon Lawler, and I stared out from the dugout at the downpour. The game was in a "rain delay," though I couldn't imagine how we'd ever get the game in. Rain bucketed down on the covered infield, and puddles formed in the outfield. A few loyal fans still remained in their seats beneath umbrellas, but most of those who'd braved the elements were staying dry in the concession areas.

The rest of my teammates were back in the clubhouse, doing the things they usually did on nights like this. And that included Jimmy Devlin. Jimmy had been giving me the cold shoulder the last two days, which I suspected had to do with Penny Sutherland. When we'd taken Penny and Jimmy's father to the airport on Sunday evening after our final game with the Royals, Penny had given Jimmy a rather perfunctory farewell. Then she graced me with a vigorous hug which I reciprocated.

"Ty," she said, "I can't thank you enough for your wonderful hospitality! And also for *this*." She held up the Celtic cross I'd given her, which she'd been displaying on her neat and tidy bosom.

Jimmy had watched her little performance stoically, and during our drive back to the city we'd barely exchanged two words. I'd had an urge to reassure him that I was not making any moves on his girlfriend. But by the end of the ride, I hadn't got around to it. If he didn't know by now that Laura Morgan was the only gal for me, he was a bigger densehead than I took him for. Besides, a few twinges of jealousy might not hurt the lad.

"Look at 'er come down, boys," Whitey said. "It's a goddamn turd floater. We sure ain't playin' no baseball tonight."

"It don't look likely," the Deacon replied. "Least it'll give Terry an extra day of rest."

"There is that," Whitey said. Then he spat a stream of tobacco juice from the wad in his cheek out onto the rain-sodden ground.

The three of us stood there for a bit in companionable silence. Then Whitey said, "Whatta ya think, Deak? Think we should start building ourselves an ark?"

"Whatta ya mean *we?*" the Deacon said.

"Ah, Deak, you sayin' you ain't gonna let me and Duffy come with ya on your floating zoo? Hell, you could stash us in steerage with all them creepy, crawly things, if ya hafta."

"I've never been much of a boat-builder, Skip," the Deacon said. "Besides, I doubt if we could find enough gopher wood."

Their joshing amused me. The Deacon and I, the two most veteran members of the Grays, were both in our seventh year with Whitey Wiggins as our skipper. Over that time my appreciation for the man had continued to grow, despite the fact that until last season the Grays had had no great success. It pleased me that in the last few years the Deacon and I had become Whitey's two main guys. He loved us, trusted us, and knew he could count on us. When you know someone feels that way about you, it makes you feel pretty damn good.

"Think we can do it again?" Whitey said softly, after a few more moments of silence. Of course the Deacon and I knew exactly what he was talking about. Whitey wanted more than anything to make it once more to the post-season. Last year was the first time he'd ever done that with any team he'd been a part of. Doing it again meant more to him than life itself.

"Jimmy'll carry us there all by his lonesome," the Deacon said. "He's a man with a mission."

"Good thing we're mostly healthy now," Whitey said. "Even you seem to be healing up, Deak. Hell, maybe you'll get in a game or two 'fore this thing is over and done with." Deacon Lawler was still on the 60-Day DL where he'd been since late June when he'd broken his thumb. We'd figured his season was over, but maybe not.

"Jimmy's been a wonder out there," Whitey continued, "but we gotta keep hittin' and playin' the leather too. Duff, you and Bobby and Spike gotta keep it goin' like ya been doin'."

Then Whitey chuckled and shook his head slowly. "So whadda you boys think about that kid Bump, huh? Who in the hell woulda dreamed he'd turn out to be a real goddamn ballplayer?"

"*You*, Skipper," I said, "that's who. You knew all along the friggin' kid would turn out to be good." I could feel Whitey next to me grinning like a chimp, but I kept my eyes looking straight out at the rain splashing and splattering on the tarp.

"Wasn't so sure, Duff, not really. But deep down, ya know, I had a good feeling about it. Sometimes in this sad life you just gotta go with your gut."

"Well," the Deacon said, "you sure have to admit that he deserves a lot of the credit himself. He sure has worked that big behind of his." Whitey and I chuckled.

As we were speaking of the devil, he suddenly appeared, clomping through the tunnel behind us. Without saying a word, Bump went down to the end of the dugout and peered up at the seats. After he'd taken a good look, he dragged his sorry carcass back towards us. He hadn't seen what he'd wanted to see.

"Holy hell, Bump," Whitey said, "you look like a lost little puppy."

"You okay Bump?" the Deacon said.

"Violet was coming to the game," he said disconsolately. "Then we were going to go and get dinner."

"It's rainin' newts and salamanders out there, son. Your gal's prob'ly smart enough to know when to stay away. Maybe you two'll get to go have some chow earlier than otherwise. Look on the bright side, son, rainouts ain't always a bad thing."

"Skipper, I think something has happened to her. I can feel it, you know. Something's wrong, I feel it. Duff, Deacon, you gotta help me. Help me find Violet."

"Did you try calling her?" I said.

"Uh huh. No luck."

"And you've heard nothing from her?"

"Nuh uh." I knew Bump didn't own a cellphone, but sometimes in emergencies the team accepted outside calls.

"Son, you oughta know by now that women can be pretty unpredictable from time to time."

"Not Violet," Bump said. "She's predictable. She's not like anyone I've ever known."

Right then Bruce Frommer, the umpire crew chief, emerged from the visitors' dugout and trudged over to us through the heavy rain. "We're calling it, Whitey. The field's no longer playable."

"Ya *think?*" Whitey shot back. "Took ya goddamn long enough!"

"Looks like we'll be playing two tomorrow," Frommer replied.

"Okie-dokie, Bruce. Hey, you wanna go and get a beer?" Frommer gave Whitey the thumbs-up.

"Okay, then," I said to Bump, "let's go change out of our uniforms. Then we can try to figure out what's happened to Violet."

"I'll come too," the Deacon said.

"Predictable?" I heard Whitey muttering to himself as we were walking away. "Oh yeah, women are about as predictable as the goddamn weather," his words nearly drowned out by the sploshing of the rain.

As we reached the end of the tunnel we heard Whitey Wiggins's voice resounding behind us. "Hey Deacon, what about that ark?"

Where was Violet? The last time Bump had heard from her was around noon when she said she'd be at the game. Bump was proud of the fact that for the first time he'd have a woman sitting with the players' wives and girlfriends. But not tonight he wouldn't.

I wondered if either Big Un or Sandy might know anything

about Vi's whereabouts, so I started by giving Big Un a call on his cellphone.

"Howdy, Duffy," he said, sounding pleased to hear from me. "Been in any good fights lately?"

"There'll be no fights for me unless you have my back, amigo, that's for sure. But hey, Big Un, you have any idea where Violet might be tonight?"

"Violet? Nope, no idea. We don't have no gigs for the next two weeks, and we've all gone our separate ways. Me and Luke are here in Wheeling visiting the homefolks."

"What about Sandy? Any idea where she is?"

"Umm, think she said she was going to Seattle. Somethin' like that. Going to see a fella, I think, since she's lost out on you."

"Thanks, Big Un. You guys have a great visit with the homefolks."

"You'll let me know if you got any more fights lined up, right?"

"You got it, amigo. I'll let you know."

When I called Sandy's number I got her recorded message. I listened to her lilting voice, then left her a brief message asking her to call me when she got a chance.

Help finally came from an unexpected quarter. From Agnes, Deacon Lawler's wife, who'd recently arrived from California for a week's visit. She'd left a message on the Deacon's phone for him to call her.

"Aggie," he said, "I got your message. Everything okay?"

"You need to bring Bump here right away. Tell him that Violet is all right and that she has important news."

"Uh, okay. We'll get there soon as we can, dear. Bye, Aggie."

Bump had fifteen nerve-wracking minutes until we reached the small townhouse he shared with Deacon Lawler. Those minutes were a bit nerve-wracking for me and the Deacon, too.

Agnes was awaiting us with the door open. She gave each of us a hug, then led Bump to their answering machine and pressed the play button.

"Hi, Deacon, hi Bump," came Violet's voice. "It's me, Vi. I'm calling from the airport. I'm catching a plane in fifteen minutes, on my way to Dublin. Oh, Bump, I'm so terribly sorry to have to miss the game tonight and our dinner. I was so looking forward to it. Here's what's happened. An hour ago I got a call from an old friend who needs my help. You know the Irish group The Wanderers? They just lost their fiddle player — a bad car accident — and they need me to come and fill in. It's temporary for now but maybe could turn into something else. I've got to go and do it, Bump. It's too good an opportunity to pass up. You know how much I love The Reivers, but this is the big time. Soon as I know, I'll tell you how to contact me. Anyway, I may be back in two weeks. In the meantime, I sure will miss you. Bye now!" Then the machine clicked off.

"Dublin?" Bump said. "She's gone to Georgia?"

"I think she means Dublin, Ireland," Agnes said gently.

"Ireland? Shoot, that's a long ways away, isn't it?"

"Not in this day and age," Agnes said. "You could be there as quick as you could be in California."

"Well, I guess that ain't so bad, then. But I sure do hope she'll be comin' back here in a couple of weeks. That's a long time not to be seeing her. I wonder who that old friend is who gave her the call?"

"It's probably a musician friend she's worked with in the past. Someone who knows how good Violet really is."

"She really is good," Bump agreed. "Well, I guess this'll give her a chance to show the world just how good. But man, oh man, I sure will miss her."

So at the drop of a hat, Violet had scooted off to Ireland. I wondered why she had to go tonight, why she couldn't just wait, see Bump tonight, and then go tomorrow. That way she could've given Bump a proper goodbye. But it wasn't any of my business.

When we'd left the dugout earlier Whitey Wiggins had been going on about the unpredictability of women. I couldn't help wondering if maybe he had a point.

29

The Grays entered the final month of the season in pretty good shape, a game back of the Sox and a game ahead of the Yankees. Jimmy was blowing away opposing hitters like Han Solo mowing down imperial storm troopers, and Terry O'Grady, Alfred King, and Jorge Comellas were pitching almost as well. Only Stan Foubert was struggling; he'd been lit up so bad in recent starts that our ever-loyal skipper was about to drop him from the rotation.

All of our position players were playing good ball, too, with me probably playing the best. I was hitting .311, ten points ahead of Bobby Radley, and I'd already racked up eighteen home runs and seventy-nine RBIs. I'd never imagined I could have twenty home runs or 100 RBIs in a season. But with a month to go, those milestones were not out of reach.

As a team we were going good and loving every second of it. Finding ourselves in the thick of a red-hot pennant chase was exhilerating. A lot of our guys could hardly wait to get out to the ball yard each day to do battle with our foes.

Our fans were relishing it, too. Our unexpected success last year had caught our fans off guard. Those poor folks hadn't quite known how to react. Most of them must have thought it was just some weird aberration, the Bay City Grays battling for the pennant. Now they'd become true believers. Our attendance was higher than it had been in decades, and some of our mild-mannered fans were becoming downright rowdy. Some had even taken to heckling opposing players!

But there were two notable exceptions to all this cheerfulness. One was Jimmy Devlin and one was Bump Rhodes. Jimmy, bless him, was pitching lights out. He was throwing his money pitch, his four-seam fastball, his vaunted heater, like bolts of lightning — 96, 97, 98 mph. His second best pitch, his hard slider, was licking at the corners of the dish like a starving dog. And now he had a third wicked weapon, the changeup his father helped him develop over the winter. Jimmy threw it with the same motion as his heater but ten miles an hour slower. Unless a hitter was looking for it, there was no way he could gauge its speed.

Off the field, though, Jimmy was behaving like a mope — irked at me, irked at Penny, irked at himself, and worried about Kat and what might be happening in Ireland. Jimmy Devlin was a conflicted lad. The little charade Penny and I had performed brought it home to him that he still had feelings for Penny Sutherland. And if he still had feelings for Penny, how could he reconcile that with the feelings he had for Kathleen Brogan?

Bump wasn't happy either. But if Jimmy could play as well as ever despite being morose, anxious, and conflicted, Bump couldn't. The great ball he'd played for the month of August had departed on the last train to Clarksville. Now Bump was inept from both sides of the plate, hitless in nineteen straight at-bats, and his throwing problems had re-surfaced. He hadn't gunned down a runner in his last five games, games in which he'd committed three throwing errors. In Bump's case what had knocked him for a loop was just one woman, not a pair of them. But that woman's absence was messing with the young lad's head.

I was a bit betwixt and between also, what with my concerns for Jimmy and Bump. But the good news for me was that Laura seemed to have gotten over her irritation about the incident at the night club. She'd sounded warmer and more cheerful in our recent conversations, and she'd even agreed to go to Ireland after the season to see the hotel and its properties that I now partly owned. She'd put in her request for a week's vacation at the end of October, a most encouraging sign. It had been a while since we'd spent a few days together, but that would soon change since we had games coming up in NYC.

I knew that Jimmy would get over his grumpiness with me. This was the first bad patch we'd had in our friendship, and I sensed he was milking it for all it was worth. Sometimes a person needs to enjoy a good sulk. He couldn't keep it up. His innate ebullience was a force of nature too strong for him to subdue for long.

Bump's angst was that of a kid suffering his first romantic setback, which I knew could be rough. But I also knew that Violet had the power to remedy Bump's blues in a heartbeat. If Violet hadn't returned by the end of the season, I'd drag the kid to Ireland to make sure she provided a remedy for his blues.

It was the second weekend in September and we'd taken the first two of three from Tampa Bay. In the final game we'd face Buck Rutledge, the Arkansas Toothpick — all six-feet-seven, 170 pounds of him, a guy who always pitched with a toothpick in one corner of his mouth. Buck was a right-handed side-wheeler whose pitches seemed to come from the hole between third and short rather than from the mound. Left-handed hitters feasted on his tosses, but for right-handed batters, his sidearm slants were evil personified.

"Not *that* sumbitch!" Lou Tolliver grumbled as we watched the human beanpole complete his pre-game warm up. It pissed Lou off that Todd Cottington, a lefty hitter, and switch-hitting Bobby Radley, were licking their chops with anticipation.

"Bastards," Lou mumbled. "Wait'll those bastards get Black Jack Jurgens," he said, referring to the Yankees' side-arming lefty reliever who specializes in terrorizing left-handed batters.

Bump Rhodes, who'd been playing horribly, was slated to ride the pine again today. But then Whitey, playing a hunch, decided to insert Bump into the lineup at the last minute. Whitey must've noticed that Bump Rhodes had emerged from his doldrums. And there could only be one reason for that — Bump must've received good news from a Celtic fiddle player in Ireland. For Bump Rhodes a misty, moisty morning had turned into a bright and sunshiny day — no matter that we were playing a night game.

Terry O'Grady, who was on the hill for us, set the Rays down in order in the opening frame. Since his call-up back in June when he'd replaced the injured Jumpin' Jack, Terry had gone seven and three and was averaging a strikeout per inning. He'd blossomed into the talented hurler Dave Rubenstein had always believed was possible.

But now in the bottom half of the inning we had to face the Arkansas Toothpick. So Juan Flores, our leadoff guy, stepped into the batter's box, took two quick called strikes, swung feebly at strike three, and trudged on back to the dugout. Then it was time for victim number two, me.

I rarely alter my batting stance, but against Rutledge I do, shifting my front foot fifteen inches to the left and pointing toward third base. By opening up like that it makes his pitches seem less like they're coming from left field. Doing that hadn't resulted in a lot of success, but it helped to lessen the fear factor.

I stepped in, fouled off two pitches, swung feebly at strike three, a wicked heater with late movement, and trudged on back to the dugout. After me it was Bobby Radley, who'd been hitting in the three-hole since coming off the DL. Batting from the left side, Bobby thwacked Rutledge's first pitch so far over the centerfield fence that it nearly hit the scoreboard.

"You bastard," Lou Tolliver said to him as he gave Bobby a congratulatory fist bump. Then mighty Lou stepped up to the plate, took two called strikes, and waved feebly at strike three. After uttering a few choice obscenities, he slung his bat away and waited by the dugout for someone to bring him his glove.

That was the game in miniature. Terry gave us seven strong innings; our right-handed batters were thoroughly humiliated; and our lefties knocked the crap out of the ball. Bobby Radley socked a homer and a pair of doubles, but Bump did even better. First time up he hit a frozen rope down the right-field line that landed five rows up in the bleachers. Second time up he hit a moon shot that ricocheted off the brick building way out beyond right center. Third time up he lunged at a ball a foot outside and whacked it into the left-field upper deck. With strong pitching from Terry, Bump's trio of dingers, and solo shots from Bobby and Todd Cottington, the

Grays came away a five-to-one winner, all our runs coming on solo home runs.

In the showers Bump, Zook, Bobby, and Todd were belting out the tune that'd become our victory anthem: "Jo-lene, Jo-lene, Jo-lene, Jo-le-ee-ene!"

"Making a joyful noise unto the Lord, those boys," a smiling Deacon Lawler said to me. "Make a pretty darn good barber shop quartet!"

"They sound more like a butcher shop quartet to me," I said.

Whitey Wiggins, a puckish grin radiating from his countenance, shouted at me, "How ya like our little ol' songbirds, Duff? They sound even better'n that opera stuff you're so fond of."

"Skip," I said, "I've got two tickets for *Tosca* next Sunday night. You coming with me?"

"Uh . . . no . . . better take a raincheck, Duff. Why doncha take Bump? You know, might help the lad with his love life."

It might at that, I thought.

That night, as I was teetering on the edge of asleep, I found myself thinking about my father. There he was, sitting uncomfortably in the stands beside my mother, who had unexpectedly turned up for my twelfth birthday. Billy and I were playing a crucial Little League game, Billy at second base, me playing short.

It had been a good six months since we'd last heard from Mom; maybe Dad knew what she'd been up to, but Billy and I didn't. Her suddenly being here made the three of us nervous, since in the last couple of years we'd gotten quite used to her not being here. Now she'd become an intrusive presence in our normal world. Dad acted kind and deferential towards her, as usual; Billy gave her the cold shoulder; and I couldn't help my feelings of both affection and resentment.

It was the bottom of the last inning. We were down by a run, but we'd loaded the bases with two outs. I was perched on third base with what would be the tying run, hoping for a wild pitch I could score on. Coming to bat was my ten-year-old brother. For a ten-year-old, Billy was a darn good player. But it was a tough situation for him — big game, bases loaded, two outs, tying run on third.

Billy hung in there like the tough competitor he was, taking a couple of pitches, fouling off a couple, finally working the count full. Then came the payoff pitch. The ball was in the dirt, clearly ball four. Billy had worked a walk and my run was going to tie the game. Except that the umpire had called the pitch a *strike!*

Strike three, three outs, game over. Our coach went ballistic, rushing at the umpire and screaming his head off. "Are you bleeping kidding me? Are you out of your bleeping mind? That's the worst call I've ever seen!"

Billy was in tears. Mom, along with all our other fans, was shouting abuse at the totally inept umpire. And there, in a split second beside home plate, was my dad, hugging Billy to him, holding him and rubbing his back gently. "It's okay," he said. "You did a great job, William. It was the umpire who messed up, son, not you. You did a great job."

Poor Billy was inconsolable. His little chest convulsed with sobs as dad continued hugging him. It wasn't easy for the rest of us to go out on the field and exchange post-game handshakes with the players on the other team.

Billy didn't join in. "Screw 'em," Billy said to Dad. "Screw those crappy losers!"

"They were trying their best too, son. No reason to blame them."

"It isn't fair!" Billy bleated. "Dad, it isn't fair!"

"No," Dad said, agreeing with Billy, "you're right. It isn't fair at all."

We were not a happy household that evening. Billy didn't join us for supper but went straight to his room, closed his door, and refused to speak to anyone. Dad told us to leave him be, so we did. Conversation at the dinner table was desultory. At one point I said, "Maybe I should've tried to steal home. Waited until the catcher threw it back to the pitcher and made a dash for it."

Dad shook his head no. "Billy came through just fine. He's hurting now, but he'll learn something important from the experience."

"And what will he learn?" my mother asked. My father stared at her for a long moment but didn't answer.

Mom, I could tell, was wanting badly to get Dad alone to talk to him about something, so after supper I took the hint and made myself scarce. I'd suspected that my birthday wasn't the only reason Mom had turned up. My suspicion was that she needed something, and my birthday gave her the excuse to come and work her magic on Dad to get it.

Oh, Dad, I thought, what a sucker you are. And yet I knew that his soft-heartedness was one of his finest traits. I only wish I hadn't inherited it from him.

30

Two weeks to go, and everything on the line — the pennant, the wild card, the postseason. We'd play one series in Boston, another in New York, then be at home for our final games against the Jays and Yankees. In those same two weeks the Yanks and Sox would also face each other in three crucial games. The entire season had now been reduced to just twelve games.

We entered the series in Beantown one game back of the Sox. And when we came out of it, we were found ourselves in front by two whole games — the result of a three-game sweep! When we'd exited the Hub City, a deathly pall had descended upon all of New England.

I got to Laura's apartment a little before nine. A candle-light supper, Mozart's Clarinet Concerto playing softly in the background, a jug of wine, a loaf of bread — and Ms. Laura Faye Morgan with the light brown hair, the light blue eyes. I quickly discovered that I was back in Ms. Morgan's good books.

That weekend we took two of three from the Bombers. Our loss came on Friday night when Jimmy had his first bad outing in a long time. When he'd walked out to the mound in the bottom of the first, a small band of Grays' fans were chanting "Cy Young, Cy Young, Cy Young," referring to the award Jimmy was likely to win. But an avalanche of boos from Yankee fans soon silenced them. It was going to be a raucous evening in the Bronx.

You aren't always on your game, and on that particular September night Jimmy Devlin wasn't. He was missing his spots and letting the Yankee fans get under his skin. Several of the Yankees' finest bench-jockeys were giving Jimmy the works before he'd even thrown a pitch, especially Gentleman Jim Breyreitz. For a guy with a limited vocabulary, he was a veritable thesaurus of vulgarities.

Things went bad for Jimmy right off — a walk to Mickey Waters, a ball that grazed Darren Jennings' bloused-out jersey, a three-run bomb from Arturo Carrasco. Whitey stuck with Jimmy as long as he could, though it was clear this wasn't his night. By the bottom of the fourth, after Jimmy had given up six runs and walked the bases full, Whitey gave him the hook.

With his head down, Jimmy trudged back toward our dugout as a torrent of abuse rained down. "Cy Young! Cy Young! Cy Young!" some smart-asses were chanting. Just before he'd reached the dugout, Jimmy stopped and stared up at the stands. "Oh, crap," I said to myself, "don't do it, Jimmy boy, please don't do it!" The lad paused a moment, took a deep breath, and stomped on down into the dugout and headed toward the clubhouse. "Whew," I said. "He didn't do it!"

That night in the Bronx the Yankees handed us our lunch. But we turned things around on Saturday and Sunday taking a pair of close games behind the able hurling of Alfred King and Jorge Comellas. A year ago those two guys had been September call-ups. Now their success was vital to our success.

Sunday night and I'd just come out of the shower in my Bay City apartment, getting all set for bed. That was when I heard a gentle rapping at my apartment door. Not the George and Lennie Collection Agency again, I hoped. If it was those weasels, I wasn't going to give them another red cent — no matter *what* my mother had done!

It wasn't George and Lennie. It was my neighbor Chuck. And the guy looked a wreck.

"Chuck, what the hell! C'mere, man." Chuck stepped in and accepted my embrace. I led him straight to my sofa and sat him down. "Scotch or bourbon?" I said, remembering I still had some of the latter left over from Jimmy's dad's visit.

"Right now, Tyrus, I'd take any blessed thing you might want to hand me," he said. "Any blessed thing at all. But, Tyrus, what I need most of all is a friend." I filled two glasses with Jamison and handed one to Chuck. His hand was trembling.

"Sláinte," I said, lifting my glass.

"And to you, Tyrus," he said, raising his glass shakily and sipping needfully.

Over the next two hours, Chuck poured out his heart. I'd never known a lot about his personal life and hadn't wanted to. But right then my shoulder was his to cry on. Chuck didn't spare the gory details about his forlorn lovelife, and as I listened, I gave him drink and a sympathetic ear.

After being in full verbal spate for about an hour, Chuck finally began to run down. Then he did a total collapse. I laid him out on my sofa, placed a pillow behind his head and draped a blanket over him. Chuck was a goner.

I tiptoed out and went next door to check on Boog the cat. The Boogster was glad to see me, purring to beat the band and rubbing his lithe self against my legs. After I'd fed him, I sat with him for a while, too. He curled up on my lap and purred happily, then Boog the cat dropped off to sleep.

So Chuck was asleep on my sofa and Boog was asleep on my lap. I wondered if anyone else in my apartment complex was in need of my tender ministrations. What the hell, come one, come all.

On Tuesday night I hit my nineteenth home run, picked up my ninety-fourth and ninety-fifth RBIs, and Terry O'Grady tossed a strong game. And yet when it was over, Toronto had edged us four to three. One bright note, though, was that Deacon Lawler took pre-game batting practice and said his thumb felt good to go. He told Whitey he wanted to be placed on the active roster, "gol darn it."

Wednesday night I saw the ball really well and rapped out three singles, all line drives, raising my hit total on the season to 200 on the nose, reaching that magic number for the third time. Bump hit a solo homer, Bobby Radley had a couple of hits, and Jimmy Devlin pitched a lot better than he had in New York the previous Friday. But as well as Jimmy pitched, it wasn't good enough. Toronto won by the score of 3-1. It was the first time this year Jimmy had lost back-to-back starts.

On Thursday night, I hit my twentieth home run and raised my RBI total to ninety-six, and Lou Tolliver hit a solo dinger. Alfred King pitched his heart out, in the process punching out ten Blue Jays. And when the game ended the final score was Jays three, Grays two. Toronto had just swept us in the three-game series.

Meanwhile in Boston, the Sox took two of three from the Yankees. When the week had begun we'd been three up with six to go. Now, with three games remaining, our lead was just a single game over the Sox and two over the Yankees. The New York Yankees — who were en route to Bay City for the regular season's grand finale.

Our first two contests with the Yankees were terrific games. Jorge Comellas and Randy Smalley went at each other on Friday night like Hamlet and Laertes dueling to the death. This time Laertes won. And while we lost to the Bombers, the Sox downed the Blue Jays. The Grays and the Red Sox were tied for first.

On Saturday night Terry O'Grady struggled from the outset, but our bats came alive and kept us in the game. Bump and Spike Bannister hit home runs; Nick Gurganis had three base knocks including a triple; and Juan Flores made several sensational plays at short. We were sitting pretty, up six to four, when Jesus Hernandez came in in the top of the ninth to close things out. But he *didn't*. For once, Jesus didn't save. He blew the save, only the third time this season, and the Yankees edged us 7-6.

Holy Mother of the Divine God! The Bay City Grays had just dropped five straight games. We'd totally squandered our three-game cushion, and we now faced a good chance of elimination.

With only a single game left to play, the Red Sox were one game up on us, and the Yankees, who'd been three games back of us just three games ago, were now tied with us. *Holy crap.*

◆ ◆ ◆

The game had been over for nearly an hour. Our dispirited fans had departed and most of our woebegone players had fled the ballpark. But Whitey Wiggins, still in uniform, remained all alone in the dugout. He leaned on the railing and stared at the partially darkened field, where a groundskeeper was tamping down the mound and another removing the bases.

I padded up softly and leaned on the railing beside him. Whitey glanced over at me and gave me a tight-lipped smile but didn't say anything. Only a minute or so later Deacon Lawler joined us. Whitey gave him a nod of acknowledgment but didn't say anything to him, either. There wasn't a whole lot to say.

The Deacon put his hand on Whitey's shoulder, gave it a gentle squeeze, and kept it there.

Then we heard more steps coming towards us from the passageway that led to the clubhouse.

"Skip?" a voice said, breaking our long silence.

"Yeah?" said Whitey.

"Skip, I want the ball tomorrow." The voice belonged to Jimmy Devlin.

"What?"

"I want the ball tomorrow. You gotta do that for me, Skip."

"On three days' rest?"

"I don't care if it's no fucking days' rest. I want the ball tomorrow. That goddamn game is going to be mine."

Whitey didn't say anything for a minute. When he did, it was Deacon Lawler he spoke to, not Jimmy. "Whatta ya think, Deak?"

The Deacon hesitated for a moment before saying said, "Skip, I want to play tomorrow also. Yes, you should give the ball to Jimmy. And you should have me in there behind the dish. You asked me what I think, Skip, and that's what I think."

"What about Bump?" Whitey said. "You want me to sit Bump?""

"You don't have to sit him," I said, adding my two cents. "You can DH him. Jimmy pitches, Deacon catches, Bump's the designated hitter."

"You takin' over my job, Duffy? Well, goddammit, you can have it. After the fine job I done this week, you couldn't do no worse. Christ almighty, Duffy, five straight losses in the most important week of my life. Christ almighty."

"You giving me the ball or what?" Jimmy snapped.

"Hell yes, I'm giving you the ball! And you better pitch the best goddamn game of your life, son. And you better catch the best goddamn game of your life, Deacon. And as for you, Duffy . . . well, I don't know what. Just keep playin' the way you been playin'. I got no complaints about that."

"Skip," Jimmy said, "you won't regret it." He spun on his heel and made a hasty retreat.

"I sure as hell better not regret it!" Whitey shouted after him.

The Deacon still had his hand on one of Whitey's shoulders, and I put my hand on his other shoulder. After a bit Whitey let out a mighty sigh.

"You don't know how much I appreciate you two fellas standing by me," he said. "Means a whole helleva lot."

After a bit I said, "Skip, I think we're due to play a good game tomorrow."

"I think we're due to play a *darn* good game tomorrow," Deacon Lawler said.

"Darn good, huh Deacon?" Whitey said. "Not just good but darn good? Well, son, that sounds pretty darn good to me. I sure as hell hope you're right."

I woke up early on Sunday morning and decided to take a long walk to clear my head. I pulled on some sweats and was out the door in a jiffy. Few people were out and about on this crisp, early-fall day, and before long I found myself strolling around the Inner Harbor, gazing at the piers, the boats, the cold gray water. I tried to think about anything but baseball — about Laura, about my father, about the Glen Tiernan Priory Hotel in Ireland — but it didn't work. My thoughts came charging back to the game we'd be playing in a few hours. That game meant a great deal to me; it meant the whole world to Whitey Wiggins.

After meandering for an hour or so, I pushed through the door of Maggie's Grill and plopped down at the counter. A couple of early birds nodded to me, though I'm pretty sure they had no more idea of who I was than I had of who they were.

The waitress who came over was an old, old friend. Not so much old in years, though she was probably ten years my senior, but old in the sense of long standing.

"Hi, Susan," I said.

"Well, look what the cat drug in. If it isn't the man himself."

I'd known Susan since my rookie season with the Grays, back at a time when I'd been struggling with a whole lot of things, the biggest of which was the unexpected death of my father. During that time Deacon Lawler had proved my truest friend on the team; the good old Deacon was always there for me when I needed him. But Susan had also emerged to provide aid and comfort. It was friendship, pure and simple. Neither of us had wanted it to be anything more, but at the time it served the needs of both of us.

"So what is it you're wanting this morning, Duff?" she said.

"The biggest darn cup of coffee you got, and the cheese omelet platter with whole wheat toast."

"Anything else?"

"Yeah, a large orange juice."

"Anything else?"

"Yeah, a win today over the Yankees." That brought a small smile to her lips and tiny crinkles to the corners of her eyes.

"Anything else at all?"

"Nothing I can think of right now."

"You never did have a whole lot of imagination," she said, giving me a faint wink. She poured me a huge mug of coffee, then hustled off with my order.

Susan came back and set my food down in front of me and pushed a small caddie filled with sauces and condiments closer to me.

She stood across from me and studied me for a while, her arms folded across her chest. "Pretty big game today," she finally said. "Will Jimmy Devlin be pitching?"

"That's the plan."

"It's a good plan," she said. "Must not've been Whitey's idea. He has even less imagination than you do." I sure as heck didn't rise to that bait.

"You going to the game?" I said.

"Don't have a ticket."

"Would you like one?"

"I'd like two. Could you do that? For old time's sake?"

"I think maybe I could swing it."

"I always knew the day would come when you'd be good for something, Duffy."

"Back then, Susan, you always had more faith in me than I had in myself." She nodded her head slowly in agreement.

"Okay, young man," she said, grinning, "you'd best eat up. You're going to need your strength today." Then she scurried off to attend to another customer.

31

The crowd arrived early, many of them early enough to watch us take pregame batting practice. Our fans were as jittery as we were; they hadn't given up on us, but I suspected they were steeling themselves for the worst. As the stadium filled, it was obvious that at least a third of the on-lookers would be Yankee fans. There was going to be as much contentiousness amongst the folks in the seats as amongst the players on the diamond.

Deacon Lawler took a lot of cuts in the batting cage, more than a player's usual allotment, but no one minded. He'd started taking BP earlier in the week in hopes of getting into a game, but today it would be major-league pitching he'd have to face, not batting practice pitching. That would be tough, especially since the Yankees were pitching Mike Prokosch, a hard-throwing righty against whom the Deacon had a .180 career average.

As we came off the field to change from our practice jerseys to our game jerseys, I glanced up at the guest section to the left of the first-base dugout and saw a lot of familiar faces — Jimmy's dad and mom, along with Penny Sutherland; the Deacon's wife Agnes; Dave Rubenstein's friend Rachel; Lou Tolliver's willowy blonde whose name I forget; even my neighbor Chuck and his mother. Next to Chuck sat Susan from Maggie's Grill, and beside her a boy of maybe ten or eleven.

"Go get 'em, Banjo!" bawled out Jimmy's father, embarrassing Jimmy's mother. And then the boy beside Susan yelled out the same thing: "Go get 'em, Banjo!" prompting applause and laughter. I just grinned and headed on into the clubhouse.

I sat in front of my locker and began the pregame ritual I'd followed forever and a day. I pulled off my practice jersey and chucked it in the direction of a huge hamper; then, as I'd done hundreds of times before, I reached into my locker and pulled a folded gray tee-shirt off the top shelf. I unfolded it and held it up for a moment in front of me. It was threadbare from a ton of washings, and you could just make out the words "Waverly College Baseball."

I'd worn just such a shirt beneath my uniform in every professional game I had ever played. This poor old tee-shirt was ready to join its predecessors as car-washing rags, but there was no chance I wouldn't be wearing it today. It was my talisman, my amulet, my rabbit's foot, my whatever-you-callit — never mind that I'd worn one in more losing games than winning ones. Wearing it wasn't a habit, it was a necessity. I pulled it over my head as I'd done so many times before, then finished getting suited up and joined my teammates.

One thing the Grays had lacked all year long was a strong vocal leader — someone who had the respect of his teammates and the dynamic presence to rally the team behind him. The Deacon and I were stabilizing forces who kept things on an even keel, but neither of us was a rah-rah guy. The Bay City Grays lacked that guy. And on this final day of the season, he finally turned up. Bobby Radley.

Robert Xavier Radley; RXR; our own special X Factor. A year ago Bobby had come out of nowhere to blossom into a late-season star. Bobby was the one piece of the puzzle we'd lacked last year, and once he'd been deployed in right field, we suddenly became a complete ball club. It was Bobby who in the final game had sunk the Yankees' ship with a game-winning home run. And this year, despite missing a month with injuries, he'd had a brilliant season — .302 batting average, 25 home runs, 81 RBIs, and quite likely a Gold Glove in right field. During the last two months Whitey had batted Bobby in the three-hole, a move no one regretted. Bobby's standing with his teammates was now so high that when he spoke, most guys listened.

"The New York *Yankees?*" Bobby shouted out to the room, catching us all off guard. "We've whipped their sorry asses nine times this year. We beat 'em today, we take the season series. Mike *Prokosch?* We're two and two against that asshole! Today we make it

three and two. So COME ON, YOU GUYS! Get psyched! Act like
you care! Get pumped! Damn it, get mad!"

"Let's beat those shit-eaters!" Lou Tolliver yelled.

"Let's rip out their guts and ravish their women!" Zook Zulaski
shouted, raising his eyes for a moment from the video game he was
playing.

"Let's *do* that!" the Deacon shouted, to everyone's surprise.
"There's a time to laugh, a time to cry, and a time to rip the enemy's
heart right out of his chest! Let's go do it, gol darn it!"

"Come on, you guys!" Bobby shouted again. "Get psyched,
dammit, get pumped. Act like care!"

"I'm psyched!" Bump yelled. "I'm pumped. I'm psyched and
pumped!" His jaw, stuffed full of Dubble Bubble chewing gum, was
going up and down twenty to the dozen.

Jimmy stood over in one corner taking all this in, a bemused grin
on his face. He glanced over at me and gave me a thumbs-up. I gave
him one back, then shouted, "Let's wipe these scummy bastards off
the face of the earth! Come on, you guys, today we're gonna *win*!"

The Bay City Grays, their arms clasped about each others'
shoulders, started bouncing up and down chanting: "*Win, win, win!
Win, win, win!*"

Whitey Wiggins stuck his head through the door. Looked.
Raised his eyebrows. Then retreated to the sanity of his office.

As we jogged out to our positions the stadium organist broke into
the theme from *Raiders of the Lost Ark*: "Bum-ba-bum-bumm, bum-
ba-buhh . . . ." Suddenly, apropos of nothing, my brother's favorite
line from the film popped into my mind: "Snakes, why did it have to
be snakes?" Billy loved that movie, and he and Sarah'd named their
daughter Marian after a character in the film. But we didn't have
Indiana Jones on the mound for us today, we had Jimmy Devlin.
And he was pitching on short rest.

Pitching Jimmy was a big risk, and yet the guy definitely deserved
to be out there. He'd been our go-to guy all season long. He had

more wins than any other pitcher in the AL and the second lowest ERA; until this past week, he hadn't lost consecutive starts all year. But Jimmy Devlin, like the Grays, had a lot on the line today. Lose, and there'd be no postseason. Lose, and Jimmy would've ended the season with three straight losses. Lose, and he could probably kiss the Cy Young Award goodbye.

After Jimmy completed his warm-up tosses, the Deacon and I both headed to the mound. "Just make 'em hit the ball, son," Deacon said. "No need for strikeouts today, let your fielders do the work. Spot your pitches on the corners. Don't go leavin' anything out over the plate. Stay ahead in the count so they'll have to be hacking. Okay, son, the first pitch'll be a four-seam heater on the outside corner. You got it?"

"Deak," Jimmy said impatiently, "c'mon man, let's play some ball, okay?" Which was exactly what Mac Maitland, the home-plate umpire, shouted out at us: "C'mon, fellas, let's play ball!"

I waited a split second till the Deacon was gone, then said, "All right, you Irish son-of-a-bitch. Time to kick some Yankee ass!"

Jimmy chuckled. "Get stuffed, you Irish son-of-a-bitch!" Then he flashed me the grin I'd been hoping to see.

"Make 'em hit it to me and Juan and you won't regret it," I said, and jogged on over to my position between first and second.

Jimmy's struggles began immediately. He gave up a leadoff single to Mickey Waters; he grazed Darren Jennings' jersey with an inside fastball; and then, after fanning Paul O'Sullivan, he walked Arturo Carrasco. The sacks were filled with only one down when Junior Jackson drilled the ball toward the left side of the second base bag. Juan Flores took one step and dove. Somehow he speared the ball! Without even looking he flipped it over his head to me at second where I caught it in my bare hand and rifled it to Todd at first. It was a six-to-four-to-three twin killing, a thing of beauty. We were out of the inning with no harm done, thanks to Juan's incredible piece of fielding.

In the bottom of the first Mike Prokosch made short work of the

Grays, fanning Juan on three pitches, getting me to tap weakly back to the mound on a split-finger fastball, and retiring Bobby Radley on a lazy fly to center. They'd threatened and we'd done zilch; but the score was 0 to 0.

It was in the top of the fourth that things finally happened. Arturo Carrasco led off for the Yankees and Jimmy walked him again — violating one of baseball's most sacred rules: never walk the leadoff hitter. With Jackson coming up, Juan and I drew in to double-play depth. On the third pitch to Junior, Carrasco suddenly broke for second. What was he doing? The guy hadn't stolen a base all year. Jackson swung and smacked the ball toward the hole between first and second. I lunged for it as Carrasco flashed in front of me. The ball nearly hit him before thwacking against the heel of my glove and rolling away toward short right field. By the time I'd run it down, Arturo was on third and Junior was on first. And there were no outs.

Jimmy shot me a what-the-hell-was-that look. *Crap.* It was a lousy time to be making my first error in nearly two hundred chances. I expelled a big breath, gritted my teeth, and avoided the eyes of my teammates.

The next guy up slapped a clean base knock to left scoring Arturo and putting the Yanks up 1 to 0. Jimmy Devlin was steaming mad, but he bore down and fanned the next two batters. That brought up the number nine guy in the Yankee order, the light-hitting Phil Dorset. Phil stepped in and swung feebly at Jimmy's first pitch, a four-seamer well off the plate. The pitch was just what the Deacon wanted, but the ball found the tip end of Dorset's bat and lofted softly down the right-field line. It landed just inside the foul line. *Holy hell* — a two-out double that scored two more runs. When we trotted off the field one batter later, we trailed by three. Two of those runs were unearned, courtesy of me.

Big Mike dominated us through six innings, limiting us to just three hits, none by Bump, the Deacon, or me. But Jimmy, pitching his heart out, somehow managed to hold the Yankee lead at three.

Jimmy was pitching on fumes, but I knew he would never take himself out and that Whitey wouldn't either, not as long as we were still in the game.

When we entered the bottom of the seventh, our ever hopeful fans got to their feet for the seventh-inning stretch and the singing of "Take Me Out to the Ball Game." That was followed by John Denver's "Thank God I'm a Country Boy," always a fan favorite. That song blaring over the stadium PA system brought the Bay City faithful alive; they were hooting and hollering like they still believed we could do it. Well hell, a few of us in the dugout believed it, too.

Bump Rhodes, hitting in the eighth slot, would be leading off. He'd walked in the second, and in the fourth he'd whacked a mighty shot down the right-field line that cleared the entire upper deck and left the stadium. It would've been one of the longest home runs in baseball history except for one thing. Bump's swing had been a tad too quick and the ball had curved foul by a foot. So all it was was a very impressive strike, a very impressive strike followed by two much less impressive strikes as Bump went down swinging.

So now in the bottom of the seventh, with the Grays down to their final nine outs, Bump moved once more toward the batter's box. Take away his batting helmet and dress him in an old-fashioned baggy uniform and Bump could've been a ballplayer from another era. Bump wore no batting gloves, no wrist bands or arm protectors, no eye black; he had no tattoos, no unshaven jaws, no lower lip puffed out with dip. What he didn't eschew was a mouth crammed full of Dubble Bubble gum. Bump chomped away in deadly earnest, a look of intense concentration on his boyish, almost cherubic, face.

Just outside the batter's box he bent over and scooped up a fistful of dirt and rubbed his hands together. Then, stepping into the box, he carefully worked each foot to the point of comfort, first his back foot and then his front.

"If I was you, busher, I wouldn't be digging in," snarled Joey Scarlotti, the Yankees' promising young catcher.

"Good thing you ain't me," Bump replied, at the same time shooting a quick glance toward our third base coach, Ray Stutz, who was working through a complex series of signs. With none on and none out, Ray's signs were all bluff. Bump was on his own.

Big Mike's first pitch came in high and hard, and Bump leaned back away from it just in time. "Told ya not to be digging in, busher!" Scarlotti sang out gleefully.

"And I told you that you ain't me," Bump replied with equanimity. He stepped out for a moment to get some more dirt on his hands, then moved back in and began working his feet to positions of comfort.

"Some guys never learn, right Mac?" Scarlotti sighed, addressing his remark to Mac Maitland, the home-plate umpire.

"I got nothing to say," Maitland said.

The next pitch was also high and tight, though not quite as high or tight as the first. But this time Bump didn't lean away from it. This time Bump stepped toward it and took a mighty cut.

The ball shot off the bat with the sound and velocity of an artillery shell. It rocketed toward the right-field corner, whammed against the façade of the second deck, and rebounded back onto the field. It had been fair by maybe ten feet. Whoa baby, that ball was long, long gone!

Our fans went bananas. It was only one run, but goddammit, it was a start! In the dugout we mobbed Bump, pummeling him black and blue. Bump had ignited us and now we had to find a way to keep it going, even if it killed us.

Deacon Lawler, batting ninth, was the next Gray to step up to the plate. Scowling, Mike Prokosch stared in at the Deacon. Big Mike was pissed. He'd been hurling a gem and then some fucking busher goes and mars the goddamn thing. Never mind that the Yankees still had a two-run lead. Mike Prokosch was pissed, never a good thing.

Lou Tolliver, whose hatred for Prokosch was legendary, was up against our dugout railing dishing out some prize-winning abuse.

Mike glanced over and glowered at Lou, then stepped back onto the rubber and looked in for Scarlotti's sign.

Deacon Lawler hadn't fared so well thus far, fanning twice, once looking and once swinging. But he stepped in and got settled, took a couple of practice cuts, and then cocked his right arm up behind him at shoulder height, the bat held motionless in a nearly vertical position. Prokosch went into his windup and blazed the ball toward the plate. It was high and hard and heading straight at the Deacon's head.

When the ball is coming right at you, all your instincts are to fall backward away from it. That's the instinct that saves you. But once in a while something else happens. Once in a while you simply freeze. And that's what the Deacon did.

The ball met his batting helmet with a horrendous crack, then ricocheted up to hit the screen behind the plate.

Deacon Lawler dropped like a felled tree, his bat and helmet landing in the dirt beside him. A huge collective gasp escaped the throats of forty-eight thousand fans and players.

"Oh, Jesus," Whitey whispered into the stunned silence, "not the Deacon."

Jimmy and Bump were two of the first to reach the Deacon, a step or two ahead of me. "Don't touch him," Mac Maitland ordered. "Wait for the guys who know what they're doing."

We heard the Deacon groan and saw him try to roll over onto his side. "Lie still, Deak," Jimmy ordered. "Help's on the way."

"I think I'll live," the Deacon moaned and put a hand to the side of his head, touching an area a little above his ear. "Ooh, ah, feels kinda tender right about there."

The training staffs from both teams arrived in a hurry and applied cold packs to the swelling on Deacon's head. "How many fingers?" a guy asked the Deacon, holding up three.

Deacon Lawler hesitated a moment and then said, "Looks all shimmery, kinda like the Holy Trinity might look."

Suddenly in our midst loomed the big frame of Mike Prokosch.

"Lawler," he said, "look, man, I'm really sorry. I didn't mean it."

I grabbed on to Lou Tolliver and pulled him away. What we didn't need right then was a brawl. Given half a chance, Lou would've liked nothing more than to rip Mike's head off.

"What the hell, Duffy? What the hell?" Lou said.

"Cool it, man, just cool it," I said.

Deacon Lawler sat up slowly. "Hey Mac," he said to the umpire, "okay for me to take my base?"

"No way you're taking your base, Deak. Not till the hospital releases you."

The ambulance arrived. They lifted the Deacon onto a gurney and strapped him down. As they were wheeling him inside the vehicle, he lifted his hand and waved as forty-eight thousand people gave him a standing ovation. They'd allowed Agnes, the Deacon's wife, to come out on the field, and now she climbed into the ambulance and went off with her husband and the paramedics.

When a semblance of normality returned, we still had a ball game to play. Moe Torgerson, the Yankee skipper, went to the mound and removed Prokosch, a prudent move for a lot of reasons. Manny del Rio, our chief utility guy, trotted out to first base to run for the Deacon. So after about a twenty-minute interruption, it was time to resume the game.

The new pitcher was Jake Weaver, the Yankee setup guy, who was coming in an inning earlier than usual. Weaver wasn't a hard thrower, but he had an assortment of breaking balls that he mixed to perfection, along with a cut fastball that had the backward movement of a screwball. Juan Flores was his first victim, lofting a weak popup to short.

I stepped in next with a specific plan. I'd look for only one pitch, the cutter, and if I got it in on my hands I'd try to get out in front of it and drive it toward the left-field corner.

I knew there was a good chance that with one out Whitey would send Manny on the second or third pitch, so I planned to be patient

— unless I got that one pitch I really wanted. Jake started me off with a teasing curve ball just off the outside corner. Ball one. Then he threw another, this one catching the corner for a called strike. Manny was dancing off of first base, acting like he was going to steal, but I still didn't see the steal sign. So I took another pitch, this one a front-door slider that stayed inside. Ball two.

With the count two and one, Manny had to be running. And he was. And there came the very pitch I'd been hoping for and there was no way I was going to lay off it — a ninety-mile-an-hour cut fastball right down the middle. At the last second it broke in towards me, as I knew it would. And I pulled the trigger.

I'd timed it perfectly and caught the ball absolutely on the sweet spot. In all of life there is no more glorious feeling than the one you get when your bat makes a perfect connection with a baseball. It feels better than anything else you have ever experienced — yes, even that.

What I had envisioned actually occurred. But with one difference. The ball had zoomed off the bat at something close to mach speed, and its slightly elevated trajectory not only carried it beyond the out-stretched arm of the leftfielder, but right into the webbing of the glove of a Bay City Grays fan with a front-row seat.

Holy Mother of Our Lord and Savior! The home run I'd hit in the All-Star Game had been one of my biggest thrills in baseball. This one was even bigger.

"Ya got good wood, Titus, ya got good wood!" I could just make out the joyous voice of Henry Devlin through the cacophony of sound that enveloped me. I circled the bases in a daze.

"That one was for you, Deak," I heard a voice say inside my head. "Yeah, it was, Deak," I said out loud, "it was for you."

"Great shot, Duffy," Darren Jennings said graciously as I rounded second base, though I knew he couldn't be happy about it. As I passed Arturo Carrasco at third, he gave me a tiny, squinty-eyed nod, then expectorated an impressive stream of tobacco juice.

I was mobbed at the plate. Even Whitey was there in the midst of the melee. I think I saw a tiny bit of moisture in his eyes.

It was my twenty-second homer on the season and my ninety-eighth and ninety-ninth runs batted in. I'd collected some good hits this year, but this one was miles ahead of all the others.

So the game was tied. Weaver tried to gather himself out on the mound before pitching to Bobby Radley, the hero of the season-ending game a year ago. This time there were no heroics for Bobby. Weaver got ahead in the count, then induced a two-hop groundout to Phil Dorset. Two down.

Lou Tolliver, batting cleanup, came up next. Before he stepped in, he stared over at the Yankee dugout, where Mike Prokosch was standing along with all the Yankee bench players and coaches. Before my hit, Prokosch had still been in line for the win. Now, with the score tied at 3-3, he wouldn't figure in the decision. Still, he cared as much about the outcome of this game as anyone there. As Lou glared at him, Prokosch glared back. If looks could kill, those two guys would've been, as Hamlet might say, food for worms.

Weaver toyed with Lou but then got too cute. Curve ball away; curve ball away. When he tried the same pitch for the third time, Lou stepped into it and powdered the ball deep into the stands in right center. Maybe Lou's homer wasn't as monumental as Bump's or as delicious as mine, but it made all the difference. Lou had given us the lead — a lead we never relinquished!

Joe Oliver came in for us in the eighth and did his thing to perfection, setting the Yankees down in order. Then Jesus Hernandez came in for the top of the ninth and put the Yankees away once and for all. And as he did our fans, both the devout and the not-so-devout, were cheering in unison, "Hey-soos Saves! Hey-soos Saves!"

So in the end it was a final scene of uproarious fans, unruly teammates, and general hysteria. A lot of us rushed over to greet our core of faithful friends. Penny gave Jimmy a huge hug and a long and lingering kiss, while all I got from her was a paltry little peck on the cheek. There's gratitude for you.

Mr. Devlin made up for it by whacking me so hard on the back it nearly put me on the DL. Chuck's mother, whose style definitely didn't lend itself to chaste little pecks on the cheek, also made up for it, embarrassing the heck out of me. Susan from Maggie's Grill came over and proudly introduced the lad she had with her. His name was Cody, she said, and he was her nephew. He was extremely shy, but he managed to say softly, "Thanks a lot for the ticket Mr. Duffy. You're my favorite player. I'm sorry I called you Banjo."

"I didn't mind a bit, Cody. I hope you had fun today. Let me know if you need another ticket this coming week, okay?" Cody's eyes lit up and he nodded yes.

The postgame champagne was flying, and some of it actually went down guys' throats. The press kept trying for interviews, with only marginal success.

Whitey and Jimmy and Bump all came over and hugged me. "Except for that error," Jimmy said, "you did okay today, Duffy. Ya Irish son-of-a-bitch."

"Listen, we really gotta go and check on the Deacon," Bump said.

"Yep, we do. First we shower, then we go," I said.

"Goes without saying, dumb-heads," Jimmy graciously agreed.

In the next few minutes, a huge chorus of baseball players, in various stages of inebriation, were blending their voices in a triumphant song of victory. It wasn't exactly the famous march from Verdi's *Aida*. To me it sounded more like, "Jo-lene, Jo-lene, Jo-lene, Jo-le-ee-ene." And for once, I added my voice to those of my teammates.

32

At the hospital, they wouldn't let us in to see the Deacon. They said only family members were permitted to be with him. When we refused to disappear, a grumpy-looking doctor came out and told us we'd have to leave. We told him we weren't leaving 'til we knew what was happening. He heaved a big sigh. "Mr. Lawler," he said, "is badly concussed," an observation so obvious it prompted a rude, two-word reply from Jimmy.

"How badly?" I asked. The doctor sighed again.

"He has a subdural hematoma," he said, acting as if such a phrase couldn't possibly mean anything to a bunch of dumb athletes. "We won't know for another twenty-four hours the extent of the internal bleeding or how well it's being absorbed. Obviously, he'll have to be kept under close observation. Since he doesn't have a history of serious concussions, there's a good chance he'll be fine after a few days. No guarantees, but that's the probability. The likelihood of long-term damage is small."

"Thanks, Doc," I said. "Could you tell his wife we're here and would like to speak with her?"

"I'll see," he said, reverting to his grumpy self.

A couple of minutes later an ashen-faced Agnes came out to the waiting room. Bump leaped up and enveloped her in his huge embrace, and she smiled wanly at him.

"So the Deacon is doing okay?" Jimmy asked.

Agnes nodded tearfully. "They've given him some painkillers. His vision is a little blurry but they said that isn't unusual."

"We brought you a few things we thought you might need," I said, holding up a small carryall. On our way to the hospital we'd stopped by their townhouse and grabbed a few things — the Deacon's shaving kit, a pair of pajamas, a change of clothes, and the most important item, the Deacon's Bible.

"Wonderful," Agnes said, clutching the Bible. "I'll be able to read to him."

"Read him about Joshua and the battle of Jericho," Bump suggested. "It's one of my favorites."

"I will," Agnes said, "I surely will."

"Read him that passage from Ecclesiastes about a time to laugh, a time to cry, and a time to take one for the team," Jimmy said.

"Not Ecclesiastes," she said. "Psalms might be better."

" 'By the waters of Babylon, we lay down and wept,' " I said. Jimmy rolled his eyes. "But listen, Agnes, you take care of yourself too, all right? Let us know if there's anything you need." We gave her farewell hugs and headed for the parking lot.

There wouldn't be much sleep for Agnes Lawler tonight. She would be watching over her man like a good and faithful shepherdess, guarding against the evils that lurk in the dark.

In the morning I enjoyed a long and lazy sleep-in. Then, as I sipped my coffee, I spent several minutes listening to all the congratulatory messages on my answering machine — most of them heart-felt, some pretty amusing, a few inventively obscene — but all of them much appreciated. One of the ones that especially pleased me was from someone who wasn't one of my closest pals or family members. It was from Laura's mother.

"Ty, it's Janet Morgan. I just had to call and congratulate you on your splendid victory!" came her voice through the machine. "I'll admit you had us worried there for a while. And then you smashed your fabulous, glorious home run. Oh my, a thing of pure beauty — like Sir Gareth vanquishing the Red Knight of the Red Laundes. And Ty, thank you for eliminating those dratted Yankees! If you end up facing the Red Sox next week in the ALCS, I'm not sure who I'll be rooting for. It might be you. Oh, and Ty, we certainly hope your teammate will be all right. That was a horrifying moment. Anyway, I just wanted to call and congratulate you. Bye for now."

Jack Strachan's call came as I was fixing myself a double-decker BLT. But good old Honest Jack wasn't calling about the ballgame.

"Duffy?" he said. "It's Jack."

"Jack! Where the heck are you, man? You're not in Bay City, by any chance?"

"No, not hardly. I'm on the N6 heading toward Galway, just a bit beyond Athenry."

"Really? Wow, Athenry? So how are the fields, Jack?" a feeble wisecrack referring to one of Ireland's most famous old songs.

"The fields're grand, Duffy. Still lyin' a bit low. But you can forget the feckin' fields, okay? I'm on my way to see Kat."

"That's grand," I said. "Say hi for me."

"Duffy, I t'ink we got problems, laddy."

"Problems? How so?"

"The lads know what ya been up to. They ain't a-tall pleased."

"You mean the hotel?"

"Yah, that's what I mean."

"What's that got to do with them? They had their shot at the hotel. In their wisdom, they said no."

"It's Kat it's got to do with."

"How so?"

"They ain't so happy with Kat, Duffy. They t'ink she's been doin' a lot of stuff behind their backs and all."

"Jack, what she and I have been doing with the hotel hasn't got a damn thing to do with those fellows."

"That's not how they see it. Lookit, Duffy, Rory's been wantin' an excuse to give Kat some major shite. Ever since she told him to feck off and leave her alone. Real personal, he took it. Rough on the lad's ego, ya know. And a lot of the other lads still t'ink Kat was the one what did for Mick. So anyways, they all got their reasons. And now this stuff with the hotel's kinda become the last straw."

"What do you think is likely to happen?"

"Don't know, Duffy. Looks like Mick's old empire is headin' for a big bustup. Some of us ain't so keen on Rory and Declan runnin' things. Some of us would prefer it to be Kat."

"So if there's a big bust-up, you'll be siding with Kat?"

"Aye, that I will. Me and Roddy and Liam and a handful of others. And o' course Ned Taafe." I didn't know who Liam was, but I knew and liked Ned Taafe, and I remembered Roddy, the huge dude with all the tattoos on his arms from the Book of Kells — a guy who came very, very close to clobbering me a year ago.

"What about Seamus?"

"Now, what would you be supposin' about Seamus?"

"I'd be supposin' that Seamus will side with whomever he thinks holds the most money and power."

"Your da didn't raise no fool, Duffy," Jack said. "Anyway," he went on, "just wanted to fill you in a bit. On me way now to see Kat and let her know just what's been happenin'. Want her to know I'm gonna be in her corner. Mick couldn't help feelin' a strong family obligation to Rory and Declan; but it was Kat he really loved. In the end, Mick would've stuck by Kat. So, I gotta do that too."

"I'll be coming over once the season's finished, Jack."

"I figured as much. You should be all right, Duffy, but I don't t'ink it'd be such a grand idea to bring Devlin. They blame him as much as Kat. And believe me, they ain't forgot that Devlin was the one who took down Mick." That didn't surprise me. The feckin' Irish have a knack for never forgetting a grievance.

"It's been more than a week since I've heard from Kat. Tell her to email me when she gets a chance. Oh, and tell her that Laura will be coming with me. We'll be there by the end of October, or a few days before."

"Good luck with your games, Duffy. You get over here, laddy, and I'll teach ya all about hurling. Now, there's a real game for ya."

"Bye, Jack. Thanks for calling. It's good to talk to you." That was the truth, too. And what a relief to discover that Honest Jack would be siding with Kathleen Brogan; for when clan warfare breaks out amongst the Irish, it can get nasty in a hurry. It's a whole lot better to have the Jack Strachans of the world with you than against you.

For the rest of the day I found myself humming "The Fields of Athenry." Couldn't get the feckin' thing out of my head.

33

We would open the postseason out west against Oakland, who'd nipped the Angels in the final week to take the AL West. At the same time, the Red Sox would be hosting the Detroit Tigers, who'd bested the Twins and White Sox in a dramatic Central Division race. In the NL, it was the Phillies versus the Giants and the Cardinals against the Braves. Of those eight teams, the common view was that the Phillies and Red Sox were the ones most likely to reach the World Series. The Vegas odds-makers gave the Bay City Grays the least chance of the eight to take it all. But what the hell did those useless wankers know, anyway?

Deacon Lawler, after being observed for twenty-four hours in the hospital, was released and sent home to his Bay City townhouse to enjoy the tender lovin' care of his wife. There was no way the Deacon could travel with the team this week, and he'd already been replaced on the active roster by Miguel Torres. Bump would do most of the catching in the ALDS, with Miguel backing him up.

"Geez, Deak, I hope you haven't looked in a mirror lately," Jimmy said with his usual level of sensitivity, as we eyed the man propped up against the cushions of his living room sofa. But Jimmy was right — the Deacon really did look like shite.

"Aggie says the Frankenstein monster ain't got nothin' on me," the Deacon replied with a smile. "No way I'm looking in the mirror. Might be too much of a shock to my system, discovering I don't look like Gregory Peck no more."

"Gregory Peck? You've never looked like Gregory Peck," Agnes said playfully. "Maybe a bit like Van Heflin."

"*Shane!*" Bump blurted out. "Van Heflin in *Shane!*" Jimmy and I exchanged surprised glances. *Shane* was a film from my father's childhood, one of his all-time favorites.

"If the Deacon is Van Heflin," Jimmy said, "I guess that makes me Alan Ladd."

"I guess it doesn't," the Deacon and I said at the same time.

As we were driving to the airport, out of the blue Bump said, "Really makes ya think about poor old Ray Chapman, don't it?" Jimmy and I exchanged wide-eyed looks yet again, surprised that Bump had ever heard of Ray Chapman. First he brings up *Shane*, then Ray Chapman. Who was this kid, anyway?

"Ray Chapman?" Jimmy said.

"You know," Bump said, "the guy got killed way back when? Ray Chapman, you heard of him, right? I think that was his name. The guy got whacked by a pitched ball?"

Of course Jimmy Devlin and I knew about Chapman, the only major-league batter ever killed by a pitch. And, coincidentally, it was a big mean Yankee pitcher who'd thrown the ball. In fact, just as soon as the Deacon went down in the game, the first thought shooting through my head was Ray Chapman, though I did all I could to quell such morbid notions.

Chapman was killed in 1920, long before anyone ever thought about protective batting helmets. His death led to some changes in the game, particularly changes involving the ball — like the regular replacement of dirty ones with clean ones during the game; and like having the umpire rub down the balls before the game with a white clay in order to reduce glare and improve the pitcher's grip. It would be another fifty or so years before hitters were required to wear batting helmets. Thank goodness the Deacon had one. It probably saved his life.

"Sure glad things turned out better for the Deacon than they did for Ray Chapman," Bump said.

"That makes two of us," Jimmy said.

"If you count Agnes, Whitey, and me," I said, "that makes five of us."

"If you count all the Bay City fans . . . ," Bump began.

"Okay, okay, enough already," Jimmy interrupted.

◆ ◆ ◆

Over the next sixteen days we played eleven baseball games. The first four were against the A's, a series in which we did everything right. We got strong pitching from Alfred King, Jorge Comellas, and Terry O'Grady; we got a lot of timely hits, and we took the series three games to one. Whitey had kept Jimmy back, holding him in reserve in case there was a fifth and final game. But there wasn't one. Which meant that Jimmy would be fully rested to pitch the opener in the ALCS.

In that first game in Boston, Jimmy completely stymied the Red Sox. His heater had the kind of hop on it that it'd had early in the season, and he was bringing it consistently at 97 MPH, occasionally following it with his devastating changeup. But the Sox bounced back taking the next two games. They shellacked Terry O'Grady in Game Two and did the same to Alfred King in Game Three.

Game Four was a slugfest. The Sox hitters knocked six balls out of the park, and we got homers from Bobby, Lou, Spike, and Bump. It was Bump's grand slam that made the difference. Our pitching had been horrible, but we'd still won, 11 - 9, and now the series was knotted up at two games apiece.

I'd given Susan from Maggie's Grill a pair of tickets for that game, and after the game Bump gave Cody a signed baseball. A lot of happy Grays' fans left the stadium that day, but none was happier than a young lad named Cody.

In Game Five Jimmy wasn't the pitcher he'd been in Game One, and the Sox beat us 6 - 4. So the outlook wasn't brilliant for the Bay City Grays. We were down three games to two, with the final game (or games) to be played in Boston. And then Jorge Comellas tossed an absolute gem! — a complete game in which he yielded just one run on three hits. We won three to one. *Madre mea*, one more win and the Bay City Grays would be going to the World Series.

And we got that win! In Game Seven Alfred gave us four strong innings, Terry three, and then Joe and Jesus wrapped the damn thing up in a five-to-three win for the Good Guys.

More champagne, more clubhouse jubilation, more rousing victory songs in the showers. But the most important thing for me was spending a quiet moment with Whitey Wiggins, who'd remained all alone in the dugout after the game.

"Goddamn it, Duffy, I never thought it would happen. Not in a million years. Us — going to the World Series. Goddamn it, us. Don't want to rub my eyes cuz I might wake up and discover the sad truth."

"The truth, Skipper, is we're heading back to Bay City to take on the San Francisco Giants. Us. You, me, Jimmy, Bump, and all the rest of your desperate pirate crew."

"They're all good boys, Duff, not a single pirate among 'em. Well, maybe Zook. But all good boys, and all of 'em pretty goddamn good ballplayers, too."

The Skipper was right. We weren't a collection of all-stars, far from it. But during the past two years we'd meshed into a solid club. Our starting pitching was thin and we had no bench to speak of, but with everyone healthy and with Bump's phenomenal emergence, the guys in our everyday lineup could hang in there against anybody.

The Bay City Grays were going to the World Series. It wasn't a fluke. We'd earned it.

34

I hadn't had a chance to spend any time with Laura since our last trip to New York, a week before the end of the regular season, which was almost a month ago. But now, with a two-day break before the start of the World Series, Laura was coming to Bay City. She'd arrive on Friday evening and stay through Sunday night, the night of our first game against the Giants.

Her flight landed at nine on Friday, and we were back in my apartment by a little after ten. After our victories over the A's and the Sox, I figured I had earned a reward like none other. And Laura was the reward I'd been longing for — a reward like none other.

Lucinda Williams has a song called "Passionate Kisses," and there are times in life when one fully comprehends the sentiments expressed in that song. This was one of them. Before we had even removed our jackets, we were clinging to each other fiercely, her face against my chest, my arms encircling her slender body. Slowly, I ran my hands upward from her hips to her shoulders and then back down again, lovingly tracing the gentle contours of her body, contours I had long since memorized, contours I could never experience too much.

When Laura tilted her head upward toward my face, I tilted mine downward. A first kiss, soft and gentle, can contain a degree of passion that its softness may belie. But of course a first kiss, soft and gentle, is often just a harbinger of things to come. And so it wasn't long before Laura and I were no longer wearing our jackets.

I woke up to the smell of coffee.

Laura was sitting at my breakfast table, working on a crossword puzzle I'd already started.

"I corrected one of your mistakes," she said. "You really should do the puzzle in pencil, you know."

"Thanks, professor, I'll keep that in mind. So, where does one get a cup of coffee in this here joint?"

"Try the coffee carafe that's sitting on the counter," she said. "I discovered it on the top shelf of your cupboard." I'd forgotten that I had one, something not even Penny Sutherland had discovered. Score one for Laura.

"Umm, you do make a tasty cup of coffee," I said. "And that's not all that's tasty about you." I bent over and kissed the side of her neck.

"Hey, don't break my concentration. I'm trying to sort out this puzzle you've totally messed up."

"I have not totally messed up any puzzle. You are totally exaggerating."

"Okay, you've only messed it up a little bit."

"You better watch out or I'll totally mess you up."

"Oh my. Aren't you the manly man this morning. You must've been feeling your oats last night."

"I was feeling a lot of things last night. But hey, let me see that blasted puzzle. Where's this so-called mistake you say you found?"

For the next hour we drank coffee, breakfasted, joshed and teased, took turns with the crossword puzzle — acted like a couple of teenagers who couldn't get enough of each other's company. It felt pretty good.

"Put on some music," Laura said. "Mozart?"

"Wolfgang Amadeus it is," I replied. I put on *The Magic Flute*, my personal favorite, and cranked up the volume.

"Is this in honor of the magic we shared last night?"

"It's in honor of Papageno discovering his Papagena," I said.

"I wonder what you mean by that?" Laura said.

As we listened to Mozart, Laura amused herself by subjecting my bookshelves to an intense scrutiny.

"You actually arrange your books by authors?" she said. "I'm sure that says something about you, though I'm not quite sure what."

"It says that when I want to find a novel by Nabokov I know

where to look. *There*," I said, pointing to one section of a bookcase, "you have your mysteries; *there* you have your serious fiction; *there* you have your poetry; and *there* you have your non-fiction. It's not the Dewey Decimal system, but it's a no-brainer, ya know."

"And what's that one?" she said, pointing to a small bookcase with a lamp and some photographs on top.

"That's the you-name-it bookcase. Whatever doesn't fit neatly elsewhere goes there."

"So you're telling me that when you've finished reading a book you actually return it to its proper place?"

"I am," I said, "indeed I am."

"You are a marvel. All the time I've known you you've never struck me as being compulsively organized."

"I'm definitely not that. Only in regard to books. Okay, and my CDs, too. My father was compulsively organized only in regard to his tools. 'After you use it, put it back,' he drummed into us. Which is definitely a good approach the next time you need a Phillips screwdriver. Or a Nabokov novel."

Laura wandered down the hall and into my study where I found her staring at my Turner watercolor. I'd told her a bit about it in the days following its surprise arrival. I'd described it to her and told her that my mother had had a hand in procuring it, though beyond that I hadn't chosen to elaborate.

"It's a truly lovely watercolor," she said. "I'm envious. How much do you know about its provenance?"

"Um, not so much, actually."

"No paperwork on it?"

"Um, just a record of purchase," I said, referring to that worthless piece of paper I'd gotten from Little George and Big Lennie.

"I'm no expert," Laura said, "but it does look real to me. Maybe I could find someone to authenticate it for you. Then you could be surer of its true value. You said your mother told you she thought she'd gotten a steal on it, right?"

That had been my little joke, telling Laura that the watercolor had been "a real steal." It almost certainly had been, in one sense or another.

"My mother has a knack for getting things on the cheap," I said. "It's how she makes her living."

"There are a lot of people in the art world who love to wheel and deal. If you're good at it, you can definitely do all right for yourself. It requires a certain flair."

Laura knew only a little bit about my mother, just the very few things I'd chosen to divulge. But being no dummy, I felt sure she suspected that my mother was one of those folks who operate very close to the margins of the law. But she also knew that Ty Duffy, unlike his brother Billy, was perversely protective of his mother. And so, to her great credit, Laura never pushed me to reveal more than I freely chose to reveal.

I left Laura to her own devices for a few hours while I went to batting practice and afterward put myself through a rigorous workout in the team weight room. Then I showered and headed for my car.

In the stadium parking lot the Giants' team bus had just pulled in, so I stood there and watched as their players came piling off, nodding to players and giving verbal greetings to the handful of guys I knew. The last one to step off the bus was Tim Elfinstone, their star pitcher and the guy we'd be facing tomorrow night in the World Series opener. He saw me watching and grinned at me, undoubtedly remembering the home run I'd hit off of him in the All-Star Game back in July.

"Hey, Duffy," he said, stepping over to me and reaching out so we could slap hands.

"Guess I'll be seeing you tomorrow night, Tim," I said.

"Oh yes," he replied. "I've been looking forward to it."

"Not too much, I hope."

"Yes, quite a bit." He grinned at me and slapped my hand once more, then headed on inside the stadium. Tim Elphinstone was now in his mid-twenties, a couple of years older than Jimmy, but he looked about sixteen. He looked like he should be busing tables, not busting fastballs in the major leagues. But that was one of the great things about baseball — you didn't need to be a humongus stud to be good. Tim Elphinstone reminded me of the ancient hero of Irish legend named Cuchulainn. He looked like a mere stripling lad; but if you were foolish enough to do battle with him, you were likely to get your ass handed to you in a sling.

When I got back to my apartment I found Laura sitting on my sofa, working on her laptop computer while listening to Gounod's *Faust*, the opera we'd be seeing tonight. As I came in she put her finger up to her lips. Marguerite was just beginning to sing "The Jewel Song," one of the opera's most famous arias. I stood stock still and listened, my eyes upon Laura all the while — Laura with the light-brown hair, Laura with the light-blue eyes. When the aria was finished, I went over and gave her a soft kiss on the lips.

"I'm glad you're here," I said, pulling back and looking into Laura's eyes.

"I'm glad I'm here too," she said, reaching her hand up and touching my cheek.

"Some men," I said, thinking of Faust, "would exchange their immortal soul for the love of a beautiful woman."

"Your immortal soul? I thought you'd already traded that to get your win over the Yankees?"

"No," I said, "you must be thinking of some character in some old Broadway musical. Besides, I don't think your name is Lola."

"You mean I don't get whatever I want?"

"From me, Lolita, you can get any little thing your heart desires."

"I'm neither Lola nor Lolita," Laura declared. "I've been wondering if I should go ahead and tell you who I really am?"

"I think you should go ahead and tell me who you really are," I said. "I can handle it."

"Well, okay. Who I really am," Laura said, "is Morgan le Fay."

"Your mother already told me," I said.

"Yes," Laura said, "and she should know."

While sipping our Sunday morning coffee, Laura and I read through Kat Brogan's latest emails. She'd decided to make a few small changes at the hotel, mostly just to put her own stamp on things, but also to let folks know who was in charge. She'd retained most of the hotel and restaurant staff but wasn't so happy with the management of the golf course. She planned to make some personnel changes, and Jack Strachan suggested some people she might consider. I figured Larry Berkman's Irish contacts might be worth talking to also.

Kat didn't say a single word about Rory and Declan. Or about any particular difficulties with Mick's old crew. I guessed that was good news, though I couldn't be certain. She was also taking it for granted that Jimmy would be coming over when Laura and I came to Ireland. I suspected that was what he intended, though we hadn't discussed the matter. I knew for certain two people who really hoped he wouldn't do that — Penny Sutherland and Jack Strachan. Jack had already warned me against bringing Jimmy. Still, if Jimmy wanted to come, I couldn't stop him.

I also didn't know what had been happening in regard to Bump and Violet, but Bump's current level of exuberance and ebullience suggested that things were going well for them. Since Violet hadn't been around, I guessed she was still in Dublin playing with that Irish group; which probably meant that Bump planned to go and see her after the Series wrapped up. Bump hadn't said a word about it. Sometimes he was too verbal for his own good; and sometimes he was too tight-lipped for my own good.

But there was one thing I *had* heard about, alas. And that was that some of my teammates decided to invite themselves over to play golf. When they heard about the hotel and the golf course, they got pretty excited. "Shit, man," Spike Bannister had said, "we're gonna go over there and check out your new place, Duffy, all right with you? You're gonna give us the Society for Homeless Athletes group-rate discount, ain't ya?"

"You mean you want to stay for free?"

"You're gonna find us some Irish chiquitas, ain't ya?" Lou said.

"I didn't know you knew Gaelic," Jimmy said.

"Lou," I said, "it's a hotel, not a whore house."

"I was just kiddin' ya," Lou said. "We can probably find our own Irish chiquitas."

Spike and Todd and Lou, all single guys, were champing at the bit, and I figured what the hell, why not? It sounded like fun to me too, so long as the bastards didn't trash the place and didn't offend the paying customers. It also dawned on me that if Jimmy ended up coming, which seemed inevitable, it might not hurt to have a few of his strapping teammates hanging around. No, it might not hurt at all.

35

The Battle of the Bays, as the writers dubbed it — the West Coast's "City by the Bay" versus the East Coast's Bay City — pitted two unlikely opponents. We'd made the post-season by winning the AL wild card, the Giants by winning what most experts considered the NL's weakest division. But the Giants had terrific starting pitching, and good pitching plus solid defense wins ball games. Their starting lineup had even fewer stars than ours, but like us, they'd meshed together to form a solid club.

In Game 1, in our ballpark, it would be Jimmy Devlin versus Tim Elphinstone, two quite contrastive hurlers. "The Elf" was a right-hander, short and slight, but with a vast array of pitches; Jimmy, a tall and lanky lefty, relied mostly on just two pitches, his four-seam fastball and his hard slider, though he now mixed in the occasional straight change. Tim was imperturbable, Jimmy highly volatile. Both of them recorded lots of strikeouts, though Tim was more a ground-ball pitcher, Jimmy more a fly-ball pitcher. On chilly nights like this one, with the air cool and heavy, fly balls shouldn't pose much of a danger for Jimmy. Besides, he had Spike Bannister, Bobby Radley, and Nick Gurganis to chase 'em down.

Tim and Jimmy dominated Game 1, both pitchers working eight innings, both recording double-digit strikeouts, both giving up a couple of hits and a couple of walks. In the top of the sixth, though, the Giants parlayed a walk, a sacrifice bunt, and a single into a run. In his eight innings Tim had allowed no runs, and he'd retired me three times in a row, twice by strikeouts.

I came up for my final at-bat in the bottom of the ninth with two down and none on. The Giants had their closer in there, a hulking brute named Kareem Gibran, a guy I'd never faced. He'd made short work of Zook Zulaski, who was batting ninth for us, and of Juan Flores, our lead-off hitter. I stood in the batter's box and watched Kareem's first four pitches carefully, each one a blazing fastball, each one right at the letters or just above. And after those four pitches the count on me was two and two.

I felt sure the next pitch would be just like the previous four. If it was, the only question was whether I could catch up to it. And there it came, and it was indeed a letter-high fastball. I timed it right and caught it on the barrel of the bat. The ball shot toward left center, and I shot down the baseline toward first, thinking that all I wanted was a two-bagger.

As I rounded first, I heard the big gasp from the Bay City faithful. The Giants center fielder had collided with the wall. But when he'd risen to his feet, the ball was snug in his glove. The guy had made a sensational catch! I was out and the game was over.

"Ya got good wood, Titus!" Jimmy's father shouted out. "Ya got darn good wood!"

All the same, it was an out. And not any ordinary out. It was the final out of the game. You never want to make outs, but if there is one out you *never* want to make, it's the one that ends the game. That one hurts the most and that's the one that I'd just made. *Crap.*

My only consolation that Sunday night was that Laura was still there with me. I was one grumpy fellow, not fit company for man nor beast. But Laura was neither man nor beast.

Monday night's game pitted the Giants' number two pitcher, Marcus Kane, against Jorge Comellas, the Tijuana Teaser. Kane is a power pitcher who'd notched seventeen wins, Jorge a consummate junk dealer who'd kept us in games all season long. But on that night the Bay City Grays got a huge emotional lift. For appearing in our dugout loomed the figure of Deacon Lawler, back in uniform for the first time.

And when Whitey handed him the lineup card to take out to the umpires, our fans gave the Deacon an earth-shattering ovation. Even the umpires slapped him on the back, and the Giants' manager gave him a warm handshake.

The Deacon's presence made all the difference. We scored early and often and ran away with the game. Jorge was his usual tricksy self, and we took a 7-2 win. After the first two games, the Series was tied at a game apiece. Now it was San Francisco, here we come.

I'd never played in San Francisco, nor did I know the city well, though I'd made brief explorations a couple of times when we'd had games across the bay in Oakland. On sunlit, crystal-clear days, the City by the Bay sparkles. Most of the times I'd been there, though, it had been gray, damp, and chilly, reminding me of Mark Twain's crack about the coldest winter he ever experienced being the summer he'd lived in San Francisco. On the good side, the Giants no longer played in Candlestick Park, reputed to have been the coldest, windiest place to play in all of baseball.

No sooner had I settled into my hotel room and stretched out on the bed than the phone rang. Don't answer the dang thing, I told myself. And yet, thinking it was Laura making sure we'd arrived safely, I did. It wasn't Laura. Nor was it anyone else I would have expected it to be or wanted it to be. The voice on the other end belonged to Seamus Byrne. Good old smarmy solicitor Byrne.

It had been more than a year since my last direct contact with Seamus. That was that October day in Dublin when I'd tracked him down in the law offices of Gallagher, Slaney, and Byrne, the day I told him to leave Laura and me the hell alone or I'd skewer him atop the Dublin Spire like a feckin' Irish shish kebob. And my aggressive, go-right-at-'em approach that day even seemed to work, at least enough to get the callow youth who'd been dogging my footsteps to disappear in the Irish mist.

"Mr. Tyrus Duffy," came Seamus's distinctive voice over the line. "Laddy, you've been playin' some very grand baseball, now haven't ya just. Sure, it would be grand indeed if you and the lads could win just another few games. You'd be the champeens of the world, so you would."

"Seamus, me old pal, wonderful to hear from you," I said. "See you around, pal." And I hung up the phone.

The telephone immediately rang again. I waited a moment, then picked it up and said, "Joe's Bar and Grill."

"Ah, Tyrus, me lad, good ta see ya haven't lost yor fine sense o' humor."

"So what are you wanting, solicitor Byrne?"

"Oh, now laddy, could we not be havin' a wee friendly chat? Could we not, me dear sor?"

"Why would we want to do that?"

"I'm havin' some news you'll be wantin' ta hear, Tyrus. Good news, sor, naught but good news. Could we not be walkin' over to China Town? Havin' ourselves a wee bite? Just like old times? Like we did the first morning we met in Bay City?"

"And you are where?"

"Right here in the lobby of yor hotel, sor. Matter o' fact, it's my hotel too."

I sighed. Well, what the hell, I thought, might as well deal with it and get it over with. Good old solicitor Byrne, good old slippery solicitor Byrne.

Seamus was waiting for me in the lobby, and he leapt to his feet as I approached. I'd forgotten just how short he really was. He looked like an oversized leprechaun or perhaps a tall-ish hobbit. He was grinning like an imp, looking for all the world like he was delighted to see me. The feeling wasn't mutual. I trusted solicitor Seamus Byrne about as far as you could sling a rat.

As we walked down O'Farrell toward Union Square, I asked him what'd brought him to San Francisco. "You've strayed a bit far from your patch, haven't you?"

"Ah, well, one of the lads went 'n got himself into a bit of a scrape," he said. "The embassy didn't want to touch it, so the family asked if we could help out a wee bit."

"So the lad's part of the Mick Slattery clan?" I asked.

"No, no, not really. But he's from a wealthy and well-connected family," Seamus admitted, not wanting to go further into details. Okay, fair enough, I thought, this time you're in it just for the money. I was glad, anyway, to know that Seamus's presence had nothing to do with me — or with an acquaintance of mine named James Patrick Devlin.

A couple of minutes later we were strolling through the ornate archway that leads into San Francisco's Chinatown. It's more impressive than anything in New York's Chinatown; and yet for me the area south of Canal Street in Manhattan has always had more appeal than the tacky souvenir shops and glitzy restaurants that line San Francisco's Grant Avenue. Still, you can't deny there are plenty of terrific places to eat there, and eat we did, Seamus matching me every bit of the way.

"Do ya mind if I just take that last wee egg roll?" Seamus asked.

"You hungry or something, Seamus?"

"Well, sor, ya don't get food like this in Ireland's little take-away shops, do you now?" No, I had to admit, you certainly do not.

"So best get it while you can, eh?" Seamus continued.

A little while later, as Seamus noshed vigorously on his moo shu pork, he finally got down to business. "So rumor has it, Mr. Duffy, that you've gone and got yorself into the hotel business. You and Kathleen Brogan."

"The Glen Tiernan Priory Hotel?"

"That would be the place."

"I'm one of a group of backers, Seamus, that's true enough. Thought it looked like a pretty good long-term investment."

"I t'ink yor surely right. I told Mick just that. So did Kathleen. Which was probably why he chose not to buy the place. Much as he loved Kathleen, Mick hated it when she contradicted him, and he 'specially hated it when he knew she were right and he were wrong."

"So you advised him to buy it?"

"Yes, though when I realized how strongly he felt about it, I let the matter go." Yes, I'll bet you did, I said to myself, you sycophantic bum-licker.

"So what's this good news you have for me?"

"Part of it was just to tell you that you made a wise purchase with the hotel."

"I'm glad you approve, Seamus, but you could have told me that over the phone."

"Ah, but then I wouldn'ta got to enjoy your most delightful company."

"And what else?" I said, knowing there had to be a what else.

"Nothing much, really. Though, how would you feel about buying a castle?"

"*What?*"

"Well, sor, you already own a most lovely Irish hotel. Surely the next step would be to have your very own Irish castle?"

"Some cold, dank, weed-grown pile of stones?"

"Well, yes, there is that. But in the case of this particular pile of stones, there's already been a substantial effort at renovation. Quite close to completion, actually, and it won't require much more to turn it into somethin' quite special. You could t'ink of it as a grand adventure. Or you could t'ink of it, sor, as something out of an old book about knights and damsels, with you, sor, as lord of the manor."

"So what you're saying, Seamus, is that a client of yours has ruined himself financially pursuing his pipe dream, and now you're casting about to find some gullible American to take it off his hands so he can recoup his losses."

"Well, yes, you could say that," Seamus admitted. "Or you could say that the terrible downturn in our economy has made it impossible for my client to continue his noble effort to restore one of Ireland's most historic buildings, to the sad detriment of Irish heritage. And you could say that here's a golden opportunity for a wise investor, one such as yorself, sor, to acquire a stunning property at a most reasonable price. If that wise investor were to do that, he would be doing both my client and the Republic of Ireland a large and grand favor."

"This castle," I said, "it's not the Grail Castle, by any chance?"

"Which one would that be?" Seamus replied, flummoxed by my remark.

"You know, the one with the Fisher King? The one that's been waiting all these years for the Grail Knight to arrive and ask the question to be asked in order to heal the Maimed King?"

"Em . . . er . . . that one," Seamus said, not having a clue what I was talking about. "Well, no, p'rhaps it's not that one. In fact, it's really more a Norman tower house than what you probably t'ink of as a true castle. Still 'n all, sor, it's quite a stunning place and a stunning opportunity."

"So Seamus, where is this stunning place located?"

"Why, it be right there in County Clare. Indeed, not so very far from the Cliffs of Moher. Not such a very long drive from yor own hotel, so it is."

"What would you think if a wise investor named Jimmy Devlin were to step forward and take advantage of this stunning opportunity? How would you feel about that?"

"Em, er . . . well sor, that might not be such a grand idea. No, not so grand a-tall. Devlin's a bit out of favor with the lads, don't you know."

"The lads? You mean Rory and Declan? Speaking of those lads, Seamus, I guess they were out there on the boat the night Mick had his accident. Do you think one of those fine lads might've had a hand in that so-called accident? You were there too, right? What's your version of what happened?"

"Nah, nah, the lads had nothin' ta do with it. We were all together when Mick wandered off by hisself. They loved their Uncle Mick. They would never've done such a t'ing."

"So you really think it was just an accident?"

"What else could it have been, sor?" What else indeed, I thought. One thing it could have been was a textbook case of kin-slaying.

"You ever heard," I said, "of an old Irish tale called 'The Sons of Turin'?"

"Rings a faint bell, but I don't recall the details."

"It's about Brian and his brothers, about how they murdered Lugh's father, bringing down a curse upon Ireland that can never be removed. It's known as one of the Three Most Sorrowful Tales of Ireland."

"So what's yor point, sor?"

"I think you know what my point is, Seamus. Do you know how that story ended? With Lugh paying those fellows back big time."

"No, sor, the lads surely didn't do for Mick. Now, there's them that t'ink Kathleen Brogan mighta had a hand in it. But I don't agree with them, neither. It were an accident, sor, and not anyt'ing else."

"So," I said, drastically changing the subject, "will you be coming to our game?"

"Em, no, no, alas no. But I'll be watchin' ya on the telly, that I will. And may the luck o' the Irish be with ya."

"Thanks, Seamus. And I hope it's not the same luck that Brian and his brothers had at the hands of Lugh."

The luck of the Irish was with us in San Francisco. All three games were well-played, well-pitched ballgames, and all three were decided by a single run. We won the first game behind the solid, steady pitching of Terry O'Grady; then lost the next, despite the fact that Alfred King held the Giants to three runs. In the third, which was Game Five in the Series, Jimmy went against Tim Elphinstone for a second time. This time it was Jimmy who came away the winner, three to two. That game featured the only home run we hit in San Francisco, a monstrous bomb off the bat of Bump Rhodes that *kersplashed* into McCovey Cove.

So, the luck of the Irish being with us, we'd taken two out of the three games in the City by the Bay. And when the Bay City Grays baseball players boarded the plane at the San Francisco airport

to fly back home, we held a three-games-to-two lead in the World
Series. Just one more measly win — one more measly win! — and
we'd be the champeens of the world.

During the long flight home to Bay City, we were a fairly subdued
bunch. We knew we were on the brink of achieving something
remarkable, remarkable for each of us individually, and remarkable
for the city whose uniforms we wore. But there would be no
premature celebrating on this flight. Counting your chickens before
they'd finished incubating was the biggest jinx in baseball. So the
drinking and card playing were less raucous than usual. Jimmy and
I played a game of cribbage, and then I worked on a crossword
puzzle for a while as Jimmy dozed, slumped against the airplane
window.

"What's a nine-letter word for carriage?" I asked Bump, who was
seated across the aisle from me. "Starts with c."

"You're asking me?" Bump said.

"I am," I said, "I'm asking you."

"Nine-letter word for carriage, starts with c. Uh . . . how about
cabriolet?"

"Nope. I thought of that but it doesn't work. Good guess,
though."

"Uh . . . how about charabanc?"

"Charabanc?"

"Yeah, one of them French things? You know, for sightseers?"

"Wow. Bump, I'm impressed! Thanks, dude, you're a whiz."

"Just got lucky, Duff. Don't ask me no more, okay? I'm quitting
while I'm still battin' a thousand." Bump Rhodes, I thought, with his
high school education, knew words like 'cabriolet' and 'charabanc.'
Who the heck *was* this kid?

"Hey, Duff?" Bump said.

"Yeah?"

"Listen, Duff, I just want to tell you how much I appreciate all
you done for me this year."

"I haven't done anything," I said.

"Yeah, Duffy, you have. If it wasn't for you and the Deacon, I'd still be playing in the minors somewhere. Or maybe not even playing anywhere at all. Man, gettin' me to try hittin' left-handed, that was 'bout the best thing ever happened to me. I really didn't want to do it, neither. Boy, I sure am glad you made me give it a try."

"It wasn't that big a deal, Bump, not after discovering that your left eye was your dominant eye."

"Yeah, but you were the guy who went 'n figured that out. And you were the guy who made me try hittin' from the left side when I really didn't want to. Shoot, Duff, you went 'n saved my worthless hide. But you know what else? Aside from savin' my worthless hide, you sure have been a good friend to me. Can't tell ya how much that means to me." This conversation was beginning to embarrass me, so I did my best to shift it in another direction.

"What are you going to do after the Series?" I asked him. "You heading home to see your folks?"

"Oh yeah, but not right off. Violet wants me to come to Dublin. So I think I'll do that first." That was what I had expected, but up 'til now he hadn't said anything about it.

"Did you know that a bunch of us will be in the west of Ireland?" Bump nodded that he did. "So you and Violet would be more than welcome if you wanted to come too."

"Thanks, Duff. That'll depend on her. Don't know much about where and when she'll be playing. I'm just gonna do whatever she wants. All I want is to spend some time with her. Seems like forever since I seen her." It had been about six weeks, really, but there are times in life when six weeks can seem like forever.

"Did you hear about my castle?"

"Your *castle*? I heard 'bout your hotel. Didn't hear nuthin' 'bout no castle."

"No, I don't have a castle. It's kind of a joke, really. There's this Irish guy who's been trying to get me to buy what he says is a castle.

Jimmy wants to go and take a look at it. So does Laura. I guess it might be kind of fun at that."

Suddenly a strange look came over the face of my young friend. "No, Duffy. Don't you be doin' that," he finally said. "That ain't a good idea a-tall."

"What? Why ever not?"

"Don't know, really. But I've got a bad feeling about it, Duff. Something a-tellin' me you really shouldn't be doin' that."

"Bump, c'mon man, it's just an old pile of stones. It's not any big deal."

"No it ain't. That's not some place you should be going. Call it a premonition. But listen, Duff. You have to be stayin' away from that place. I feel certain about that."

"Geez, Bump, are you psychic or something?"

"Well, sometimes I kinda am."

So Bump had had a *premonition*? I didn't even know he knew the word, let alone words like 'cabriolet' or 'charabanc.' How could a simple country boy from lower Alabama know words like that? Had he been the spelling bee champion of Conuceh County? Who was this kid, anyway?

"Okay," I said, "I'll keep it in mind."

"I'm serious," he said. "Somethin' terrible happened there, and I have this feeling that something terrible might be a-goin' to happen there again."

"Bump, you don't even know what place I'm talking about."

"No, I don't. But at the same time, Duff, I kinda do."

36

"Tyrus, honey, it's your mother," came the voice from the answering machine. "Your team is doing so wonderfully well, hon, I just can't tell you how excited I am for you." Thanks, Mom, I thought, I'm sure you're just jumping up and down. So get to the point, Mom, what do you need now?

"Ty, honey, do you remember the watercolor I sent you awhile back? It turns out I sent you the wrong one. I'm embarrassed to say it, but I need to get that one back. I'm sure you like it – how could anyone not like it?" Then came the faint sound of my mother's lovely soft laugh, the one she's used to charm many a man. "But I have another one for you that's even more wonderful and more valuable. You'll like this one even more, I promise you."

So Mom, I was thinking, you accidentally sent me the real thing and now you want to send me a beautiful fake, figuring an amateur like me won't know the difference? Well, you'd probably be right.

"I know you have your mind on other things right now, and I apologize for bothering you. But it's terribly important I get the watercolor back as soon as possible. I can't give you a number where you can reach me, but I'll try to figure out this complicated time thing and call you again tomorrow morning, your time. I think your game tomorrow is in the evening, so I'll try to call you mid-morning. Okay? Love you, honey. Talk to you tomorrow."

I wondered if she really did send me the original Turner watercolor by accident, having meant to send me a forgery. Or maybe she'd burned through the money she'd made on the Picasso drawing and now found herself lusting after the money she'd sacrificed by giving me the Turner. Or perhaps she'd run across some sucker willing to pay a king's ransom for the Turner. Knowing Mom, it might be any of those things; or something else I hadn't thought of.

I walked down the hall to my study and stood in front of the Turner – *my* Turner. I'd come to love it and felt very possessive of it. I didn't much like the idea of giving it back.

And as I was standing there looking at it, I suddenly got the shivers. That romantic ruined castle perched on the hill overlooking the water — it brought to mind the castle Seamus Byrne had told me about in Ireland; the same castle Bump Rhodes had insisted I stay away from.

You stupid jerk, I said to myself. It's just a frigging watercolor painting. It's just a frigging pile of stones. Why are you giving yourself the shivers? Why indeed? And yet . . . I was.

It rained for the next two days. Incessantly. Game 6 of the Series, scheduled for the second of those days, had to be pushed back. That was good and it was bad. Good because now if the Series went to a seventh game, it might be possible for Jimmy to pitch again. Bad because Jorge Comellas, scheduled to go for us in Game Six, would be pitching on extra rest, and he was always more effective when his arm was a little bit tired. When he was too strong, the junk balls he served up didn't do as much. Both days we took BP beneath the stadium. The field was unusable, and once we'd finally be able to resume play, the outfield was still going to be a quagmire.

My mother's call came about eleven that first morning. I'd had a couple of hours to rehearse what I was going to say to her. But of course once we got talking, all my pre-planning went out the window.

"Hi, Mom," I said, picking up the phone, knowing it had to be her.

"Oh, honey, thank goodness. I was afraid I might have the time wrong."

"Hi, Mom," I said again.

"Hi, hon," she said. "It's wonderful to hear your voice."

"How's things in Prague?" I said.

"I wouldn't know, Ty. I haven't been there for a while. Right now I'm in Florence."

"Wow. Dante, Petrarch, and Boccaccio. The Medici. Galileo. And now Clare Laughlin too. A real rogues' gallery."

"Do you play today?" she said, ignoring my foolish maunderings.

"Off day today, with heavy rain forecast for tomorrow. So, who knows when we'll get the game in."

"Ty, did you listen to the message I left you?"

"I did, Mom."

"Oh, good. So you can return the watercolor? I'm really embarrassed that I sent you the wrong one. But you'll absolutely adore the new one. It's even lovelier than the one I sent."

"I'd return it to you if I could, but right now I can't."

"*What?*" I imagined the look of horror on my mother's face.

"The thing is, I don't have it. My friend Laura took it up to New York to have it appraised." That wasn't true, but when you're dealing with the Queen of Lies, there isn't any law against telling a tiny white lie yourself, is there? Besides, I wanted to know what her reaction to that particular possibility might be. Her initial reaction, anyway, was silence.

"Umm," she finally said, "do you think she's already done that? If she hasn't, could you tell her it won't be necessary? Maybe, if she's willing, she could send it to me from New York?"

"Mom, would you mind telling me the *real* reason you want it back?" Again there was silence.

"Tyrus, I resent what you're implying! I have already told you the real reason — I simply sent you the wrong one. Honey, why do you have to be so ungrateful?"

"Geez, Mom! I bailed you out of a huge jam — to the tune of $225,000 — and you're calling *me* ungrateful? Mom, you are really something else!"

Oh, hell. I hadn't meant to say anything like that to her. Now she was crying. So much for my carefully planned words.

"Look, Mom, I'm sorry. But I can't help thinking there's more to all of this than you are telling me." I heard my mother doing her best to collect herself, finally breathing out a huge sigh.

"Ty, honey," she said in a somewhat contrite-sounding voice, "okay, here's the truth. I need it back because the owners want it back."

"The owners? I thought *you* were the owner."

"I mean the people I got it from. The previous owners. They've changed their minds and are now willing to pay a great deal more to get it back than I originally paid." And just how much was that, I couldn't help thinking. Nothing? I was the one who'd paid for the two unspecified works of art, wasn't I?

"So what happened to the money I paid to George and Lennie? I thought that was to pay back the previous owners."

"George and Lennie? I don't know any George and Lennie. I paid the owners $75,000 for the watercolor and now they're willing to pay $150,000 to get it back."

It appeared that the Queen of Liars had found her footing once more. It was probably true that she didn't know anything about George and Lennie; but if she really paid $75,000 for the Turner, then my name is Boris Spasski.

"Okay, Mom, okay. Tell me where you'd like it sent. I can't promise it'll get there any time soon, but I'll see what I can do."

I jotted down the address, and we wound up our conversation fairly quickly. She actually thanked me for being so understanding and wished us well in our games.

But the truth, I strongly suspected, was something different from what she'd told me. I felt sure she wasn't returning the watercolor to its previous owners. No, my mother must've found a rich new buyer. But what I didn't know, and probably never would know, was whether she'd sent me the Turner by mistake, or whether she'd sent it out of a momentary fit of generosity. I hoped it was the latter. Somehow, I doubted it.

Chuck invited me for dinner that night, and he and Boog the cat greeted me warmly at the door.

"Wow, Chuck, this place looks great!" Chuck had recently had his apartment completely redecorated, and it looked stupendous. Even better was the fact that Chuck and his decorator, while working closely together, had really hit it off. The emotional upheaval I'd witnessed a month or so ago was ancient history.

Boog was doing his thing, purring and rubbing himself against my ankles. "Hey, you knuckle-headed old Boogster," I said, reaching down and petting him.

"Don't know why Boog is so undiscriminating," Chuck said. "I try to teach him, but nature always overcomes nurture."

"It's probably my catnip body lotion," I said.

"It wouldn't surprise me," Chuck said. "I think that's what turns on my mother, too."

Over dinner I asked Chuck if he could do me a favor.

"A favor? What is it?" he said. "I hope it's something delicious."

"No, 'fraid not. I need you to put something in your safe for me." I knew that in Chuck's closet was a super-duper hi-tech contraption not even James Bond could crack. Chuck claimed he needed it for business purposes, but I suspected he might also need it for personal purposes.

"It could still be delicious," Chuck said, "depending on what it might be."

"It's the watercolor," I said. "Seems it's more valuable than I thought, and that my having it isn't as much a secret as I thought."

"The Turner your mother purloined?" I had not told Chuck that she'd "purloined" it. But being no dummy, he'd figured that out on his own. "The cops are hot on your trail?"

"Not the cops. The robbers."

"See? I told you it might be delicious. Mystery. Intrigue. Danger. High crimes and misdemeanors."

"Don't get carried away, Chuck."

"I love to get carried away, Tyrus. You should know that by now."

37

Game 6 was in the books, and there would be a Game 7.

We'd had our chances in Game 6 but squandered them. I was one of the chief squanderers. In the fourth, with men on first and third and one out, I tried to push one through the hole to right. I chopped a one-hopper to the second baseman who turned it into an inning-ending double play. In the seventh, I ripped a gapper to left-center, scoring Bump. But as I rounded first I skidded on a muddy patch of infield dirt. Instead of wisely retreating to first, I tried for second. The throw beat me and I was toast. We went down five to three. The Series was knotted at three games apiece.

In Game 7, Jimmy and Tim would face each other for the third time, both pitching on three days' rest. Jimmy had done okay pitching on short rest in our season-ending game against the Yankees, and we hoped for a repeat performance. But Dave Rubenstein didn't like it. He pleaded with Whitey to use Alfred King or Terry O'Grady, both fully rested. Whitey wouldn't budge. Jimmy was the guy. Win or lose, Jimmy was the guy. Whitey was implacable. That turned out to be a bad thing.

Jimmy's father and my brother Billy, who'd been in Bay City for Game 6, stayed on for the final game. Sarah was home with Marian; Penny Sutherland couldn't afford to miss any more days of teaching; and Laura had a major opening at the museum in New York. So it was just us guys. Which was fine, for Billy and Henry Devlin are the perfect companions in times of high stress. With those two around, I'd have no problem staying loose.

In the morning, the three of us walked over to Maggie's Grill for breakfast. It was Hank Devlin's kind of place, and Billy, who'd been there several times before, loved to banter with the waitresses, especially with my friend Susan.

"Coffee all around?" Susan said, as we slid ourselves onto three stools at the counter. "Hello, there, baby brother," she said to Billy. "Haven't seen you in a while."

Henry Devlin guffawed at the baby brother remark.

"Hey, good lookin', what ya got cookin'?" came Billy's predictably cornball reply.

"I can see it's going to be one of those days," I said to Jimmy's father, grimacing.

"Oh well, let these two youngsters have their fun," he replied. "No harm in a little innocent fun."

"Innocent?" Billy said. "Nothin' innocent about it."

"Innocent?" said Susan as she filled our mugs, "Nothin' innocent about it, sir." Then she gave Henry a big wink. "By the way, I appreciate being called a youngster."

"Banjo," he said, "I think you brung us to the right place. Folks 'round here seem mighty friendly. Actually, now I think of it, I think I seen this young woman at some of your games. Wasn't she with a kid?"

"Her nephew Cody. I've already left them a pair of tickets for tonight. They'll be sitting just a few seats from you guys."

"Works for me," Billy said.

"Yeah, but son," said Mr. Devlin, deciding to get in on the thing, "I got a feeling she's way too much woman for you."

Several people close by had been paying attention to our conversation, because right then they all broke out laughing.

"Oh, man," Billy said, "now ya gone and hurt my feelings."

"How 'bout I buy you a beer at the game?"

"How 'bout you buy me two?"

The atmosphere in the ballpark wasn't at all like it had been in our season finale against the Yankees. Then there'd been a lot of tension, even hostility, between the Grays fans and the Yankees fans, and that went for the players, too. Now the mood was festive. Our fans never really believed we'd get this far, and every advance was a delightful bonus. That was true even for Whitey Wiggins. It had been his ultimate desire to *play* in a World Series, not actually to *win* one. And yet. . . .

Jimmy went through his usual pre-game regimen of stretching, followed by long-toss, followed by twenty minutes of hot towels, then more stretching, and finally a slow and proper warmup out in the bullpen. We'd learned long ago it wasn't a good idea to talk to Jimmy before a game, not unless you wanted to have your head chewed off. Today it was the Deacon who caught his warmup pitches, and the Deacon's remarks were limited to "nice one, Jimmy," "that's the stuff, kiddo," and "now you're bringing it, son!"

Behind closed doors that morning there'd been a heated argument about who would pitch after Jimmy had gone as far as he could, regardless of whether it was three innings or six. Dave Rubenstein, who'd wanted Alfred King out there to begin with, favored bringing in Alfred. Ray Stutz, our third base coach and a close personal friend of Whitey's, pushed for Terry O'Grady, who'd pitched well in Game 3. But both of those guys were rookies – in Terry's case, he'd only had half a season in the big leagues – and that gave Whitey real pause. Whitey wanted it to be a veteran of the wars. By game time, I wasn't sure how the matter had been settled, or even if it had been.

As the players and coaches from both teams were introduced, they trotted out to stand on the first and third base lines. The fans cheered for both teams, but their loudest ovation was for Deacon Lawler. Then, when a local high school choir launched into a stirring rendition of the National Anthem, I became just as teary-eyed as the next guy, which in my case was Bump Rhodes, who was pretty damn teary-eyed. As the notes of the music faded, forty-eight thousand throats shouted "Play Ball!" It was Game 7 of the World Series – a little boy's dream come true.

As Jimmy was making his final warmup tosses to Bump, he had a get-the-hell-away from me look on his face, so I didn't trot in for a final encouraging word, as I usually did. Nor did Bump. Jimmy feckin' Devlin was on his own.

Jimmy started strong, with a strikeout, a fly out, a walk, and another strikeout. And in the bottom half we scratched out a run with Juan's walk, my sacrifice bunt, and Bobby Radley's run-scoring single.

Jimmy staggered through the second, yielding a pair of singles and a walk to fill the bases, before getting out of the inning by means of a five-to-four-to-three double play. It was worse for him in the third. A single and a pair of homers gave the Giants a three-to-one lead. The Elf, on the other hand, appeared to be settling in.

In the half top of the fourth, Jimmy got the first two guys out. And then he hit the wall — a walk, a hit batsman, and another walk. Dave trotted out to the mound, and as he did, Whitey was on the phone to the bullpen, where we already had a couple of guys loosening up. Staring into the first-base dugout from my position at second base, I could actually read Whitey's lips: "Tell Stan he'll be coming in." Stan? Whitey wanted Stan Foubert? What about Alfred King? What about Terry O'Grady? Oh, geez.

Stan Foubert was our forgotten man. Up until August he'd been our number two starter, right behind Jimmy. And in August, when everyone else on the staff was pitching well, Stan pitched poorly in five straight starts. Suddenly, he had *nada*. And so that was it for Stan. Whitey sat him down and only used him for mop-up duty the rest of the year. In the entire post season, Stan had only thrown two innings. And now, in the deciding game of the World Series, Stan was the guy that Whitey wanted? Oh, geez.

Jimmy stayed in to pitch to the next hitter, who worked him to a full count. Then Jimmy unloaded an inside fastball that brushed the guy's shirt. Jimmy had hit the batter with the bases loaded!

Whitey walked out slowly. Jimmy's eyes remained on the ground as Whitey asked him for the ball. Jimmy Devlin had given it his best shot, but today it wasn't to be. It was only the fourth inning, and we were already down four to one. Jimmy trotted off the field to a standing ovation. The fans were acknowledging his fabulous year, surely a Cy Young-winning season. The only person in the stadium who was disappointed in Jimmy today was Jimmy. I glanced over at where Mr. Devlin and Billy were seated, and both of them were giving Jimmy two thumbs-up. But I doubt if Jimmy saw them.

In came Stan. The wily old veteran. Until Jimmy arrived on the scene last year, Stan Foubert had been our number one guy. He'd done well this year, too, until his August collapse. Did he have anything left in the tank? We would soon find out. The first guy he faced ripped a wicked line drive in my direction. I leaped as high as I could and snared it, ending the inning and ending the Giants' biggest threat so far.

Tim was able to hang in there a bit longer than Jimmy had, but now he too was flagging. In the bottom of the fourth Spike Bannister hit a solo homer, and Bump whacked a double, though he ended up stranded on second. Giants four, Grays two.

In the fifth Stan Foubert started slowly, yielding a bloop single, benefitting from a double play, walking a guy, giving up another soft single, and finally getting a fly-ball out. Two hits and a walk for the Giants in the fifth but no runs. In our half, Zook Zulaski singled, stole second, moved to third on Juan's ground out, and scored on my single to center. After five complete it was Giants four, Grays three.

We were still very much in the game, and suddenly Stanley Foubert found himself and became the French Chef of old, slicing and dicing like nobody's business. In order for Stan to be successful, he needed to locate his pitches to perfection. Now he was. He was painting the black, moving his pitches in and out, up and down, keeping the hitters guessing. Bump wasn't even calling the game; Stan was calling his own game. Bump Rhodes was just along for the ride. And it was a hell of a ride.

In the sixth and seventh innings, Stan retired six men in a row. He recorded no strikeouts, and yet not a single batter hit a ball out of the infield. Stan was inducing nubbers and pop-ups. Juan and I had a lot of work those two innings, work which was absolutely our cup of tea.

Still, we were down by a run, and although Tim Elphinstone was no longer out there, we weren't faring so well against the guys who were. We hadn't had a hit since the fifth.

When Stan trotted back out to start the eighth inning, I think everyone felt we were pushing our luck. Why not bring in Scotty Evers or Joe Oliver, our normal setup guy? Or the hard-throwing Alfred King? But no, it was Stan who was still out there.

He gave up a lead-off triple on a ball that hit high up on the right-center field wall and bounded away from Spike. Then he walked the next guy. Oh geez. But with remarkable aplomb, the French Chef went right back to work. Up to that point he hadn't had a single strikeout. Three batters later, Stan Foubert had recorded a trio of strikeouts, and the Giants hadn't scored!

But we didn't either. We got a couple guys on but left them out there. So going into the ninth, we were still down a run. Now all eyes were on the bullpen, where Jesus Hernandez was tuned and ready to go. And all eyes watched in amazement as Stan Foubert walked slowly back out to the mound.

Against all odds, Stan, after a shaky start in the fifth, had given us three glorious innings. Wasn't that enough? Wasn't it time to return to our normal play book? Apparently not.

On Stan's first pitch, the Giant batter drilled a ball toward the left-field corner, and Nick Gurganis, at full gallop, made a very sweet backhanded grab before banging into the wall. *Whew.* One out. When the next guy singled sharply to right, even Whitey had seen enough. He came out to the mound and took the ball. He gave Stan a little pat on the rump, then motioned for Jesus. As Stan Foubert walked slowly back toward the dugout, he received the same thunderous ovation as Jimmy. Stan's career was all but over, but he'd given us a last great effort.

Jesus came in and struck out the first two guys, ending the inning. Now it was on to the bottom of the ninth inning. Our last chance.

I led off, my fifth at-bat on the day. Normally I look at a lot of pitches, and with us down a run, I would surely be trying to make the pitcher throw strikes and possibly draw a walk. And on the first pitch, I dropped a bunt down the third-base line. I sprinted toward first like the hounds of hell were nipping at my heels. I didn't see what happened, but apparently the third baseman, taken completely by surprise, let the ball roll, hoping it would go foul. It didn't.

So the tying run was on, and the heart of the order was coming up. And then Bobby Radley, our hitting star, proceeded to strike out. And so did Lou Tolliver. Damn and blast! There I was, still stuck on first. Now with Todd Cottington coming up, the Giants brought in a lefty to pitch to the left-handed batter. Bad move. The guy walked Todd on four pitches, moving me into scoring position. With the right-handed hitting Spike Bannister coming up next, the Giants brought in that hulking brute named Kareem Gibran. And the guy proceeded to walk Spike! Now the sacks were loaded, with me on third.

Batting for the Bay City Grays was Bump Rhodes. He'd be hitting lefty against the right-handed Gibran. Bases loaded, two outs, tying run on third base. Oh, man.

For a split second, I wondered if the situation reminded my brother of a similar time when I was on third and he was the batter? It certainly did me. I hoped this time the outcome would be different.

Bump took a strike. He stepped out and knocked the dirt from his spikes. He glanced down at Ray Stutz at third, who was shouting encouragement. Bump fouled one off, then took a pair of balls when Kareem tried to make him swing at pitches out of the zone. Bump didn't bite. Way to go, Bump.

Bump fouled off two more pitches, then took another ball. Now the count was full. The catcher scurried out to the mound and said something profound to Gibran like, "Don't you *walk* this f-ker!"

Kareem didn't walk Bump. With everything on the line, he gave Bump his very best fastball, right down the chute. Bump was late with his swing. But he caught just enough of the ball to send it my way. A soft little floater. The third baseman took two steps and dove. The ball eluded his outstretched glove. It trickled down the third base line into short left field.

I was in with the tying run. Todd Cottington, not our swiftest base runner, rounded third and scored right behind me.

We'd *won*! We'd damn well *won*! The Bay City Grays were the champeens of the world.

It was *jubilation time*, man was it ever! Our players poured out onto the field, piling on top of Bump, mobbing Todd, whacking each other for joy. And they were joined in doing that by a whole lot of fans who'd come out onto the field despite the best efforts of the security guys.

When I got the chance, I hugged Whitey Wigggins like there was no tomorrow. Our skipper was laughing and crying at the same time, crying big, wet tears of joy.

In the stands I saw Billy and Jimmy's father hugging the daylights out of Susan and Cody. And then I saw Chuck's mother plant a huge juicy kiss right on Hank Devlin's lips. Better him than me!

Yes indeed, we'd won the World Series, we'd actually won the World Series!

We'd won the World Series, and in just a few days from now, Laura and I would be heading off to Ireland together. Man, oh man, right at that moment it felt good to be alive.

38

The plane was making its final descent to Shannon Airport. Below, a patchwork of green fields spread out on both sides of the broad river estuary. It was seven-thirty in the morning, Ireland time, and a couple of sleep-deprived Americans made sure their seat belts were fastened and their trays secured in an upright position. This was the first time I'd ever arrived in Ireland when it wasn't raining. I hoped that was a good omen.

One nice thing about Ireland is that clearing passport control, picking up your luggage, and going through customs is relatively painless, and this time events at the car rental counter went smoothly also. Kat had offered to send the hotel van for us, but I'd told her not to bother. I wanted a car to get around in, and I knew there'd be sites Laura would want to visit. For her this was a vacation, and her idea of a vacation involved poking about in a lot of old places that might have article-potential for the museum's publications.

"Much of a drive to Galway?" she asked.

"About an hour if we head straight there. But why do I have this feeling that you've planned a few stops along the way."

"Only one," she said. "And it's hardly out of the way. It's near the town of Gort, an old monastery called Kilmacduagh. Has a round tower I'd like to photograph. Supposedly one of Ireland's best."

A year ago, when Laura was researching and photographing Ireland's most famous high crosses, we'd also seen some impressive round towers in the places we'd visited – Monasterboise, Kells, and Clonmacnois, which had a pair of them. But I'd never heard of Kilmacduagh.

The road northward toward Galway, the N18, now has dual carriageway all the way to Gort, which is about halfway to Galway, so we reached our turnoff about twenty-five minutes later.

"Gort," I said, "a most melodious name."

"Comes trippingly off the tongue," Laura said. "Probably named for some wild and wicked old Celtic chieftain now lost in the mists of time."

"Old Gort," I said, "Yes, I remember him well. Definitely not a guy to mess with. Not unless you have Bump Rhodes covering your back. Rory and Declan McManus can't hold a candle to old Gort."

"Rory and Declan? Mick Slattery's feckin' nephews?"

"Mick Slattery's feckin' nephews."

"Think we'll run into them?"

"Not if I can help it. I'm praying right now to the spirit of old Gort that we'll give those two lads a miss."

"No," Laura said a moment later, "never mind praying to old Gort. The town's not named for an ancient Celtic chieftain." Her nose was buried in her pocket guidebook. "Turns out 'gort' is a Gaelic word meaning 'a tilled field'."

"Don't believe everything you read," I said. "They just don't want people to know the terrible truth about old Gort — Gort the Mortifier we called him back then."

Laura glanced at me out of the corner of her eye, then decided the best course of action would be to ignore me.

We followed a narrow lane that was well signposted to a local golf course, the entrance to which we soon passed, but which was less well signposted to the monastic site. After a dozen or so twistings and turnings we reached our destination.

There, soaring above a scattering of gray-stone buildings, was a most impressive structure. "Oh goodness," Laura said, "what an inspiring sight!"

"It is," I agreed, "even for pagans like me and old Gort."

I swung the car into a small graveled parking area and switched off the engine. Laura was out the door in a flash, armed with two cameras and her guide books, a happy and excited young woman.

It was about 8:30 in the morning and Laura and I had this peaceful place all to ourselves. Those early Christian monks had loved their solitude, and they'd certainly found it here. The only ones enjoying that solitude now were a pair of jet-lagged Americans and some languidly grazing cows.

I left Laura to her investigating and photo taking, and after I'd meandered about the old buildings for a few minutes on my own, I decided to get the kinks out and circumambulate the entire site. I followed a little path which led from the parking area and took me in a wide circle. It felt great to give my legs a proper stretch after that long night in a cramped airline seat.

A chorus of songbirds regaled me from the adjacent glade. I recognized the lilting notes of a lark but not any of the others, and made a mental note to pick up a book on Irish birds. With little scheduled for the next few days, Laura and I should have plenty of time to explore Galway's bookshops.

As I walked, it dawned on me how fortunate I was. Here I was in a place of pastoral perfection with a beautiful woman I really cared about, a woman who, despite all logic, hadn't given up on me. Not only that, I was a member of the team that had just won the World Series! For me, those two facts were absolutely amazing, astounding, and stupefying. Suddenly appearing inside my head were lines I remembered from an Andrew Marvell poem — "*Meanwhile the mind, from pleasure less, / Withdraws into its happiness . . . To a green thought in a green shade.*"

But before long my thoughts returned to more immediate and mundane matters — to Kat Brogan, who was expecting us by late morning; and to Jack Strachan, who was now lending a hand with the golf course. Jack and Kat, I knew, had formed a fresh alliance, and Jack had even managed to bring a good few of the lads along with him into this new configuration. Losing Kathleen Brogan and Jack Strachan must've been a major blow to Rory McManus and to Mick Slattery enterprises. Now Kat and Jack seemed to be forming their own scaled down version of Mick Slattery enterprises, one in which I played an indirect but rather key role.

One thing I wasn't sure about was how James Patrick Devlin was going to fit into this arrangement. I guessed we would soon find out, since Jimmy would be arriving in a few more days, despite what everyone — with the sole exception of Kat — wanted. Maybe, since he'd gone back to Missouri first for a brief visit with the home folks, Penny would work a minor miracle and convince him to stay. Not bloody likely. Still, one could always hope.

Arriving on Jimmy's heels would be Lou, Todd, and Spike. Kat had reserved a large family room for them at the hotel, though I doubted we'd see much of them. They'd be playing one golf course or another from dawn till dusk, before making the rounds of Galway's pubs and clubs every night.

By the time I got back to the car park, Laura had had her fill. She looked cheerful, pink-cheeked, and extremely desirable. Once again the thought crossed my mind that I was one lucky bastard.

Before we climbed into the car I pulled Laura to me and held her for a moment. She seemed quite happy to be held.

"I know what," she said. "Why don't we run away to Ireland?"

"That's a grand idea, lass. It surely is."

As we stood there embracing, I couldn't help noticing a dark green Ford Fiesta drive past the car park, a car I'd already seen roll by a few minutes earlier. I had no reason to think that car had anything to do with us; yet seeing it twice in the space of five minutes in the remote countryside gave me a twinge of uneasiness.

We pulled out of the car park and drove back toward Gort, going in a direction opposite to that of the other car. In only a few minutes we were back on the N18 to Galway. But a little later, when I glanced into the rear-view mirror, two cars back of us I saw a dark green car. Was it the same car? I couldn't be sure.

We skirted Galway's city center and picked up the N59 that heads north toward Outherard. The hotel is a few miles out that road, north of the university and overlooking Lough Corrib, one of Ireland's largest lakes. When we spotted the sign for the Glen Tiernan Priory Hotel, I turned off onto the quarter-mile drive that leads to it. To our left was an expanse of green grass dotted with trees and shrubs, to our right one of the golf course fairways, where a couple of guys were just now trudging toward their balls, pushing their trolleys ahead of them. As was true for many of Ireland's courses, golfers had to walk the course because motorized carts weren't allowed.

"Look there, Ty Duffy, it's your hotel!" Laura declared. "And it looks exactly like the photo on the website."

It was a Victorian-looking rusty-red brick structure with Virginia Creeper, now in its full glory, covering large sections of the outer walls. Several high chimneys loomed above a slate roof; there were a couple of large oriel windows, and on the top floor, a series of dormers. Most of the building only dated back to the nineteenth century, but it had been erected on the site of a medieval priory, and some of the priory's original arches and masonry had been worked into the architectural design.

The driveway led us around the hotel's far corner, where the main entrance was located, and into the guests' car park, where maybe ten or twelve cars were parked. Standing by the pro shop and watching us, arms akimbo, was a hatchet-faced bloke with a lean and hungry look — Honest Jack Strachan himself.

39

"Ya made it, then," Jack said with a grin. "Come ta take a look at your hotel in the flesh. And ya won the big ballgames, too, didn't ya just. The drinks'll be on me, lad, they surely will."

"Jack, you old son of a gun, I'd like you to meet Laura."

"Nice ta meet ya, Laura," Jack said, a big smile on his lean and craggy face.

A moment later Kat Brogan came hurrying towards us from the hotel's main entrance. She and Laura exchanged hugs, and then it was my turn.

"Oh, Ty Duffy, ya went and won the World Series! What a grand and glorious thing that is."

"Thanks, Kat. The luck of the Irish was with us."

"No luck about it. You and Jimmy are the best, the very best. So, now," she said, turning to Laura, "what is it you'll be wantin'? Grand tour? Nice cup o' tea? Warm and cozy nap?"

"Cup of tea, grand tour, and then the nap," Laura said.

"Drink about half six?" Jack said to me. "In the lounge bar?'

"Works for me," I replied.

"Back to it, then." And Jack was on the move toward the pro shop.

As Kat, Laura, and I walked up the steps to the hotel entrance, I noticed a dark green car coming slowly down the drive. It stopped, did a U-turn, and headed back toward the main road. It looked like a Ford Fiesta. There seemed to be loads of the feckin' things in Ireland. Or maybe just the one?

"I've put you in a third-floor room with one of the best views of the lough," Kat said. "No lift, I'm afraid, but Sean'll help you with your bags. Come back down for tea whenever you're ready."

"Back in ten minutes," Laura said.

"C'mon, Sean," I said to the lad who was hefting Laura's suitcase, no easy task. "Tote that barge, lift that bale. You manage that one and I'll get these." Sean grinned as he began lifting and toting. Laura, holding the old-fashioned room key, bounded up the stairs ahead of us like a leggy young deer. I shared her excitement.

The large, high-ceiling room had a delightful charm. It was sparsely furnished with a four-poster double bed, an ornate wardrobe (in lieu of a closet), a tallboy chest of drawers, a wing chair and reading lamp, and a couple of wall mirrors with intricate wooden frames. There was no telephone, and the TV was discretely tucked away inside an ancient-looking wall cupboard. If Sean hadn't shown me where it was, I never would've found it.

From the one large dormer window we had a perfect view across the golf course toward Lough Corrib. The hotel property didn't extend as far as the lakeshore, along which I could see a scattering of white-washed cottages.

Sean hefted Laura's suitcase onto a small stand that groaned in protest but didn't collapse. I tossed my bag and backpack into a corner. Sean showed us the extra blankets and pillows on the top shelf of the wardrobe.

"This is grand, Sean." I handed him five euros. "Thanks for lifting and toting."

Laura checked out the bathroom, hung up a few outfits in the wardrobe, and declared herself ready for tea.

Kat's office took up one corner of the first floor, not far from the registration desk now being staffed by a teenage girl named Nadia. Kat had already been busy with the tea, which she now poured for Laura and herself, since I had declined.

"Ty Duffy," she said, "I fear you are strictly a coffee man."

"Not strictly. But I don't want anything right now, thanks."

"Coffee's the drink of the body," Kat said, "but tea is the drink of the soul."

I guess I'm more a body kind of guy, I thought, admiring the beautiful women in whose presence I now luxuriated — Kat Brogan, with her auburn hair and peaches and cream complexion; lovely

Laura, with her light-blue eyes and light-brown hair. I sat there with them for a few minutes as the two of them chatted away. Those two had formed a strong bond during that weekend in New York, way back in the early part of the season. My presence, obviously, was entirely superfluous.

"Think I'll wander a bit," I said, "then take a nap." They nodded at me dismissively and went right on with their chattering, not missing a single beat.

Behind the pro shop was the driving range. A couple of guys were hitting balls, and they looked even worse than I am. Maybe Jack would lend me some sticks and I could give these guys a few pointers.

"Help ya, sor?" came a deep and gravelly voice from behind me. I turned around and standing there, big as life, was my favorite member of Satan's Seraphim, Roddy Doolan, with shaved head, bulbous nose, piratical earring, and those Book of Kells tattoos on his massive forearms and bulging biceps. Roddy recognized me almost as soon as I'd recognized him.

"Well, if it ain't the big fella hisself. Come to check on yor hotel, then?"

"Hello, Roddy. I'm flattered that you remember me." The first time I'd run into him was in a coffee shop in Dingle called The Abbott's Habit. Later that same day, out on the Great Blasket, we'd nearly come to blows, which wouldn't have had a happy ending. Now, apparently, we were allies. One could hope, anyway.

"Wanna strike a few balls?"

"Not now, thanks, but in the next few days for sure." If I really were going to play a couple of rounds with Lou, Todd, and Spike, all good golfers, I would definitely need to sharpen up my game.

"Hey, Liam!" Roddy called out, "come on over and meet the big fella." A gangly, string bean of a lad with an unruly mop of red hair came loping over. "This here's Mr. Duffy, Liam. He's in charge, along with Miss Brogan." When I reached out my hand, the lad shyly did too. "Liam's a quiet one. Makes a nice change from Miss

Brogan and Jack," Roddy said with a grin.

I bid them adieu and wandered about the hotel grounds — well-tended grass, a scattering of trees I struggled to identify, clumps of shrubberies that probably bloomed in the spring, including some rhododendrons and fuchsias.

Okay, now it was nap time. Never mind the grand tour. Back in our room, I splashed water on my jet-lagged face and stared into the mirror where I saw an early-middle-aged guy staring back at me, a guy that a little freckled-faced, sandy-haired kid had somehow turned into. He was no beauty, but not so awfully bad, I told myself. Billy, ironically, was the one who'd inherited my mother's beautiful, distinctive, gray-green eyes. I'd got my father's washed-out blue ones. Still, I'd much rather share traits with my father than my mother.

Jack Strachan was sitting alone at a table in a far corner of the lounge, the pint glass in front of him already empty.

"More of the same, Jack?" I said, as I approached.

"That'd be grand. Pint o' Guinness, if ya please."

"Two jars of Guinness," I told the round little barman. There was already a full pint settling on the counter. He'd anticipated Jack's next order.

I set our drinks on the table and sat down across from Honest Jack. "To your very good health, Jack," I said, lifting my glass.

"And ta yours, Duffy." We drank, me drinking even more deeply than Jack. That first taste of real Irish Guinness is always a special treat. Makes going to Ireland worth it just for that.

"So Jack," I said, after wiping my mouth with the back of my hand, "what's the deal with all these dark-green Ford Fiestas I keep seeing all over the place?"

"Ah, ya spotted 'em, did ya? Good on ya, Duffy. What's the deal with 'em? Think they're bein' smart, tryin' ta spook us, is all. That's a real laugh, that is. Those pansies ever get up the nerve to try anything, Roddy and I'll sort 'em out in a hurry."

"Rory's boys?"

"Oh yeh. Not exactly the best and the brightest."

"You don't think they'd try to do anything rash, do you, like burn down the hotel?"

"You're not fully insured?" Jack said with a wink. I assumed I was, though Jack's question made me nervous. Still, Larry Berkman and his pals would never have overlooked something as crucial as that.

"Nah, I don't think they'd go so far as that," Jack went on, "though we do keep a sharp eye out. And we got some pretty good security cameras too, ones that ain't too noticeable to the ordinary Joe." I guess not, since I hadn't spotted any of them.

"Why should they care that you and Kat have chosen to go it alone?"

"Various reasons. A matter of loyalties, for one, though I'd say we've been more loyal to Mick and his ideals than they have. But jealousy's a big one also. Kat did somethin' smart that they were too dumb ta do. Rory hates it that she's better at the business than he is. And that she's gone and stuck her thumb in his eye. And he don't like it so much that I've chosen her over him. Sure, it's a big family feud, it is. And family feuds can be the best donnybrooks of 'em all."

"It'll blow over eventually, though, won't it?"

"Em . . . I wouldn't be too sure. T'ings don't always blow over with the Irish. Harborin' a hurt, deserved or not, 'tis bred in the bone. And lookit, Duffy, if yor pal is comin' over here, that just might give 'em the excuse they're looking for."

"Excuse to do what?'

"That's what we'll be findin' out, now, won't we?"

Three drinks and a plate of fish and chips later, I was hailed by Nadia from the reception desk. "There's a message for you, sir," she said, handing me a slip of paper.

It was from my brother Billy. What it said was: "Mom wants you to call her. I didn't tell her where you are but said I'd try to track you down. She sounded worried. But then, why else would she bother to call? Sorry to intrude upon your good times. Cheers, Billy." Then there was a phone number.

The girl said I could use the phone in Kat's office and showed me how to get an outside line. "Thanks a lot," I said, and waited until she'd closed the door before punching in the long sequence of numbers.

"Tyrus?" said the anxious voice on the other end of the line. "Is that you, honey?"

"Hi, Mom. Yep, it's me."

"Oh, honey, thank goodness. Honey, that watercolor I asked you to send? Have you sent it yet?" She was referring to the Turner watercolor I liked so much, the one she'd given me before having the gall to ask for it back.

"Actually, I haven't. I've been kind of preoccupied lately with a little thing called the World Series." My loving, caring, oh-so-sensitive mother skipped right over my mention of the World Series. No questions, no congratulations, no nothing.

"So you haven't sent it yet? Oh, thank goodness for that. Don't send it, Ty, please don't send it."

"*Don't* send it?"

"No, honey, please don't send it. It turns out that there are some not very nice people here who are looking for it. I've sworn to them that I don't have it. Which is true." Yeah, I thought, but just barely.

"Could you put it somewhere safe? Somewhere no one is likely to find it?"

"I already have," I said, thinking of Chuck's secret, super hi-tech safe. Even if someone were to ransack my apartment in my absence, they wouldn't think of doing that to Chuck's apartment. Besides, Chuck's apartment had about as much security as Fort Knox.

"Oh, that's wonderful, honey. I can't tell you how much of a relief that is."

"We aim to please," I said.

"Oh, Tyrus, you please me so much. I'm the luckiest mother in the world. I didn't deserve to have two such perfect sons." No, mother, you didn't, I thought — though Billy and I fell well short of being perfect.

"Ty, honey, if someone comes and asks you about the watercolor, just show them the second one I sent you. It should be arriving there any day now. Keep an eye out for it, okay?" It was Chuck who'd be doing that, a fact my mother didn't need to know.

"Okay, Mom. You take care."

"Love you, honey. I'll talk to you soon." We both hung up. Neither of us asked where the other one was. It was probably just as well that we didn't know.

40

My body's clock was out of kilter, which is why at three A.M. I found myself staring out of the hotel window across a dark expanse of golf course. In the distance, a couple of lights glimmered along the lake shore. In between everything was bathed in shades of purple. No stars were visible. Rain was in the offing, though for now everything seemed eerily silent.

Rather than crawl back into bed and risk disturbing Laura, I curled up in the wing chair, pulled one of the extra blankets about me, and retreated into my thoughts. I'm not one of Planet Earth's more introspective guys; for me, self-examination has never been very profitable. I normally try to avoid it. Still, now and then I fall off the wagon.

As I sat there in the darkness my thoughts journeyed back to Bay City and to the glorious end of our season. I saw myself standing in the dugout beside Whitey Wiggins. Tears were streaming down his weather-beaten cheeks. "God damn it, Ty," he said, "now I can die happy."

"*Nunc dimittis*, huh Skipper?" I said. Whitey reached out and gave me a gentle poke in the shoulder. He had no idea what I'd just said, though in his own way he kind of understood.

We stood there in silence for another lengthy moment before he said, "There's talk they may ask you to manage the team."

"*What? Me?* Shoot, Skip, my playing days aren't close to being over. I've got some good years left. Manage the team? Man, oh man."

"It would be a great honor, son. You'd be one of the youngest managers in baseball history."

"Actually, Skip, I have a confession to make. It's crossed my mind that this might be the perfect time for me to walk away with you and the Deacon. There are no guys I'd rather do it with. I'll never have another season like this one. World Champs. My eighth straight

.300 season. My fourth 200-hit season. Bigger power numbers than I've ever had. Maybe the three of us should go out the door together."

"You could do that," Whitey said. "Go out the door, hang up your glove and spikes — and take over the managerial reins of the team. I'd be mighty proud, Duff, to have you as my successor."

I'd always thought that when I stopped playing ball I'd go back to my old college, volunteer to teaching a writing class or two at no salary, and help out the friend of mine who coached the college baseball team. Such a future held a lot of appeal to me. *Manage the Grays?* That possibility had never entered my head. I hadn't even intended to stay in pro ball after my playing days were over. Not as a scout, not in some front office job, and certainly not in managing. Geez, manage the Grays?

But other than Whitey, no one else had mentioned the idea to me. Until our GM, Pete Paulson, did, there wasn't any point in worrying about it. And yet, what if he did? What would I do then?

But I knew that from this point forward, playing for the Grays wouldn't be the same — not without Whitey Wiggins and Deacon Lawler. And so I'd begun to realize that I had come to an important crossroads.

In addition to my situation with the Grays, there was also the crucially important matter of me and Laura. I knew how wedded she was to her career and to New York City. I would never ask her to give those things up. But I couldn't see myself living permanently in New York — despite all the glorious operas they have there. So where did that leave us? I supposed I should find out what her thoughts were about our future, although it scared me to do that. It was simpler just to cruise along mindlessly and let the future take care of itself.

Suddenly my reverie was ended by a tremendous *crash* — a mighty thunderbolt that rent the firmament and illuminated the whole room — a peal of thunder that was merely the opening note of the overture. For the conductor had cued the timpani, the cymbals, the tubas, and the bassoons. The sky opened and unleashed its contents. Nature's symphony was now in full-throated spate.

"Ty! What in the world?"

"It's okay," I said. "It's your basic rainy night in Galway."

"I'm cold," Laura said. "Come warm me up."

"I might just do that," I said, "as long as you don't go putting your cold feet on my warm legs."

I slipped into bed and discovered a most desirable person curled up in there.

"Hey! I said don't do that!"

"Cold feet," Laura said, "but warm heart."

The hotel van, driven by shy Liam, dropped us off at Eyre Square in the center of town. It was ten-thirty in the morning, but only the stout of heart were braving the windy, rain-swept streets. Still, the weather suited our goal of browsing in bookstores. I'd been in Galway a couple of times before and figured I could find Charlie Byrne's, one of the best second-hand bookshops in Ireland.

Our plan to spend a rainy day inside a cozy bookstore wasn't unique to us. The clerks already had customers lining up at the counter, and in the store's many nooks and crannies book lovers loitered and lingered. Over the sound system came Paul McCartney singing "Blackbird" from *The White Album*. I left Laura at the bargain table and, humming along with Sir Paul, went to find the fiction section, since for once I hadn't brought along a single good novel.

I browsed a while and settled on an early Graham Greene, then drifted off to the crime fiction section where I found a Michael Dibden I hadn't read. Figuring those two paperbacks should hold me for the next week, I set about tracking down Laura. Now coming over the sound system was Gram Parsons and Emmylou Harris singing "Love Hurts," a song whose lyrics contained more truth than I wished to hear.

I found Laura in the poetry section, a stack of books beneath her arm. I knew her approach was to snatch up every book that appealed to her. Then, before she got around to making any purchases, she'd review her stack and winnow it down to three or four.

"There you are," she said. "Mind holding a few of these?" a purely rhetorical question since she'd already held them out to me. "I'd like another ten or fifteen minutes, okay?"

I nodded and added her books to mine. In her stack were slender volumes on Irish birds and wild flowers, on Irish round towers, and on Irish tower houses. The last one brought to mind the so-called castle Seamus had dangled before my eyes. The same castle about which Bump Rhodes'd had a strange premonition.

I wondered where Bump was now. In Dublin with Violet? I hoped so. I wished the two of them well. But as Gram Parsons' song states so bluntly, love hurts and scars and wounds and mars. Not always, I thought, not always. Though in my father's case it certainly had. He'd tried to hide his wounds and scars, but I'd always known they were there.

"All set," Laura said. "Let me just see if there are any of these I don't want." She ran her eyes over her stack and ruled out about half of them, leaving her with seven books, including the three I'd noticed before.

"Irish tower houses?" I said. "You don't really want that one, do you?"

"Of course I do. Maybe it has a picture of your castle."

"I don't have a castle! I don't intend to have a castle! You and Seamus can't bully me into having a castle! My apartment in Bay City, *that's* my castle. I don't want or need any other castle!"

"You amuse me, Ty Duffy. Perhaps this is a case of someone protesting too much? Perhaps deep down you really want a castle?"

"And why would I want a castle?"

"Because you love Malory, and Malory is filled with castles. Because you love Tolkien, and Tolkien is filled with castles. Because deep down every little boy wants a castle."

"You saying I'm still a little boy?"

"It wouldn't hurt to go and see it, would it? Surely there's no harm in doing that." I was beginning to get the feeling I didn't have much say in the matter.

We spent the next hour in Galway's City Museum. I love museums almost as much as Laura, and this one was a gem, located near the Long Walk and the Spanish Arch and looking out across Wolfe Tone Bridge toward the area known as the Claddagh, an area which once suffered the horrific consequences of the potato famine.

We wandered together for a while, then separately. I waited for her in the gift shop, where I spotted yet another small book on Irish tower houses — a book I surely wasn't going to buy. By the time Laura had had her fill, it was nearly one, and I was famished.

In McDonagh's fish and chips place we ordered at the counter and found seats at a sturdy, heavily lacquered, picnic-style table. A pungent aroma of fried fish, chips, vinegar, and wet garments filled the place. Diners occupied most of the tables, crowding together with the casual friendliness of the Irish. An elderly couple was already seated at the table we chose, though it looked like they were nearly finished.

"Wet weather today," the geezer said, acknowledging our presence. He nudged the plastic ketchup and vinegar bottles over closer to us.

"Good drinking weather," I said, dosing my platter with malt vinegar.

"Aye, 'tis that, 'tis that," he replied, grinning. "You a Yank, then?" I refrained from saying no, I'm a Gray, and nodded in agreement.

"Got some cousins in America," he said. "Ferrell's their name. Haven't seen 'em in ages. Perhaps ya'd be knowin' 'em?"

"Wes and Rick?" I said facetiously, referring to one of baseball's celebrated sets of brothers, one a catcher and one a pitcher.

"Aye, that'll be them. So how're they gettin' on?"

"Okay, I think, though like all of us, they're not getting any younger. If I see them I'll tell 'em you said hello." Telling them would be a good trick, since Rick and Wes Ferrell had probably been deceased for twenty or thirty years.

"Well, all the best o' luck ta ya," he said, as they began gathering up their bits, preparing to depart. Laura and I gave them warm farewell smiles.

"Shame on you, Ty Duffy," she said when they were gone.

"I was just humoring him. No harm in that."

"You were making fun of that kind old gentleman."

Before I could defend myself further, we were joined at our table by two more diners, this time a pair of young men who looked to be in their twenties. "This okay by you?" one of them said.

"Of course," Laura and I said at the same time.

Speaking of brothers, these two guys looked very much like brothers — dark-haired, dark-eyed, wiry builds. The guy I guessed was the older of the two was a little smaller and quite good-looking, with a shrewd, intelligent, yet slightly arrogant-looking face. The younger guy was larger all around — taller, broader of shoulder, more muscular in build, though with coarser features. His eyes, nose, and mouth seemed a little too large for his head. For a fleeting moment these two brought George and Lennie to mind, though there wasn't really much similarity.

"I'm Rory McManus," the good-looking one said, holding out his hand. "This is my brother Declan."

"I thought you might be brothers," Laura said. I wasn't sure if she'd realized yet who these guys were, but I certainly had.

"Yeh, kinda obvious, I guess."

"I'm Duff," I said. "She's Laura."

"Oh, now I know," Rory said, as if he'd had a sudden epiphany. "You're the ball player from the States. You two are friends of Kat Brogan's. Isn't that right?"

"Yes," Laura said, glancing first at me and then at them, "we are friends of Kat's. How is it that you know her?"

It was Declan who spoke up. "Yeh, well, we've known Kattie," he said, "since we was lads in nappies." The lummox's thick lips and over-sized teeth were grinning wolfishly. I wasn't sure which of them I found more repulsive, the slick S.O.B. or the scuzzy one. It was a near-run thing.

"You're involved in the hotel," Rory said addressing me. "One of Kat's partners or something?"

"We're just Americans here on holiday," I said.

"Buying that hotel was brilliant," Rory said, "and Mick knew it, too. But his humble origins and biases wouldn't allow him to do it. Always fancied himself a latter-day Finn McCool, the outsider who fought his way up from nothing. For Mick, owning a fancy hotel wouldn't've been right. Mick always preferred catering to the common folk. He was never one for havin' grandiose notions."

That wasn't exactly how Jack Strachan had described the matter, or how Seamus Byrne had described it, either. But it did fit the image Mick Slattery always wished to project of being Western Ireland's very own Robin Hood.

Neither Laura nor I gave any indication that we knew what Rory was talking about. I had no intention of discussing Kat, the hotel, Mick Slattery, or any other thing with these two losers. I resented them intruding upon us and wasn't about to allow Rory to draw me in. I would've loved to find out what they could tell us about Mick's drowning accident, but that was a topic I knew I shouldn't touch.

So, not wishing to be in their company any longer than necessary, Laura and I quickly finished and snatched up our things.

"Hope we haven't offended you," Rory said. "Ireland's a casual place and we don't stand much on ceremony. If we've been overly forward, we apologize, eh?"

"Nice to meet you fellas," I said, not offering my hand.

"Listen, Duffy," Rory said, "tell Kathleen we want her back. We need her, and that's the honest truth. She's better than any of us, and we want her back. With no hard feelings. You can get someone else to run yor hotel. Tell her, eh? Could ya do that for us?"

"Why don't you tell her yourself," Laura said coldly. "You don't seem to lack for the gift of the gab."

While Rory just smiled, Declan gave Laura the big eyes. Her

sudden assertiveness had startled him. I supposed he liked his
women submissive. When up against women like Laura Morgan
and Kathleen Brogan, Declan was out of his depth.

As we walked up Quay Street heading for Eyre Square, Laura
and I reflected on our encounter with the brothers McManus.

"What did you make of all that?" she asked.

"Don't know, really. At least they weren't overtly hostile."

"But didn't you sense an implied threat? Tell Kat Brogan to get
herself back in line, or else?"

"Yeah, maybe. From what Jack's told me, I know that Rory
and Kat have a bit of a history, romantic and otherwise. I can
understand, I guess, why they're upset with her. And with Jack.
And with Jimmy. But I can't see why they should have any bone to
pick with you and me."

"Surely they lump us all together."

"I guess. Anyway, I don't see how they can do us much harm."
Laura, I sensed, wasn't so sure about that.

"That Declan really creeped me out," she said. "Did you get the
impression that maybe he wasn't quite all there?"

"He did seem a bit strange. Anyway, let's hope that's our only
encounter with them."

When we got to Eyre Square, the hotel van was idling at curbside.
Liam looked nervous, since he was parked illegally. As soon as we
hopped in, he zipped right out of there, heading back to the hotel.

While Laura and Kat were sharing another cup of tea and another
good gossip, I went over to the driving range to hit a bucket of balls,
hoping to groove my swing a bit, then get in nine holes while there
was still enough light. Laura said she'd walk the course with me
when she'd finished her tea. The wind and rain were gone now, and
it had turned into a decent afternoon. That's Eire for you. The sun
had come out and so had all the birds of Ireland, *chirp, chirp.*

Jack, Liam, and Roddy were staring at me as I stood on the first
tee box with the set of loaner clubs Jack had arranged for me. Geez,

guys, don't put any pressure on me! I got lucky and hit a straight-ish drive of about 220 yards, bringing whoops of approval from my fans. Good thing none of 'em was watching fifteen minutes later when I scuffed my shot from the second tee, dribbling the ball along the fairway for maybe thirty yards. "These wet fairways don't give much roll," I said to Laura, who wasn't paying attention anyway.

"There's a warbler," she cried out, not in reference to my drive, "a blue-winged warbler." She was clutching her bird book, more engrossed in nature than in my effort to play the devilish game of golf. By the time I'd finished the fifth hole, Laura's bird list included collared doves, wagtails, and northern lapwings. During those first five holes I'd managed a par, three bogeys, and a never-you-mind — no birdies in sight.

As we moved toward the sixth tee I shouted to Laura, "Look! Did you see it? It was a sparrow. I'm pretty sure it was a sparrow."

"Oh, you are good!" she replied sarcastically. "But Ty, right there — quick! right there! — oh darn, it's gone. Did you see it? It was a hoopoe. Did you see its crest?" The only thing I saw was an excited, rosy-cheeked woman whose very existence caused my heart to sing.

A little later I tried again, this time calling Laura's attention to several hooded crows meandering on the grass about forty yards ahead near the edge of the fairway. "Look at them, Laura! Hooded crows! Look at those beauties!"

Laura laughed. "First sparrows, now crows? You do have a knack for spotting exotic species. But to be fair, hooded crows *are* rather special. Common in Ireland and Scotland but almost never found in England."

"They're *Celts*," I said, "You know, *Gaels*. In fact, what they really are are ancient, pagan druids who've shape-shifted into birds. Those old druids were partial to crows and ravens. See how they're eyeing us? Have you ever seen such intelligent-looking birds? I hope they're going to come down on our side and not on Rory and Declan's."

"If they're druids, don't go hitting them with your ball," Laura wisely advised. I didn't, since my pitiful slice landed on the opposite side of the fairway.

I finished my nine holes just as the light was fading. Never mind my score, though it was slightly better than I'd feared it would be. Maybe I could get in another round before Todd, Lou, and Spike turned up the day after tomorrow.

When I entered the hotel lounge bar half an hour later, who should be sitting there with Jack Strachan but Seamus Byrne.

"Duffy," Jack said, "ya looked like Ben Hogan out there today. Broke the course record, did ya?"

"Hello, counsellor," I said to Seamus, ignoring Jack's gibes. "Exchanged California's nasty weather for the balmy clime of Ireland?"

"Come ta sell you a castle, Mr. Duffy," Seamus said with a malicious grin, looking like an evil little leprechaun. "Ah, and here come the ladies," he said, as Kat and Laura walked over to join us.

"What was that about a castle?" Kat said.

"Just what this young fella's a-needin'," Seamus declared. "Just the t'ing that Mr. Ty Duffy's been a-longin' for."

"Well," Laura said, either ignoring or not noticing me shaking my head no, "I would enjoy seeing it. I love seeing Ireland's ancient sites."

"Ah, now there's a woman after me own heart," Seamus said, beaming at Laura.

"Is it far from here?" she asked.

"Not a-tall, not a-tall. Close to Doolin, it is. About an hour's drive."

"I think I know the one you mean," Jack said. "Overlooking the sea? Not so far from the Cliffs of Moher?" For a fleeting moment the Turner watercolor depicting a delapidated castle overlooking the sea flashed through my brain. And at almost the same time, so did Bump's dire warning.

"So why don't we be plannin' an outing, then?" Seamus said. "When would be convenient?"

"Not tomorrow," Kat said, "nor the day after. Jimmy arrives tomorrow, and we should give him a quiet day before we all go gallivanting off."

"Then why don't we make it the day after that?" Seamus declared.

"We could all go in the hotel van," Kat said. "And if the weather's grand, we could picnic by the sea. I know several good spots."

I couldn't help thinking about events of a year ago, when Jimmy and Kat and Laura and I had taken a picnic lunch out on the Great Blasket, off the tip of the Dingle Peninsula. Packed into that one day were more dramatic events than in any other day of my life, adventures I had no desire to reprise.

As Seamus nattered on about this and that, I couldn't get Bump's dire warning out of my head. Bump had never seen this castle and knew nothing about. So why did the lad have that strange presentiment? What in the hell did Bump Rhodes know that the rest of us didn't? Who *was* Bump Rhodes, anyway?

41

Before dawn, Kat was off to meet Jimmy's flight at Shannon Airport. Laura and I planned to spend the day in no one's company but our own, driving out into the rugged Connemara countryside and checking out a couple of ancient sites. By mid-morning we'd reached the old monastery at Inchagoill. We had to take a little ferry to get there and had the place to ourselves. It was worth it, for its weather-worn ogham stone made my companion especially happy. Funny how ogham stones can do that.

We lunched at O'Dowd's pub in Roundstone and got a local to take our picture with the Twelve Bens of Connemara forming the backdrop. Later we found a dilapidated old castle Laura had wanted to see — where we were promptly chased off the site by a shotgun-wielding farmer. Even Laura's charm didn't work on the guy, which proves that not *everyone* in Ireland is a sweetheart. I couldn't help wondering if our brush with the angry farmer was an omen warning us to steer clear of castles and tower houses.

On our way back to Galway we had a leisurely meal in Outherard and so didn't reach the hotel till nearly ten. We peeked into the lounge but didn't see anyone we knew, so we wearily climbed the stairs to our room. Tonight Laura wasn't bounding up those stairs like a leggy young deer. It had been a perfect day, aside from the angry farmer, and it ended with two exhausted wanderers crawling under the duvet on their double bed. With Laura snuggled up cozily against me, it wasn't five minutes before we were both goners.

Jimmy Devlin and I high-fived each other and shly embraced. Until seeing the big galoot, I hadn't realized how much I'd missed him.

"Duffy, you look great."

"It's the soft Irish climate. Does wonders for my complexion. How was your flight?"

"Awful. But it's nice to be the hell out of Missouri."

"Not a good visit?"

"No, it was a good visit. Well, mostly. But I may have left a broken heart behind me."

"You *rat*. Why do you do that to her?"

"Duff, she brings it on herself. Why can't she get it through her lovely head that what she wants isn't what I want?"

"And what is it that you want?"

"You know damn well what I want. And here it comes." Kat, followed by Laura, was just now coming to join us for breakfast. And despite myself, I had to agree with Jimmy that Kathleen Brogan was a remarkable woman. Women like her don't come along every day.

Laura gave Jimmy a kiss on the cheek and gave me one on the lips. What a lucky guy I am, I thought for the umpteenth time.

A young Polish waitress brought Jimmy and me our full Irish breakfasts, Laura and Kat their bagels and juice. It felt wonderful to be sitting there with my closest friends, joshing, noshing, and slugging down coffee. I'd been hoping, though I knew it was a long shot, that Jimmy would've had a change of heart and decided not to come to Ireland. Now that he was here, I was glad he was.

"Jimmy and I are going boating on the lough this morning," Kat said. "Want to join us?"

"Thanks, but I'm going to decline," Laura said. "I kind of overdid it yesterday. I'm going to have a day of reading and relaxing."

"It'll be golf for me," I said. "The dudes'll be turning up later today. It'll be my last chance to sharpen my game before making a fool of myself."

"Won't be anything new about that, will there?" Jimmy said.

"I'd like to see *you* play golf," I said.

"Forget that," Jimmy said. "When I'm eighty I might give it a shot. You won't catch me out there before then."

Half an hour later I was standing in the parking lot, my loaner golf clubs on a pull-cart, getting set to walk over to the first tee. Jimmy and Kat had just climbed into Kat's car and were pulling out of the parking lot. A moment after that another car, a dark green one, pulled out of a slot at the far end of the lot and followed them up the driveway. It was a Ford Fiesta. Yesterday no one had followed Laura and me, which I took to mean we were no longer persons of interest. We weren't, because other persons had now replaced us.

I'd just rolled in a twenty-five foot putt on the eighteenth green — only my second par of the day — when I looked up to see Spike, Todd, and Lou admiring my handiwork. I was glad I hadn't known they were there before I stroked my putt.

"Hell, Duffy," Lou bellowed out, "I'm not playing against you! Not for a hundred dollars a hole I'm not." I gave my teammates a wave and went over to them. It was big grins and fist bumps all around.

"Grab yours sticks, fellas," Todd said, "and let's be getting out the cobwebs. We've got time to play nine, maybe eighteen. You ready to go around again, Duff?" They hadn't even taken their bags to their room and they were raring to go. They'd probably find this little course kind of tame, but it would give 'em a tune up before they faced some of the really challenging links courses.

Kat and Jimmy returned a little before dusk — safe and sound and merry as grigs. I'd been watching for them since I'd finished playing nine holes with the guys, who were still out there finishing a second nine. Them being jet-lagged and me being at the top of my game, I managed not to humiliate myself.

Tonight the seven of us — the five Grays plus Kat and Laura — would have a proper dinner in the hotel dining room, something Laura and I hadn't done yet. It meant I'd have to dress up a bit. But I supposed I could make an exception this once.

I was showered and dressed long before Laura, so I went down to the lounge for a pre-dinner drink. There, seated with Jack Strachan in the far back corner of the large room, were Seamus Byrne and Rory and Declan McManus. When Jack saw me come in, he waved me over. Since the room was otherwise empty, I didn't have much choice but to have a drink with a trio of blokes toward whom I felt very little amity.

"Ya clean up good, Duffy," Jack said. "You folks goin' to La Scala tonight?" Rory and Seamus chuckled at Jack's feeble witticism; Declan looked clueless.

"Howdy, gents," I said. "So the brothers have come to pay Kat a little visit?"

"Decided to follow up on your friend Laura's advice," Rory said, "and come and tell Kathleen in person how much we want her back. Far as that goes," he said with a foxy grin, "we might even be willin' to take Jack back as part of the deal."

Just then Kat Brogan, looking as ethereal as a faerie princess freshly come from the Celtic Otherworld, glided over to join us. I couldn't help noticing Declan McManus gazing upon Kat with awe, adoration, and more than a hint of lust.

Jack got to his feet and offered Kat his chair.

"Need to go 'n close up the pro shop," he said. "Hope those pals o' yours, Duffy, have finally finished their round."

"They have. Saw 'em on the stairs a few minutes ago."

Jack nodded his farewells to the others and quickly departed. I had a feeling he wasn't hugely comfortable being around Rory and Declan.

"Kat," I said, "I was about to get myself a drink. What can I get for you?"

"Glass of house red?" Then she joined the others at the table.

As I was ordering our drinks, the early news was just winding up on the TV mounted on the wall above the bar. Right at that moment *The Angelus* came on. It was six P.M., when the national network pauses to sound the angelus bells and show a restful, peaceful scene. Although I wasn't raised in a devout household, I've always found that an appealing custom. Not a bad idea to take a break from the hurly-burly of our lives and be soothed by the sound of the bells and a few seconds of peaceful silence. Like me, the barman paused in his activities and took in the gentle scene on the TV.

Then, it was back to the hurly-burly of our lives. Indeed, it was back to it with a vengeance. For as I was carrying our drinks back toward the table in the far corner, Kat's impassioned voice rang out across the room.

"So you think *I'm* the one who did for Mick?" Kat was glaring at Rory. She'd transformed herself from otherworldly princess to Celtic warrior-woman. "Rory McManus, you mean to tell me that you, of all people, don't know who it was that did for Mick?"

Kat's words halted me in my tracks. This was surely a conversation I was not supposed to be hearing — though a conversation I greatly desired to hear. I took two sideways steps and positioned myself behind one of the room's large pillars, hoping it would shield me from view.

I glanced back toward the barman, who was paying no attention. Then I looked toward the far corner of the room and discovered that from my shielded position I could observe what was happening in the large mirror on the sidewall of the lounge bar.

Kat was silently staring daggers at Rory. Then her fierce gaze shifted from Rory to Declan. And when it did, the lad's entire face — from his expansive forehead and outsized ears down to his broad protruding chin — turned a fiery red.

"You're telling me, Rory McManus," Kat said again, this time with steel in her voice but with her eyes still fixed on Declan, who had no intention of meeting her gaze, "that you don't even know who did for Mick?" Her statement was more an accusation than a question.

Seamus was squirming uncomfortably. And yet it seemed to me that the implications of what Kat was saying hadn't especially startled him.

No, Rory McManus was the only one there whose face bore a look of shocked surprise. For in that moment it was suddenly dawning on him that of the four of them, he was the only one there who hadn't known what'd happened to Mick. And now, as he looked at his brother's beet-red face, he *did*.

Declan kept his eyes turned downward, staring at the pint of Carlsberg lager he cradled in his massive hands. Declan McManus, it seemed quite clear, had kept a hugely important secret from his brother.

But if he was the one who'd been the agent of Mick's demise, which now seemed highly likely, why had he done it? He surely hadn't done it on his own hook; someone else had to have put him up to it. And if that person hadn't been his brother Rory, then who had it been? Seamus Byrne? Or had it been Kathleen Brogan?

42

The dining room was two-thirds filled. Some of the diners were hotel guests but most weren't. The hotel's restaurant, one of the finest in Galway, always attracted a crowd no matter the day of the week.

Laura was already seated at our table, visiting with Todd and Spike. Lou Tolliver, gregarious soul that he is, was standing beside another table, chatting and laughing with the folks there. It didn't take Lou long to make new friends, though somehow I suspected he was also on the lookout, or should I say the prowl, for what he called chiquitas. I didn't think he was likely to find them here in the hotel dining room. But you never know.

When Kat Brogan entered the room, looking once more like a princess from the land of Tir na Nog, all eyes were drawn to her, including Lou's. Kat stopped for a moment at each table to say hello to the diners, and I couldn't help admiring the warmth and informality of the Irish that allows for intimate contact with people one doesn't even know. I was also a bit stunned by how Kat could go, in just a few minutes' time, from Celtic warrior-woman to the charming hostess she now was. Kat Brogan was awfully damned quick on her feet. Maybe she should have been a middle infielder.

Still no sign of Jimmy. Had he fallen asleep back in his room? Maybe I should go and hunt him down. I hoped he hadn't run afoul of Rory and Declan.

I had a quick look in the lounge bar but Jimmy wasn't there, nor was Seamus, Rory, or Declan.

I found him at the registration desk talking to Nadia. Jimmy looked peeved. He said he'd had a call from Penny. He shoved a slip of paper into his jacket pocket and rolled his eyes at me.

"Why me, lord, why me?" he said.

"Why *not* you?" I said.

"Why not *you?*" Jimmy retorted. "Better you than me, mate."

"C'mon, mate, time to eat."

All the others were now seated at our table, a grinning Lou and a smirking Spike having nabbed the seats on each side of Kat. I magnanimously motioned Jimmy toward the unoccupied chair next to Laura and plunked myself down between Todd and Spike, making me the only guy not seated beside a good-looking woman. Now and then you have to share the wealth.

Lou Tolliver held forth for the next hour. His non-stop patter was amusing and sometimes drew laughter from the folks around us who couldn't help overhearing Lou's not-so-soft voice. I'd been afraid that my compatriots might embarrass us, but they were a big hit. Lou even refrained from telling any off-color jokes. I didn't know he had so many clean ones in his repertoire. Or maybe he'd made an extra effort to sanitize them. "So an Irishman, an Englishman, a Texan, and a Broadway showgirl are in an elevator in the Empire State Building when the blackout occurs," he said. And Lou was off and running.

Throughout the meal Jimmy seemed uncharacteristically glum. He must've been upset by Penny's message. A couple of times I saw Kat give him searching looks. No fool she, Kat intuited that something was up with the lad. But she knew that whatever ailed him, it was probably something she could cure.

Several diners, after they'd finished their meals, came over to say their goodbyes to Kat and to shake hands with the famous American baseball players. A couple of the ones who were especially in the know asked Jimmy for his autograph, an honor that brightened the lad up just a bit.

"Devlin," one man said, "now that's a name ta make one proud." And he clapped Jimmy softly on the shoulder.

"And now to bed," Lou declared, not quite stifling a huge yawn. And not a moment too soon, I thought. These guys have been going non-stop since they got off the plane this morning. And that included eighteen holes of golf.

"Where to tomorrow?" Spike asked.

"Lahinch," Todd said. He was the one who'd made all the golf course bookings.

"Lahinch?" said a man at a nearby table. "I hope ya've brought plenty of balls. Hit 'em low and hit 'em straight, that's all I can tell ya. And pray that the winds be soft."

Kat and Laura, Jimmy and I set off from the hotel in my rental car a little after nine-thirty. Since it was just the four of us, there was no point in using the hotel van. Seamus had made our appointment at the tower house for three, so we had plenty of time to get there and have a picnic along the way. There was a storm coming in off the Atlantic later in the day, but until then the weather was supposed to be grand. Seamus wouldn't be there, but the owners planned to meet us and show us around. Not only that, they hoped we'd be willing to spend the night.

I recognized a clever sales ploy when I saw one — get the suckers to spend a night in a castle that could be their very own and get them hooked. I tried to put the kibosh on the overnight idea but was outvoted three to one.

We turned off the main road and headed toward the Burren, a desolate landscape like none other, and passed through the little town of Kinvarra. At Ballyvaughan we swung onto the coastal road that eventually leads to Doolin. In one direction we had spectacular views of the Burren, in the other spectacular views of Galway Bay. When we'd passed Black Head, off to our right we could just see the low-lying outlines of the mist-enshrouded Aran Islands.

"The place I have in mind," Kat said, "is another four or five kilometers. There's a small pull-off where we can park. Then we can walk down and picnic beside the water. It's quite a perfect spot."

The events of the last couple of days, if anything, had made Kathleen Brogan even more of an enigma to me than she'd been before. She could be delightful, charming, wholesome, normal, in every way the perfect woman for Jimmy Devlin, and I couldn't help admiring her intelligence and fiercely independent spirit.

But then there was the other Kat, a woman with a dark side I had only glimpsed, a fearless and terrifying Celtic warrior-woman. I honestly didn't know if Kat Brogan had used Declan McManus to exact her vengeance on Mick Slattery. Declan was clearly under her spell, a spell comprising adoration, wonderment, and sexual desire — a potent mixture. If she'd manipulated the lummox and used him to do her dirty work, Kat Brogan was nothing short of a murderer. But I didn't know if that was what had happened. And until I did, I would suspend all judgments.

We picnicked atop a great flat slab of limestone, the sea lapping the rocks fifteen feet below us. Looking down into the clear blue water, we could see fish, jellyfish, and other creatures beyond my ken. Beneath the water, the great flow of limestone upon which we were sitting continued on out to the Aran Islands, which were part of an extensive rock formation that had begun far behind us in the Burren. For geologists, this was an area of great fascination.

"Castles," Kat was saying, "have become a most grand attraction for the tourists, ya know. The big package tours nowadays lure folks with the invitation to 'Spend a night in a real Irish castle.' Gettin' in on that could be quite a lucrative t'ing. If the price is right, Ty Duffy, I think you should consider the matter."

"I'm pretty happy with the Irish real estate I have a stake in now," I said. "The hotel seems to be going really well, Kat, thanks to you. I'm happy just sticking with that."

"Anyway," Laura said, "it'll be fun seeing it, even if we aren't serious customers. You know how much I love seeing the old things."

"Yeah, I've been getting that impression. But I'd love to see the look on Larry Berkman's face if I called him and said, 'Larry, I need you to scrape up another twenty mil so I can cash in on a feckin' Irish castle.' "

"Here's what you should do with your feckin' Irish castle," Jimmy said. "Instead of serving up one of those cheesy medieval banquets everyone offers, you could offer 'em the real damn thing. Your advertising could say: 'Enjoy a TRUE medieval experience. Spend a night shackled in the dungeon of an Irish castle. Touch the slimy walls, smell the stench of the moldy, lice-infested straw, experience real rats gnawing on your manacled feet. Yes! — treat yourself to a REAL medieval experience, one you'll never forget!'"

"If I'm ever dumb enough to buy a castle, amigo, I'll be sure to make you my PR guy."

"I doubt if it has a dungeon," Kat said. "Just a dank cellar."

"Close enough," Jimmy said.

We spent two pleasant hours lazing by the sea. Laura tans quickly, and the warm autumn sun put some color in her cheeks. The breezes off the ocean were soft and refreshing. I hoped they weren't any stronger thirty miles down the road at Lahinch, where my pals were whacking golf balls on one of Ireland's most challenging courses.

As we trekked back to the car I said, "Why don't we just skip the castle. We could spend the evening in Doolin listening to music and sipping traditional brews. How's that sound?"

"Why don't we do both," Kat responded. "Doolin's not so far from where we'll be."

"We're *going* to the feckin' castle!" Jimmy declared.

"Of course we are," Laura said. "And I'm betting that Ty Duffy will enjoy the experience as much any of us. If I'm wrong, I'll give you anything in my power to give."

"*Anything?*" I exclaimed. "In that case, bring it the hell on!"

"Well . . . ," she said, " . . . *almost* anything."

Kat was laughing at us. "Jaysus," she said, "how did I ever get mixed up with t'ree such bloomin' idjits?"

"C'mon," I said, "if we're going to that effing castle, let's do it. But I want you to remember one thing. When Perceval got to the Grail Castle, it was the politeness that'd been drummed into him that led to his undoing. I'll go to the effing castle and I'll spend the night there, but don't expect me to be polite. I'm not making Perceval's mistake, okay?" The three of them looked at me blankly.

"Who the heck is Perceval?" Jimmy said. "Reliever who used to pitch for the Angels?"

"The Perceval I'm talking about might well be pitching for the angelic host right now," I replied. "But he never played for the L.A. Angels of Anaheim."

As we were putting things back in the car, Kat's mobile phone sounded. Its ring tone was Wagner's "The Ride of the Valkyries" theme, evoking a vision of Odin's handmaidens hovering over a battlefield littered with corpses. I hoped it wasn't an omen.

"That's grand," Kat said, "let me just jot it down." Laura fished a pen and an old receipt out of her bag and handed them to Kat, who scribbled down a number and then read it back. "Grand, grand. T'anks, Nadia. See you tomorrow, then." She pressed a button and folded her phone.

"That was Nadia. Seems one o' yor pals called the hotel, tryin' ta track ya down. Wants ya to give 'im a jingle. Some fella named, em, Bump? So ring 'im back, why doncha?" and she handed me her mobile phone.

"Another country heard from," I said.

"Lower Alabama ain't a country," Jimmy said.

"Hello?" I said, after I'd gotten all the numbers punched in, "it's Ty Duffy." Violet was on the other end. They'd just finished a gig in Limerick, she said, and having a free night, they hoped we might meet up somewhere. I suggested we try rendezvousing in Doolin.

"Tell 'em ta find McGann's pub," Kat said. "Once they get ta Doolin, anyone'll know where that is. Tell 'em we'll plan ta get there 'round about eight." So that was settled. Tonight we'd be seeing the Bumpster and his gal Violet.

We turned down the narrow lane leading to our destination, and after several twists and turns, there it was, perched on a bluff overlooking the sea — a four-sided gray-stone tower enclosed within a fifteen-foot-high wall. Framed by a bank of dark clouds over the sea behind it, it was an impressive sight in a rather forbidding fashion. A pair of chimneys rose up above the crumbling parapet, and narrow windows and arrow loops in the shape of slender crosses seemed randomly scattered about the tower's tall sides.

"Wow," said Jimmy, "home, sweet home."

The menacing structure bore no resemblance to the misty, romantic-looking castle depicted in my Turner watercolor. This so-called castle had a coldness and a starkness that took one aback. Home sweet home indeed.

We drove in through an open gateway and parked beside a light blue Land Rover which probably belonged to the owners. The little courtyard within the castle's outer wall was paved with cobblestones and slightly slanted for drainage. Aside from a couple of small utility sheds snugged up against the outer wall, the area around the tower house was open to the elements.

From the high-arched doorway facing the courtyard emerged a smiling man and woman. "It's Mr. Duffy, then, is it?" the man exclaimed in a bluff and hearty voice.

"Yes, it is. Hi. Mr. Thomas Riordan?"

"Call me Tom. And this is my wife, Siobhan."

Introductions were made all around, and then the genial, talkative Riordans ushered us into the tower house. It was obvious they'd gone to great lengths to give the place an authentic medieval feel, though as we were soon to discover, they'd also done a lot to make the living areas on the upper floors comfortable and modern.

"The laws are quite stringent," Tom Riordan explained. "The exterior cannot be modified in any way, aside from measures to prevent further deterioration. The interior walls must be preserved and maintained just as they are, though new structures can be placed within them following clearly defined specifications. You'll be relieved to know we've installed electricity on all floors and modern plumbing on the top three."

On the ground floor the Riordans had attempted to recreate a medieval castle's great hall. Two long refectory tables, flanked on the outside by wooden benches, dominated the room. At the head of the tables, on a low stone platform, was a high-backed chair with carved armrests and a purple cloth draped dramatically over its back. High up on the wall at the opposite end of the room perched a wooden minstrels' gallery. Banners emblazoned with coats of arms hung on the side walls; crossed swords and halberds filled the spaces between them. Unlit rush torches angled out at forty-five degree angles from the wall sconces, though electric lights were discretely positioned behind them.

"It was grand fun tracking down the furnishings for this room," Tom Riordan said. "The tables and benches and most of the wall hangings actually date to the fifteenth and sixteenth centuries. The little gallery, however, isn't at all old. We added it about ten years ago. But doesn't it look grand? We were quite pleased with how it turned out. The craftsmen, we thought, did a superb job."

"Not too shabby," Jimmy said, nodding his agreement. "But how do you get up there?"

"Normally, you don't," Tom Riordan admitted. "It's mostly just decorative. You'd need a ladder, really."

"A cute fake, eh?" Jimmy said.

"Well," Mrs. Riordan said, "we quite like it."

"I do too," Laura said generously. "Gives the room a special flair." Siobhan Riordan beamed at Laura Morgan.

Tucked in one corner of the room beneath the minstrel's gallery was the entrance to the original stone staircase built into the castle's external wall. The ancient stone steps, we soon discovered, twisted tightly in a clockwise spiral, the only handrail being a thick rope secured to the outer wall by metal loops.

Emerging from the stairwell we entered a large room furnished completely differently than the room below. Here everything was brand-spanking new, and the space was efficiently subdivided into a stylishly appointed sitting room and adjacent kitchen and dining spaces.

"This is our everyday living area," Siobhan Riordan said. "If you were to turn the castle into a hotel, which we'd been planning to do, this floor could be for the guests' general use and where you'd serve breakfast and other meals. The next two floors, as you'll see in a moment, are arranged as small private suites. Your rooms for this evening are on those floors also."

After proudly pointing out all the amenities the second floor had to offer, the Riordans led us on up to the top two floors, each of which was subdivided into four en suite guest rooms. The space was laid out so that each of the rooms included two of the tower's small windows, one of which had a sea view. These rooms were furnished more along the lines of the rooms back at the GlenTiernan Priory Hotel, though to me they weren't as inviting. I knew that castles weren't palaces, that they'd been built for defense, not comfort, and that the more comforts you added, the more defense you sacrificed. Still, these rooms seemed cold and cheerless. I'd take my own apartment back in Bay City any day of the week. *That* was my castle.

Our tour ended on the tower's rooftop where we had striking views of the sea off to the west. As we gazed out from the battlements, it was obvious that a weather front was approaching, its huge, dark clouds looking ominous.

"Pretty cool place to have a barbecue," Jimmy said. "My dad would be in hog heaven up here — I can just see him, listening to Hank Williams and sizzling some big old steaks. Look, if you don't want this place, Duff, you could always consider buying it for my old man."

Imagining Hank Devlin up here listening to Hank Williams, grilling huge slabs of beef, and happily sipping his Jim Beam, brought a smile to my face, the first one I'd had since setting foot in this accursed heap of stones.

"But Mr. Riordan, where's the dungeon?" Jimmy said. "You've shown us every darn thing except the dungeon." Jimmy had dungeons on the brain.

"Ah, well, sorry to disappoint you there, lad. Still, if one really had a mind to contrive one, wouldn't be so hard ta do. There's a narrow stair from the ground floor down to an old storage cellar. With a bit of ingenuity, you could rig up an impressive dungeon down there, so you could."

"That's a relief," Jimmy said. "No castle should be without a proper dungeon."

The Riordans left us to wander about on our own for a while, then tracked us down to say their farewells. Their actual home was half an hour's drive away.

"We'll be off then," Tom said. "Best be gettin' to Lisdoonvarna before the storm hits." He gave us keys to the outer door and all the guest rooms and told us to make ourselves at home. "Fix yourselves a meal here, if ya'd like to. The fridge is fully stocked. Or head on over to Lahinch. There be lots of good restaurants over there."

"We'll be goin' to Doolin," Kat said. "Maybe listen to a little music."

"Even better," Tom said. "Just be careful on the twisty lanes. Specially after ya've done some drink-takin'." And he winked at Kat.

The Riordans departed, and we had the castle to ourselves. For a while, anyway.

43

When you picture an Irish pub, what you're picturing is McGann's. Nothing much to look at, really, inside or out. Perched on high stools at the ancient wooden bar, three or four regulars. The folks behind the bar, hustling like mad to refill drinks and place the customers' meal orders. A smallish main room with four or five low wooden tables and low stools. A couple of other rooms, including the loos, out toward the back of the building. In the front corner by the window looking out on the street, a spot reserved for the musicians. We wandered into McGann's a little before eight, hoping to enjoy our meal before the musicians got going between nine and ten.

Half an hour later, Bump and Violet turned up, looking like a pair of shy and innocent kids — slender, dark-eyed Violet, dressed in a black silk blouse and black Levis, with her long, straight, shiny black hair; bulky Bump, with the forearms of a blacksmith and a countenance like a cherub — both extraordinarily appealing and extraordinarily talented in their own ways.

With Jimmy and Kat dominating the conversation, Violet and Bump happily settled into their comfort zone, listening, nodding, and smiling. Laura caught my eye and winked. The contrast between these two couples, one animated and effervescent, one silent and bashful, seemed to amuse her. But I was suddenly struck by something else altogether. For I realized, to my surprise, how comforted I was by the simple fact of Bump's presence. A sense of well-being came over me, the same kind of well-being I often felt in the presence of Deacon Lawler.

Jimmy Devlin, he of the one-track brain, had returned again to the topic of dungeons. "We could turn that cellar into a totally cool dungeon," he was saying. "I know a guy in Missouri who could do all the iron work. He'd make it look just the way we'd want it to look. I'm telling you, it could be really cool."

"I don't get you," Bump said. "A castle dungeon? What're you talking about?"

"A dungeon, you varlet, a castle dungeon. That's where you and Violet will be spending the night tonight, sleeping in the dungeon. You didn't know that? Geez, I thought Duffy told you all about it."

"We're sleeping *where?*"

"He's teasing you," Violet said.

"He is," Laura said. "But we're serious about wanting you to stay at the castle tonight. There's gobs of room and the owners have given us the run of the place. There's no need for you to have to find somewhere else to stay."

"It would be grand if you would," Kat said.

"It would," I added. "The more, the merrier." And besides, Bump's solid, reassuring presence would give me greater peace of mind — though I didn't say that.

Bump looked stunned. "A castle?" he said.

"Let's do," Violet said to Bump. "Let's stay there. It sounds like a lot of fun."

Bump Rhodes didn't reply. A strange and far-away look had come over his face. His eyes were open but completely glazed over. He seemed to be staring off into space.

"Bump? Earth to Bump," Violet said. "Come in, Bump." But the lad remained lost in his brown study.

"Bump!" Violet said again, this time tugging at his sleeve. Slowly, the lad's eyes began to focus and then he was back with us again, back from wherever he'd been.

"Sorry, Vi. What'd you say?"

"That I'd like to accept their offer of staying at the castle tonight. That be okay?"

Bump shrugged. "Yeah, I guess. I mean, sure. Anyway, my first thought was that it was a terrible idea. But now . . . well . . . now I know different. Everything's going to be okay after all."

I had no clue what Bump was talking about. But what I did

know was that if Vi wanted to do it, Bump wasn't likely to say no. Pleasing his gal was pretty damn important to the varlet from lower Alabama.

Eventually the musicians wandered in and spent a few minutes setting up. Then, after a bit of tuning and warming up, the three of them — fiddle, guitar, tin whistle — started going at it. They began with a soft and lilting instrumental piece and then modulated in some toe-tapping stuff, perhaps a jig or a reel. A little boy came forward and perched himself on a stool right next to them, his feet unconsciously moving to the Celtic rhythms. He was enthralled. One day not so long from now he would be up there performing with them, on the tin whistle or the Celtic fiddle.

Two hours later, as the musicians were winding down and the crowd thinning out, the few people who remained began taking turns singing songs of their own choosing. One guy offered up a respectable rendition of Johnny Cash's "Forty Shades of Green," and when an old woman began singing "The Fields of Athenry," everyone joined in with her on the chorus. Bump Rhodes didn't know the song, but it soon set the tears to rolling down his cheeks. After that another old gent sang a soft and heart-rending tune entirely in Gaelic. It didn't matter that we couldn't understand a single word he sang.

"Come on, you Yanks," someone said, "yor turn to pitch in." Violet whispered something to Laura and Kat, and then the three of them — tentatively at first but with growing confidence as they got into it — served up a respectable version of "Down in the Valley," their blended voices reminding me of the McGarrigle Sisters. When they got to the lines about "Build me a castle, forty feet high / So I can see him, as he rides by," I looked over at Bump, only to see that the knucklehead had disappeared again — off to cloud cuckoo land. The L.A. Kid had a beatific smile on his face.

The storm hit with a vengeance just as we were leaving McGann's. The wind-driven rain lashed at our faces as we sprinted to our cars.

As good a driver as I was on the wrong side of the road, this time I was happy to leave the driving to Kat. I kept Bump and Violet, in the car behind us, in my prayers. Fortunately, all they had to do was follow our tail lights. Assuming they didn't get blown into a ditch.

"As the centaur said to the innkeeper," Jimmy murmured, "it's not a fit night out for man nor beast."

"Ah, shite," Kat said, "any more of that and yor walkin', storm or no storm."

"C'mon, that's a good one," Jimmy said.

"No, it isn't," three voices replied.

As we navigated the back lanes of County Clare, the headlights of another car came rushing up behind our little two-car caravan.

"Someone's in a feckin' big hurry," Kat muttered. "They always are. It's why there's so many ghastly traffic fatalities in this godforsaken country. Everyone just has to go fast as they feckin' can." The car remained right on Bump's tail, which must've been nerve wracking for the lad.

Reaching the tower house in one piece, we discovered that the gateway, which we had carefully latched and locked, was standing wide open. A large car was parked inside and it wasn't the Riordans'. And when we pulled our cars in, the car behind Bump drove in also. It stopped behind us blocking the gate.

"What the bloody hell," Jimmy said. "Someone's looking to get a punch in the mouth."

The downpour hadn't let up, and the four of us made a mad dash for the protection of the tower doorway, with Bump and Violet not far behind us. To our consternation, we found the door unlocked and partially open. Lights were on inside. The only light we'd left on was the one illuminating the courtyard.

"Hello?" Kat shouted. "Who's here?"

"We are," came a voice from the courtyard behind us. Five men followed us inside, two of whom I immediately recognized — Declan and Rory McManus. The other three, I figured, must comprise their goon squad.

"You aren't welcome here, Rory McManus," Kat said fiercely. "Ya'd best be off with ya. Be off with ya now, or I'll be callin' the Guards." She already had her mobile phone out and was getting ready to call the Irish equivalent of 911.

"That would make me very unhappy, Kathleen. You don't want to make me unhappy. It'll take the Gardai at least forty-five minutes to get here. If you make that call, it will be forty-*one* very unpleasant minutes for you and your friends."

"Just go, Rory. Ya've no business bein' here."

"We'll go when we're good and ready," he replied, with a vulpine smirk. "Why don't you all just sit down so we can be havin' ourselves a little chat. Let's see if we can't be getting a few things ironed out amongst the lot of us."

"There's nothing a-tall to be ironin' out. I'm tellin' ya, Rory McManus, I'm finished with ya. So just be leavin' and goin' on with yor grubby little activities. Ya won't be havin' any problems with me. "

"But we have a rather *big* problem with you, Kathleen. You see, the time has come to get things square in regards to Mick Slattery. Kat, ya just can't go killing a man like Mick Slattery and be gettin' off scot-free. Where's the justice in that? You just can't be doin' that."

Kat glanced at Declan, whose unprepossessing face was blank as a plank. "Rory," she said, "you *know* who did for Mick. So why're ya still tryin' to pin the feckin' thing on me?"

"It was you, Kathleen." Rory turned and looked at Declan. "It was Kathleen, yeah?"

"Nobody else," Declan declared. "Saw her do it myself, I did. Saw her push 'im right over the railin' and down inta the sea. Poor Mick, sick as a dog, he were. And it were like a dog she treated 'im. Pushed 'im right over the rail and down into the sea."

"Ya lyin' bastard!" Kat shouted. "Ya feckin' lyin' bastard!"

Kat looked about her wildly. Then her eyes lit upon the crossed halberds hanging on the wall. She rushed over and grabbed one of them and turned to face Declan.

"I never did for Mick," she said in a steely voice. "But I'll sure as hell do for you, ya lyin' bastard."

As Kat began to move toward Declan, one of the goon squad guys tried to intercept her. When she made menacing movements with the sharp blade atop the halberd, he took two steps back and held up his hands as if to say, "Okay, have it your way."

"Get yourself a weapon, Declan McManus," Kat Brogan growled. "Just you and me. Let's determine who's tellin' the truth here."

What Kat was proposing sounded a lot like a judicial combat, the kind of duel they describe in the old chivalric romances. In those old stories, the person who is in the right always wins because God is on his side: the phrase *Dieu et mon Droit* popped into my head. Unfortunately, this wasn't one of the old stories.

It took Declan a few seconds to process all of this, but finally he reached for another halberd. Gripping it with both hands, he held it nervously across his chest.

"Stop!" Jimmy shouted. "This isn't the Middle Ages, for Christ's sake. Put those things down, you jerks!" It seemed weird for Jimmy Devlin to be the voice of reason.

"Why put them down?" Rory said calmly. "Why not settle the matter precisely as Kathleen has proposed?"

"The hell with that," I said. "Why don't you and me settle the matter between the two us, Rory?"

"And there's another good idea," he said, a little too quickly for my comfort. "Since they're using the halberds, Mr. Duffy, why don't you and I use the swords?"

"Ty!" Laura shouted. "Listen to Jimmy, for goodness sake. Don't make things worse!"

"It's going to be okay," came Bump's calm voice. "There's no need to worry. Everything's going to be okay. It is, it really is."

"What are you *talking* about?" Violet stormed at Bump. "These silly fools are going to kill each other! Bump, you have to stop them!"

Now even Bump began to look a little worried. He'd seemed so sure before, but now his confidence was ebbing.

Kat, paying no attention to anything else, was stalking Declan, rotating the tip end of her halberd in small circles in front of her, and Declan, looking flustered, was slowly backpedalling. His face said he wanted no part of this Celtic warrior-woman, not when her dander was up. And it was up.

Rory was taking practice swooshes with one of the swords, and the bastard appeared to know what he was doing. He looked at me, smiled, and said invitingly, "Lay on, MacDuff?" It was a relief to know I was MacDuff and not MacBeth — though not a very big one.

"Not swords," I said, "fists."

"Not fists," he said, "swords." And he extended his arm toward me, the tip end of his sword almost touching my chest.

"If I might be allowed to have the honor?" Bump said. He'd taken hold of the other sword and now advanced toward Rory. Rory glanced at him with a look of surprise. He'd correctly read me as a completely inexperienced swordsman. Bump appeared to be another matter.

"Bump, I said *stop* them, not join them!" Violet screamed.

"I *will* stop them," Bump said. "Been a while since I held one of these, but I bet I can still do it. Like riding a bicycle is what they say."

Rory was nonplussed by Bump's aplomb. So was I. Who the hell did he think he was, d'Artagnan?

"Lay on, McManus?" Bump said, assuming a fencer's stance.

"No!" boomed a loud voice from up above us. "*Lay off!*"

Everyone halted right where they were and looked up. There, standing in the dim light of the minstrels' gallery at the far end of the hall, was a dark figure. Holy Mother of the Divine God, where did *he* come from?

44

Two other figures emerged from the gloom to flank the first figure. The one on the right looked distinctly like Honest Jack Strachan; the hulking, bald-headed one on the left could only be Roddy Doolan. It wasn't the Holy Trinity. But under the circumstances, it was probably the next best thing.

"*Mick?* My God, is that really *you?*" The sword in Rory's hand clattered to the floor.

Holy Mother of God, I thought again. It *was* Mick Slattery — *resurrected!*

Declan looked as thunderstruck as I was. His over-sized mouth hung crookedly agape. He dropped the halberd, spun on his heel, and lumbered toward the castle doorway, the other goons right behind him. But Rory McManus remained rooted where he was.

"Yes, Rory," Mick Slattery said, "it's really me. Back from my watery grave to torment yor miserable soul. Oh, Rory, ya didn't actually think you could kill me, did ya laddy?"

"Mick," Rory stammered, "it weren't me. Honestly, it weren't me."

"Oh yeah, it were you. Not directly, mind you. Maybe it were Declan who carried it out and maybe it were Seamus who put him up to it. But it were you, too, Rory. And tryin' to pin it all on Kathleen! That isn't our code, laddy, that isn't our way. So you'd best be following the others out that door. You're finished, Rory. You're out. If you were anything other than kin, it would be far worse for you than that. So go on with ya, lad. But here's my final piece of advice. You'd best stay far, far away, 'cause the day could still come when I won't be feeling so charitable."

Rory looked around him. He stared at Kat. He looked back up at the three figures standing there on the gallery. Then, without another word, he slouched toward the door and was gone.

Those of us who remained stood there in silence. We needed to catch our breaths and collect our wits.

Then Jimmy said, "How the hell did they get up there? I thought that damn thing was just decorative."

"I think they call it a ladder," I said.

We were all in the second-floor sitting room — Kat and Jimmy, Violet and Bump, Laura and me; along with Mick Slattery, Jack Strachan, Roddy Doolan, and off in a corner by himself, Liam the Silent.

Everyone now had cups of tea, cups which in some cases had more in them than tea. The sounds of the storm, though muffled by thick walls and triple-glazed windows, could still be heard.

Mick's fingers, consciously or unconsciously, played back and forth across the scar above his thinning hairline. That scar had been there for over a year now, since Jimmy's immaculate stone toss on the Great Blasket, and it would be there until Mick Slattery's dying day. Mick's thin lips bore a faint smile, and all the time he couldn't keep his eyes off of Kat Brogan.

"Much as I might have liked to see it, Kat, and much as he may have deserved it, I couldn't have you skewering my pitiful nephew. It were quite a sight, though, seeing you stalking the lad. He looked so scared I thought he might piss his pants." Then Mick, Jack, and Roddy all guffawed in unison. Liam grinned.

"Yor quite the gal, Kat. Worth the lot o' them. I won't blame you if you say no to what I'm about to propose. But listen here, Kat, there's nothin' that would mean more to me than havin' you take charge and be runnin' things altogether. I can't do it anymore, and frankly, I've lost my desire to. Them useless nephews of mine, they are out. They had their chance. Now they are out."

Kat sat absolutely still. But under her mask-like face, emotions had to be roiling. As Mick reached for his tea cup, I saw that his hand was just slightly trembling.

"You are so much like your mother, Kat. God, did I love that woman. God, did she break my heart, choosin' yor da over me. But she were right. He were the better man. I was too hard, too cold, too ambitious. Much as I loved Kev, I always believed he were a little bit too soft, more fool me. What I took for softness, yor mam took for what it was — kindness, warmth, generosity, a heart full o' goodness. He were a gentle man, yor da. That was what yor mam needed, not a hard-drivin', hard-chargin' son of a bitch like me." Mick took a big sip from his Bushmill's-laden tea cup.

"That hurt me somethin' terrible, Kat, when I discovered I was odd man out. The three of us had been closer than close since we was little uns, and all that time I'd never dreamed that Niamh would pick Kevin 'stead o' me. Oh god, did that hurt. But in the end I forgave 'em. I still loved the both o' them, and I've never stopped loving them.

"Kat," Mick said, then paused for a moment before continuing. "There's somethin' you got to understand. I didn't do for yor da. His death were an accident. It were on a night like this one, too. Jack'll tell ya. He and I were together when the word came."

"Only time I ever saw Mick Slattery cry," Jack said somberly. "He were too distraught to be the one to tell yor mam. I had to do that. Hardest thing I've ever done."

"I remember," Kat said. "Oh yes, I remember." And she stared silently into her cup of tea. Everyone else remained silent.

It was Bump, surprisingly, who finally broke the silence. "Sir," he said, addressing Mick, "if you'll pardon me for asking, what did happen that night out there on that boat? Did that feller really push you over the rail and into the sea?"

Mick thought about that a bit before replying. "I'm guessing Seamus was the one who planned it. He were the one brought me the fateful drink. But that's the big joke, isn't it. If I'd been conscious when they tossed me inta the water, I woulda surely drowned. But because I was unconscious, I floated.

"Don't know how long I was in the water. Hours, likely. First thing I knew, I was lying in a bunk in someone else's dry clothes.

A rescuin' angel'd plucked me from the sea, more dead than alive. Took me to Nantucket and let me lie low there.

"The newspapers said I was presumed dead, so I figured it might be good just to leave it that way. See how things would sort themselves. Even Jack didn't know, not until two weeks ago."

"Ya bastard," Jack said, smiling at Mick with affection.

"It were nice stayin' there with my rescuin' angel. Helped ta change my perspective on things. I owe her a lot, I do. She and me . . . well, who knows. But I certainly owe her a lot." Mick's fingers were rubbing against the scar on his forehead.

I looked around me at all these silent folks, all of them as astonished as I was by Mick's remarkable tale. And as I did, my imagination began getting the better of me, as it is wont to do. Here was Bump Rhodes, who possessed all the qualities of an innocent young Grail Knight; and right alongside him was his girl Blanchflower, better known as Violet. And here, too, was King Mick, who bore a distinct resemblance to the Maimed King — or maybe he was the Fisher King, I wasn't quite sure which — each of them with their entourage, and all of us together here in the Grail Castle while the storm continued to rage outside.

Okay, okay, so it didn't perfectly fit the old story. Still, it wasn't *completely* ridiculous. It was in the ballpark, so to speak.

"Why are you looking so gleeful?" Laura whispered to me. I was too embarrassed to say, so I didn't.

Instead I said, "Do you think maybe I should go ahead and buy this castle?"

Laura's eyes got big. She stared at me a moment before saying, "Why in the world would you want to do that?"

"Beats me. Maybe Kat and Mick should buy it. After all, it is the Grail Castle and he is the Maimed King."

"Ah," Laura said. "Now I know why you were looking so gleeful. You are one big knucklehead."

"Are you calling me a *knucklehead?*"

"'Fraid so," she said. "Sometimes you have to tell it like it is."

45

Mick and the boys had headed off, and now just the six of us remained. It was late. Exactly how late I had no idea, but the adrenaline was still pumping and sleep was a long ways away.

"C'mon," shouted Jimmy. "Let's go up topside. Grab your beverages and let's go!"

"It's storming out there!" Violet protested.

"Don't make no never-you-mind to me. C'mon, you pathetic little wusses. C'mon, you lazy lollygaggers."

"Let's go!" Kat shouted, and she and Jimmy were already making for the stairway.

"I'm game," I said.

"Me, too," Laura declared.

"Why the heck not?" added Bump. And then the four of us were right on Jimmy and Kat's heels.

The wind was blowing a gale, the rain was whooshing down, and thunder and lightning rumbled off in the distance. Even though the storm was showing signs of being on the wane, it took just seconds before all of us were soaked.

"Such a gentle little rain," Jimmy yelled, "so good for the roses."

"Blow winds and crack your cheeks!" I shouted out to the elements.

"Into each life a little rain must fall," Laura declaimed.

"His rain descendeth on the just and the unjust," Bump said, sounding more like the Deacon than Bump.

"Some people," Kat said, "just don't know enough to come in out of the rain."

Then Violet began singing at the top of her voice, belting out the words of a famous tune by Lerner and Lowe. "Ma-ri-a," she sang out, "Ma-ri-a . . . ." Without a moment's hesitation, the rest of us joined right in — " . . . they call the wind Maria."

◆ ◆ ◆

We stayed on the tower rooftop for at least an hour, singing, cavorting, philosophizing, joshing, soaked to our skins. I don't think any of us had any dry clothes to change into. But right then we couldn't have cared less.

The storm finally moved off to the east, though the wind still blew. We could hear the sounds of the sea, and off to the west we could see waves pounding against the shore. Eons from now there would be no Ireland, for the sea would have claimed it entirely.

"I *like* this place," said Bump. "This is my first time in Ireland, and I like it here. I been a lot of places before but never Ireland. Yeah, I really do like this place."

"What do you mean you been a lot of places before?" Jimmy said.

"Oh . . . well . . . ," Bump said, sounding embarrassed, "I don't know. It's not important, really." Jimmy was staring at the L.A. Kid, trying to figure him out. Good luck with that.

"Anyway," Bump said to me, changing the subject, "what do you reckon you're going to do, Duff? Are you going to say *yes?*"

"Yeah, I'd like to know that, too," Jimmy said. "What's it going to be, Duff?"

"If you're asking whether or not I'm going to buy this effing castle, the answer is you can take this effing castle and you can shove it — ."

"No, that ain't what we're asking," Bump said.

"Don't play coy, Duff," Jimmy said. "You know what we're asking. Are you going to manage the Grays or not?"

"*Manage the Grays?*" Laura said. "Ty, you haven't said anything about *that.*"

"These friggin' guys seem to know more than I do, Laura. No one has asked me to manage the Grays."

"C'mon, man," Jimmy said, "everyone knows that's what's going to happen. All the guys know, and it's what all the guys want. So what are you going to say?"

"I'm a ballplayer, darn it. I don't want to be a *manager*. I'm a player."

"You would be one of the youngest managers in baseball history," Bump said. "That would be pretty dad-gum cool."

"It would," Laura said, "it would be pretty dad-gum cool."

"You're siding with *these* guys?"

"Course I am. At least, I am if it's what you want."

But was it that I wanted? I still didn't know. And anyway, no one had offered me the job. But it sounded like they would. And what if I took the job and turned out to be a lousy manager? Well, if that happened, I supposed I could still follow my plan of going back to Waverly College and lending a hand here and there. And maybe, just maybe, I wouldn't turn out to be a lousy manager.

One thing I did know. When I was no longer a member of the Grays, I sure would miss these guys.

"If I were to say yes," I said, "do you think there's any chance I could talk the Deacon into coming back to help out? I mean, how many souls can a guy save, anyway? That's got to be tiring work. He can't keep that up forever."

"Not next year," Bump said, "but the year after." We all looked at Bump. When he realized we were staring at him he said, "I mean, that's what I'm guessin'. Knowing the Deacon, I don't suppose he'd wanna to take a break quite so soon. The Deacon's got a lot of staying power, you know. Anyway, that's what I'm supposin'."

"I'm wet and cold," Violet said. "Do you think maybe we could go back inside?"

Yes, it was time to do that. We were all wet and cold and running on fumes.

It had been a long day. And I figured we all still had some long days ahead of us. But I suddenly found myself looking forward to them. I had no idea what those days would bring. But I was eager to find out.

CPSIA information can be obtained at www.ICGtesting.com
Printed in the USA
LVOW11s2131170815

450538LV00001B/70/P